Dakota

Annabelle Stewart, all tight leather skirt and hot lace panties, thundered into my life for one night after a rock show and calmly drove away the next day. She should have been like any other one-night stand I've had over the last ten years touring with Balefire. But she wasn't. At odd moments, I catch myself thinking about her, wondering if I made as big an impression on her as she did on me.

Then I walk into the rehearsal for our drummer's wedding, and who's standing with the bride? The hottie who keeps me awake with thoughts of our one night together. Beautiful, smart, and sassy as hell, Annabelle sets me on fire with her kisses and leaves me hanging. But I've got plans for her.

Annabelle

I never expected to see him again. Two years after hooking up with Dakota Perri after a Balefire concert, I'd convinced myself that night was a fantasy. But the way he looks at me during Jack and Clio's wedding, like he remembers every second of our one-night stand, lights me up. Too bad I blew it.

Then I score an management internship with the band, an opportunity guaranteed to land me a scholarship with a top graduate program—if I don't earn a reputation for sleeping my way to success. Which is a problem. I see Dakota every day. Every time we're together, the sparks fly faster and hotter. If I want to achieve my goals, I have to resist him. But how can I resist a man as panty-meltingly hot as Dakota Perri when he says he's wild for me?

Other Books by Tam DeRudder Jackson

The Talisman Series
Talisman
Warrior
Prophetess
(novella)
Bard
Druid

The Balefire Series
Play For Me
Sing For Me
Wild For Me

Wild For Me

Tam DeRudder Jackson

*For Grady
and for Austin and Trey—
the rock stars in my life.
I love you.*

Chapter One

Dakota

WHEN I STROLLED into the rehearsal for the monk's wedding, I was knocked flat on my ass. Metaphorically speaking. We didn't start the evening with a brawl. Kind of amazing considering how much grief my little joke caused Jack for a while. Now the joke was on me. The girl who haunted my dreams stood laughing with a couple of other women, oblivious to my presence. It left me with an ache in my chest so intense it threatened to choke me.

Last time I saw Annabelle, she tossed me a wave as she drove away in her sweet blacked-out Mustang. After checking another experience off her bucket list, an after-concert night of sex with a rock star, she drove right out of my life. Too bad she left all those incredible memories behind.

Closing my eyes, I could see her again, haltingly giving her first—and I hoped only—striptease. Then she climbed up my body where I lay on the bed, leaned in and kissed me so hot and deep and dark I almost came in my jeans. For the rest of the night, we torched my sheets to the point we could have set off the hotel fire alarms.

As the sun sneaked in under the drapes the morning after, she gathered her clothes like she assumed she was another one-night stand in a decade of one-night stands for me. Except in unguarded moments over the last two years, I'd caught myself thinking about her, dreaming about her. That girl gave me the best night ever—and the next morning she calmly walked away like banging a rock star was something she did every other day. No begging for a selfie to prove her night to her girlfriends. No slyly hinting I might want her number. No outright asking to join the band on tour. Maybe she did bang rock stars regularly. Hell, I didn't know. As I watched her with the monk's fiancée, for some reason the thought burned like acid in my gut.

Whether he planned it or not, Jack revenged me well, saddling me with his fiancée's friend MandMs for the wedding. The girl was so starstruck she could barely look at me let alone speak to me when Clio Barnes soon-to-be Whitehorse introduced us. Instead of taking my arm to walk down the aisle the way every other bridesmaid did at the wedding rehearsal, she let her fingers hover somewhere near my elbow and studiously watched the grass as we walked to the pretty arbor in the Whitehorse family's backyard. I was going to have to work on relaxing her, or she might fall flat on her face at the start of the ceremony the next day. What I would have rather been doing was talking Annabelle back into my bed.

As I stood beside our bass guitarist Adam Tron and lead singer Blu Connolly, the other members of Balefire, I knew I was supposed to be listening to the justice of the peace explain what all would be happening tomorrow afternoon during the ceremony. Instead, I couldn't help but remember my earlier encounter with the only girl who'd ever been more than a blip on my radar once I finally approached her.

"Annabelle."

"Dakota."

"You two know each other?" Blu had asked, looking from one of us to the other like a spectator at a ping-pong game.

As we stared at each other, I watched her eyes widen a fraction and felt my own mirror hers. Damn, she was cool.

"Not really," we said in unison.

"We met after the concert at Red Rocks," I said.

"The same night Jack and Clio managed the first of their reconciliations," Annabelle added with a little smile.

Blu tilted his head. "Huh. Wonder how I missed all that."

"It was a big night, playing in front of our home crowd and all. I think you were celebrating." I was addressing Blu but never took my eyes off Annabelle.

What whirred around in her pretty head? What did she truly think about the night we met?

Before I could pursue the topic any further, Lori Whitehorse, Jack's mom, interrupted us to let us know the JP had arrived and we were needed in the rehearsal.

Now, Blu hissing at me under his breath jerked me back into the present.

"You get that?"

"What?" I asked, confused.

"Where'd you go?"

I shrugged. What was I gonna say? That I was reliving moments with Annabelle since she'd unexpectedly walked back into my life?

"When the JP says, 'This is a union of love,' that's our cue to grab our guitars to play Jack's song to Clio. Pay attention, dude."

"Got it," I whispered back as I tried not to stare at Annabelle across the aisle.

That's when I caught her sneaking a look at me, and I couldn't help it. I grinned and winked. Of course I wanted her attention. What I really wanted was to know if she'd give me another night like that one magic night we spent together two years ago.

Annabelle

When we gathered at the back door to Jack's parents' house, Dakota Perri slipped behind me and whispered in my ear. "Annabelle, can I hope for another private striptease later?"

Since the man was a walking, talking ad for hot sex, I shouldn't have been surprised. I could hear laughter in his voice, but Clio saved me from answering when she interrupted to pair up the wedding party. I'd be walking in with Adam Tron, the bassist for Balefire. We'd walk ahead of Stacy Newhouse, our sorority sister and the maid of honor, and Colin Whitehorse, Jack's older brother and best man. I couldn't decide if I was relieved or disappointed about not walking in with Dakota.

Good thing I didn't have to answer his question. What could I say? I had no idea what he thought about what happened between us. I'd earned my reputation for wildness, but that strip show I'd given him the night we first met was a one-off. I couldn't decide if he was teasing me or actually wanted a repeat performance.

Even though I'd played it cool, I couldn't stop shifting my gaze across the aisle to that man. Damn him and his bona fide rock star gorgeousness, those incredible sea blue eyes, that shock of sun-kissed brown hair, that lean muscular body decorated with tats in the most interesting places. It would help if I didn't remember every detail about him. When he grinned and winked at me, my heart jumped and I struggled not to lose my breath.

Yep, Dakota was definitely laughing at me.

But I remembered the way he groaned and shouted his pleasure during that one magical night I spent with him after a Balefire concert two years ago. Not only was the man a virtuoso guitar player, he was also a master at pleasuring a woman. My skin tingled, and my core tightened and wept at the sound of his voice so deep and warm in my ear when we saw each other at the start of the rehearsal.

Since he'd undoubtedly had countless women over years of

touring with Balefire, I was under no illusions about him remembering much of what happened with me. After all, I'd been a junior in college, hardly a worldly woman when I slept with him. Certainly, my little strip show couldn't have been the first—or last—private show some woman had given him either.

Still, I never thought I'd actually see him again even after it came out that my best friend Clio's baby daddy was Jack Whitehorse, Balefire's drummer. Yet here we were, meeting again nearly two years after that incredible night following the Red Rocks concert.

From some distant place, the sounds of the string quartet playing and people moving jerked me back to the present. We filed down the aisle between the chairs Jack's army of brothers had set up in the Whitehorses's back yard. Adam Tron and I walked out ahead of Dakota and my sorority sister MandMs, who fluttered beside him, apparently starstruck. I understood the feeling, but for a different reason. The heat on my backside told me his gorgeous eyes were trained right there, and I couldn't wait for the rehearsal to end. The girls and I had planned one last single ladies' night with Clio, which meant I could escape Dakota Perri until I could process all the emotions skittering through me at seeing him in person again.

Too bad Dakota had other plans.

Cornering me away from the others, he asked, "Annabelle, you are planning to save me a dance after the ceremony tomorrow, aren't ya?"

"I think the entire wedding party is expected to dance together at least once."

"I meant a private dance."

When he deepened the timbre of his voice, dripping seduction into the delivery of the word *private,* I couldn't miss what he meant. But I pretended to anyway. "If you want to dance with me at the reception tomorrow, Dakota, just ask."

He moved closer, nearly but not quite touching me yet stealing all the available air. "Last time, Annabelle, I didn't have to ask."

Since Dakota stood somewhere north of six feet while I topped out at five five, I had to look up into his eyes. The desire I saw there tripped my pulse into overdrive. Maybe he remembered that night better than I thought.

Blu's fiancée, Ashleigh Baker, saved me from giving in to temptation and probably making a fool of myself.

"Hey, Annabelle, you riding with us?" she called.

Sliding awkwardly beneath his arm where he had me partially caged in beside the house, I mumbled, "Excuse me. The girls and I are taking Clio out for one last fling. I think I'm holding up the show."

"I heard. Have a good time, Annabelle. I'll see you tomorrow."

The deep rumble of his voice, the promise in the word *tomorrow*, sent shivers straight through me. I heard more than saw the smile on his face, and a little voice inside me screamed, "Run! Run for your heart!" But of course I didn't. I walked away with as much bravado as I could pretend and knew I'd spend the rest of the evening thinking even more than usual about Dakota Perri.

CHAPTER TWO

Annabelle

"WHAT'S THE DEAL with you and Dakota, Annabelle?" Stacy asked almost before we found a table in the dimly lit club we'd chosen for the night's festivities.

"Jack used Annabelle's acquaintance with Bailey Saunders to set us up the night we made Angel after the Red Rocks show," Clio helpfully supplied.

"Who's Bailey Saunders?" MandMs asked.

"Balefire's head road engineer," I said.

Stacy kept pushing. "How do you know Bailey?"

Slanting her a look, I said, "I met Bailey at a party once. He took a picture of me and apparently caught Clio in the background." I glanced around the room for our table. "I guess he showed the picture to Jack who saw Clio and hatched a plan that included giving me tickets and backstage passes to the concert, on the condition I brought Clio with me."

"So that's why you'd only offer those Red Rocks tickets to Clio. Now it all makes sense." Stacy arched a brow. "Did you meet Dakota that night?"

Clio and I exchanged a look.

"It's your story," Clio began. "I assumed something happened, but I never asked."

"Of course something happened." We were talking about Dakota Perri and me after all. Geez. Then I remembered myself. "But it was a long time ago. Tonight, we should be focusing on you."

Turning away from the conversation, I led us to the big semi-circular booth at the back of the bar. The large gold and black "Reserved" sign smack in the middle of it told me I had the right one.

Mandy MacLean, aka MandMs, was the quiet one of our little quartet, which made the vehemence in her voice so jarring once we all slid into our seats. "He didn't hurt you, ask you to do something you didn't want to do, did he? I've heard stories about how some of these privileged rock 'n' roll players take advantage of women." Her eyes saucered and her face turned cherry red as she looked around at our friends, two of whom were engaged to rock stars.

I had to laugh. She'd be mortified to discover what *I* initiated with Dakota that night. "No, MandMs, nothing bad happened." I waved my hand. "But it's all in the past."

"From the way he zeroed in on you at the rehearsal, it didn't look like it's in the past," Ashleigh said with a sly grin.

Before meeting Blu, Ashleigh had literally had been the girl next door, and the press still brought up the way Blu proposed to her onstage during a Balefire show in Miami. Though a couple of years older than the rest of us, and not part of our original little group of Chi Phi sorority sisters, Ashleigh fit right in with us.

Still, I wished she wasn't so observant. "You know Dakota better than I do. The fact that he's a monumental flirt shouldn't surprise you, Ashleigh," I said with an eye roll. Hopefully, they'd all take the hint and drop the discussion.

They didn't.

"He wasn't flirting with me during the rehearsal," MandMs pointed out with an impish smirk.

"That's because you were freaking out the whole time. Honestly, MandMs, you can take his arm like the rest of us. He won't bite—much. Right, Annabelle?" Stacy said with a laugh.

"But he's so big and intense and hot. And, oh God, he smells like heaven. I have no idea what to do with that much male perfection," MandMs gushed, breathlessly fanning herself.

I laughed with the others, but I knew exactly what she meant. Thinking about what he said after the rehearsal left me all hot and bothered. Mercifully, a waitress arrived to take our drink order. After she headed back to the bar, we busied ourselves arranging our gifts for Clio in the middle of the table. A few minutes later, our waitress returned with a tray of yummy drinks—margaritas and shots of tequila.

Raising my shot glass, I said, "Let's toast the woman—and man of the hour, which for the record is not Dakota Perri," I said with as much humor as I could. "To Jack Whitehorse and Clio Barnes. May you have the whole fairytale."

Choruses of "Oh yeah!" "Jack and Clio!" and "Congratulations!" rang out around the table as we raised our glasses to our friend.

"Now for the important stuff," I added with a wink.

Reaching across the table, I grabbed the gift bag I'd brought in with me and handed it to Clio. "Angel is evidence that you and Jack are quite compatible between the sheets," I began, "but we don't want you two becoming boring old married people. This should help."

I handed my gift to Clio with a wicked grin over the top of my margarita.

Clio pinkened, anticipating the naughtiness she would have to share with the rest of the group. Of course, I didn't disappoint. I'd found the sexiest white lace camisole, garters, and stockings set—no panties of course—exactly perfect for a honeymoon with a rock god. When Clio extracted my gift from the silver foil bag, people at the bar could hear the gasps from our corner table.

"Clio, your birth control had better be up to date when you

wear that on your honeymoon, or Angel is going to have a sibling before the year's up," Stacy said, with a laugh.

"This is seriously hot. Leave it to you, Annabelle, to find something like this for me." Clio grinned. "Thank you."

"My gift will complement Annabelle's. Here." Ashleigh handed Clio another bag.

"I can't imagine what could complement that." With a shy smile, Clio reached into the gift bag and pulled out a sexy black silk wrapper that looked about as long as a man's shirt.

"You have to pair those two, Clio," I said. "The hem of that wrapper might brush the tops of the stockings. Jack will lose his mind when he sees you."

She wavered. "If I can find the nerve to wear it."

"Oh, you have to wear it. Guys love to look, and you're going to look sooo amazing in that outfit." Ashleigh bobbed her head.

"This will be for the next night." Stacy handed Clio another gift bag.

Clio parted the tissue paper to reveal a turquoise satin teddy cut nearly to the navel. "Oh my. I think there might be a scrap of material here." She laughed nervously.

"It will look stunning with your auburn hair. That's mainly why I chose it. You could even wear the black wrapper with it for an added surprise," Stacy said.

I winked at Ashleigh who gave me a discreet thumbs-up.

"These gifts presuppose Jack will want you any way other than naked for the entirety of your honeymoon." I waggled my brows over the rim of my glass and took a sip of cool strawberry deliciousness.

Clio laughed too, but she didn't look any of us in the eye.

As I watched her reaction, I couldn't stop the teasing. "You know, for a woman who's the mom of a one-year-old daughter, I think you're the most virginal of us all."

"Except for maybe MandMs." Stacy slid her a side-eye. "Speaking of, what do you have for the blushing bride?"

"Oh, just this."

MandMs's cryptic tone should have alerted us, but we are talking MandMs here, which presumed something practical or at the least something innocent.

MandMs handed Clio a rather large, nondescript black matte gift bag that appeared to be filled with black tissue paper. The wrapping was intriguing, especially given the occasion and the giver.

Clio pulled out a wad of tissue paper and gasped. "MandMs! I thought Annabelle would give me this, not you."

When Clio didn't immediately reveal the contents of the bag, Stacy, Ashleigh, and I prompted her. "Come on, Clio. Show us."

"What's in the bag, Clio?"

"Spill it, girlfriend."

With an audible sigh, Clio pulled out a set of fur-lined handcuffs, a large purple vibrator, a pile of red silk scarves, and several small pots of flavored body paint.

"Did not see that coming, MandMs." I nodded in admiration. "But it looks like you brought the most useful gift of all."

Smiling, Stacy added, "Jack and Clio certainly shouldn't be bored on their honeymoon."

"Like that would happen anyway," Ashleigh said, raising her glass to her lips.

"What a surprise coming from you," Clio repeated, staring at MandMs.

MandMs shrugged and took a sip of her margarita.

"All right, MandMs, give it up. How do you know about all this stuff?" I demanded.

"I paid attention when we were all living at the Chi Phi house. And I've dated a few guys too," she replied with an enigmatic expression.

"There's a story there, one you need to share, Miss Innocence," Stacy said.

"I'll follow Annabelle's lead tonight and keep the focus on the woman of the hour. Clio, you don't have to give us details about your honeymoon, but maybe you could tell us Jack's reaction to our gifts? That would be fun," MandMs said before she demolished her margarita.

"Easy, girl. We need to be coherent tomorrow afternoon." Ashleigh inclined her head toward MandMs's empty glass.

"Afternoon being the operative word," MandMs replied, signaling the waitress for another round. "Tonight, we celebrate our friend's happiness."

During the evening, several men in the club approached us, drawn by the exuberant way we drank and danced together. With both Clio and Ashleigh engaged to two of the most gorgeous men on the planet and the other three of us there to support Clio, we flirted but kept our party mostly to ourselves. No doubt that was doubly unfair to the male clientele considering how hot we all looked in our short skirts and sky-high heels.

Some of the hangdog looks we received when we turned down the guys' more creative lines kept us going for the ride back to our hotel suite. Having closed down the club, we were still giggling when we exited our town car.

"I loved the guy who told you he could get you out of it after you told him you were in a relationship," Ashleigh said to Clio.

"I know, right?" She giggled.

"I liked the one about 'aside from being sexy, what else do you do for a living?'" I added and nearly tripped on the curb outside the hotel lobby.

"You do look sexy in that tight green dress, Annabelle," Stacy said. "But he didn't see you nearly miss that curb." Her laughter unleashed a fit of giggles from MandMs.

"Keep laughing, MandMs. But I thought I heard one of those guys, the one with the horn-rimmed glasses and his shirt buttoned to the collar, ask you if you were religious, 'cause you were the answer to his prayers. How did he zero in on you like that?"

"He wasn't the only one coming on to MandMs," Stacy said, her words slightly slurred. "I overheard that built cowboy tell her she might be asked to leave the bar soon since she was making the other women look bad. Way to go, MandMs!" She offered a fist bump, but they missed, unleashing another fit of laughter.

"I liked the guy who told you to stop drinking, Stacy, because you were driving him home," Clio added.

"I liked him too. That line was actually a good one."

Clio keyed us into the hotel suite where we were spending the night together, and we fell inside still laughing at the lines we'd heard during our evening. She dropped her gift bags on a side table while the rest of us collapsed onto comfy couches and lounge chairs artfully arranged around the living room.

"Clearly, that club attracts guys who spend too much time on pickup line sites or something." Ashleigh smirked.

"Yeah, well not all of us are lucky enough to find a rental next door to a rock star like some people we know," Stacy said with a sly wink.

"There is that." Ashleigh sighed. A smile spread over her face as she stared dreamily at the huge diamond on her left hand. With a little shake of her head, she said, "We picked the right place for a bachelorette party since that crowd assured that all of us would make it home together. Is that why you chose that particular venue, Stacy?"

"Maybe," she drawled.

"Don't be coy, Stace. You know that's exactly why you picked that club." I leaned back against the cushions on the couch and dangled the heel of my shoe off my foot.

"You have to admit, it was entertaining." Stacy snuggled deeper into the cushions on the other end of the couch.

"A good time was definitely had by all," MandMs said from the lounge she'd draped herself over.

"Time for bed, girls." Clio stood and stretched. "We have an early wake-up tomorrow."

"Ugghh! Don't remind us," I groaned, but I hauled myself up

off my comfy seat and headed down the hall to the bedroom I was sharing with MandMs.

♪

A picture-perfect day dawned for Clio's wedding. Or maybe it didn't dawn that way—but that's how we found it when we finally dragged ourselves out of bed at the butt crack of ten o'clock after someone from room service banged on our door. When we opened the drapes in the living area of the suite, we could see blue skies for miles.

"Today is going to be perfect," Stacy pronounced from where she stood before the floor-to-ceiling windows. "The perfect day for the perfect couple."

Her words fell on deaf ears as the bride in question stepped back into her bedroom, her phone tight against her ear. As I walked farther into the living room, I caught part of her conversation.

"We had a great time, but I miss you and Angel. That's the first night I've ever spent away from her. I can't wait…"

I lost the rest when Clio softly closed the door behind her.

"The perfect bride is being the perfect mom at the moment, Stacy," I said as I arranged myself on the lounge.

"She is, isn't she?" Stacy handed me a flute of orange juice.

I took a sip. Make that a mimosa. Yum.

"That's exactly the way we should start this perfect day. Your roommate up yet?" I asked.

"Ashleigh's in the shower. I take it MandMs is in yours."

"Yep. Which means more yummy healthy alcohol for us."

"Healthy alcohol?"

"Of course. You made this with orange juice, didn't you?"

Stacy cracked up.

"What's so funny?" Ashleigh asked as she stepped into the room, towel drying her hair.

Stacy walked over to the room service cart and produced another mimosa, handing it to Ashleigh. "Here's some 'healthy alcohol,'" she said, air quoting me.

Ashleigh pulled a face, and I explained, "It's made with orange juice. Orange juice is good for you. So—healthy alcohol." Punctuating my words, I took a large swallow, smacked my lips, and grinned.

"You are one of a kind, Annabelle." A wicked gleam slipped into Ashleigh's eyes. "You really are kind of perfect for Dakota."

I nearly dropped my drink at her comment but tossed back the entire contents of my glass to cover my reaction.

"Uh-huh. There's definitely more to your story than you've told us," Stacy began.

The back of my neck grew hot. "I, uh, you know, it's not…"

Bless MandMs. "Hey, Annabelle. Can I borrow some of your lotion? I seem to have forgotten mine."

"Sure. Let me grab it for you."

I all but ran down the short hallway to our shared room.

♪

We all congregated in Clio's bedroom to dress for the wedding. I was helping MandMs with her hair when I heard Ashleigh open the door of the suite to Lori Whitehorse, Jack's mom, who arrived with Clio's baby Angel. We'd all showered and finished the breakfast she'd so thoughtfully ordered from room service. Stacy allowed Clio two minutes to reconnect with her daughter before she sat Clio back into the chair so she could finish her makeup. A sense of déjà vu washed over me as I remembered another day when Stacy made up Clio's face in anticipation of seeing Jack Whitehorse.

"This is the scene I always hoped to see in my own home," Lori remarked with a sigh as she surveyed the chaos of Clio's bedroom. Bridesmaid dresses hung from closet doors and Clio's wedding dress took up the middle of her bed. We'd dragged extra chairs from other rooms into the suite as we helped each other fix our hair and makeup. Laughing and talking, we were completely at home with our informal set-up as we prettied ourselves.

"Jack mentioned something about that when he called me this morning," Clio said around Stacy's hand as she applied lipstick to Clio's mouth.

"I'd like to know what you were doing talking to Jack this morning," Lori demanded. "The bride and groom are supposed to remain separated until the wedding." Her tone was stern, but her eyes danced.

"Couldn't help it. If your son weren't so h"—she caught herself—"wonderful, I wouldn't need to call him the morning of our wedding," Clio responded. "Besides, I needed to check on Angel."

At the mention of her name, the toddler in question crawled up into her mother's lap and reached for the makeup brush Stacy wielded as she touched up the contours she'd highlighted on Clio's cheeks.

"She lived right up to her name as usual," Lori cooed at the baby. "Angel is the most precious little person on the planet." She smiled lovingly at her granddaughter who fisted her tiny hands in Clio's bathrobe and babbled happily.

"I almost forgot. The photographer will be here in half an hour, so I hope you're ready for the dressing photos," Lori added.

"You sure are, Lori. You're one stunning mother of the groom. No wonder your sons are so gorgeous," Ashleigh said as she dropped her rose-champagne bridesmaid dress over her head. Due to her time on the road touring with Balefire, she had perfected a routine that rendered her sensational in half the time it took the rest of us to look decent.

"They are a rather gorgeous lot, aren't they?" Lori beamed with pride. "Now one of them is finally bringing women into the family. Has Jack mentioned he's currently my favorite?"

"Only about a thousand times since our engagement last Christmas," Clio said laughing.

"If I'm lucky, girls will outnumber boys in the Whitehorse

household before all is said and done," Lori added, waggling her eyebrows wickedly.

We finished our wedding toilet right as a knock on the door announced the photographer's arrival. He took several photos of Stacy and Lori fussing with Clio's veil and of the rest of us admiring the garter we'd insisted she place high on her thigh rather than below her knee where she demurely tried to put it. Then the photographer concentrated on Clio and Angel. For some weird reason, those poses of my friend staring into her daughter's eyes with so much love caused a picture of Dakota Perri to invade my mind. Shaking my head to clear it, I made myself useful by gathering up the bouquets the florist had delivered on the heels of the photographer's arrival.

A short time later, our happy, giggly trek through the hotel lobby stopped all conversation as people smiled at the gorgeous bride and her entourage. A stretch limo awaited us in front of the hotel, and I pulled Clio aside as Lori stepped in to buckle Angel into her car seat.

"Remember the last time we rode in a limo together? I couldn't understand why you weren't having as much fun as the rest of us, but that's not the case today, is it girlfriend?"

"Honestly, Annabelle, I was terrified to see Jack that night. Today, I can hardly wait to see him, to make our life together official." A speculative gleam in her eye should have warned me. "As I recall, you couldn't wait to meet a certain lead guitar player that night. That still the case, Annabelle?"

"Didn't we give that topic a rest at your bachelorette party?"

"You *are* looking forward to seeing him again." Clio grinned. "Good for you. He's definitely hot, and you know exactly how to handle your heart around a guy like him," she added with a whole lot more confidence than I felt.

My friends appreciated that I was choosy yet also enjoyed men. After all, God put them on this earth to make life fun for us girls. But for some reason I didn't want to think about too much, I wanted to keep my night with Dakota to myself. Hold those memories close.

Fortunately, we had the distraction of the wedding to change the subject as Stacy lifted Clio's train, and together we helped her into the car. Gathered in our wake, the hotel lobby crowd cheered as I closed the door, and all of us waved back. The strangers' enthusiastic send-off seemed an auspicious beginning to Jack and Clio's marriage.

CHAPTER THREE

Annabelle

MANDMS NUDGED ME, and we both stole a glance at Clio's parents, Harrison and Meredith Barnes, as the three single members of Balefire launched into their raucous, acoustic version of "Missing You." Jack had written the song for Clio between one of their reconciliations and asked the guys to play it during the ceremony, a plan kept secret from Clio's parents. Mr. and Mrs. Harrison Barnes considered themselves among Denver's elite, and they probably were, but their insistence on strict decorum for the ceremony, complete with a string quartet, irritated Jack. I'd overheard him say something about it to Tron before the rehearsal last night.

This little show apparently was his way of giving his new in-laws the finger while simultaneously honoring his bride and friends.

Meredith Barnes pursed her lips and glared at the back of Clio's head, but I thought I detected the ghost of a smile on Harrison Barnes's lips before he blanked his face altogether.

Clio, on the other hand, laughed out loud when Balefire started playing and leaned up to kiss Jack on the cheek.

Blu appeared to be trying to sing to the happy couple, but I noticed his attention kept straying to Ashleigh. My heart fluttered at all the love flowing through the music, and my attention drifted to Dakota.

He played his guitar like a sorcerer, conjuring incredible sounds from a wooden box and steel strings. I couldn't look away as he tore up a solo in the middle of the song where Jack usually blew a listener's mind with his drums. Dakota's long fingers were a blur as they traveled up and down the neck of his guitar, mesmerizing me with movement and sound. Somewhere in the back of my consciousness, I remembered those hands playing my body with exactly as much skill.

Like he'd somehow tuned in to my thoughts, Dakota looked away from his guitar only once, his eyes zeroing in on me. I couldn't read the expression in their sea-blue depths before he gave me a tiny nod and returned his concentration to playing. Could the sorcerer read my mind? Yet I couldn't stop staring until the song ended and the band returned their instruments to their hiding place behind the justice of the peace.

Jack and Clio concluded the ceremony with a kiss so scorching it should have been X-rated. Jack's grandmother was still fanning herself as the last of the wedding party walked up the aisle and over to the reception area under a banquet-size tent. That kiss made me wish for a private moment with a certain lead guitarist before I took a deep breath to shut down my libido. Sensing Dakota's eyes on the bare skin my dress exposed on my back as we walked up the aisle didn't help much.

The reception began with the toasts. Stacy gushed about what a great couple and what great parents Jack and Clio made. Jack's brother Colin told Jack to enjoy his favored son status while he could, leaving everyone to guess what he meant by that. Then I caught the telltale signs of a blush staining Stacy's cheeks beneath her carefully applied makeup, and I wondered.

Next, Jack and Clio cut the cake without all that smashing-cake-in-the-face nonsense. Jack's four younger brothers grumbled their disappointment, but Jack simply smiled and leaned in to kiss imaginary cake crumbs from Clio's lips, eliciting a sigh from the women in attendance. He looked up from the kiss and winked at his brothers, slipping an arm around his bride and pulling her close to his side.

I tried my best to keep my attention on the bride and groom, on the wedding traditions they enacted, and on Adam Tron, my partner for the day. Even though I found the man interesting and sizzling hot in his quiet, understated way, my thoughts and my eyes kept straying down the table to where Dakota sat. Unable to keep my eyes away from him, I mentally kicked myself. Seeing MandMs ignoring him made me too happy to be nice, but I couldn't help it. The idea of Dakota with MandMs, especially after her little surprise present at the bachelorette party, had invited the green-eyed monster into the dark recesses of my mind. The feeling left me uncomfortable. MandMs was one of my best friends, and I certainly had no claim on Dakota Perri after one night of spectacular sex.

Not long after the cake distribution, Jack's old band Rude Awakening set up their instruments, and the party started in earnest, rescuing me from my wayward thoughts.

Dakota

Unfortunately, I'd been seated at the opposite end of the table from Annabelle for the toasts and cake. Which meant I couldn't acknowledge let alone do something about the hot desire she let me see when she stared at me as I played my guitar during the ceremony. MandMs hadn't relaxed with me at all, so I didn't even have conversation as a distraction for the lustful thoughts Annabelle stirred in my head.

I'd promised Blu and Tron I'd remain on my best behavior today, so I had to wait until after Jack and Clio danced their first dance before I could approach Annabelle. Anticipating the wait might actually kill me, I downed my glass of champagne and reached for the magnum on our end of the table for a refill. If the preliminaries continued to drag on, I'd be well into that bottle to maintain my sanity.

Nonchalantly leaning forward to sip from my glass, I turned my head to check on Annabelle and caught her staring back at me. Good to know she couldn't stop thinking about me either. I acknowledged her with a nod and a wink, and she leaned back in her chair so fast, I was afraid she might topple over. Maybe she wasn't so cool where I was concerned. I liked knowing that. Chuckling to myself, I took another healthy swallow of champagne and settled back into my chair.

"W-what's so funny?" MandMs asked from beside me.

"Circumstance," I replied before catching on that she'd initiated conversation. "Hey, you talk."

"Of course I talk. What kind of comment is that?" she huffed.

"Since Clio paired us up at the rehearsal yesterday, you've been completely silent."

"Well, you've been completely intimidating."

She drained her champagne, and I didn't waste time refilling her glass.

"Drink up. Maybe when you relax, you won't find me intimidating."

She cocked a brow at me and drained half the refill I'd poured for her.

"Slow down, sister. We still have to dance."

"I know. I'm getting ready."

"You need to be smashed to dance with me?" That was a new one.

"You do have a reputation, you know. One I think you've earned. I'm trying not to embarrass Clio by running away from you."

Huh. I'd never had that effect on a woman. Usually, they were crowding around me, not trying to keep themselves from running away. Then again, I did just watch the sexiest woman I'd ever met nearly knock herself out of her chair when I caught her staring at me. I grinned to myself again.

I knew I shouldn't but I couldn't resist teasing Clio's nerved-up friend. "Relax. I promise not to ravish you—much—on the dance floor."

When I said that, I swear MandMs squeaked. She downed the rest of her champagne and didn't wait for me to refill her glass, doing the honors herself instead.

Damn. I wore a tux, covering up all of my ink. I'd replaced the big-ass diamond stud I usually wore in my ear with an understated gold hoop. I'd even brushed my teeth and washed behind my ears in the shower this morning. Yet this girl acted like I was some ravaging ogre from a fairy tale. Oh, yeah, here was some fun to be had.

Jack's old band started warming up on the dais near the portable dance floor under the tent, and Jack and Clio rose to take the floor for the first dance. Nonchalantly reclining in my chair, I slid my arm along the back of MandMs's seat and smiled wolfishly at the way she sat forward like she might run through the table any minute to escape me.

A few bars into the song, Dez Amarillas, lead singer of Rude Awakening, invited us onto the dance floor. "Our buddy Jack and his new wife—damn, that's kinda hard to say—his new wife Clio would like the rest of the wedding party to join them out here."

"That's our cue."

I stood and reached a hand out to MandMs who stared at it like it might morph into a serpent or something before she waved hers over it and stood by herself. So of course, I had to go there. "Time to face the music, little girl," I growled at her.

She squeaked again when I set my hand lightly on the small of her back and propelled her ahead of me for our obligatory dance. As much fun as it was to tease her, her responses were starting to bug me. What I wanted—needed—was the breathy encouragement of a certain brunette with eyes the most beautiful shade of light green I'd ever seen.

Since the wedding party took the dance floor in the middle of the song, I didn't have to endure MandMs's stiff body and jerky dance moves for long. When the song ended, though, I couldn't resist a parting shot. I snapped my teeth near her ear, and she nearly jumped out of her dress. "Thanks for the dance. The Big Bad Wolf will leave you alone now," I whispered.

Without waiting for her response, I turned on my heel and headed for my prize. After being a good boy and putting up with the goofy bridesmaid, I deserved some alone time with Annabelle.

During a quiet moment at the rehearsal last night, I'd casually asked Clio about her. The fact that she'd remained unattached since I met her gratified me. I didn't want to have to take out some schmo who thought he stood a chance with her. Plus, her attending the wedding dateless gave me the green light for enjoying another night—or two—with her. Knowing she'd be here was one of the reasons I came stag. Of course, attending any function with a date would have meant giving up opportunities, and that never figured into my MO.

By the time I finished teasing MandMs, Annabelle had nearly made it off the dance floor. Snagging her hand, I tugged her back to me.

"Annababy, I think it's my turn to dance with you."

I couldn't help but smirk at her wide-eyed stare in response to the endearment I'd made up on our one night together. "Hey, you told me last night if I wanted to dance with you, all I had to do was ask."

Though the band kicked into something up-tempo, I pulled Annabelle close, wrapping my arms around her, probably holding her way too close for a polite dance at the start of the evening. Not that I gave a shit. I'd been waiting a long time for this moment.

She held herself stiffly, her hands barely resting on my biceps. I needed her to relax, be herself with me.

"I heard you girls had a good time last night."

"We did, thanks."

"You give Clio some special stuff to encourage Jack on their honeymoon?" I couldn't rein in the wicked chuckle that escaped me.

Annabelle shivered deliciously against me, and I pulled her body flush with mine as I swayed us to the music.

"Definitely," she replied with a knowing smile. "MandMs surprised the heck out of us with the bag of tricks she gave Clio."

"MandMs?" I pulled back enough to catch her eye. "From my experience with that one, I'd think she gave Clio a blanket masquerading as sleepwear." I couldn't help the accompanying eye roll. Honestly, that woman had tried my patience almost to my last nerve.

Annabelle laughed. I couldn't tell if she laughed at me or at her friend, but I didn't care. Her laughter made me think of champagne bubbles, all light and round. When she laughed, she relaxed, her full breasts pillowing perfectly against my chest. It was all I could do to keep my hands wrapped around her waist rather than let them explore further south over her pretty round ass.

Her expression turned positively naughty as she described MandMs's gift to Clio. My eyes widened as she shared the details of flavored body paint and fur-lined handcuffs.

"Get out! Are we talking about the same person here? The one who needed two glasses of liquid courage to dance half a dance with me a few minutes ago?"

"She thinks you're scary." Annabelle smirked.

"I know." I sighed dramatically. "She told me when she finally started speaking to me." I leaned in close, rubbing my jaw lightly against the side of Annabelle's face. "You don't think I'm scary though," I purred into her ear.

Again with the full-body shiver. I have to admit, I liked the way the woman couldn't help but respond to me.

She sighed and pulled away, leveling a look at me. "I know you're scary. When it comes to women, you're a pirate, stealing all our common sense. I've seen your show live, remember? Every possible style of women's lingerie literally carpeted that stage and the floor in front of it at Red Rocks."

"Except for your sexy black lace thong." I quirked a brow. "That hung off my guitar for most of the show."

She gasped. "You remember what I threw onto the stage that night?"

"There were three hotties in the front row whose attention I wanted later. One of them turned out to be Clio, who obviously was spoken for. The other one tossed up a red lace bra, and I had a notion to follow up on her invitation." She shot me a look, and I chuckled. "You tossed up those incredibly sexy panties. But I gotta say, Annabelle, you were definitely the prize."

She blinked at me.

"Usually, I'm not a big fan of weddings, but I was looking forward to this one when I found out you'd be attending it."

No doubt my eyes gave away my desire for her since she sucked in a breath when she looked into them.

The song ended, and the lead singer announced the bride and groom were to dance with their parents. Since my whole goal for the evening involved a repeat of the night after Red Rocks, I took Annabelle's hand in mine and led her from the dance floor over to where I'd been sitting with MandMs. Mercifully, that woman had vacated her seat, ensuring I could keep Annabelle close to me.

Apparently, some little drama played out with Clio and her parents, something that riveted Annabelle's interest. She sat on the edge of the chair I pulled out for her, and when I leaned in to ask her about champagne, she shushed me.

"What's going on?" I whispered.

Speaking out of the side of her mouth, she explained, "I don't know what Jack's told you, but Clio's parents don't exactly approve of this marriage. Because of Angel, they're stuck though. I hope Clio's dad doesn't humiliate her at her own wedding."

At her pronouncement, I noticed she sat like she could bolt any second. Not what I had in mind at all.

"Are you planning to do something about it?" I asked more casually than I felt.

"I think all the women in the bridal party plus Jack's mom are ready to do something about it."

Leaning back in my chair, I looked around the reception, and sure enough, all of Clio's friends showed a keen interest in Harrison Barnes's reaction to the lead singer's invitation.

Taking his time, he stood up from the little table where he and his wife sat apart from the rest of the party and walked with purpose to Clio and Jack's table. Silently, he held his hand out to his daughter, and I swear, I heard a collective sigh of relief circle the backyard.

Clio glanced at Jack, and he nodded before he stood and walked over to her mom. The woman hesitated, and it was my turn to feel protective.

"She wouldn't…" Annabelle began, echoing my thoughts.

Mrs. Barnes looked around at the rest of the party guests and placed her hand in Jack's. I relaxed and turned my attention to Annabelle.

"I take it this little scene had people worried."

"You were worried too. I felt you tense up when it looked like Mrs. Barnes might not dance with her new son-in-law."

I shrugged.

"We can all relax and have some fun now that Clio's parents have publicly acknowledged Jack and Clio." She sat back in her chair and let out a long breath.

Handing Annabelle a glass of champagne, I said, "I'm all about having fun. Dancing with you, among other things, is fun."

I kept my tone neutral, but I slid my arm over the back of her chair.

When she downed a slug of champagne, I couldn't help but grin. Leaning toward her, I whispered, "Just so you know, you get to me too."

Slowly, she turned her head to stare at me with round eyes.

"I'm not kidding about wanting a repeat of the first time we met." I let my eyes roam over her face and the artistic mass of shiny curls piled on her head before I zeroed in on her pouty mouth. "In case you were wondering."

She took a deep breath. "I gotta be honest, Dakota. I'm surprised you even remembered me."

"Remembered your panties onstage and that incredible strip show you gave me later." I smiled over the rim of my glass and downed half my champagne.

"Shhh! You don't have to say that so loud," she hissed and looked around for who else might have heard me.

"You're embarrassed by that? How could you be embarrassed by that?" Seriously, I couldn't understand how doing something so off-the-charts hot could embarrass her. Leaning close, I said, "That night was one of the most incredible nights I've ever spent with a woman, Annabelle."

Again with the surprised eyes. "It was?"

"Definitely. And I let you get away without knowing your last name or number. I read the wedding program, so now I know your name is Annabelle Stewart, but I still don't have your number."

"You want that?"

How could this woman who put herself out there to give me a private show and radiated confidence in the way she carried herself and interacted with her friends—yes, I was watching—not believe my very real interest in her?

I pulled my phone from the front pocket of my suit pants and pulled up a new contact. "Your number, Annabelle."

She blinked a couple of times, and I wanted to kiss her. Not because her full lips were such a temptation or because I knew exactly how soft they felt beneath mine but because she wasn't one of those pretentious women who knew the only thing in the world I wanted was her number.

A slow smile curved those luscious lips as she caught where my eyes had wandered. Then she grabbed my phone and programmed her number into it—at least I hoped it was her number.

After she handed the phone back to me, she arched a brow, leaned in close to me, and whispered, "We're going to keep that night between us, right?" A sudden thought took her and she sat back and gasped. "You haven't already told the other guys in the band, have you?"

Her strapless dress only hinted at her cleavage, but it exposed her chest, where a distinctly rose tinge bloomed on its way to her neck. Fascinated, I watched as it climbed up to her cheeks. Without conscious thought, I traced my fingertips along that blush and cupped her face in my hand. She stilled at my touch, seeming not to breathe.

Setting my lips on her skin, I spoke for her ears only. "Annabelle, there are some experiences that are too special to share with anyone. That night with you was one of them." Settling back in my chair, I eyed her. "I take it you didn't share it with your friends either."

"N-no."

"Bet we're on the same page about this too."

Lowering my mouth to hers, a tiny puff of air gusted over my lips as she let it go. Those full ripe lips of hers were beneath mine, and the whole party disappeared. So soft, so sweet. A faint taste of champagne and the dark promise of feminine heat overwhelmed my senses, and I deepened the kiss, sliding my tongue across the seam of her mouth, teasing her to let me in.

When she opened for me, I couldn't stop the groan that rumbled deep in my throat. Jesus, the woman could kiss. Her tongue moved over mine as aggressively and insistently as mine moved over hers. Somewhere along the line, her hand rose to my face, holding me to her the way I held her to me. I could have kissed her like that for hours, but from some distant place, someone rather loudly cleared his throat, interrupting my concentration.

Tron stood right behind my chair. "I'd tell you to get a room, but I know you'd take me up on that suggestion, and the party is a long way from over," he said laughing.

"Oh, I agree with that," I replied, my eyes never leaving Annabelle's. "What do you want, Tron?"

"To remind you that you're seated at the front of the party."

"And?"

"And you might want to remember that you promised to behave today—and tonight. Show some solidarity with Jack on his big day."

Rolling my eyes, I sighed and pulled back. "Yeah, yeah. I remember. You can move along now. Nothing to see here."

Tron laughed again. Addressing Annabelle, he added, "Apparently, you made an impression on our boy that night after Red Rocks."

"What are you talking about?" she demanded, leveling a suspicious look at me.

"You were with Clio that night. Dakota was jerking Jack's chain about her before you snagged his attention, which was good. Kept me from having to step in the middle of those two." He smiled. "Guess you're reconnecting."

"And we don't need a chaperone," I grumbled.

"You kinda did a few minutes ago," he said with a chuckle. "Enjoy yourselves, kids, but humor the rest of us and keep it PG."

"Who died and made you dad?" I said under my breath.

Tron exploded in laughter and walked away.

All the good feelings we'd been sharing seemed to have dried up with Tron's interruption.

"I thought you said you didn't share anything about that night with the rest of the band," Annabelle said quietly, her eyes on her lap.

I'd been on the receiving end of that kind of frost a time or two, and I wasn't having it from her. "I didn't say one damn thing about us to anyone, Annababy."

She arched a brow and sat farther away from me.

"Like Tron said, he remembers you from that night too. Kinda hard not to with as hot as you looked in that leather skirt."

"You remember what I wore that night?" It was kind of cute the way her voice rose with each word.

"I remember everything about that night. Which is why I hope you didn't fuck with me when you programmed your number into my phone. I have plans for us that don't end with this party."

Annabelle

That kiss I couldn't resist left me wet and needy, distinctly uncomfortable for the earliness of the evening. The way Dakota touched me, so gentle yet with so much intent almost got me off as much as his kiss. Good thing Tron interrupted us, or who knows how far things could have gone. It was one thing when I thought he might have a passing idea of who I was. It was something else to know he remembered the same details I did—and for the same reason.

Sleeping with Dakota Perri after Balefire's Red Rocks concert had been my own personal dare, a private challenge I thought would end there. I hadn't counted on how he'd make me feel—or apparently how I'd make him feel too. Thinking about it now, I hadn't treated him fairly. In my mind at the time, he was a rock star, someone not quite real. The night itself had become almost a fantasy in my head, something that only happened in my dreams.

Our conversation after Tron interrupted us reminded me that in spite of his celebrity, his incredible musical ability, and his reputation, Dakota was first and foremost a man. An intense, incredibly hot man who wanted another night with me. A real night, not a fantasy.

Total shock would be the understatement of the year to describe how that revelation made me feel.

Of course I'd go there. No woman in her right mind would pass up a night with the sexiest lead guitarist in the country. But what about afterward? Considering the way I'd obsessed over Dakota after spending one night with him, how would I ever handle the aftermath of spending a second one with him? Especially since I understood he was a player, a wild-ass rock 'n' roll star who would move on with the band's next tour.

Sure, he'd asked for my phone number, and if he ever called it, he'd find I'd played him straight. I blinked at him. I was fairly sure he'd never call it. A guy like him would do the pretty and ask for a number to keep a girl from feeling used. After all, he might run into her again at a wedding or something. Still, the possibility of another incredible night in Dakota Perri's bed would tempt a saint to sin. Everyone who knew me knew I never aspired to be a saint.

"Annabelle, what are you doing sitting here? We need you for the bridesmaids dance." When MandMs breathlessly spoke to me, I had a fleeting notion she did so to drag me away from Dakota, probably for my own protection.

"The what?" Dakota demanded.

"You know, when the bridesmaids all dance together—without guys," she emphasized like everyone should know what she was talking about.

Actually, we made up the dance at the bachelorette party when all of us were pretty well hammered. I'm surprised anyone remembered.

"Come *on*, Annabelle." She punctuated her command by grabbing my arm and nearly dragging me out of my chair.

Throwing an apologetic smile at Dakota, I followed my friend to join the others already on the dance floor. Ashleigh met me with a shot of tequila while Stacy handed one to MandMs. Shooting the girls a wicked grin, I downed mine, wiped my mouth with the back of my hand, and shook my head. Out of the corner of my eye, I caught Clio's mom gaping in horror at my antics, and I burst out laughing. After we shot our shots, the four of us lined up facing the head table to perform our dance for the bride and groom.

Chapter Four

Dakota

BLU WANDERED OVER to me as we watched the girls do some serious booty shakin' for Jack and Clio's benefit.

"Those are some smokin' hot moves out there," I commented with a grin over my champagne glass.

Neither of us could hold in our amusement at the campy way they danced together in something resembling a line until it morphed into extra sexy with them pairing off. My mouth went dry at the way Annabelle moved her ass, and I had to discreetly adjust the front of my tux. I heard Blu clear his throat, so I glanced at Ashleigh and knew exactly what was on his mind as we enjoyed the show our girls put on with their friends.

"Your girl or mine?" Blu asked. The sly smirk on his face didn't fool me for a second.

One of the circulating servers stepped out onto the floor with a tray of shots, and the girls stopped dancing long enough to down two each before resuming their dance.

"They're all sizzling out there, laughing and dancing like that,"

I replied. "Hell, even scared little MandMs is drawing attention to her cute ass."

Blu cocked a brow. "You aiming to have two of the bridesmaids tonight? I thought your attention centered on the one you already knew."

"I'm not blind, and I'm not dead. Each of those girls is gorgeous. But Ashleigh is taken—"

"Damn straight."

"I think Colin has designs on Stacy."

Blu smiled. "You caught that too."

I nodded. "MandMs thinks I'm the Big Bad Wolf."

"You, of course, did nothing to encourage that idea," he said, laughing.

"Possibly." I smirked. "And Annabelle and I have a rather sweet history I'd like to revisit. I'm confining my play to one girl tonight. Satisfied?"

"You may have competition for that," Blu said as we watched the lead singer of the band step off the dais to join the girls, singling out Annabelle to dance with him.

When Balefire first started out, we played lots of weddings too, so I knew all about hooking up with bridesmaids. Which meant I needed to put a stop to the lead singer's intentions immediately—or sooner.

A waiter bearing another tray of shots interrupted the singer before he could move in my girl. While the bridesmaids downed two more shots each, I made my move to the dance floor. Blu trailed right behind me.

"Hey, I don't need a chaperone here. I said I wouldn't make a scene tonight. I'm only going to cut in on the booty dance and make sure that singer understands his place at this party," I ground out over my shoulder.

"'Course you are, Dakota my man. I figured I'd join my girl too," Blu replied, a smile on his lips that didn't match the wariness in his eyes.

Apparently, Tron and Jack's brother Colin had a similar idea—or they were worried about the way the lead singer tried to move in on Annabelle. Either way, they arrived on the dance floor at roughly the same time Blu and I did. Tron took one for the team as he danced with MandMs, leaving Annabelle to me.

"Another wedding party dance?" she asked as I smiled at her and took one of her hands in mine.

"Something like that. You girls were having too much fun without us, so we thought we'd join in."

With a lopsided grin, she twirled around me. "Now we're having too much fun with you."

"Not sure I could ever have too much fun with you, Annababy," I said, pulling her in close.

"Shh! That's our secret, remember?" Her loud stage whisper drew the attention of Stacy and Colin who were dancing near us.

"Keep talking, Annabelle. You know we want to hear all about that," Stacy said over her shoulder as Colin spun her away from us.

"Oops!" Annabelle giggled.

The song ended, and I led her back to our chairs at the wedding party table.

"Maybe we need to put some food in you. What do you say?" I asked as I seated her.

"That would ruin the good buzz I have going right now. Did you know we were doing shots of tequila last night too? We heard some funny stuff when we were doing those shots." A coy smile played over those luscious lips of hers.

Humoring her, I asked, "What did you hear?"

"Pickup lines. The whole club was filled with guys spouting pickup lines. I think it must have been pickup line night or something." She giggled and reached for her flute of champagne.

"Yeah? Did they work?" I pretended humor, but for some reason, it bothered me that she might have picked up someone at the club. Especially after the guys and I spent Jack's last night as a single man playing high-stakes poker with some card sharps masquerading as Jack's brothers and no women in sight.

"We laughed all the way back to the hotel. Silly boys and their pickup lines," she answered, mischief dancing in her eyes.

As I watched and listened to her, it occurred to me I might have acquired an interest in a woman startlingly close to my own temperament. Someone who enjoyed a good time with no strings attached. Love 'em and leave 'em behind. Except I hadn't left her behind. She'd touched something inside me, and I discovered to my growing consternation that I didn't want to share her.

"Did they work?" I asked.

She blinked in surprise at the harshness I didn't try to disguise in my voice.

"Of course not. Our hen party rules included no guys allowed. But I have to admit we enjoyed how hard those guys were working their lines."

"Bet I've got one that would work on you." I shot her a wicked smile and waited.

"Uh-huh. I think you already used it at the rehearsal last night. Got you two dances so far tonight."

I smiled knowingly, holding her eyes with mine until at last, she broke the contact.

"Hey darlin', over here. I need something with more kick than champagne," she said to a passing waiter.

She ordered a hop-skip-and-go-naked, her expression challenging me, so I asked for one too. If she wanted to do shots with me, I was all for it. Whatever she wanted to do—drink, dance, sneak away for some off-the-charts sex—as long as she wanted to do it with me, I was game.

For whatever reason, Annabelle decided to party hard to celebrate Jack and Clio's marriage. Turned out, we drank too many shots, danced too few dances, and didn't even get to the sex. At some point, Stacy helped Annabelle stagger to the ladies' room, and neither of them returned to the party. After all the shots I did with her, it took me a while to figure out she'd disappeared. By then, it was too late. When I asked where the girls had gone, Tron informed me that Sam, Jack's dad, had driven Annabelle, Stacy, and MandMs back to the hotel to sleep off the wedding. How the fuck did I let that happen?

Chapter Five

Annabelle

AFTER WAKING UP in the hotel suite in my underwear and stockings the next morning with no idea how that happened, life returned to normal. I'd moved into the apartment above my parents' garage right after college graduation. Now it was time to work on securing an internship in marketing and management. Squandering an opportunity for another night with Dakota Perri by drinking too much too early at the wedding reception still tortured me whenever I thought about it. After all, it wasn't like I'd had so many opportunities to repeat the incredible experience of spending a night with him.

Yeah, I remembered the part early in the evening when he'd asked for my number, but that had been over a week ago. I had no delusions about what he thought. He'd let me down easy with the phone number request.

The chiming of my phone interrupted my thoughts, and one look at the unfamiliar number sent my heart into overdrive. Taking a couple of deep breaths to calm down, I answered. "This is Annabelle."

"Hello Annabelle. This is Garrett Phillips, manager for Balefire. We met briefly at Jack and Clio Whitehorse's wedding last weekend."

Clearing my throat to hide the disappointment in my voice, I said, "Yes, I remember. How are you Garrett?"

"Listen, this isn't a social call. I've been informed that you're looking for an internship in marketing and management, so I took the liberty of checking into your credentials, and I'd like to offer you an opportunity."

"W-what?" I sputtered and immediately wanted to kick myself. "I mean, yes, I am looking for an internship." I hoped I sounded at least somewhat professional.

"You would be working in the front office with our marketing people for the first month before working closely with me when the band heads out on tour after Jack and Clio return from their honeymoon."

Wow. Oh wow. I could be going on tour with Balefire. I would be on tour with Dakota Perri. I did a little happy dance around my chair before I sobered up.

Damn. I'd be out on tour with Dakota Perri. How awkward would that be when I had to watch him hooking up with other fans like me, knowing what those women were going to experience with him?

"Um, what all would that entail?" I asked.

"More than I want to discuss on the phone. Are you available to stop by the band's studio tomorrow afternoon, say two? We'll talk about it then."

I consulted my nonexistent calendar. "Sure, that'll work."

"Emory, our office manager, will have something drawn up. If you're game, we can sign the paperwork after our meeting."

He gave me directions to the band's studio and rang off.

I alternated between bouncing around my apartment, jumping up and down on the floor and the furniture, and trying to control my excitement with realistic thoughts of what it would mean to watch Dakota with the hordes of groupies the band attracted after every show. The idea of being part of Balefire's entourage sent me over the moon. Then I thought about what that probably meant—being the help, not part of the band—and my enthusiasm crashed to earth. As much as I wanted to see Dakota again, even after the fool I made of myself at Clio and Jack's wedding, I had to be realistic. I wouldn't be touring in the same way Clio and Ashleigh did. Probably, I'd be walking around with my phone glued to my ear and an iPad glued to my hand as I took notes from Garrett about what needed to be done, how, when, and where.

Still, the offer was an incredible chance to beef up my résumé and make me stand out from all the other MBA candidates when I applied to graduate school. I knew the minute Garrett offered it, I'd say yes, but I had to play it cool at the meeting he scheduled.

I didn't know how or when Clio had given Garrett my number, but I had time before she returned from her tropical honeymoon to make plans for the best way to thank her. No doubt this was her way of giving back after the way I helped Jack reconnect with her. The thought made me smile.

♪

Balefire's studio was housed in a Quonset hut-looking building in an older, mostly residential area in Denver. The studio had no signs or markings of any kind to distinguish it from being anything other than the mechanics shop it used to be. If not for Garrett's precise directions, I'm not sure I'd have found it.

I walked in through the side door and down a short nondescript hallway that opened into the understated elegance of the studio's front office. It took a couple minutes to acclimate my eyes to the subtle flames woven through the area rug on the floor and licking up the walls in the corners and across the ceiling of the room. A massive black and chrome desk took up the space in the middle of the floor while a series of private offices with large windows looking out into the central area surrounded it.

The stunning Asian woman seated at the massive desk looked up from her telephone conversation to acknowledge me with a finger. A minute later, she concluded her call and walked around her desk to greet me.

"You must be Annabelle Stewart. I'm Emory Murakami, office manager and general girl Friday for Balefire. It'll be great to have a person with your particular skill set working for us."

She spoke as if the internship was a done deal even though I'd yet to see, let alone sign, any papers.

"Nice to meet you," I returned, shaking her outstretched hand.

Though the cut of her slim pencil skirt and silk blouse proclaimed professional attire, the oversized black-and-white herringbone print of the skirt and deep magenta color of the blouse left no doubt she worked for a rock 'n' roll outfit. I felt kind of old-fashioned in my navy blue suit and fitted ivory silk blouse. Even though my pencil skirt sported a deep back vent that showed off my legs in sheer black stockings, my outfit was the epitome of understated compared to hers. Clearly, there was an expectation of some wildness even among the business professionals on the staff. I could do that. Much of my college wardrobe would be right at home at the band's headquarters. Inwardly, I grinned.

As if she read my mind, Emory laughed. "Don't worry. You've already made a good impression both on paper and at Jack's wedding."

"Oh my gosh! You were there. I remember you from the receiving line following the ceremony." My short-lived elation at recognizing her quickly gave way to chagrin. "That means you saw that though I gave it an honest try, I can't exactly party like a rock star."

"You and your girls were certainly entertaining. I thought you fit right in." Emory soothed me with a smile. "When we saw your college transcripts, I have to admit you blew our minds. Double major in finance and marketing and management, and you finished in four years with honors. Impressive."

"Thank you. Clio set a high bar at the sorority." At her question-ing look, I clarified. "She led our house to the Pan-Hellenic academic cup every year we were at CSU. Her friends thought we needed to at least pretend like we could keep up."

"You girls are close." It wasn't a question.

"We're the best of friends. Though it does feel a little weird to have her married now."

"There you are. Right on time too. That's good, really good," said Balefire's manager and my potential boss as he entered the reception area from a side door. "I see you've met Emory. She's the backbone of the management side of this rock 'n' roll show."

I extended my hand to him. "Hello Garrett. Nice to see you again," I said like the last time I'd seen him I hadn't been smashed out of my mind.

The smirk he returned told me he hadn't forgotten exactly what I'd been like the last time he'd seen me. Damn. I could sense my face growing warm, especially as he stood there with my hand in his, his thumb gliding over the back of my hand as he stared into my eyes for an uncomfortably long minute.

Abruptly, he seemed to come to a decision. Gesturing around the room, he said, "This is the reception area for the studio. Most everyone is back in the kitchen having lunch unless they're working out upstairs in the gym. Let me show you around and explain what you'll be doing during your internship," he said, smoothing over my embarrassment.

As he led me out of the reception area, I called over my shoulder, "Nice to meet you, Emory."

"Likewise. I'm sure we're going to work well together."

I didn't know what Clio said or did that gave these people so much faith in me, but the way they made my internship sound like a done deal left me uneasy. What if I didn't perform to their expectations? Then there was the way Garrett looked at me, like maybe there could be additional "management" expectations. What was I going to do with that?

What truly worried me was looking a fool in front of Dakota.

Snorting a laugh at myself, I came back to earth. Probably, he wouldn't notice one damn thing I did to help manage the band.

Garrett led me down a long hallway decorated with framed gold and platinum albums Balefire had recorded over the years. At the end of it, we stepped through a door into a room big enough to house Jack's massive touring drum kit and the hydraulics and scaffolding needed to lift it two stories into the air. The rest of the stage gear and instruments the band used in concerts was arranged in the middle of the hangar-like space. Comfy couches lined two walls. Garrett explained they were oversized to accommodate the band sleeping in the studio as they wrote and rehearsed new music. He pointed out the shower room to the left of Jack's drums and said the band kept lockers for extra clothes there. I questioned him with a look, and he told me rehearsals could stretch into weeks at a time when the band was in the zone.

There was something about the way he looked at me as he described the accommodations that held me back. Under any other circumstance, I'd be doing a happy dance at seeing all the cool, behind-the-scenes glimpses of the band's way of life. I'd probably try out the couches and check out the showers, even when I knew I should be professional. But I kept catching Garrett eyeing me up and down, and my skin crawled from my scalp to my toes. No way would I be overnighting at the studio when the band dropped into the zone.

He directed my attention to the state-of-the-art recording studio located directly behind Jack's drums. Past the recording studio, a set of stairs led to the upper story that housed the gym, game room, theater, and conference room.

"Wow," I said, impressed. "From outside, this space doesn't look like much, but it's amazing in here. Does everyone use the upstairs?" What I truly wanted to know was if any of the band—read that, Dakota Perri—was hanging around the studio at the moment.

"When the band is in the zone, we're all on call." He nodded.

"It's nice to have space on-site to recreate and unwind. Plus, you'll discover that the guys are generous with the people who work for them. In fact, they keep their original tour bus parked out back to remind them they weren't always a megaband."

"I'd like to see that," I said with a smile.

"I'll show you after lunch." The way he said that made me regret my words. Then he patted his stomach. "The chef made some kind of fancy stuffed hamburgers. The smell has had my stomach growling since I arrived an hour ago."

He indicated a short hallway and placed his hand on the small of my back as he ushered me to the kitchen. I tried to ignore my creeped-out reaction to his touch and concentrated on the mouth-watering smells of lunch growing stronger with each step we took down the hall.

With our meeting scheduled at two, I'd eaten lunch at the regular time for regular people. But all my experiences with the behind-the-scenes world of Balefire so far told me that nothing about the workings of the band was regular.

Stepping through another door, we entered a magnificent kitchen with stainless steel appliances and a long butcher-block island separating the cooking area from the eating area. Various styles and types of stoves and cooktops lined an entire wall. The chef stood in front of an indoor grill with an enormous exhaust hood above it. He flipped burgers with so much flair he seemed to be doing some sort of burger barbecue dance rather than cooking.

"That's Jeff, our chef. As you can see, he can rock it behind a grill," Garrett said with a smirk.

Jeff nodded in my direction but maintained his focus on the food.

"All that movement shows up in the food though, so we humor his *Dancing with the Stars* fantasies." Garrett chuckled. "Come on. I'll introduce you to the rest of the office staff."

He stepped around the island to the dining area situated a step down from the cooking area. A long table surrounded with twelve high-backed chairs was centered in the space with a few tables for four grouped around it. Three men and a woman sat at one end of the long table. Their laughter punctuated their lively conversation, and I relaxed a bit.

Garrett interrupted their hilarity to introduce me. "This is Annabelle Stewart, our new management intern. Annabelle, this is Dan Cook, our finance manager."

A blond man who looked to be in his early thirties with laugh lines bracketing his eyes stood to shake my hand. "Pleasure, Annabelle."

Garrett continued around the table. "This is Trevor Wyatt, Dan's assistant, and beside him is Caroline Zanetti, our merch and marketing manager."

The two of them smiled and nodded at me. They also looked to be in their early thirties. The way Caroline leaned against Trevor's shoulder made it clear they had something going together.

"Hey, are you two holding hands under the table?" Garrett asked.

"At least that's all we're doing," Trevor responded with a smirk. He turned to Caroline and gave her a smacking kiss on the mouth. "Mm, Jeff's burgers taste even better on your lips."

Caroline laughed merrily and returned her attention to me. "Trevor, she's new. We need to break her in slowly."

I smiled, liking her on the spot.

Beside me, Garrett snorted before recovering enough to finish the introductions. "This is Josh Wilson, our transportation manager and the old man on the crew." Leaning in close to me, he stage-whispered conspiratorially, "He has kids in high school."

He made it sound like Josh might have one foot in the grave. Ironic, since Garrett didn't look much younger than Josh.

Josh appeared average seated next to the others, but when he stood to shake my hand, I had to look way up at him as he towered over both Garrett and me. The table hid his incredibly long legs.

The man must have topped out at six feet four at least. The few strands of gray sprinkled through his black hair gave him a distinguished air, and his warm handshake set me at ease. "Nice to meet you Annabelle. You might as well know, we're always like this." A mischievous smile played over his features. I knew right then that no matter what my feelings for Dakota, feelings I hadn't made up my mind about yet, interning for Balefire was going to be a good time.

# Chapter Six

Dakota

I FINISHED THE TUNE-UP on my tricked-out four-wheel-drive pickup and headed over to Blu and Ashleigh's place. The restlessness I'd felt since Jack and Clio's wedding rode me hard, and I needed an outlet. What I'd wanted, of course, was incredible sex with a smokin' hot babe with chestnut hair and gorgeous green eyes. Problem was, I didn't exactly know where Annabelle's head was. She'd danced with me and kissed me like she wanted a repeat performance of our one night together. The next thing I knew, she'd left the party with her girls, and I hadn't seen her since.

My fault, of course. After all, I hadn't tried her number to see if she'd played me or not. For the first time in my life, I was unsure with a woman and it drove me batshit crazy. Wanting her as much as I did, but not knowing for sure what she thought had me climbing the walls.

So I did what I always did, what my dad always did when we needed to work something out in our heads—I added or changed or intensified moving parts on my truck. The thing roared in my driveway as I gunned it and put it in gear. It was so loud it wasn't quite street legal, and the torque and horsepower were more than enough to win any local or regional race if I ever cared to enter one. But what I loved to do with it involved covering every square inch of the pristine white and screaming lime green exterior with mud.

Hopefully, I could talk Ashleigh into giving Blu up for an afternoon. Or more likely, I was going to have to talk Blu into sparing his lifelong best friend an afternoon of his time. Tired of being alone with my thoughts, I wanted company. And I needed mudding therapy.

When we finished touring in the spring, Blu moved Ashleigh into his big-ass house. In the several times I'd been over to visit them since then, I hadn't noticed she'd done much to make his place girly, which I would have expected of her, especially since I knew Blu gave her permission to decorate it any way she wanted. Then again, we were talking Ashleigh who dragged all of us through every garden she could find during our tour of Europe last fall.

After roaring up Blu's driveway and killing the engine on my truck, I can't say I was surprised to find her on her knees in the flower bed in front of their house. As I bounded out of my ride, Blu rounded the corner of the garage carrying a giant bag of what he told me was mulch, whatever that was, before he dumped it on the ground behind Ashleigh.

"Yeah, so how 'bout you take a rest from all this manual labor and go out to the mud flats with me?" I said as I watched the two of them distribute wood shavings around the plants she'd stuck in the ground.

I'd long ago given up trying to understand Blu's newfound interest in gardening. After all, he had the girl. He didn't need to keep impressing her. Yet there he was on his hands and knees beside her playing in the dirt.

"We need to finish mulching this bed. If you sit your ass down here, get your hands dirty, it might leave me some time to go out with you for a while," Blu said. He didn't even crack a smile as he said it. Damn, was he ever whipped.

Sighing, I knelt beside him. Apparently, the only way I was going to spring my best friend was to surrender to the desires of his pretty jailer…even if I was the only one who viewed his situation that way.

♪

We tore up my favorite play area, covering my truck with at least an inch of thick dark mud. Roaring through axle-deep puddles, sliding through mud slicks, testing the traction of my knobby new tires, we laughed our asses off. I was so happy to have my head clear of everything except our wild-ass ride that I even turned the wheel over to Blu for a trip through the boggy course.

After finally wearing ourselves out with our dirty fun, we headed back to Blu's place. Ashleigh had chosen to stay home, leaving us to our crazy. After all, she'd already ridden with us once on one of our escapades. We were still laughing when I tipped the car wash attendant fifty bucks extra to take on my filthy mess.

Blu, who always could read me like a book, said, "Is this one of those nights when I need to pocket your keys and call Ashleigh the second we walk through the doors of the bar?"

"What the fuck are you talking about?"

Yeah, I totally knew what he was talking about, but after freeing my mind of Annabelle for a couple of blessed hours, I wasn't sure I wanted to go there.

Blu did. "You know—Annabelle Stewart. Your interest in the woman was kinda hard to miss at the wedding."

"She's fuckin' hot, all right?" I bared my teeth. "Can we leave it at that?"

"She is, and we could, but what would be the fun in that?" Blu's eyes danced. "You've got a thing for her."

"Like I said, she's hot. Now can we drop it?" I tried to keep the exasperation out of my voice. After all, I needed my friend to be my distraction not my torment. Unfortunately, neither of us had ever been any good at keeping our thoughts from the other. It's how I'd known to jerk Blu's chain about Ashleigh the first time I met her.

"It's going to take several beers to scrub the image of you checking out Annabelle's tonsils with your tongue at the head table during the reception."

"Fuck you."

Blu's laughter filled the cab of my truck and echoed in my head as we entered our favorite bar in our old neighborhood.

Thinking about what a bad idea it was dragging Blu out to play, I nearly didn't see Vaughn Hamilton sitting at the bar. Which is kind of surprising considering the man is built like a truck. Not to mention he likes to wear badass leather vests to show off all his ink when he's not in the office slaving over some engineering problem. He'd hooked up with one of Ashleigh's friends last summer, so it came as a surprise to find him by himself.

"Vaughn! What are you doing here—alone?" Blu asked as he took the seat beside our old buddy.

We flanked Vaughn, and the bartender magicked two beers in front of us. A spark of hope that Vaughn's story would draw attention away from me flickered out when he replied, "Jamie's at some teaching conference or some shit. Left me home alone for a week. Can you believe that?" He fist-bumped Blu. "Nice to see you man." He tossed back the last of his beer and signaled the bartender for another. "How's Ashleigh?"

"She's with me. Enough said." Blu laughed and took a swig of his beer.

"How 'bout you, Dakota?"

Caught with a mouthful of beer, I couldn't answer right away. Not that that would have stopped Blu.

"He's got woman troubles. It's why we're here."

Vaughn nearly snorted his fresh beer. "Woman troubles? Dakota? Pull the other one."

"See, Blu? Vaughn believes me. No troubles at all for this boy." *Except I can't stop thinking about her.*

Blu grinned evilly over his beer. "Oh, he knows. Takes one to know one, right Vaughn?"

"Tell me about this mysterious creature. I didn't think a woman existed who could keep Dakota's attention for more than one night, if that." His smirk made me consider how satisfying it would feel to put my fist in his face. "Have you ever even had a girlfriend?"

"What kind of fucked-up question is that?" I grumbled. But I knew exactly what he was on about.

Twenty-eight years old, and I'd never had a real girlfriend. When we'd started out, I didn't think a couple of girls who tagged along with the band but confined their sleeping arrangements to my bed counted as actual girlfriends. Truth was, I'd seen up close and personal what it looked like when you gave your heart to a woman and she didn't want it anymore. I'd seen how it tore up my dad when my mom walked out on us when I was eight. I never forgot for one single day how much it stung to have the most important woman in the world walk away and never once look back. Opening myself up to that kind of heartbreak wasn't in the cards for me. At. All.

The thoughts I'd been having about Annabelle since seeing her again did not fall into the category of warm and fuzzy. White picket fence and fucking gardening. Having a girl's name tattooed over and through some of the sweetest ink I'd ever seen on Vaughn's arm. Not for me. What I wanted was another night of sizzling-hot sex with a gorgeous woman who had no trouble walking away. Who didn't make a big deal of it—or of me. But I didn't want to come across as an asshole for wanting that.

Yeah. That's the story I was going with.

"Girlfriends cramp your style. Get all up in your grill for wanting a night out with the guys, for appreciating a great rack on another woman, for making a mess of your truck when you go out to play. No thank you very much," I muttered.

Those other two assholes burst out laughing.

"My style's all kinds of cramped. What about you, Vaughn?" Blu smirked.

"Regular, off-the-charts sex with a woman who likes to kick my ass at the pool table so she can make it up to me in bed? Sucks, man. It really does," Vaughn deadpanned before the two of them erupted into more guffaws.

The casual tone of Blu's voice should have warned me. "Ashleigh stopped by the studio this morning 'cause she likes to chat up Emory."

"That's another thing. Girlfriends love to gossip," I said.

Ignoring me, Blu plowed on. "Seems Annabelle signed the paperwork to do a management internship with the band. She starts Monday."

"Annabelle, huh? Pretty name. Bet she's gorgeous." Vaughn tipped back his beer and winked at Blu.

Blu jumped right in. "She's a little shorter than Ash with dark hair down the middle of her back, beautiful eyes, and a rack—"

"Shut it, Blu. Shut the fuck up."

He smirked and finished off another beer.

Between them, Vaughn and Blu had me seriously reconsidering my choice of friends.

"So, that's the way of it, Dakota," Vaughn said like he was a judge pronouncing a sentence on someone in court. "Bartender, we need a round of Jack Daniels. We're celebrating our friend's descent toward a ball and chain."

"You know, Vaughn, you're a big guy, but I have money. I bet I could find people who would dispose of the body for the right price." I wasn't entirely sure I was joking.

Vaughn clapped me on the shoulder and grinned. The bartender set three shots in front of us. Vaughn and Blu didn't seem to mind that I didn't clink my glass with theirs when they toasted the "lovely Annabelle." I signaled for another round, and somewhere after that, the night became a blank.

I woke up Sunday morning lying on the couch in my living room fully dressed. Whoever dropped me off hadn't even removed my muddy boots. With a groan, I thought about the nasty note my housekeeper would leave me and the huge tip I'd need to leave her. I groaned again when I sat up and my head started pounding out a rhythm bigger than anything Jack had dreamed up so far. For several minutes I sat still with my head in my hands and tried to wait out the worst of it. As I shifted to rest my aching head against the back of the couch, I noticed a pitcher of water and a glass on the table beside me.

There was a note under the glass:

We'll be by this afternoon to help you get your truck. Ashleigh says not to worry. Everyone at the studio is jacked about working with Annabelle. Ha. Ha. —Blu. PS Take all the aspirin. You're going to need it.

Three tablets lay beside the glass on the table. I took them all, drained the pitcher of water, and said to the empty room, "Asshole."

It took me about an hour to lever myself off the couch and into the shower. By then I needed coffee and food. Wandering out to the kitchen, I found a fresh pot of coffee and a box of croissants stuffed with all kinds of eggy breakfast goodness. There was also another note:

Girlfriends usually know exactly how to help you take care of a hangover. You can thank Ashleigh for thinking of this. I would have just dumped your sorry ass at the front door. You're welcome.

—Blu

"Fucker."

But I poured myself a huge mug of steaming coffee and ate all four of the egg-stuffed croissants in the box. If the two of them had plans for joining me for breakfast, they'd need to bring more food.

♪

The next morning found me sneaking through a side door into our studios. Walking through the front office would have been too damn obvious. I'd driven my Lexus to avoid announcing my arrival in my usual fashion. When Blu and Ashleigh had driven me back to the bar late yesterday afternoon to retrieve my truck, he'd kept it toned down. Guess he thought he and Vaughn had had enough fun at my expense even after I became too obliterated to defend myself at the bar.

I made my way to the recording studio, adjusted my favorite pair of headphones on my head, picked up my axe, and started noodling around with a melody that had been wandering through my mind ever since seeing Annabelle again. Within minutes, I did what I always did when it was only me and my guitar—lost myself so far in the music that the rest of the world didn't exist.

Somewhere along the line, I located a pad and pencil and busily scratched down some notes when a flash of color caught my eye. Standing right outside the window of the recording studio was Annabelle. She was wearing a green dress the exact color of her eyes and looking so hot, my dick perked right up at the sight of her.

Her deer-in-the-headlights expression told me she didn't expect to see me here. Before she could rally and do something ridiculous— like disappear again—I crooked my finger at her, a gesture I knew instinctively would draw her to me. She questioned me with her eyes, and I grinned and nodded. Never breaking eye contact through the glass separating the recording studio from our rehearsal space, I walked over to the door and opened it.

Annabelle took her sweet time walking around the corner of the studio to me. Time that let me know I affected her too. Nice not to be in this thing alone, I thought as she finally stepped through the door.

"I thought you guys were on vacation until Jack and Clio came home from their honeymoon," she said.

"We are."

"Shouldn't you be somewhere exotic, on a beach with a monster margarita and bikinis for miles?" She smirked.

"Why would I want to do that when I could be hanging out in the studio with a sassy intern wearing a sexy tight green dress, hmm?"

"You'd pass up all that skin for a dress?" The look on her face said she didn't believe my bullshit at all.

"I would if I were thinking about how the girl would be stripping off that dress sometime soon."

"And we're back to that."

She sounded flustered, but her confident stance didn't waver. Have I mentioned how hot it was that the girl could play it so cool?

"You disappeared from the wedding reception before the party was over."

"Yeah, well, those shots caught up with all of us fast. Jack's dad apparently took one look at the bridesmaids as we gathered in the kitchen for another round and decided we were done." A laugh puffed out of her. "He put us in a car and delivered us to our hotel. I don't think we even said goodbye to the bride and groom." She sobered. "I can hardly wait to explain that to Clio and Jack when they come home."

I couldn't help the grin that spread across my face at finding out she hadn't ditched me after all.

"Good to know."

She arched a brow.

I smiled. "We'll have to watch your shot intake when we're on tour."

"You know about my internship? How?"

"This operation lives on gossip. Ashleigh and Emory are good friends. I spent some time this weekend with Blu and Ashleigh, so there you have it."

I hoped like hell Ashleigh kept some things to herself when

she talked to Emory next time. I didn't need Annabelle to know I'd drunk myself into a stupor on Saturday night because I couldn't get her off my mind.

"What do you think of the job so far?" I asked, crossing my arms over my chest and leaning back against an amp near the door.

"A lot goes into keeping you guys on the road and on the public's mind."

She'd slipped her hands behind her back and leaned against the doorframe to the studio. So sexy cool it was all I could do not to step over and haul her up against me, kiss that banked flame I knew lived inside her into a raging firestorm. But not today. I needed to take it slow, bide my time, take her on my own personal tour of our studios when there was no chance of an audience.

"What are you working on? You seemed really into it."

I shrugged. "A little something that's been crashing around in my head for a while."

"May I hear?"

"Sure. But not today."

"Oh. Okay."

I could tell from her sad little smile that she didn't understand. "It's a rough draft, Annabelle. It needs work before I even share it with the guys."

She nodded and pushed away from the door. "Well then, I should stop interrupting your creative genius."

"Creative genius, huh? I like that." I grinned.

With an eye roll, cool Annabelle replaced vulnerable Annabelle. She turned to leave.

"Were you headed back to the kitchen?"

"As a matter of fact, yes."

"Mind if I join you?"

"'Course not. This is your rodeo after all."

"That it is, pretty girl, that it is."

Chapter Seven

Annabelle

WITH THE BAND on hiatus while Clio and Jack enjoyed their honeymoon in Fiji, I couldn't have been more surprised to see Dakota Perri in the studio when I walked through the rehearsal space to the communal kitchen behind it. Though I couldn't hear the sounds as he played his guitar, I could feel them as I watched his long fingers fly over the strings. The play of the muscles in his arms fascinated me as he tore up and down the neck of his guitar. The almost orgasmic expression on his face, his eyes closed, his jaw thrust forward, the sinews in his neck on prominent display reminded me of a night long ago when he played my body the same way he played his song in the quiet of the recording studio. I wouldn't have been able to tear my eyes away if the place had caught fire.

Which I think my lady parts did as I watched him play. It didn't help that I always responded to his musicianship like this. Even watching him on YouTube videos left me all hot and bothered. When I'd seen him perform in person, I almost creamed myself in my front row seat. Especially when he winked at me after I shot my thong at him. As memories collided with the present, I was fanning myself—literally—when he opened his eyes and caught me staring at him through the studio window.

Then he crooked his finger at me, and like every other woman I imagine he'd ever met, I went where he wanted me to go.

Pathetic.

He'd asked for my number at the wedding reception, but he hadn't called it. Not that I expected him to. Still, I'd kept my phone on my person since the wedding, even tucking it into my bra on my first day at work since my dress didn't have pockets. Hope springs eternal and all that bullpucky.

So pathetic.

Inviting himself to join me for lunch had everything to do with my convenient proximity and nothing to do with any true interest the man had in me. Though I needed someone to tell that to my pussy again, please, because the heat of his hand at the small of my back as we walked down the short hallway to the kitchen left me uncomfortably wet.

Caroline and Trevor were seated together same as on the day we met. The sight of their dark heads leaned in close as they conversed did not invite guests to their table. At another table sat Garrett and Dan Cook, a laptop between them as they went over some spreadsheets. Chef Jeff hummed as he busied himself at the butcher-block island plating something fancy. When he glanced up at our entrance through the kitchen door, he whipped out two more plates and drizzled dark sauce over their surfaces to start preparing our meal.

Dakota guided me to one of the small tables away from the others and shocked me by pulling out my chair for me. I don't know why the gesture surprised me so much. I guess I'd spent too much of my fantasy life thinking of rock stars as so far above the rest of us they wouldn't need silly little things like manners.

"Thank you," I said, glancing up at him.

He nodded as if he knew exactly what I was thinking and seated himself in the chair directly to my left.

For several seconds, he waited me out, staring at me with such intensity it made me want to squirm. But I planted my feet flat on the floor and stayed still—a tiny victory since my mouth didn't get the message.

"Do you ever take time off?"

"I'm taking time off now."

"Writing new music in the studio? That didn't look like time off to me."

"Depends. If what you do for a living is a job, then you need time off. If what you do for a living is who you are, then you're never working."

I smiled at him. He definitely didn't look like he was working when I watched him through the studio window.

"Besides music, what else do you like to do?"

"Beautiful women in sexy dresses." He leaned his elbow on the table beside me, his jaw in the palm of his hand. The naughtiness in those sea blue eyes of his dared me.

"That goes without saying Dakota. I attended one of your concerts, remember?" I said, taking up his dare.

"You were wearing another sexy dress then too." He leaned in close to me. "I enjoyed that one, especially as you took it off."

"You do remember that I'm now employed by you, right?"

"So?"

"So, there's probably some clause or something in your studio contracts that warn against fraternizing with the help."

I mean, really. The man always put inappropriate thoughts about him in my head. But I didn't need a bad evaluation out of this internship. If anything, I needed something glowing to make this opportunity stand out for me even more. Which meant I needed to keep my distance from Dakota Perri.

"Nah. We don't run that kind of organization. If we did, we'd have to do something about those two." He jerked a thumb in Caroline and Trevor's direction. They happened to be enjoying a kiss right at that moment. "Which would be criminal considering the cool merch Caroline designs and the creative ideas Trevor dreams up to help us make more money."

He leaned in closer. "You got a closet full of sexy dresses, Annabelle?"

Chef Jeff interrupted to announce our lunch awaited us. Which gave me a minute to try to sort out Dakota's keen interest in my wardrobe. We all rose and made our way to the island where we found he'd plated salmon mousse that was almost too pretty to eat and lovely spinach and arugula salads lying on top of whatever sauce I'd seen him squeezing onto the plates when we walked in.

We carried our meals back to our table, and Dakota asked me for my drink preference. Again, since I was at work and professional, I asked for water. But I couldn't stop staring as Dakota ambled with easy grace to an industrial-size stainless steel refrigerator from which he extracted a bottled water and an icy cold beer. Watching his ass in the jeans he wore, not too tight, not too loose, had me crossing my legs under the table. He stopped beside the island momentarily, and I realized he'd uncapped his beer when I heard the tinny sound of the cap joining others in a bucket beneath the opener.

I stared longingly at his throat as it worked to down the first swallow he took while he handed me my water. The gleam in his eyes when he sat down beside me told me he didn't miss what I forgot to hide in mine.

"The food here is sensational. How did you guys land such an amazing chef?" I asked to distract him from what we were both thinking.

"Jeff's an old friend. We went to high school with him. When he finished culinary school, he needed a place to practice, and we'd just opened this studio." Dakota forked a mouthful of salmon, holding it just above his plate. "We invited him on board, and he's been here ever since. He likes the travel."

"He goes out on tour with you guys?"

"Of course." He savored a bite of fish. "We need decent food at weird hours, so he takes care of us. Plus, he likes to check out the food scene everywhere we tour."

"The whole world."

"Yeah," Dakota said with a grin. "It gives him ideas, and the rest of us benefit."

"This fish is borderline orgasmic," I moaned over a bite.

"Careful. He doesn't need those kinds of ideas." Dakota shot me a look from beneath his brows, and I couldn't decide if he was playing with me or not.

"Oh, I don't know. Makes me excited for what he's whipping up over there for dessert."

"Dessert excites me too," he said, the sexy rumble of his voice reverberating through me, momentarily making me forget where we were and that we had an audience as I stared back at him. Damn the man. He kept turning up the heat—like *that's* what I needed.

I didn't realize I worried my lower lip with my teeth until I caught where his attention strayed. Closing my mouth and clearing my throat, I gave my lunch my entire attention. After a few seconds, I heard his quiet chuckle.

"Glad to know we're on the same page, Annabelle."

"I'm not convinced we are," I said bravely and chanced another foray into the sea of his eyes.

"Meaning?"

"Meaning I didn't play you when I gave you my number. Something you obviously only asked for to be polite."

Chef Jeff stopped by our table bearing a tray of dessert cups containing homemade berry sorbet. Dakota grabbed two off the tray. "Jeff, my man, you are a rock star. That salmon has my girl here all twitterpated. You've outdone yourself as usual."

Jeff nodded at Dakota and turned to me. "You're the intern. Jeff Scott." He balanced the tray with one hand while he extended his other hand to me.

"Annabelle Stewart. Very pleased to meet you and your amazing food," I said with a smile.

"If it keeps beautiful women like you happy, then my work here is done," Jeff said, returning my smile.

Dakota cleared his throat. "You should prolly deliver those other desserts before they melt, my man." He gazed pointedly at where our hands still touched and I swear the wattage of Jeff's smile could have lit up the room all by itself.

With a slow, deliberate movement, he dropped my hand and turned away to deliver the rest of his desserts to the others.

"Where were we? Oh yeah, did you mean this number?" He pulled his phone from his pocket, scrolled through it, and showed me a screen where my number still existed in his contacts.

"I don't seem to have any missed calls or texts from a number I don't know," I countered, pulling my own phone from its place in my bra. I scrolled through my recent calls and text messages, showing him the screen as I did so.

Not that he noticed. He was still staring at my cleavage from where I'd retrieved my phone.

He shifted in his chair. "Do you always keep your phone there?"

"Only when I don't have pockets. Now pay attention. Those nonexistent communications? For the record, I'm here at the studio for management. I'm not here for your convenience, Dakota."

Yes, I wanted him. Oh, how I wanted him. But since I assumed I'd be working and touring with the band on their fall swing through the US, I didn't want to be his fallback whenever he didn't have a convenient groupie. After all, I had firsthand experience with how much he liked his fans.

Ignoring my comment, he grabbed my phone. After programming in his number under "Hottest Guitar Player Ever," he handed it back and said, "You want communication, Annabelle? We'll communicate—both of us."

Dakota was telling me something with his eyes, but for the life of me, I didn't have a clue what it was. I nodded anyway and busied myself with my dessert.

♪

I spent the rest of my first day on the job shadowing Caroline. While I thought I'd be working more with Garrett, it seemed that to start, I'd be doing marketing for the band. As Dakota had accurately described, Caroline was a whiz at merchandising. She was the creative genius behind the ad campaign that had filled stadiums during their tour through Europe and the Eastern United States last year and put Balefire posters in dorm rooms and bedrooms across the world. After one day with her, I knew I'd learn more from her than I ever had in a college classroom.

Emory also took a particular interest in me. In my short time at the studio, both when I toured it with Garrett and on my first day on the job, it was clear the place pulsed through her, which made me super glad I'd made a good first impression on her.

When I exited the studio at the end of the day, Dakota was leaning against the hood of my Mustang, one foot casually crossed over the other. His dark sunglasses kept me from reading his expression beyond the grin playing about his sculpted mouth. That he was up to something, however, I had no doubt.

"So, gorgeous, where do you want to go for dinner?"

"I'm sorry, Dakota, but I promised my mom I'd eat with the family tonight."

"At your parents' place?"

"Yeah."

"What's your mom cooking for dinner?"

"I don't know, but whatever it is, it'll be delicious. Maybe not Chef Jeff fancy, but definitely food I don't pass up. Rain check?"

"Or you could be polite."

I slanted him a look, and he had the audacity to laugh. "Get in, Annabelle. I'll follow you."

He held my car door open for me, and that mischievous grin playing around his mouth morphed into a smile made even more wicked with his eyes hidden behind his aviator shades. After slapping the roof of my car twice, he bounded over to a sweet blacked-out Lexus and slid in. I was so busy trying to process Dakota Perri driving such an understated car that I forgot what I was doing or what he obviously intended to do. My phone buzzed an incoming text in my bra, startling me out of my thoughts.

Come on, Annabelle. Let's get this show on the road. I'm starving.

Seriously? The man had invited himself to dinner—with my parents. As though we'd done something like dating rather than only enjoying a one-night stand together. What the hell was that?

Chapter Eight

Annabelle

"HI, MOM. LISTEN, is it okay if I bring a friend with me to dinner?"

"Sure, sweetheart. Someone from work?"

My mom sounded distracted, which was good. I didn't dare tell her who my guest was, or the whole family would freak out, my dad and little sister especially. My dad's hobby, his real passion, was playing his guitar. He spent time most evenings working out riffs from his favorite professional guitarists, Dakota Perri included. My sister Emma fell asleep every night gazing up at the life-size poster of Balefire she'd tacked to the ceiling above her bed. I could hardly wait for my family to embarrass the hell out of me with their star-struck responses to our dinner guest.

With any luck, Dakota wouldn't let on that we'd met before Jack and Clio's wedding. My family had already freaked at the wedding photos I'd shared with them, the ones where I stood beside Adam Tron as part of the wedding party. I'd knocked them out with news of my internship. Adding Dakota as a dinner guest would probably send them to the moon. Discovering I knew Dakota intimately? I didn't want to imagine what sort of disaster that would create.

The man in question followed me into my parents' driveway and parked directly behind me. He hopped out of his car and loped up to open my door for me. He had incredible manners, something I struggled to reconcile with his bad boy rock 'n' roll image. And his sexy body. And the way he moved. And the way he put my secret parts on high alert every time he opened his mouth to speak or laugh.

"Hey, Annababy, what do I need to know about your family before we join them for dinner?"

I sighed. "I have a typical suburban American family. Dad's a structural engineer. Mom's a technical writer for the same engineering firm Dad works for. My sister is a senior in high school and quite possibly Balefire's biggest fan. She ranted at me for weeks after I didn't take her to the Red Rocks concert with the tickets Bailey gave me."

"Yeah, yeah. But what are their names?"

"Oh. My dad is Alan, Mom is Ellie, and little sis is Emma."

"Cute. Your parents named you guys with their initials. See, those are the important things to know," he said, nodding sagely, but I could see the smirk lurking on his lips.

I had to smile. "You're quick. Most people don't catch that."

As we entered the house, I braced myself for the nuclear fallout I knew would happen the second my family discovered who I'd brought home to dinner.

"So formal, Annabelle. Who's so special you couldn't come in the regular way?" Emma's sarcasm preceded her entrance into the front foyer.

When she stepped around the corner from the kitchen at the end of the hallway, she stopped dead in her tracks, her eyes rounding into dinner plates before she let out the mother of all ear-piercing screams. How she didn't break glass is a mystery for the ages.

I turned and covered Dakota's ears only to see the laughter dancing in his endlessly sea blue eyes. He reached up and removed my hands, but only dropped one as we stood together facing Emma.

"Ohmygod, ohmygod, ohmygod! It's Dakota Perri! In our house! Ohmygod!" Emma screamed.

Leaning down, Dakota whispered in my ear, "I'm hoping that will be you screaming sometime soon. Preferably somewhere more private, but not limited to that."

I gaped at him for several seconds then slammed my jaw shut, the clacking sound of my teeth echoing in my head. Emma must have rubbed off on me.

Or something.

Her racket brought both of my parents into the foyer. The round-eyed expressions on their faces would have been comical under any other circumstances. For this once, though, I wished they looked like the professionals they usually were instead of cartoon caricatures of themselves.

Composing myself, I said, "Well done, Emma. You've made my guest feel right at home. Dakota, this is my family. My dad, Alan, my mom, Ellie, and the six-alarm screamer is my sister Emma."

Emma drew her eyes away from Dakota long enough to narrow them at me before going back to stare at him. Maybe his presence would preempt her usual annoying behavior.

With his left hand, Dakota maintained his hold on my right hand as he extended his right hand first to my dad, then my mom, and finally to my sister.

"Pleasure to meet you all. Thanks for having me over for dinner."

Several seconds of awkward silence fell as my family continued to stare at him. Then each of my parents seemed to have the same thought as they stared down at where he still held my hand. Anticipating my attempt to pull away, he squeezed my fingers, and I wondered if he entertained second thoughts about inviting himself to dinner with my family.

"What's for dinner?" I cringed at the fake brightness of my voice, but Dakota holding my hand so firmly in his caused all sorts of shivery sensations to skim through my body.

Mom blinked out of the trance she'd fallen into with the arrival of a celebrity rock star in her house. "Your favorite. Stuffed pork chops."

"Yum! But you do know those are Dad's favorites," I said with a grin. "Not that I'd ever pass them up, mind you."

"Yes, well. They're ready, so we should probably eat them." Mom sounded breathless like she'd been training for a marathon rather than cooking dinner. I couldn't blame her. I was feeling a little out of breath myself.

♪

Stunningly, dinner was relatively normal, all things considered. Emma insisted on sitting beside Dakota and asking too many obnoxious questions like how many other celebrities he knew, which ones he hung out with, which ones he dated. The last question she aimed at me even though she asked Dakota. I shrugged at her and chuckled to myself at the way he deflected her. He'd been answering obnoxious questions from the press for a decade, so no doubt he was used to her line of interrogation.

Instead, he asked my parents about their work. He shocked me with his in-depth knowledge of the structural engineering needed for Jack's hydraulic lift for his drum kit, which opened Balefire's concerts so spectacularly. When he and Dad started talking about the engineering required for the band's stage, the atmosphere in my parents' kitchen returned to a regular family dinner, Dakota fitting in like he'd always been there. I fought with myself about how to feel about that.

Afterward, Dad invited Dakota to his "office," the last bedroom upstairs that Mom called "the escape hatch," where Dad spent far more time playing his collection of acoustic and electric guitars than doing any kind of work. I could hear Dad talking animatedly,

Dakota's rumble sounding patient as they discussed several riffs Dad wanted to learn, their voices fading as they climbed the stairs.

I wished I could have escaped the kitchen as easily as Dakota.

"You couldn't give me a heads-up that you were bringing a celebrity home? We could have eaten in the formal dining room at least," Mom hissed when the men were probably only two steps up the hallway.

"I don't think he minded that we ate like normal people in the kitchen, Mom."

"Well, I minded. I would have liked to have given him a better first impression."

"I think your stuffed pork chops impressed the heck out of him. Poor Dad's not going to have any leftovers for his lunch tomorrow."

Mom softened at that. "He did seem to enjoy my food." She smiled and glanced toward the stairs. "I don't think your dad will mind that he's doing without for lunch tomorrow."

"Geez, you two. None of that is important," Emma interrupted. "Are the two of you dating? After knowing him what, a week?" She apparently had no intention of limiting her obnoxious questions to Dakota.

My heart stuttered. Carefully keeping my gaze on the dishes I rinsed and the tone of my voice even, I said, "No, we're not dating."

"Then what was all the hand-holding you were doing when you walked into the house?" Her expression was a sarcastic *Uh-huh* as she sat on the counter beside the sink, swinging her legs as Mom and I rinsed dishes and loaded the dishwasher.

"Panic, I think."

Emma's brow shot up. "Really." The thick sarcasm in that one word could best anything Daniel Tosh could emote in an entire episode of *Tosh.0*.

Mom laughed. "I think what Annabelle's referring to is that glass-shattering scream you let out when you saw who she'd brought home with her."

"Exactly," I added, relieved. Dakota holding my hand as I'd introduced him to my family felt too much like bringing home someone important to me, someone who could possibly be permanent. Which of course did not describe Dakota Perri. Not. At. All. Hot, wild sex in a hotel suite after a concert? Yes. Going home with a girl to meet her parents? Not so much.

"Pooh. He hears that kind of reaction on a nightly basis when he's on tour," Emma scoffed, but I noticed a faint pink stain on her cheeks.

"True. But those decibels in a huge arena are easier to take than in the close confines of a hallway in someone's house." I smirked.

"Whatever."

She hopped down off the counter and walked over to the door to listen to the music coming from upstairs. Soon, Mom and I joined her. By silent agreement, the three of us found ourselves upstairs in Dad's office.

I'm not sure how long they played because it was so fun to listen to them riff off each other. Dakota couldn't hide his virtuosity, but he dialed it back and let Dad take the lead occasionally. The way Dad's face lit up when the two of them connected on a rhythm or a progression sucked me further inside the gravitational pull of Dakota's orbit. If I'd thought him sexy as he whispered naughty things in my ear or winked at me during a wedding—or drove me out of my mind in a hotel suite—he out-sexied himself with the encouraging way he treated my dad's decent but still amateur guitar-playing skills.

Finally, Dad remembered himself. "Dakota, this has been awesome. Never in my life would I have thought I'd have a private master class from a true professional. Thank you."

"Oh my gosh, yes, Dakota. He won't be able to stop talking about this for weeks," Mom gushed, her face shining. For as much as she teased him about his "escape hatch," she loved to listen to Dad play because of how much he loved playing.

"My pleasure. I learned a few things too, so thank you. It was the least I could do to repay that delicious dinner, Mrs. Stewart."

Jesus. Again with the manners. The man continued to systematically shatter all my preconceived notions about him. Dammit. I didn't want to like him as much as I did. Wanting his body was one thing. Liking his personality was something else entirely.

"Please, call me Ellie." The demure look on her face told all about how Dakota had charmed my mom too. "You're welcome to join us for dinner whenever you'd like."

Really, Mom? Really? I hadn't figured out yet how to deal with Dakota at work, and now Mom extended him a standing invitation to dinner? After the way he'd invited himself over tonight, I had no doubt the man would take her up on it too. Soon. And often.

On cue, Dakota said, "I'm all over that."

The wicked gleam in his eyes as he slanted me a look told me he knew exactly what I thought of Mom's standing invite. So he piled it on. "Annabelle, you gonna walk me out?"

Emma smirked at me and piped up, "I'll walk you out, Dakota."

He didn't even blink. "Two gorgeous Stewart girls, one for each arm? Can't pass that up."

I rolled my eyes and stood to lead him from the room.

I caught Mom exchanging a look with Dad. "Emma, I need you in the kitchen, actually."

"Now?" Emma whined.

"Thanks again for a great evening," Dakota said to my family as he reached for my hand when I walked ahead of him out of the room.

He didn't let go until we were outside on the front porch.

"That wasn't exactly what I had in mind when I invited you out to dinner, Annabelle," he began.

"I'm sure," I said, chuckling.

"But I did have a great time meeting your family. They're so normal. How is it again that you're from these people?"

"The stork works in mysterious ways," I deadpanned.

"You gonna walk me to my car?"

I shot him a side-eye and caught a glimpse of my sister at the front window. Dakota nodded in her direction, and I took the hint. Curious about what he wanted to say to me privately, I walked with him down the driveway.

"You live with your parents?" he asked.

"Not really. I've taken up temporary residence in the apartment above their garage." I pointed to the space. "The previous tenants moved out right before I graduated college, so I asked if I could move in until I found a job or started graduate school and could afford my own place."

"Basically, your bedroom is detached from the rest of the house."

"It's a full apartment with two bedrooms," I said with a smirk.

I couldn't figure out the look on his face. Guess I must have overshared or something.

"What about your privacy?"

"I can't imagine why you'd be worried about that."

"You can't? Let me remind you."

The tease in his voice should have warned me, but I wasn't quick enough. He slipped his hand around the nape of my neck and held me while he dipped his head to kiss me. And he didn't start slow. The press of his lips to mine insisted on a response. With a sigh, I gave him what he wanted, opening my lips to welcome the play of his tongue. With his other hand, he cupped my face, his thumb tracing patterns over my cheek as he deepened the kiss still more, our tongues tangling in a wild dance. In the space of two heartbeats, we were all but devouring each other.

At last he broke away. Leaning his forehead on mine, he panted. "Your place doesn't allow for much privacy is all I'm sayin'."

"Dakota, what are you doing?"

"Making up for lost time. Which clearly isn't going down

tonight since I just met your family. Wouldn't want them to get the wrong idea about me."

The wicked grin on his handsome face so at odds with his words left me off-balance.

"What are you talking about?"

"See you at the studio tomorrow, babe."

As he stared at my mouth, a weirdly intense look crossed his features. He leaned in and brushed his lips over mine once more before he opened his car door, slid in, and drove away.

I stared after Dakota for several long minutes then turned and went up to my apartment. Having caught a glimpse of Emma still blatantly watching me from the living room window, I opted not to subject myself to the third degree masquerading as my family for the rest of the evening. Especially since I had no clue how to answer their most pressing question: was I dating the lead guitarist of Balefire?

CHAPTER NINE

Dakota

WHEN I LOOKED up from playing my axe in the studio and saw Annabelle standing there in that tight green dress her first day, I knew I couldn't wait to spend some one-on-one time with her. What I didn't bargain for was her family. Alan Stewart could actually hang with me on some of the riffs we played, and he made a damn fine rhythm guitar player. I'd enjoyed that evening we spent playing together so much it passed in a nano-second. Ellie cooked almost as well as Blu's mom Diane, and that's saying something, considering Diane's gourmet restaurant had a wait list months in advance. Emma acted like I always thought a kid sister would act, which of course meant she amused me as she did her damnedest to annoy Annabelle. When I was little, I dreamed of belonging to a family like Annabelle's. Time to face facts. I liked her family way more than a wild-ass single guy should even think about.

Damn.

Growing up with only my dad, I'd never seen what a so-called "traditional family" looked like up close. Blu had always been my best friend, and he grew up with only his mom, so I spent my early years thinking most people either had a mom or a dad but not both. By the time I reached middle school and started hanging with Tron and our old drummer Dave Brubaker, I saw that a lot of people grew up with both parents. But Dave's dad drove over-the-road trucks, so he wasn't around much. Tron's parents were so busy running Tron's dad's mechanics shop they mostly left us to our own devices, which meant I didn't see of either of them much when we were at Tron's.

Spending time with Annabelle and her family left me even more restless than I usually was when the band wasn't rehearsing or touring. Fine. Not the time I spent with them but the walking away from them. Sure I wanted to spend time with Annabelle. Of course I wanted her back in my bed. That became the number one goal after we reconnected at Jack and Clio's wedding. Spending more time with her family? Definitely not a side benefit I'd ever expected to want.

Even though I had a perfectly decent sound room in my house, during our hiatus, I went in to the studio every day to play. At times, I even forgot to keep my eyes on the window to watch for her if she walked by. For some reason, Annabelle didn't walk by the recording room much. But with the studio located as it was between the offices and the kitchen, I could catch her on her way to lunch, which of course meant joining her. I'd ask her about her job, what she was learning, tease her of course. Then she'd excuse herself and go back to work. Not wanting to make my intentions too obvious to the rest of the staff, I kept my attention to her in check and only at lunchtime. After three days of fantasizing about taking off whatever hot dress she wore to work and baiting her with innuendos and references to that one hot night we'd shared, I'd waited long enough.

Clearly, Annabelle intended to treat me professionally, like I was her boss or something. Not the plan I had in mind for Balefire's first-ever intern. Driving up to the studio in my sweet—read that loud—pickup instead of my Lexus, I announced myself to the whole team.

Emory greeted me as I strode through the front office.

"Are you guys starting rehearsals today?" she asked. The way she tilted her head and knit her brow simultaneously told me I'd confused her. "I thought you weren't starting back up until next week."

"Hello to you too, Emory. You're right. Rehearsals start next week. Annabelle around?"

Glancing over at the office she'd assigned to Annabelle and finding it empty, Emory turned back to me. "She was here a few minutes ago. She must have slipped out. Shall I page her?"

"Don't worry about it. I'll catch up with her. Enjoy your day, Em."

Ignoring the quizzical look on her face, I headed out of the office and down the hall to the rehearsal space. As I walked that hallway for the thousandth time, I broke into a grin like always. Seeing all that bling announcing the band's popularity with the fans never got old. Then I thought about catching Annabelle alone, and my grin spread over my whole body.

She walked out of the ladies' room directly into my chest. Wrapping my arms around her, I said, "Whoa there, Annie-girl."

"Dakota!" she gasped. "I'm sorry. I didn't see you."

"You mean you didn't want to hold me just now?"

She huffed out a sigh. "You can let go of me."

Instead, I pushed her up against the wall behind her, caging her in with my body. "I've missed you, Annabelle." I brushed my lips along her temple.

"You saw me yesterday."

Her words held exasperation, but the breathy way she said them told me something else entirely.

"Mm, yeah. I *saw* you and talked to you while we ate lunch together, but I haven't been with you—only you—since the other night in your driveway. We need to do something about that, Annababy."

She looked into my eyes, a question in hers. A question with only one possible answer.

I leaned down and kissed her. I meant it to be a promise, a little taste of what was going to happen between us in the near future. When she opened her mouth and welcomed me inside, she pre-empted the hell out of my good intentions. Our tongues tangled, each of us desperate to touch the other. She tightened her arms around my waist, pushing her full breasts into me as though she couldn't get close enough to me. My cock went rock hard as the whimpers coming from the back of her throat turned to moans. Breaking away from her mouth, I trailed kisses down the soft skin of her neck.

As I slipped a hand between us to palm and tease her breast, I heard a door slide closed somewhere in the rehearsal space. Until then, I hadn't heard anything above the roaring of blood in my ears. Resting my forehead on Annabelle's, I panted. "Hang tight. Who-ever came in will pass by without seeing us."

But the intrusion of someone else in the space broke the spell. With her hands at the sides of my hips, she pushed me away from her. "I have to get back to work, Dakota," she whispered.

"Uh-huh. You might want to make a return trip to the ladies' room first." I couldn't help but grin at her.

Her shining eyes, flushed face, and kiss-swollen lips advertised exactly what we'd been doing. Her hand flew to her mouth. "Oh, shit!"

Before I let her slip from my arms, I murmured, "We're not done. Though I loved meeting your family the other night, tonight is going to be much more private. I like what you're wearing, by the way. It's perfect for where we'll be going to dinner."

Her eyes widened, and she opened her mouth to say something, probably something ridiculous like she couldn't go out with me since I'm technically her boss, but the sound of voices coming from the kitchen shushed her. She hustled back into the rest room, treating me to the sexy sway of her sweet ass in the tight black miniskirt she wore over black stockings with some sort of pattern running over them and sky-high heels. As I stepped over to the recording room door, I formed a plan to have a better look at that pattern after she got off work.

A couple of seconds after I flipped the lights on, Dan and Garrett walked in.

"You've been spending a lot more time around here than usual for a hiatus, Dakota," Garrett began. "Could it have anything to do with the pretty intern we took on? Not to say I blame you. Annabelle is one seriously hot mama."

The look I gave him had Dan backing up. Garrett didn't get the hint.

"Wouldn't have ever thought you'd tangle yourself up with someone you're going to have to see regularly," he pushed.

"Aren't you supposed to be setting up the dates for our tour?" I grumbled. Garrett might have been an ace manager, but sometimes he could be a douche.

"Testy," he continued, a speculative look on his face. "Does that mean you're getting some or that she shot you down?"

"Fuck off, Garrett."

I turned my back on him, picked up a guitar, and started tuning it.

"I bet Dakota's never been shot down before in his life."

"I think we should probably leave Dakota to what he does so well that puts food on all our tables," Dan said as he edged his way toward the door.

Without looking away from the guitar in my hands, I said, "Good idea."

Garrett laughed, but it sounded off somehow. "Temper over a woman? Didn't think I'd live to see the day, Dakota."

"Like I said, Garrett. Fuck. You."

I wasn't playing this time, something Dan seemed to have figured out.

"About those numbers we were running Garrett. They're in my office," he said.

Garrett smirked. I crossed my arms, cocked a brow, and dared him to keep it coming. After staring me down for several seconds, he shrugged and followed Dan, leaving me in peace.

♪

I spent the afternoon working on the new song I'd started earlier in the week. But I couldn't push the conversation with Garrett out of my head. What *was* I doing pursuing someone I couldn't escape easily by hopping on a tour bus or catching our plane afterward? Scenes from the only night I'd spent with Annabelle and her hot glances at the wedding and the way she couldn't take her eyes off me when I jammed with her dad after dinner bounced around in my head. Images of her laughing with her friends, humoring her family, fitting into the Balefire staff like she'd started with the band all collided in my head. I hadn't been paying attention, and she'd slipped in under my skin. The question was, what did I plan to do about it?

Whipping out my phone, I shot off a quick text: *Don't even think about leaving the studio without me tonight.*

Annabelle

I'd purposefully tried to avoid Dakota at work since he invited himself to dinner and rocked my world with that good-night kiss. He'd managed to have lunch with me every day except for today, but otherwise, we hardly saw each other. Thankfully. I didn't ever want to be known as the girl who slept her way into any corporate situation. I mean, how cliché was that?

Then Garrett and Dan nearly caught me making out with Dakota—at work no less. Yeah, no cliché there. After having had my number for nearly two weeks he finally decided to use it to threaten me into joining him for dinner? The man had no boundaries. Obviously, he also didn't care about what anyone at work might think of me if they knew Dakota and I had something going on.

Which we didn't, not really. I couldn't figure out what he wanted. Though he'd insisted on having my number, he didn't call or text until today. Emory once mentioned that him hanging around the studios this much during a hiatus was unusual since he normally traveled somewhere exotic to relax during his time off. Yet he'd worked in the studio every day since my first day on the job. Maybe that meant he wanted to start something with me—or maybe he had some songs inside him that he needed to let out right now. I didn't know.

What I knew was that Dakota kept me off-balance. Believing that night would be the only one, I'd deliberately redirected my thoughts whenever Red Rocks pushed its way into my head. Since Clio's wedding, images of that night swirled around my thoughts like a merry-go-round I couldn't control. Dakota checking me out at the after-concert party before slinging an arm around me and leading me to his hotel suite. Dakota so cool and sexy lying on the bed fully dressed while I stripped for him. Dakota rocking my world as he gave me the best sex of my life. Dakota walking me to my car the next morning, so polite and decent when I didn't expect it, when he didn't have to be.

Until he kissed me like he needed my breath to save his life, in full view of my sister no less, I would have thought I'd brought home an entirely different person. He charmed the socks off my whole family. And since then, all three of them talked nonstop about Dakota whenever I saw them. Last night for a break from all the Dakota Perri worship at Mom and Dad's, I caught a movie after work and climbed the stairs to my apartment after all the lights were out in their house.

I should have known when he gave me a break today by leaving me alone at lunch that he had something else in mind. Of course I knew it wasn't a good idea to go out with the boss, even if only for dinner. Which it wouldn't be. He'd served me a warning with that kiss outside the recording space. Our business ethics profs drilled it into our heads at every opportunity that we never ever fraternized with the boss. Yet here I was, checking the clock and willing it to speed up so I could spend some private time with him. What was *wrong* with me?

I'd made a good impression on the staff at Balefire's studios. I knew that. It was something I shouldn't—didn't—want to jeopardize. Caroline and I had hit it off like we'd known each other forever. Emory treated me like one of the staff from the moment I met her. Dan and Trevor were friendly and helpful, even though I didn't work closely with either of them. Going out with Dakota meant potentially screwing up my fledgling relationships with the people I needed most in my job and for any future career I wanted in management. Yet I knew I'd never resist him even if I wanted to. Being honest with myself, I didn't want to resist a man so hot and sexy, a man who with one kiss could make me feel like he was my lifeline to the world.

Garrett's cologne announced him several seconds before he interrupted my thoughts. Did he bathe in Drakkar Noir? Didn't he know the younger crowd had moved on from wearing it years ago?

"Annabelle, there you are!"

What the hell? Where else would I be than in my little office with its plate glass window looking out on the elegantly appointed reception area?

"Is there something you need?" I asked, my tone carefully neutral.

He made me uneasy, like he wanted to pounce. Everyone else on the staff had been so great except him. With his "casual" brushes against me when he invaded my personal bubble, with his innuendos, with his weird sense of style—like he couldn't decide if he wanted to be a rock star or a corporate raider—the guy creeped me out. But I was smart enough to keep my thoughts to myself. In my short time at the studio, I'd observed that everyone on the staff deferred to him and genuinely seemed to like him. So maybe it was just me.

"I like your ideas for marketing the band's upcoming tour. The social media push to encourage all the fans to attend the concerts in Balefire T-shirts is brilliant. Photographing the crowds wearing the cover of the band's latest album will make people feel like they're a part of the show."

Well, damn. There I'd gone cataloging my problems with Garrett, and he showed up with awesome compliments.

"Even though you came highly recommended," he continued, "when we first took you on, I didn't know what to expect. Now I see what a smart move we made."

"Thank you."

Okay, so if he praises everyone like this, maybe that's why everyone seems to like him so much.

"Sexy and smart. Most men can't resist that."

He caged me in with one hand on the back of my chair, the other flat on the desk in front of me. And I stopped feeling guilty. With morbid fascination, I watched his eyes as they deliberately dropped from mine to take in the hint of cleavage revealed by the sweetheart neckline of my favorite magenta knit T-shirt. Slowly, he raised them back up to stare at my mouth like he was contemplating kissing me.

"That's an interesting look you prefer," I said, interrupting his blatant perusal of my assets. Since I couldn't decide if he was trying to intimidate me or date me, I leaped on the offensive. "Cutoff band shirts tucked into dress slacks. Not sure what you're trying to say with that look, but it does grab people's attention." I didn't even try to keep the sarcasm out of my voice.

If Garrett were my only fraternizing temptation, I could do my business professors proud with my amazing self-control and ethics.

He blinked a couple of times before his eyes narrowed, and a tiny awareness of dread shivered through me.

"Like I said, Annabelle. You're worth keeping an eye on."

He straightened and rolled his shoulders in an obvious effort to make me look at them. After shooting me a speculative look, he turned on his heel and walked away. Only after he crossed to the other side of the reception area did I let out the breath I'd been holding in hopes of dodging another whiff of his cologne.

CHAPTER TEN

Annabelle

"HELLO ANNABABY. I thought we'd take my ride this time."

At the end of the workday, my silly heart leaped when I found Dakota leaning casually on my Mustang again.

He pushed away from my car and grabbed my hand in one smooth movement. I tugged against his hold when he led me around my car and over to a behemoth of a pickup truck. He wanted to take me out in *that*? The top of the cab to midway down the doors and box was searing white while the bottom of the truck and one glowing flame up the middle of the hood screamed electric lime green. Even in the slanted afternoon sun, the truck's paint job made me squint.

Recovering my shock at the sight of his truck, I said, "I thought you drove a Lexus."

"That's my stealth car." He grinned. "This is my daily driver. Sweet, huh?"

The truck definitely drew the eye. Like its driver. Not a coincidence, for sure. The loud paint job utterly fit Dakota.

"Yeah. I like the flame. But, um, Dakota, how am I ever going to ride in it?"

With the truck's massive tires and six-inch lift, its doors must have been at least three feet off the ground. Raising my foot that high, even in my four-inch sandals, would mean showing off that I wasn't wearing underwear beneath my patterned pantyhose. Not going to happen.

Dakota grinned and opened the driver's door. Positioning me in front of him, he put his hands on my hips and said, "Bend your knees and give a little hop."

He chuckled at my squeak when he launched me up onto the seat. When I tried to scoot over to let him in behind me, a huge gearshift in the shape of a guitar neck stymied my progress. "Annabelle, I can understand why you'd want to drive my awesome truck, but it's your first ride in it, so maybe you should let me do the honors." The laughter hiding in his voice told me he knew exactly why I still sat in the driver's seat.

"Maybe if you'd boosted me in on the other side, I wouldn't be in your way," I huffed. In a most unladylike fashion, I lifted my right foot over the shifter, scooted over with the thing between my legs, and finally moved far enough to lift my left foot over it.

Before I could accomplish that last move, Dakota sat beside me, his big hand on my thigh stopping me. "Where do you think you're going, babe?"

I arched a brow. "You want me to ride with this thing between my legs?"

He stared deliberately at the gearshift between my thighs. "That's one of the sexiest things I've ever seen. You do know I need to put my hand there to drive."

If I had any doubt about the outcome of this dinner date, his innuendo made his intentions clear. Closing my eyes tight, I willed my legs not to clamp together, telling him exactly what his words did to me. When I opened my eyes, Dakota was smiling at the view of my legs sprawled open around the guitar neck of his gearshift.

"I wondered about that pattern on your stockings. Roses. I like the idea of you hiding your pretty pussy in a rose garden."

"Dakota!"

His laughter filled the cab as he let go of my thigh long enough to turn the key in the ignition. When the monster masquerading as his truck roared to life, the thunder of the engine in the confined space next to the Quonset hut blasted away any further conversation. Not that I knew what to say to Dakota's blatant come-on. Yet I couldn't hide my smile as his hand "accidentally" grazed the inside of my thigh every time he needed to shift the truck as he took his time driving up the lane from the studios to the street.

"Where are we going to dinner?" I asked after we reached a wide boulevard where the truck could cruise at speed without him having to shift so much. My voice sounding normal surprised the heck out of me considering the way my blood fizzed through my veins at the touch of his warm hand on my thigh.

As though he knew exactly what he was doing to me, he gave my thigh a tiny squeeze and took his eyes from the road long enough to wink at me. "No you don't, Annabelle. No matter how hot those stockings are on your gorgeous legs, you're not getting information out of me that easily."

Emphasizing his words, he ran his palm down to my knee and back up to the hem of my skirt, settling his hand there as he traced the pattern of a rose with his fingers. Gasping at his touch, I tried to pull my legs together, but the infernal gearshift between them impeded my movement.

"Hey, Annababy. Leave some air in the cab for me, would ya?" He smirked.

The sound of his laughter, the rumble of the truck vibrating the seat beneath my ass, his hand tracing patterns on my thigh combined to make my core so tight I worried I might explode on the spot. But I didn't earn my reputation in college by accident. Taking a deep, though circumspect, breath through my nose, I casually slid my hand over the soft denim of his well-worn jeans. Enjoying the play of his thick strong muscles beneath my fingers, I mimicked his hand movements, tracing patterns with my fingers, giving his thigh a squeeze, reveling in the feel of all that powerful muscle under my palm.

Now it was his turn to suck in air, but I didn't say a word. With my eyes trained on the scenes passing outside the windshield, I smiled as we drove to Dakota's secret destination.

Dakota

I had to hand it to her. Annabelle could hang right in there with me, play the game as well as I played it, which made her even sexier. Too bad I'd already made a reservation, and not one I was willing to cancel for a quickie in the front seat of my truck. Besides, I had bigger plans for my reunion with her sexy body. Still, I slid my fingers beneath the hem of her skirt high up the inside of her thigh. At last, she gratified my teasing by clamping her thighs together with a little squirm.

Catching a glimpse of her thighs tightened around the guitar neck gearshift nearly ruined my resolve about how the evening would go. So fucking hot. Definitely an image I knew I'd replay in my head often in the future. Definitely an image that gave me ideas for the evening.

Annabelle said nothing. Just kept her delicate hand on my thigh and her eyes on the road.

We arrived at Signals, Diane Connolly's new gourmet restaurant, a few minutes before our reservation. Since the woman had practically raised me with Blu, I knew she'd have our table ready even though, judging from the parking lot, the place was packed. As usual. The buzz about it since she opened her place at the beginning of the summer ensured a full house every night. Blu told me at Jack's wedding that the restaurant ran her ragged and he'd never seen her so happy. Clearly, Ashleigh Baker's positive influences extended beyond her fiancé to his mom since from what Blu said, Ashleigh had been the one to convince Diane to open the place.

Of course I'd attended Diane's grand opening and eaten at Signals several times since then, but tonight was special. Tonight I had Annabelle with me. In a way, on our second date I was bringing Annabelle home to mom the way she had taken me home to her family.

I slipped my arm around her waist and led her to the front door.

"Signals? I heard the wait for a reservation here is weeks," she said, not bothering to disguise the excitement in her voice.

"I have connections."

Her face clouded for a second. "Oh, yeah." I watched with alarm as her enthusiasm deflated. "Sometimes when we're at the studio, I forget that you're a rock star."

"That's not it at all, Annie-girl."

The skepticism in those raised brows was killing the mood.

"Blu's mom owns this place and is the executive chef. Any one of the guys in the band has a table whenever we want it. It's called family, Annabelle."

"Oh." Then, "Oooh! Blu's *mom* owns this place," like she got it.

"It's famous for her food, not the band," I said dryly as I ushered her through the door.

LeShaun, Signals' very correct maître d', greeted us at the door. He had me by an inch and at least forty pounds, which meant he could be the bouncer if someone made the poor choice of acting up in Diane's place—even in the awesome tux he wore so well. His perfectly smooth brown skin always left me wondering if he was closer to Blu's and my age or to Diane's. His extremely proper manners had me leaning toward Diane. Or maybe it was the way he looked at her the couple of times I'd seen him with her in the kitchen.

At any rate, it made me happy to find him working the front door.

"LeShaun! Good to see you, man," I said, extending my hand. I'd tried fist-bumping him once, and he'd looked at my hand like it belonged to an alien. Like I said, very proper.

"Good evening, Mr. Perri. We're happy you could join us tonight. Your table is ready. Is this your young lady?"

I had to suppress a smirk. Did I mention proper? "This is Annabelle Stewart, my date. Annabelle, LeShaun Greene, the maître d' of Signals." In a stage whisper I added, "He's in charge, so keep yourself under control for once, would ya?"

Annabelle rolled her eyes at me and extended her hand to LeShaun. "A pleasure to meet you, sir."

He inclined his head at her as he briefly took her hand. With two of Diane's oversized leather-bound menus in his hand, he stepped in front of us. "Follow me, please."

Judging from the pointing and whispering, a few people recognized me as we wove our way through the tables in the central seating area. LeShaun led us to a banquette on the raised platform at the back of the restaurant. Being separated from the main floor by the platform and a low railing along it afforded patrons privacy from the general crowd seated at tables at tasteful distances from each other on the main floor. Of course, that didn't stop a group of people at one of those tables from trying to snap a photo of us with their phones. LeShaun stood between the cameras and us as he handed out our menus and mentioned that Diane insisted on serving us and would be out shortly.

Turning on his heel, he purposefully walked over to the table of gawkers, and though we couldn't hear what he said, he made his point obvious as the waitstaff appeared as if by magic with to-go boxes presumably filled with the patrons' food. When one of the men at the table tried to protest, LeShaun crossed his arms over his impressive chest and nodded once at the door. Immediately, the man stopped arguing.

Annabelle watched the scene in awe. "It's not his size that

intimidates people. It's his manners. How can you argue with some-one who knows exactly how to act?"

I smirked. "I think that's why Diane hired him. She drilled man-ners into Blu and me regularly. Not that all of them took."

"That explains it."

"Explains what?"

"The way you acted at my parents' house the other night." She arched a brow. "Not the inviting yourself to dinner part."

I interrupted her with a self-satisfied grin.

"But the way you acted during dinner and afterwards impressed the hell out of them. They're still talking about it."

"You're welcome."

"Are you always so full of yourself?"

"By full of myself, you mean awesome, right?"

I watched in fascination as she tried not to let it loose, but a smile twitched over her lips anyway.

A server interrupted to ask about drinks. I ordered a beer and a glass of water—I wasn't completely irresponsible—and Annabelle ordered a vodka lemonade. So my girl wasn't afraid of me. Good.

While we took a minute to peruse our menus, Annabelle com-mented on all the "yummy"—her word—choices. I already knew I'd order whatever special Diane described since I could count on whatever it was being delicious. The woman didn't know how to cook anything that didn't leave a guy begging for seconds. How she'd remained unmarried all these years after Blu's dad walked out was an unsolvable mystery.

As if I'd conjured her with my thoughts, the woman herself arrived at our table.

"Dakota! I'm so happy to see you!" Diane gushed like she hadn't seen me in months instead of last week when I came in alone for dinner.

I stood and hugged her then turned to Annabelle. "This is my date, Annabelle Stewart. Annabelle, Diane Connolly."

"We met briefly at Jack and Clio's wedding," Diane said with a smile. "It's nice to see you again, Annabelle."

"Thank you. It's nice to see you too."

"I take it the two of you hit it off at the wedding?" Diane asked, a sly smile crossing her lips.

"Pretty much," I said, trying to head off the third degree I knew she wanted to inflict on us.

For as long as I could remember, Diane had been trying to fix Blu and me up with "nice young women." She'd finally managed it with Blu, introducing him to the girl next door who turned out to be the girl of his dreams or some shit. I just wanted a good time for a while.

Apparently, Annabelle agreed with me since she changed the subject. "I'm so excited to be here. I've heard rave reviews about your place, but I didn't know the owner of Signals was *that* Diane Connolly. This place is amazing," she said as she glanced around the dining room. "I love the old-world feel of it. All the rich wood and bold floral upholstery and brass accents make me think of old romantic movies."

Running her hands along the leather of the banquette seat, she added, "The intimacy of these banquettes makes me feel special, like a VIP or something."

"You are a VIP," Diane said warmly. "Thank you. Ashleigh and Blu encouraged me to go for this, and though I worried I might not be ready, it's doing all right so far."

"Better than all right. You must have known why I invited myself to dinner at your place so often when Blu and I were kids." I winked.

"Inviting yourself to dinner is a habit with you?" Annabelle asked with a smirk on her pouty lips.

"Only when I know I'm going to eat great food."

She narrowed her eyes at me. "You didn't know that before you invited yourself."

"You're a cook too, Annabelle?" Diane asked, interest lighting up her face.

"Not really."

"There's a story there," Diane began, but I cut her off.

"Yeah, but we don't want to hold you up with all the boring details. What's for dinner tonight?"

"I'll get the details out of you later," she threatened.

"Uh-huh."

I had no doubt she'd try. But she didn't need to know how Annabelle and I met or about my current pursuit of the gorgeous brunette seated across the table from me.

Diane sighed dramatically. She was such a mom. Though I'd never admit how much I liked that, I think she knew.

Instead of pursuing our conversation, she rattled off the specials. As I already knew I would, I opted for yak medallions cooked in a whiskey reduction special. After considering for a minute, Annabelle chose the seafood linguine. Diane had practiced that dish on us a few times when Blu and I came in from the road over the years, so I knew I'd be stealing a bite or two from Annabelle's plate before the meal was over. I ordered a bottle of the house wine, and Diane hustled off to start cooking. If it weren't for the fancy atmosphere of the place, the familiarity of her cooking our dinner made me feel like I was home.

Annabelle watched Diane walk away. "You two seem really close."

"She practically raised me. Diane's the one who talked my dad into guitar lessons for me when I was eight."

"Seriously?"

"Yeah. Blu and I demonstrated a knack for finding trouble from the minute we met. Diane thought if we did something constructive together, we might not get in it as much. Good thing she's never gone on tour with us." I snickered.

"Bet she has a clue," Annabelle said dryly.

I grinned and slid around the booth to sit closer to her. I couldn't seem to help myself when it came to Annabelle. Whenever she was near, I wanted my hands on her. Keeping my distance as much as I had at the studio this last week had been pure torture. But I had plans for the night that would make up for it.

Chapter Eleven

Annabelle

NOT SURPRISINGLY, DINNER with Dakota turned out to be an adventure.

"Annabelle, check it out. I think that's John Elway being seated in the next booth," Dakota said, gesturing with his fork.

When I looked over, I only saw one of the servers pouring water. But when I returned to my meal, I discovered Dakota spinning my linguine around his fork and popping a generous bite into his mouth.

"That's why you moved so close to me, so you could eat your dinner and mine too." I slapped at his hand when he came in for seconds. "Keep your fork in your own food." Though I tried to sound tough, his attempt at an innocent expression with his mouth stuffed full of my dinner twitched a grin out of me.

Before I could protest more, Dakota forked up a bite of his meal and offered it to me. When I closed my mouth around a succulent piece of yak meat, he slid the fork from my mouth with slow, sensual deliberateness. Leaning in, he touched the tip of his tongue to the corner of my mouth. I stopped chewing and sat still as a mouse as the big cat played with me. He eyed my lips with a lazy sexy stare that made me forget all about how good my food tasted.

At last, he sat back and casually said, "Yep, just as I thought. Diane's food tastes even better when we share."

His businesslike tone defied the smoldering heat in those gorgeous blue eyes of his as they darkened from their usual summer sea to deep midnight while I tried not to squirm under the intensity of his stare.

"Is there anything else I can grab for you, sir? Dessert, perhaps?" The guy serving us looked to be my age, but his starstruck demeanor made him seem younger when his voice rose half an octave in the course of his question.

Dakota finally looked away from me long enough to ask, "Does Diane have any hot berry compote left back there?"

"I-I'm not sure."

"If she has any, bring us one and two spoons. Thanks," Dakota said with a nod.

The server hustled directly back to the kitchen even though the patrons at the banquette beside us tried to grab his attention.

"Now, where were we? Oh yeah, we were talking about how good your dinner is and how much you've enjoyed sharing it with me." He nonchalantly speared a bite of lobster from my plate.

"You are incorrigible," I huffed.

"That's a compliment, yeah? Because I like to share too." He held his fork in front of my mouth, leaving me no choice but to enjoy another taste of his meal.

By the time the server returned with our dessert, Dakota had finished his dinner and a good portion of mine. But thanks to the way he'd wanted to share, I wasn't sure I even had room for dessert. That also could have been because of all the butterflies fluttering around in my stomach from the press of his thigh against mine and the sexy sensuality of trading bites of our dinner.

When the server set the warm compote in front of us, the smell of fresh berries in thick, rich custard with a buttery crust topping made me rethink my ideas about enjoying dessert. Though the server placed a spoon in front of each of us, Dakota deliberately reached for mine and spooned up a bite for me. I couldn't stop myself from closing my eyes and licking my lips around the decadent flavors of tart blackberries, raspberries, and blueberries in vanilla custard. Blinking my eyes open, I caught Dakota's gaze zeroed in on my mouth.

I reached for his spoon and scooped up a bite of berry goodness to offer him. Without taking his eyes from mine, he opened his mouth for the treat, and I took my time feeding him. Turnabout being fair and all that. But I wasn't prepared for the way my body reacted to watching him eat from my spoon. My nipples hardened beneath my thin knit shirt, and wet heat gathered at the apex of my thighs. In the farthest recesses of my consciousness, I was aware that if LeShaun or Diane or a server interrupted us, they'd see the proof of my arousal, but I didn't care. The only thing on my mind was how beautiful Dakota's full, sculpted lips looked wrapped around my spoon, how deep I was falling into the oceans of his eyes, how my body heated when sharing dessert with him.

Before sitting down to dinner with him, I had no idea how sensual a meal could be. The whole experience felt almost as intimate as sharing that hotel suite after the Red Rocks concert when we first met. I knew I played with fire. The mere thought of dating my boss could put my nascent career on the line. Not to mention my heart could quite easily do something stupid like fall in love with Dakota Perri. Those thoughts didn't slow me down as I allowed him to lead me by the hand back to his truck after we gave our compliments and said our goodbyes to Diane Connolly.

The deliberate way he walked, the way he squeezed my waist as he handed me back up into his truck, the way he didn't even pretend subtlety as he played his fingers over my thigh on the ride back to the studio told me exactly where we were headed. And I went willingly, even eagerly.

After he turned off the engine of his truck, the world seemed to stand still as he stared out the windshield, his hand still firmly squeezing my thigh. He blew out a breath. "I want to show you something. Inside the studio."

He looked so serious that I couldn't help but nod in agreement, my curiosity overriding my good sense. Guiding me around the side of the building, he led me through a side door, which he carefully locked behind us. With a tug of my hand, he steered me through the dark up the stairs to the theater room. We stopped before what I assumed was some sort of panel in the wall, and after he keyed in a few commands, a soft glow lit the edges of the room. The surround-sound speakers came to life with Hinder's "Better Than Me."

"Dance with me, Annabelle," Dakota said as he took me in his arms.

He pulled me close, our bodies touching from chests to thighs, and all the heat I'd experienced in the restaurant as we fed each other dessert rushed over me. Unable to help it, I pushed myself even closer to him as the music segued into Apocalyptica's "Not Strong Enough," and if I'd listened to the words rather than only to the music, I might have caught a clue about where things between Dakota and me would end up.

Dakota

Jesus, this woman. I meant to tease her a little at dinner—and enjoy as much of Diane's food as I could. But Annabelle couldn't seem to hold back. Those tiny whimpers of pleasure at the back of her throat when I fed her a piece of succulent yak, the outright groans of ecstasy when she wrapped those plump lips of hers around a taste of berries and custard. Did she even know how she killed me? It was all I could do to make it through dinner without jumping her right there in the restaurant. Bet Diane would have loved that. I chuckled to myself. Probably, she would have kicked me out of Signals for life.

My dick pulsed on high alert for hours. Like I hadn't blue-balled myself enough since seeing Annabelle again at the monk's wedding. As I slid my hands over the sweet globes of her ass, I said a silent prayer she'd forgive me for the damage I knew I was going to do to those sexy stockings hugging her gorgeous legs. Lifting her higher against my body, I found her full, beautiful mouth with my own. As usual with her it seemed, I couldn't start slow.

Almost as soon as I initiated the kiss, my tongue tangled with hers, a delicious taste of berries and wine and Annabelle. I kept one hand on her ass while the other slid up her back to tangle in the thick, silky mass of her hair, holding her where I wanted her as I ravaged her mouth.

Annabelle didn't remain idle as I kissed us both stupid. Even in those deliciously high heels she liked, she barely reached my chin. Still, when her leg twined around my thigh as she started to climb me, I slid my hand back down her body to grab her ass in both hands and help her wrap her beautiful long legs around my waist. Without breaking our kiss, I carried her to the nearest recliner and sat down with her straddling my lap.

Giving her ass a squeeze and a promise, I let my hands roam, pushing her shirt up over her head. She dropped her head back as I trailed my lips over her jaw and down the smooth skin of her throat. Dipping my tongue into the hollow of her collarbone, I tasted her musky perfume, her flavor driving me wild. No baby doll florals or cloying patchouli for my girl. She smelled and tasted as spicy, full, and sensual as her curves and her natural responses to me.

Her hard nipples teased my palms, and I turned my attention to her perfect tits showcased by the deep pink lace of her bra. I took one taut nipple in my mouth, laving my tongue over the lace and felt like Superman when she cried out and ground her sweet pussy against the front of my jeans. Yeah, she was in this with me, but I wanted there to be no regret afterward.

Planting my hands on her hips, I held her still as I pulled away from the perfection of her breasts. I nearly lost myself in the deep green of her desire-darkened eyes. Sliding her hands from my shoulders to my face, she held me while she traced her thumb over the curve of my lower lip. That little move required a response, and I opened my mouth to nip the pad of her thumb, pulling it inside and giving it a suck. A tightening of her thighs around mine accompanied her quick intake of breath, and I couldn't remember a time when I wanted a woman as much as I wanted Annabelle.

"Jesus, woman. Have some self-control."

"Oh, I have all kinds of self-control. It's you we're not so sure about," she said in a breathy voice.

The naughty gleam in her eyes told me everything I needed to know. I stared at her kiss-swollen lips for a long beat. With a laugh, I said, "Fuck it. Self-control is overrated."

I pulled her down for another drugging kiss and unclasped her pretty bra, taking my time testing the weight of her gorgeous breasts with my hands. After a few blissful minutes of palming her luscious body, I busied my hands with unzipping her skirt and pulling it over her hips.

Annabelle interrupted me long enough to drag my T-shirt over my head before she drove me crazy with her clever fingers tracing the contours of my chest and abs, finding my tats and following them first with her fingertips then with her lips. She had to scoot back on my lap when she found the tat of half a heart at my hip, tracing it lightly with the pad of her finger. When she opened the fly of my jeans, I kicked back and let her have her way.

The wicked smile on her lips told me what she planned seconds before she slid all the way off my lap to kneel between my thighs. I helped her by lifting up enough to slide my jeans down over my hips, and then she was there, kissing the length of my cock, exploring it with her tongue, her eyes never leaving mine. I don't know how Annabelle knew exactly how to please me, but I couldn't remember anything as wild and sexy as her eyes on mine as she pleasured me.

I didn't even try to suppress the groan that escaped my throat when she took me fully into the wet heat of her mouth.

Plunging my hands into her mass of hair, I held on and let her work her magic until she took me to the edge of explosion.

"Annabelle," I gritted out. "Come here."

Pretending not to hear me, she stroked me again, so I tugged on her hair. "Come here, Annababy."

With excruciating slowness, she pulled herself up my body, dragging her tight nipples along my dick then up my belly and over my chest. "I was enjoying that, you know," she sassed.

"Oh, I know." I cleared my throat. "I definitely know."

I slid my hands up under her skirt until I found the waistband of her pantyhose. "I loved these on you, Annabelle. I really did."

She gasped at the ripping sound as I tore them down over her hips. "Those were my favorite pair."

"We'll go shopping."

I dipped a finger inside her pussy and grinned. Pulling it out, I sucked her lovely juices from it. "Glad we're in this together," I said as I watched her pupils leave only a thin ring of green in her wide eyes.

Tugging a condom from my pocket, I ripped the foil with my teeth. While I kept my eyes on hers, I rolled it down over myself. "Lift up a little, baby."

She did, and I positioned myself where I wanted to be and guided her hips down to sheath me in all her wet, tight heat.

As she gripped my shoulders with her hands and my cock with her pussy, she closed her eyes, her head falling back as a sigh escaped her lips. "Oh Dakota, you feel so good."

I leaned forward to take one of her tight pink nipples into my mouth, and she rewarded me with a wiggle, sucking me even deeper inside her, her pussy pulsing around me and driving me wild. In silent synchronization, we moved together until both of us were panting and sweating, striving to orgasm together. She tightened around me at the same time lightning raced down my spine, both of us crying out, and I lost myself in our song of ecstasy.

Fanfuckingtastic.

I didn't think we could top Red Rocks.

I was wrong.

Chapter Twelve

Annabelle

DAMMIT. IN THE end I couldn't resist him. I knew myself—and Dakota—well enough to have made a better choice than to go out to dinner with him. When he put his hand on my thigh the first time before he'd even put his truck in gear, I knew where our evening would end. I should have stopped it then, begged off and gone home—alone. Instead, I hopped right on that crazy train and took another wild ride.

But Balefire's studio? How could I have been so dumb as to follow him into the studio? We would have had more privacy at my apartment with my nosy family at home than in the studio. He had to bypass the system after he keyed us inside, which left a hollow feeling in the pit of my stomach. I had no doubt Garrett checked with the security company regularly. The guy knew *everything* that went on with the band. So what happened when someone checking the tapes decided to give Dakota a hard time about bringing a woman back to the studio after hours, and then someone happened to notice the identity of that woman?

Granted, my date with Dakota was the best ever. And the sex? Strat-o-spheric. But was it worth my career?

Obviously, I had something seriously wrong with me to have spent Friday night the way I did. Followed by a weekend of continuously checking my phone for some sort of affirmation from Dakota that at least I'd wowed him a little too. Make the sacrifice of my favorite pair of pantyhose—or the loss of my career before it even started—worth it.

Instead, I'd spent the weekend doing my laundry, taking Emma to the latest James Bond movie, and working on the marketing plan Caroline and I had dreamed up together for Balefire's West Coast tour. At least I'd been semiproductive when I wasn't shushing my va-jay-jay about wanting more alone time with a certain lead guitar player. Honestly, I knew he wasn't the settling down type, something I believed we had in common before I reconnected with him. I needed to keep my act together and play whack-a-mole with any silly expectations that threatened to pop into my head. Maintain a hint of professionalism since I couldn't seem to do decorum. And dispense with feelings for damn sure.

Imagine my surprise midmorning Monday when the man himself waltzed into my office like he hadn't ignored me for the entire weekend.

"Annababy! There you are! Come on, I want to show you something."

Isn't that how I got in trouble Friday night?

"Hello Dakota. I'm great. How are you?"

Ignoring my sarcasm, he grabbed me by the hand and hauled me out of my chair. It was all I could do to keep up with his long-legged strides as he hustled me through the reception area.

"Good morning, Dakota," Emory said as we hot-stepped past her desk.

"Back at ya, Em," Dakota returned without breaking stride.

That was it for conversation until he had me pinned up against the wall at the back of the darkened recording studio. With him touching me from shoulders to knees, I nearly couldn't think. Nearly.

"Dakota—"

"Shhh." He quieted me with the pad of his finger against my lips. "Annie-girl, do you have any idea how long it's been since Friday night?"

He shoved his hands into my hair, holding me still while he lowered his mouth to mine and kissed every rational thought straight out of my head, taking my breath along for the ride. When at last he pulled back enough to brush his lips softly over mine, I'd forgotten everything except for possibly my name.

He leaned his forehead on mine and whispered, "Don't be mad. I meant to come see you, but my plans took a detour. I went four-wheeling with Blu and our friend Vaughn, the guy who engineers our stage for us. We started drinking beers right after lunch, and I woke up last night on Vaughn's couch. I'll make it up to you, I promise."

Wait. Where was this—all of this—going?

"You don't owe me an explanation."

Those gorgeous sea blue eyes of his took a little spin inside their space, like I'd made a silly comment. "Listen, I've gotta be out of the studio today. Garrett's lined up some radio interviews and shit for Blu and me since we're the only two in town right now. But I'll be back before you get off work."

Smiling, he let me go. Then he turned back and stole a quick kiss before exiting the studio. For several seconds, I sagged against the wall, trying to find my balance in the wake of the hurricane masquerading as Dakota Perri. In all my previous relationships, I dictated the speed, the intensity, and the duration of the experience. With the way he stormed back into my life after Clio's wedding, it was dawning on me that this time, I might be the one buffeted by the winds of the sensual storms he could create. And I had no idea what to do with that.

When I walked back into the office, Emory glanced up from her computer, gave me a secretive smile, and mercifully didn't ask me about Dakota. After closing myself in my office, I set my mind firmly on the task of marketing Balefire's West Coast tour and didn't let my thoughts whirl in a tornado of images of Dakota Perri more than once or six or maybe a hundred times for the rest of the day.

♪

As I keyed myself into my apartment, I heard the unmistakable throb and rumble of the engine in Dakota's ride. No way could that window-rattling sound turning onto my parents' quiet residential street belong to anything other than the behemoth he liked to call his truck. Instead of turning the knob and entering my apartment, I watched from my landing as a white and lime green pickup pulled in behind my Mustang and parked.

Spotting me, he revved the engine before shutting off his monster. When he exited his truck, he carried a bag that appeared to contain pizza boxes. He smiled up at me as he bounded up the stairs, taking them two at a time to the landing that served as a tiny deck for my apartment.

"I meant to catch you before you left work tonight, but Garrett lined up interviews on three different radio stations and with a couple of local reporters, as well as with a West Coast entertainment blog." He caught his breath for a second. "Anyway, I hope you haven't eaten yet 'cause I picked up pizza." He held up the bag and smiled at me with a boyishness I couldn't resist.

Then again, he should have to work for some things. "What kind?"

"Meat lover's," he said with an unapologetic leer. Before I could call him out, he added, "and vegetarian and Hawaiian. I wasn't sure what kind you liked."

"Uh-huh."

"We gonna eat these or what?" he asked, nodding toward my door.

Huffing out a dramatic sigh, I turned to let us in when Emma called from the bottom of the stairs. "You brought pizza, Dakota? Sweet! Since Mom and Dad went out to dinner tonight without me, I was going to be stuck with leftovers, but pizza is much better."

By the time she finished her little speech, she was at the top of the stairs and pushing her way past us into my apartment.

"Come on in, Emma. Join us for dinner why don't you?" I muttered as I walked through the door behind her.

Glancing over my shoulder at Dakota, I caught him grinning and gave in too.

We followed Emma into my tiny kitchen where she sat like a queen at my dinette. While Dakota set out the pizza on the island separating the kitchen from the living and dining areas, I busied myself with gathering plates and utensils. Grabbing drinks from my fridge, a couple of beers for Dakota and me and a Coke for Emma who made a face when I set it in front of her, I said, "Emma, my queen, you're going to have to rouse yourself from your throne and grab your own slice if you want any."

As I helped myself to a slice of veggie and a slice of meat lover's, I slanted a look at Dakota who openly grinned at me as he took two slices of meat lover's and seated himself at the table.

With a long-suffering sigh, Emma stood and served herself. When she returned to the table, she narrowed her eyes at Dakota's proximity to me at my card table-sized dinette. That one look should have warned me, but I was still caught up in the innuendo of Dakota's dinner choice to catch it.

"Are you two dating?" she asked around a bite of Hawaiian pizza.

"No," I said.

"Yes," Dakota said simultaneously.

"I see you have your stories straight. That's good," she deadpanned.

"Really, Annabelle, it's silly to keep the news from your family. Especially after you invited me to dinner with them last week." He smirked.

Dakota and me *dating*? He had to be messing with Emma. Quirking a brow, I shot him a look and turned back to Emma. "What's the occasion? Mom and Dad hardly ever go out to dinner."

"I think Dad got a promotion or something," she said as though her news were nothing more than a weather report. She took another bite and blinked up at me.

"Why didn't I know about this?" I nearly squeaked.

"I don't know. Maybe because you've been spending all your time hanging out with the rich and famous?"

Batting her lashes, she gifted Dakota with a smile that elicited a snort from him, but I didn't let her off the hook so easily.

"Emma, when did this happen?"

"Last Thursday, I think. You didn't come home until really late on Friday night." She stretched out *really late* as she looked between the two of us for something I had no intention of confirming for her. "And they spent the weekend with me at my soccer tournament. I guess you couldn't have found out till now. Sorry."

Filling her mouth with a rather unladylike bite of pizza, she looked anything but sorry.

As I stared at her, Dakota filled the awkward silence. "That's cool for your dad. I was kind of hoping to jam with him again tonight, but this promotion thing is good too."

Emma swallowed her huge bite of pizza. "He's going to be sorry he missed you. He brings up that night you two played together all the time. It's kind of annoying, actually."

"Emma!" I gasped. "Sometimes I can't believe you. You don't get to invite yourself to dinner and insult my guest."

"I wasn't insulting Dakota. If anything, I was insulting Dad, who you have to admit is annoying."

"As are you," I retorted. I couldn't help it. Sometimes with Emma, I reverted to my own obnoxious seventeen-year-old self. I glanced at Dakota who watched us with open delight.

"What?" I grumped.

"Don't mind me. I'm enjoying the show." He took a bite of his slice and settled back into his chair. With a wave of his hand, he added, "I'm pretty sure if you keep going, you'll get to 'I know you are, but what am I?'"

I tried to glare at him, but Emma cracked up, and I couldn't help it. Within seconds, tears of laughter slid over my cheeks while Dakota filled my tiny apartment with the rich masculine sound of his laughter.

We ate our fill of pizza, nearly demolishing the three pies he'd brought over. With a contented sigh, Emma sat back in her chair and looked expectantly at me. "What's for dessert?"

"Maybe you should go back to the big house for that," I not so subtly suggested.

"Oooh, good idea. I think there's enough of Mom's famous apple pie for the three of us. BRB."

She shot out of her chair and ran the short distance to the door, disappearing through it.

"Emma's a kick. I like her a lot. But I gotta admit, she's messing with the plan, Annabelle."

Though I had a pretty good idea, I still had to ask. "What plan would that be?"

"The one where we end up on your couch. Preferably with you on my lap and nothing between us." He waggled his eyebrows at me suggestively. "This will have to tide us over for now."

Slipping his big hand around the back of my neck beneath my hair, he pulled me to him. For a long second, he stared at my mouth then leaned in and fitted his lips to mine. He tasted of pepperoni, beer, and Dakota, the manly flavor of him overwhelming my senses. No one could blame me for sliding my tongue along his and deepening the kiss he started.

Because the million warnings I'd given myself since the first day of my internship with the band had done so much good.

The whole world narrowed to my chest pressed to the hard

planes of Dakota's pecs, our hearts hammering against our ribs as we explored each other's mouths like two lovers who hadn't seen each other in years. No one had ever kissed me the way Dakota Perri always kissed me, with fire and passion and so much hunger. Every time he touched his lips to mine, he stole all my willpower, all my wise intentions, replacing them with red-hot lust.

Of its own volition, my leg traveled up his shins and crested his knee when Emma burst in through my front door.

"Annabelle! I thought you said you two weren't dating." She shut the door with her heel. "Sorry to interrupt." The smirk on her face proclaimed the opposite. "But Mom's apple pie is to die for. I didn't know if you had any ice cream, so I brought some of that too. You gonna help me warm this up?" At last, she took a breath and stared meaningfully at me.

Reading her last question correctly, I stood with as much dignity as I could considering the heat flaming my face at Emma's little discovery. I busied myself pulling more plates from the cupboard and heard Dakota stand. A second later, he took up most of the space in my tiny kitchen as he placed our dinner dishes in the sink. With no subtlety whatsoever, he pushed the side of his hard body against mine. Though I tried to put a little space between us, he shifted enough to continue touching me. Huffing out a breath, I moved to the island and tried to ignore him as I plated slices of apple pie.

Emma, as expected, had reseated herself at the table, awaiting her minions to do her bidding.

"You two met at Clio's wedding and hit it off, huh?" she asked.

When I looked up, I caught the mischievous sparkle in her eye. Before I could head her off, Dakota slipped up behind me, wrapped his arms around my waist, and rested his chin on my shoulder.

Along my spine I felt the rumble of his voice as much as heard it. "How could I resist your sister, Emma?"

He let out an *oomph!* when I elbowed him in the ribs and stepped away from the heaven of his heat. "We're not dating, little sis. Dakota's messing with you." I grabbed my dessert and headed over to the couch.

From the corner of my eye, I caught Dakota's conspiratorial wink at Emma. "Your sister's shy. That's why she's acting so weird about us dating. Which we totally are." Something in his voice dragged my eyes to his where I saw heat and something else I couldn't quite identify.

He sat beside me on the couch, took a big bite of pie, and dared me with his eyes to contradict him again.

The two of us sitting on the couch together with our dessert enticed Emma off her dinette chair throne to join us. Since I took a corner of the couch, Dakota sat beside me with Emma flanking him. Grabbing the remote, I asked, "Netflix okay with you?"

I addressed Dakota, but it was Emma who replied, "Oh hey, are we binge-watching? 'Cause if we are, I was in the middle of season three of *Dexter* when Mom made me quit watching to finish my physics."

She sat on the edge of the cushion and stared intently at the options on the screen.

Dakota surprised both of us when he said, "I like watching that weird sci-fi series with the kids in the Upside Down."

I blinked at him. "You do? I love that show."

I scrolled through my favorites until I reached *Stranger Things.* "Any particular episode or season?"

"Ugh! You like sci-fi, Dakota? Really? Aren't you a rock star?" Emma slumped into the cushions.

Leaning forward so I could stare her down, I said, "Just because he's a rock star doesn't mean he's not educated."

"Hey, ladies, are you still trying for 'I know you are, but what am I?'"

"Sorry," I huffed. Settling back into the cushions, I added, "Let's watch the show already, huh?"

I queued up an episode and preempted any more immature

responses to my sister by stuffing my face with apple pie and melting ice cream. Even without being able to see her, I could feel Emma making a face at me, something Dakota confirmed when he burst out laughing. Somehow, once again, the evening I envisioned and the one I experienced were not in the same zip code.

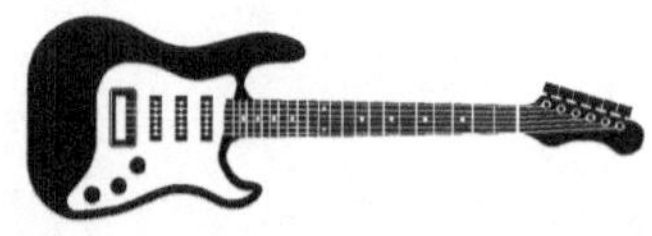

Chapter Thirteen

Dakota

ANNABELLE'S LITTLE SISTER was a kick. Seriously entertaining. And a monumental pain in the ass. When I stopped over to Annabelle's the other night, I had plans that included getting naked after dinner. Emma designating herself chaperone for the evening wouldn't necessarily have interfered with those plans until she nodded off during the third or fourth episode of *Stranger Things*. Short of me carrying her down the narrow stairs out of Annabelle's apartment and over the lawn to her parents' place, she was spending the night.

Watching Annabelle indulge her sister then fall for it whenever Emma baited her made me laugh. Watching them together also showed me Annabelle's soft center, something she tried too hard to hide. So yeah, I kind of enjoyed Emma's game. Having her stick around for the entire evening interrupted all my bad intentions, though. Growing up an only child, I often wondered what it would be like to have siblings. After my night with the girls, I figured out I needed to set some ground rules with Annabelle's sister as long as we were dating or whatever it was we were doing together.

At least I convinced Annabelle to leave Emma asleep on the couch and walk me out to my truck at the end of the evening. Where I proceeded to kiss the shit out of her. Or maybe she kissed the shit out of me. Either way, that woman left me so hard I had to take care of myself—twice—in the shower after I got home.

The last couple of days, Garrett kept both Annabelle and me so busy, I didn't have a chance to be alone with her at the studio. When I'd texted her to meet up after she got off work, she made some kind of excuse not to see me. I even resorted to driving the stealth car past her place last night and discovered she wasn't at home—just like she'd told me she wouldn't be. I guess she wasn't yankin' my chain. Didn't make me any happier that I hadn't seen her in days, and it'd been nearly a week since we last had sex.

Yes, I was keeping track. No, it's not like I couldn't get any. I had a dozen numbers I could call for a casual hook-up. But the thought of getting it on with anyone other than Annabelle didn't rev my engine. Which I knew should've made me much more concerned than I was. Her proximity and the fact that we'd only been together once since reconnecting were to blame. And the way she kissed me. Damn, thinking about those lips of hers gave me a stiffy.

When I strolled into the studio today and discovered her in the rehearsal space, I screeched to a halt, my whole body on high alert. Until I realized she was talking to someone. As I stood right inside the door listening to them, I wondered about the last few nights when she said she couldn't see me. From what I could tell, Annabelle and our head road engineer, Bailey Saunders, knew each other quite well.

"Will you be traveling with us on this tour, Annabelle?" Bailey asked with obvious interest. Obvious in the way he stood way too close to my girl.

"I'm not sure. In the meetings I've had with Garrett, it hasn't come up. From what I've picked up around the office, those of us working in marketing usually stay here in Denver and manage from the office," she replied. "It would be fun to tour with the band. I wouldn't pass up the opportunity, for sure." She let out a flirty little laugh.

Well, fuck. What the hell was that?

As I took a step farther into the rehearsal space, Garrett materialized at my side. "Jesus! How do you do that? Are you a ghost or something?" I growled to cover my reaction to the way he startled me.

"Don't blame me if you were laser-focused on the pretty intern and not paying attention to the rest of the world." Garrett smirked. "Looks like she's playing nice with the rest of the help." He nodded at Bailey who hadn't taken his eyes off Annabelle even after she turned to see who was talking near the door.

"Yeah."

I sauntered over to Bailey and offered my hand. "Good to see you, man. How you been?"

"Great. Took a little ride through the Black Hills after Jack and Clio's wedding. Since we're going to be on tour during the Sturgis Rally this year, I thought I'd take in the scenery for once, enjoy a quiet afternoon drinking at the Full Throttle Saloon. It was kind of refreshing not to have to wait thirty minutes for a beer."

The way he continued to look over at Annabelle had me thinking he had a certain kind of scenery on his mind and not the kind with trees and shit. Time to put a stop to that.

"Annabelle. It's been a few days," I said. "How 'bout you take a break and join me for lunch? Bet Chef Jeff has something delicious going in the kitchen." I casually took her hand in mine, giving it a little squeeze to reassure her she'd been on my mind—and maybe to let her know I wanted to be on her mind too.

The stiff way she held herself told me I'd done something wrong, but I couldn't figure out what exactly and wouldn't ask with our audience. So I held on when she subtly tried to extricate her hand from mine.

Garrett, the jerk, complicated things even more. "How 'bout we all have some lunch? We can talk over tour logistics and marketing together," he said. The way he looked at Annabelle made me think Bailey wasn't the only one with designs on her.

As hot as she looked in her black-and-white-striped yoga pants with the hot pink top and black knee-high stiletto boots, I guess I couldn't blame either one of them. Except I did. Did neither one notice her hand in mine? As much as I hated to pull rank, the tiny detail of me being the rock star should have meant something to both of them too.

Since we hadn't advertised that we knew each other previously—and quite intimately—before Jack married Clio, everyone else on the staff and crew thought my interest in Annabelle began with her internship. Hell, maybe Bailey and Garrett thought since they'd met her at Jack's wedding, they had as much of a shot with her as I did. Like that would ever be the case. Bailey spent most of his time with our equipment on the road. He wouldn't have much chance to see Annabelle on tour, so I couldn't figure out what his angle was. Garrett, though, had been chasing after girls—fans, groupies, merch salesgirls, pretty much any woman who came near the band—since we took him on as our manager. After his fiasco with Ashleigh Baker on our last tour, I would have thought he'd learned his lesson.

Catching him eyeing Annabelle up and down told me maybe Garrett was a slow learner.

"Whatever, Garrett. We're still a few weeks away from going out. It's okay with the band if you relax a little," I said, trying to preempt his ideas for crashing my lunch with Annabelle.

I led her to the kitchen at the back of the studio and walked in to some heavenly scent that momentarily took my mind off the way the guys were checking out my woman.

"Hey, Jeff, what's for lunch? It smells amazing in here," I called as I pulled out a chair for Annabelle at a table for four. Damned inconvenient we didn't have any intimate tables for two in the kitchen, considering Garrett and Bailey nearly tripped us following on our heels the way they did.

"I was in the mood for fish, so I whipped up some gen-u-ine Louisiana jambalaya," Jeff said with an affected Southern accent that had all of us laughing.

I hid my satisfaction at the disconcerted looks on both their faces as Bailey and Garrett figured out I'd staked my claim to Annabelle by seating her beside me across the table from each of them. Garrett corrected himself the fastest, smoothing over his expression with a smile at the two of us that left me uncomfortable. Judging from the way Annabelle shifted in her chair, she had a similar reaction. Bailey stared at her with something that looked like hurt, which made me wonder again about the conversation I'd walked in on in the rehearsal studio.

Resting my free hand high on Annabelle's thigh, I gave her a tiny squeeze. Her body stiffened beneath my touch, and I slid her a sideways look. While Jeff distracted Garrett and Bailey with steaming bowls of Cajun eats, Annabelle, staring somewhere over Garrett's shoulder, discreetly slipped her hand under the table and tried unsuccessfully to remove mine from its quite comfortable spot on her thigh.

After dipping a spoon in his bowl and tasting the food, Bailey casually said, "It was lucky for Jack and Clio that you and I met at that party a few years ago, wasn't it, Annabelle?"

At Bailey's little pronouncement, I nearly aspirated the bite of hot Cajun deliciousness I'd taken. Annabelle smacked me hard between my shoulder blades to stop my coughing while Bailey handed me my beer. Garrett looked up with a speculative smirk, a look that bothered me more than discovering Annabelle and Bailey had a history together predating hers and mine.

A long pull of beer calmed me down enough to ask, "How long have you two known each other?"

I didn't take my eyes off Annabelle who looked anywhere but at me.

"We met at a party about a year before Jack and Clio hooked up at Red Rocks," Bailey answered. "I thought Jack told you the story of how I was showing him a photo of Annabelle, and he saw Clio in it. He asked me to hook Annabelle up with tickets to the show on the condition she bring Clio with her."

Bailey had a weird look on his face as he stared across the table at Annabelle, and a bad feeling crept into my chest.

"The rest, as they say, is history," Annabelle added in a fake cheery voice. The way she focused so intently on her food made me wonder if she thought it might start to do tricks.

"You ended up with Dakota that night, didn't you Annabelle?" Bailey asked, and I could have sworn he sounded hurt about it.

"Um, yeah," she replied.

An uncomfortable silence descended over our table. I'm not sure what crossed Bailey's and Garrett's minds, but I could barely contain all the questions I had for Annabelle. Fortunately for her, Caroline and Trevor chose that moment to show up for lunch, or I might have embarrassed the hell out of her by asking a couple of them.

"Hey, Bailey, nice to see you man. You have a good trip?" Trevor asked as they fist-bumped.

"Awesome. Nothing like taking my bike out for a long ride," Bailey replied as his eyes strayed back to Annabelle.

"Annabelle, I looked over your ideas for marketing band shirts ahead of the tour, and I think you have something there. When you're free after lunch, come visit me in my office," Caroline said.

Annabelle nodded.

"I'd like to be in that meeting, Caroline." From his tone, Garrett was telling, not asking.

"Of course." Turning to Trevor, she added, "Sounds like we'd better be quick about grabbing lunch."

"Or grabbing something," Trevor said with a smirk.

"Save it for later, you two. Like your afternoon break in the conference room." Though I returned my eyes to my lunch, I didn't even try to hide my smirk. Caroline's tiny gasp and Trevor's discreet cough told me they knew exactly what I referred to. Thinking about the little tryst I caught them in on a rare quiet day in the studio last spring gave me ideas about Annabelle and me at some point before we went out on tour. Once I made sure whatever had gone down between Bailey and her was now history.

"Before you can have her, Caroline, I'm going to steal Annabelle for a little while."

Garrett raised a brow in question, but I turned my attention to Jeff who approached our table with a tray of desserts: peach sorbet he'd dressed up with raspberry syrup, real whipped cream, and a piece of dark chocolate. It was one of my favorites, as Jeff well knew, and I fist-bumped him after he set my bowl in front of me. In the end, I didn't have to worry about savoring mine since Annabelle barely touched hers. She'd hardly eaten any of Jeff's kick-ass meal.

"Mind if I finish that?" I nodded at her dessert.

"Be my guest."

"You all right, Annabelle? You didn't eat much lunch," Garrett commented. He tried to sound concerned, but I saw the avid way he sat forward in his chair as he watched her.

"I'm fine. Just not very hungry today." She smiled at him but without her usual wattage.

After finishing off our desserts, I tugged her toward a side door to the studio. I didn't say anything until we reached my truck when she silently questioned me with a quirk of her eyebrow. "We need to have a private conversation. Get in." I punctuated my command by putting my hands on her waist and nearly launching her up onto the seat of my pickup. Before she had a chance to react, I joined her on the bench seat, simultaneously slamming my door and firing up the engine. "Buckle up, Buttercup. We're going for a ride."

"You have nerve, Dakota Perri!" she huffed but slid on her seatbelt all the same.

Neither of us said anything as I drove away from the studio.

Annabelle crossed her arms over her beautiful rack and stared straight ahead out the windshield. Without thinking about it, I headed out of town toward the public lands where I'd spent the weekend with Blu and Vaughn, tearing up the dirt and mud. This time of day, traffic remained light enough that we flew along the freeway. Her uncharacteristic quietness probably should have worried me, but I was too caught up in my own thoughts.

When we reached my favorite playground, I veered to the side around and behind a hill to a stand of trees edging the boundary between public and private land. This being a weekday, there were only a couple of vehicles out in the middle where some mud still lingered after the weekend.

I killed the engine, unclipped my seatbelt, and turned to Annabelle. "What's the deal with you and Bailey?"

"You dragged me all the way out here to talk about Bailey?"

"I guess I could have asked at lunch." I lifted my eyebrow in a dare.

"There is no 'deal'"—she uncrossed her arms to air quote— "between Bailey and me. We met at a party when I was in college. He showed an interest and I didn't reciprocate. I didn't even know about that pic until after Jack and Clio were back together."

"Seems he's still interested."

She huffed out a sigh that sounded the tiniest bit exasperated. "Today is the first time I've seen him since Jack and Clio's wedding. I only said hello to him at the wedding, not that it's any of your business."

"Oh, it's my business, Annabelle. It's definitely my business."

"Meaning what, exactly?" She glared at me, issuing her own challenge.

"Meaning that in the past, I've been open to sharing a woman with another man, but that doesn't apply to you."

"*Excuse* me?"

"You heard me. I'm not sharing you."

"Listen, Dakota. I know you've been a big rock star for a long time." Her tone was exaggerated patience. "But FYI, I'm not some toy you can decide to share or not."

"Aw, Annabelle, I do like to play with you," I teased as I slipped my arm around her shoulders and urged her toward me, my eyes straying to her mouth.

"Dakota—"

"Annabelle."

She crossed her arms over her pretty rack, and I sighed.

"Babe. We're dating."

My mind had wandered to other things. Like having those plush lips of hers on mine.

I gazed into the beautiful meadow green of her eyes and watched her pupils dilate. Seeing she'd gone with me—and had done it as fast—gave me the green light. Lowering my lips to hers, I brushed a light kiss across her hot mouth, and my heart hammered at the tiny gasp she couldn't contain at my touch. I'm not sure if some afternoon delight was what I'd subconsciously intended when I dragged her away from the studio, but as usual, whenever I was with Annabelle, I wanted her. When I set my lips on hers again, I didn't hold back.

CHAPTER FOURTEEN

Annabelle

DAKOTA LET ME up for air for a second as he shifted in his seat and slid his hand down my right thigh to my knee. Pulling me over the gearshift, he seated me halfway onto his lap. He plunged both of his hands back into my hair, holding me while he plundered my lips.

The way he traced and teased his tongue over my mouth left me sighing with pleasure. The man must have been born a sex savant the way he could read me, the way he remembered everything he did before that got me off. The one long-term boyfriend I'd had sophomore year of college didn't discover all my triggers in an entire year of dating. Dakota found them intuitively and remembered after one glorious night. He revisited them when we reacquainted ourselves in the studio's TV room. Now he was just showing off, finding ways to rev me up that I didn't even know existed.

Like the way he slid his hand down my side, his fingers lightly dancing over my body while he held my head still as he explored my mouth with his talented tongue. Sliding and tangling, nipping and soothing, pulling back and plunging in, Dakota kissed me like it was his job. The combination of light and hard touch drove me wild, and I clung to fistfuls of his T-shirt as I tried to wiggle closer to him.

When the rough calluses of his fingertips played over the smooth skin on my side, I dimly registered he intended to divest me of my camisole. In broad daylight…in a semipublic place in the front seat of his truck. Somewhere in the shadowy recesses of my mind, I thought I should probably protest that idea, but the front of my mind could only concentrate on the dance of our tongues as we stroked and teased and played with each other.

Breaking the kiss, he trailed his mouth along my jaw, licking and nipping and kissing a path to my ear. Knowingly, he traced the sensitive shell with his tongue, gently biting down on the lobe and sending me off on a mini-orgasm. With that one move, he had me scrambling onto his lap.

He dropped his hand away from my half-undressed torso down to his side. I heard a whirring sound, and then we were slowly moving down and back as he lowered the seatback of the front seat to rest flush with the edge of the bench of the back seat. In a matter of seconds, he'd converted the cab of his truck into a bed.

"What—" I began and caught the naughty glint in his beautiful sea blue eyes.

The next thing I knew, I was on my back. He rested on his forearms on either side of my shoulders as he nudged his hips between my legs. "Custom design. Blu helped me install it. Sweet, huh?"

He pushed himself up onto his knees, smiled down into my eyes, and slid his hands beneath my camisole. Involuntarily, I shivered at his touch, and his smile turned wicked as he laughed and slipped my top and bra completely off me in one quick move.

When he leaned back down, I arched up to him, expecting his mouth on mine. Instead, he let go a fiendish chuckle in the back of his throat and bypassed my offering to trail his tongue along my collarbone. How did he know about the sensitivity of my collarbone? Like I said, a sex savant. As he kissed me, he explored the undersides of my arms with his fingertips, urging me to raise my arms above my head. Powerless to do anything other than his bidding, I gave in to his silent demand.

It was no secret to my previous lovers that a man's mouth on my nipples could send me into orbit. But Dakota figured out that the bottom of my rib cage was more sensitive than the undersides of my breasts. As he pulled my nipple into his mouth, kissing, sucking, licking me to distraction, he played his talented calloused fingers along my ribs, ratcheting my pleasure into the stratosphere while molten heat pooled low in my belly. I couldn't control the way I arched and writhed against him as he relentlessly continued his sweet torture, kissing his way from one erect nipple to the other.

Somewhere along the way, he slid his hands down my belly to another sexy place he helped me discover about myself. He had to bare my body to do it justice, so he sat up and lifted one of my legs high enough to reach the zipper of my boot. In two breaths, my boots lay somewhere on the floor of the truck. In another breath, my yoga pants and thong joined them.

Dakota's concentration shifted to the underside of my ass where he feathered his fingertips, making me squirm as he turned his attention to my hamstrings. By the time he reached the backs of my knees, I was panting and wild with need.

When I reached for the button on his fly, he grabbed my hands and placed them back above my head. "Haven't you heard, Annabelle? Good things come to those who wait." The low timbre of his voice gave way to a sexy laugh I felt deep in my core.

"Dakota, please."

"Love that, Annabelle. Begging might help you get what you want."

The naughty smirk on his face had me writhing and squirming again, but he wouldn't give in. Slowly, so single-mindedly slowly, he kissed his way from the back of my knee, down my calf, to the hollow below my anklebone. With an openmouthed kiss on the arch of my foot, he nearly launched me to the moon.

When I cried out, he locked eyes with me. "That's it, Annababy. When I finally give you what you're begging for, I want you to burst into flame."

The sensations his touches sent skittering over my body left me almost incoherent with desire as I shivered beneath him. Still, he showed no mercy, kissing my other leg down to the sole of my foot, and I nearly came from the mere touch of his mouth and hands on my body.

At last, he trailed his fingers lightly up the insides of my thighs, gliding up and down a couple of times for emphasis, and I hoped he would give me some relief.

Not in his game plan, apparently. He skimmed the especially sensitive skin where my thighs met my hips, skipping the tour I desired he take of my pussy. I growled in frustration, and he laughed.

Trying to give him a little taste of his own medicine, I reached for him again, this time going for one of *his* erogenous zones. With my fingertips, I tested the taut skin encasing his sculpted abs. From all his working out, the man had an amazing body, a body I'd loved exploring the night I thought would be our one and only, a body I hadn't had the chance to explore when he took me to the studio. The feel of his skin beneath my hands only fired me up more, and I pushed his T-shirt higher up his chest. Eventually, he stopped teasing me long enough to remove his shirt.

For several long seconds, he stared down at me, naked, my skin flushed, my body open to him. I did the only thing I could—I smiled.

Yeah, he'd managed to strip me bare in the front seat of his truck. Yeah, he'd deliberately driven me crazy. Yeah, this show had belonged completely to him.

Until now.

All the teasing left his eyes as he reached into his back pocket, extracting a condom and replacing his wallet in his jeans. His eyes never leaving mine, he released himself from his clothes, shoving his jeans and boxer briefs down his thighs to his knees. I experienced a new kind of heat as our eyes remained locked while he sheathed himself.

His voice harsh with desire, he commanded, "This is what you wanted, Annabelle. So watch."

Dakota had me so wound up that I would have done anything in that moment to have him inside me. Shifting up onto my elbows, I watched as he touched the head of his cock to my pussy lips and joined us together in one smooth stroke that forced his name from my mouth on a gasp. At last, he was above me and moving inside me, narrowing my whole world to one single moment and the parts of us he'd joined together.

All my senses tuned to Dakota. The scent of his citrusy soap combined with the smell of sex, the salty taste of him when I licked beads of sweat from his chest, the feel of his skin gliding over mine as his pecs rocked over my breasts, the sound of his groans as he stroked us closer and closer to paradise, the way the sunlight contoured his perfect features—the whole scene left me spellbound. Never in my life had I experienced anything as erotic as having afternoon sex with Dakota Perri in the front of his truck.

He shifted, slightly changing the angle of his cock inside me, and I lost myself in the most powerful orgasm I'd ever had. Seconds later, he joined me, our song of ecstasy harmonizing and crescendoing far beyond the confines of the cab of the truck.

When at last we came back to earth, Dakota pushed back up on his arms from the prone position to which he'd collapsed on top of me and grinned down at me. "See Annabelle? We're dating. That's why there will be no sharing." Though his tone was playful, the shadows in his eyes told me he meant something serious.

We'd circled back to the toy thing, and I thought I should be offended. Yet those shadows shut my mouth. What the hell had just happened?

Dakota

The inside of my truck smelled like sunshine and sex hours after I dropped Annabelle back at the studio. Garrett had lined up a local television interview, and Blu and I gave the fans some love. We had no idea why Garrett was so obsessed with marketing this latest tour, but somewhere in our drunken weekend, we decided to surprise the studio audience. We showed up with our acoustic axes and played an impromptu concert. I covered Jack's vocals on a of couple songs, which changed the sound and caused speculation about the band. Jack and Clio honeymooning for a month translated into a band breakup in the short attention spans of the media, I guess.

Garrett ranted at us for about five minutes afterward, but that was only because we didn't consult him ahead of time, let him control it. Sometimes I wondered who employed who. Balefire was our band. Guess we could mess with our sound if we wanted to, treat the fans to something extra if we felt like it.

When I closed the door of my truck and inhaled Annabelle's scent, all my attitude about Garrett evaporated. Her smell went straight to my dick, taking my thoughts back to the most incredible afternoon I'd ever spent with a woman. Yeah, I'd been living the whole sex-booze-and-rock-n-roll dream for the last decade. And I'd loved every minute of it. But this one woman grabbed my attention and refused to let go.

The way Annabelle responded to me, from the first time we met to this afternoon in my truck, nearly sent me to my knees. Her breathy sighs, her tiny whimpers, her full-body shivers whenever I touched her were more addicting than any liquor or drug I'd ever enjoyed. The way she screamed my name when she came made me feel like Superman and Captain America and Thor all at the same time. Sex with Annabelle was the best I'd ever had.

If it was only sex, though, I could stop thinking about her twenty-four seven. But she wandered around in my head all the damn time, smiling that secret smile whenever she teased me, calling me on my bullshit, indulging her little sister even when Emma deliberately jerked her chain, being all wicked smart about the business end of the band, looking at me with soft green eyes when she thought I didn't notice. Annabelle was a package, all right. One I wanted to unwrap and enjoy every day.

As I drove to the bar for my standing night of pool with Vaughn, I considered my next move—making sure Annabelle went on tour with us. Since she was interning in the front office, I knew she'd have responsibilities for marketing that would include handling the phones, organizing merch orders, and preparing and sending out teasers and general advertising on social, visual, and print media. Holding a business degree myself, I also understood that she could learn so much more about managing the band from tagging along on tour. Which would mean she'd be with me for at least the next two months.

Bonus.

Somewhere in the back of my mind, the old me, the guy I was before I reconnected with Annabelle, reminded me that I didn't do relationships, didn't spend more than a week or two with a single woman—if that. Catching another whiff of sex and Annabelle, I drew it deep inside me, the scent and memories filling up the empty spaces I hadn't noticed before she blew back into my life. When I walked into the bar, I didn't even care about how much shit Vaughn gave me for the goofy grin on my face. I had plans for Annabelle and me, and I didn't give a rat's ass how much my change in attitude amused my friends.

CHAPTER FIFTEEN

Annabelle

"I TAKE IT THE honeymoon was fantastic," I said to Clio when she arrived at the studio with her daughter Angel.

"Tropical islands are everything they're cracked up to be and then some," she replied with a dreamy expression on her face.

"Down!" a squirming Angel demanded, and we both laughed as Clio set her daughter on her feet to explore my office on the unsteady legs of a little one learning to walk.

"If not for my darling Angel-baby, we might still be in Fiji. But we both missed her too much, so we came home two weeks early."

"*What?* You've been in town for two weeks and didn't tell anyone?"

"Yeah," Clio said with a secret smile. "Staycations are almost as good as tropical honeymoons."

"Obviously, Jack was right. The two of you were meant to be." I rescued a pen that had fallen to the floor from Angel's grasp and set it on my desk. "Good thing he married you 'cause I was ready to kick his ass if he broke your heart again."

Clio gave me a one-armed hug. "I know, Annabelle. That's why you're one of my best friends. How's the internship going?" She sat on the chair angled beside my desk and handed her toddler a cracker.

"Great, so far. I'm thankful for the opportunity to work here," I said, giving her a look I hope conveyed my gratitude. "Between Caroline and Emory, I'm learning a ton about the behind-the-scenes part of running the band. Garrett's been…" I struggled for the right words.

Clio tilted her head and waited.

"Garrett's been—interesting," I finished lamely.

"Explain."

I hesitated to share my feelings about Balefire's manager, especially in the office. In my short time with the band, it hadn't escaped me that Garrett seemed to know everything. Discovering he had cameras or bugs in our offices, inside and outside the studio, wouldn't have surprised me at all.

"Garrett can be a little intense, you know? Sometimes he crowds my space."

She slanted me a look and I rushed on. "It's nothing I can't handle."

"Now that the band is back to rehearsing, he'll be busy with them, so things should be better. If you're having trouble with him, talk to Jack or maybe Blu. Garrett's never bothered me, probably because I came as a package deal by the time he met me." Clio stopped to gaze fondly at her daughter who was busy trying to climb onto my lap. "But he made a run at Ashleigh last fall, one that created all kinds of problems in the band. He should have learned his lesson."

"I didn't know that. No one talks much about the last tour."

Instead of mollifying me, Clio's explanations reminded me of the chances I took every time I was alone with Dakota.

"Are you here for lunch?"

"Yeah. Jack texted me about an hour ago and said things were going well. That's his hint that I should visit the studio," she said with a laugh. "Besides, I've missed Chef Jeff's cooking."

"His food is to die for. Between eating here and having the occasional meal at Signals, I had to start going to a gym."

"Signals, huh? Who would you know with connections at Diane Connolly's place, I wonder?" Clio asked, speculation in her smile.

I rolled my eyes to cover my slip. "Let's go see what's on the menu today, huh?" Wrapping Angel in my arms, I turned my attention to her. "I bet Chef Jeff has something special for beautiful little girls named Angel. Should we go check it out?"

I didn't make eye contact with Clio as I carried her daughter through the reception area and out to the rehearsal space.

♪

With Jack and Clio officially back in town, the band returned to work rehearsing for their West Coast tour. Garrett kept me hopping in the front office, though I managed to sneak back into the rehearsal space a time or two to listen to Balefire's preparations. The opportunity to hear one of my favorite bands perfect their music thrilled me.

Fine. Listening to and watching Dakota tear up his guitar thrilled me. A guitar in his hands came alive, and each of the axes in his rather large collection had its own personality, something only Dakota, it seemed, could unleash. Today he was playing a gorgeous Gibson Les Paul Standard, the guitar's color exactly matching his eyes. Both the man and his instrument flashed blue fire as he tore up a particularly intricate solo, the speed of his fingers over the frets almost more than my eyes could follow. After a few seconds of tuning my ear to his sound, I recognized the solo as the one he'd been writing during the weeks he'd hung around the studio without the rest of the band.

I'd only been in the room for what seemed like a second when he looked up, those arresting sea blue eyes focused on me as he continued to play. If anything, his music ratcheted up a notch, as though my presence ignited the sound. I might have dismissed my observation as being all in my head if the rest of the guys in the band didn't turn their attention to me when Dakota's sound made its subtle shift in intensity.

Mesmerized by the man and his music, I remained a statue as he soloed, and the whole space narrowed to the two of us. A golden net of notes and need dropped over me. Dakota's sound and the desire radiating from his eyes drew me inexorably to him. I knew he was a player—in every sense of the word—something I'd never questioned or obsessed over. After all, staying with one guy for any length of time had never been part of my repertoire either. But something about the way he played, his attention riveted on me, his sound reverberating through me, hollowed out a space inside me, a place reserved only for him. My heart pounded in my chest in time to his rhythms, and I struggled to catch my breath as he lured me deeper and deeper into his magical musical fantasy. At least that's what I told myself as I drew a deep breath in through my nostrils and tried to calm down.

Angel, bless her, jerked me back to the real world. Having caught sight of her daddy behind his massive drum kit, she let out an ear-splitting squeal and started squirming in my arms. Clio materialized at my side and relieved me of her daughter who continued to make noise as she pointed animatedly at Jack behind his drums. Angel's excitement halted the rehearsal, breaking the spell Dakota wove over me with his guitar and his eyes. Sucking in a deep breath, I squared my shoulders and walked purposefully behind Clio, ignoring Dakota and his ability to take me out of myself.

Like he'd let me get away with that. As I made my way to the back of the rehearsal studio toward the kitchen, he caught me by the elbow and dragged me into the tiny hallway leading to the stairs to the second floor.

"Why did it take you so long to come watch? You made me wait all morning to play that solo."

The low timbre of his voice in my ear, his breath playing over my skin as he pinned me between his hard body and the wall behind me dropped that golden net of desire right back over me. I tried so hard not to react to him as I placed my hands on his hips to put some space between our bodies. But he preempted my plan, using his nose to push my hair away from the spot below my ear where he lipped my skin and sucked on that sensitive place. I couldn't stop the moan escaping my lips at his touch, and I felt more than heard the low laugh rumble through him at my response.

"You can pretend with everyone else that I don't get to you, Annabelle, but we both know I do. You liked that solo, didn't you?"

"I like all of Balefire's music," I hedged.

"It's your story, babe. Tell it any way you want. But I know the truth," he murmured against my mouth and rocked my world with a searing kiss.

His kiss burned so deep and hot that my whole body caught fire. I forgot where we were, who we were, that I had a job and a professional reputation to protect as I tangled my tongue with his. My hands slipped around his narrow waist, and I clung to him as he plundered my mouth. Powerless to resist his panty-melting kiss, I couldn't stop myself from rubbing along his hard body from shoulders to knees. He tasted and teased, pressing his lips to mine before pulling back only enough to brush his mouth gently over my lips, our breaths mingling. He tugged my bottom lip with his teeth, soothing the bite with a lick and sliding his tongue back inside my mouth to tangle with mine again. When at last we came up for air, the only sound I could hear was the roaring of blood in my ears.

"I'm glad you like the solo, Annabelle." He stepped back enough to let me breathe. A curious expression crossed his face and his entire demeanor changed. "Now stop distracting me from my lunch, woman. I need my share of Chef Jeff's food to keep me going this afternoon."

Grabbing my hand, he led me into the kitchen where we found

the rest of the band tucked into their lunch. Blu watched us with an open grin while Tron's expression was more inscrutable as we walked into the room. Clio and Jack were oblivious as they tag-teamed Angel at the small corner table where they'd secluded themselves away from the rest of the guys. Mercifully, no one from the front office, notably Garrett, was anywhere to be seen.

"Now we know why you didn't find a beach during our hiatus, Dakota," Blu said with a grin as he leaned back in his chair and eyed the two of us.

"I know, right? That solo I wrote is bitchin'. I raised the hell out of the bar for your lyrics. Unless you're going to wuss out and leave 'em up to Jackie-boy," Dakota replied as he tugged me down to sit beside him at the table Blu and Tron occupied.

"That's it. You were all about writing music for the last month," Blu deadpanned and turned his attention to me. "I take it you like working this gig, Annabelle?"

Struggling to find my composure after Dakota's mesmerizing kisses, I cleared my throat. "It's been fun working here."

Blu barked out a laugh. "We can see that."

Even the usually taciturn Adam Tron sported a smirk at my comment.

Desperately trying to cover the inadvertent innuendo I'd made, I hurried on. "The whole staff has been supportive and helpful. I'm learning all kinds of things about the behind the scenes aspect of marketing and touring Balefire."

"Emphasis on behind the scenes from the looks of it," Blu added.

I dropped my eyes to check out my shirt and discovered to my horrifying embarrassment that all that rubbing against Dakota's body left me rather conspicuously wrinkled. Adding to my growing mortification, my face heated up as Dakota leaned casually back in his chair and said, "Behind the scenes is always where the best action happens. Everyone knows that, Blu."

He might have directed his comment to his best friend, but his fingers playing out a rhythm along the top of my shoulder and up the sides of my neck left no doubt he spoke to me.

Bless Tron. "So you'll be going out on tour with us, Annabelle?"

"I'm not sure if my job includes traveling with the band."

"Of course Annie's going out on tour with us. How else is she going to have the full Balefire experience?" Exasperation saturated Dakota's tone.

His response in front of his bandmates would have been enough by itself to worry me about my professional reputation. But Garrett chose that moment to walk into the kitchen, his dark stare dropping a lead weight of apprehension into the pit of my stomach. I had no idea how much of our conversation he'd heard, but from the look on his face, he'd heard enough to send my nerves into flight.

Dakota's palm on my shoulder, anchoring me to my seat was my first indication I'd tried to act on my response. Speaking low in my ear, he asked, "Where do you think you need to go? You haven't eaten yet."

I swear I felt him ghost a kiss over the shell of my ear, and I wanted to scream at every male in the room, most especially at Dakota Perri.

"There you are, Annabelle." Garrett's tone was ominous. "I need to see you in my office after lunch. Blu, Tron, Dakota…" Looking around, he spotted Jack and added, "Jack," who, at the sound of his name looked away from his daughter. "We have a dinner meeting with one of the promoters."

If I'd been any busier trying to slide down in my seat, I might have missed the thunder that clouded Dakota's face at the mention of the meeting. "Correction, Garrett." His tone was icy. "*You* have a meeting with the promoter. That's your *job*. We may or may not be finished rehearsing for the day, and if we're not done, we're not interrupting the flow to stroke some wannabe's ego."

"This guy's scheduled three sold-out shows at the LA Coliseum to open this tour. The least you can do is share a meal with him," Garrett insisted.

"At our expense," Blu added dryly. "In case you forgot, Garrett my man, without Balefire's awesome talents, there would be no show to schedule. You enjoy your dinner." He turned away from Garrett and winked at Dakota and Tron.

Garrett played his trump card, deflating the guys in a stunning manner. "I made reservations at Signals. So I imagine we *are* going to enjoy our dinner."

"Jesus, Garrett. That's low, even for you." Blu narrowed his eyes at him.

Garrett smiled like the shark I'd discovered him to be. "Annabelle, you'll want to attend this meeting. Meeting with promoters is an important aspect of the music business, as I'm sure you'll see."

Beside me, Dakota growled deep in his throat, his arm sliding around me to pull me into his side. "Fine, Garrett. We'll be there." With a nod to Blu, he added, "Make sure your reservations include Clio and Ashleigh."

Out of the corner of my eye, I saw Jack tip up his chin then Garrett snagged my attention again. A shadow rippled over his face, but he smoothed his features. "I made the reservation for nine, so you'll have plenty of rehearsal time."

He walked over to the bar separating the kitchen from the dining area, slid onto a barstool, and said in a hearty tone that sounded fake to me, "Hey, Jeff, what deliciousness have you concocted for lunch today?" The way he studiously avoided looking at Dakota or me after Dakota's pronouncement doubled the size of that lead weight in my belly as I tried to understand the undercurrents of hostility suddenly swirling around the room.

Chapter Sixteen

Annabelle

"YOU ARE AWARE of Dakota's reputation on tour."

Garrett's comment alerted me to the real reason for our meeting since I could have emailed the updates in a succinct bulleted list. Yet every reply I could make to his innuendo constituted a trap, so I kept my mouth shut.

"You've done exceptional work for us. I can envision you as a permanent part of the team—however—" This time he tried to wait me out, so I scooted to the edge of my chair and adopted my most guileless expression. I might have even batted my eyes for good measure while I worked to keep my lunch from climbing up my throat.

"My point is you can't allow your emotions to interfere with your work. Not when your goal is the Wharton School of Business." With a quirk of his brow, his meaning became staggeringly clear. "As I understand it, you've already had your groupie experience with Dakota, so now you need to concentrate on the job, build up your contacts, grow your *professional reputation*."

The emphasis Garrett put on those last two words made my blood run cold. Still, I clamped my jaws even tighter and blinked at him. At lunch he'd mentioned his expectation that I attend the dinner he'd lined up with the promoter, so for the short term at least, I still had my job.

Then he dropped his bomb. "I think it's in your best interests to stay here at the studio while the band is on tour."

I gasped in surprise, but he feigned obliviousness and continued. "You'll be a distraction to the band if you accompany us. Besides, you have some excellent ideas you and Caroline can execute best if you're here working on them together. Agreed?"

The question was rhetorical.

Placing his hands flat on his desk, he stood up and smiled down at me in that oily way of his. My skin crawled as he added, "That's it for now, Miss Stewart. I'll expect to see you at Signals a little before nine tonight so I can brief you on protocol. Wear something hot."

Before I could reply to his outrageous suggestion, he strolled out of his office in the direction of the rehearsal studio while I gaped at his back.

Slumping back in my chair, I blew out the breath I'd been holding and closed my eyes against the ugly image of Garrett Phillips with his smarmy innuendos about Dakota and me and his disgusting, deliberately obtuse demand that I throw myself at the promoter. I shouldn't be with a member of the band, but I should sleep with a promoter? His veiled threats about my career goals were another matter. More than anything, I wanted to scream my frustration, but with the outer office full of Balefire employees, that indulgence was out of the question. *How dare he?* Oh yeah, he held the key to my future, and I harbored no illusions about how he'd use it to get what he wanted.

♪

When I walked into Signals at eight forty-five on the dot, Garrett was waiting for me in the foyer. The venue precluded him from exploding, something the dull red color riding his cheeks alerted me he wanted to do—badly. "I thought I told you to wear something hot," he hissed.

Widening my eyes at him, I asked, "A tight skirt and a silk shirt aren't hot?"

I knew I played with fire when I slipped on the knee-length black pencil skirt and demurely cut emerald green silk blouse, but no way did I intend to throw myself at the promoter. As Blu had pointed out so well at lunch, without the band, the promoter had nothing. Balefire didn't need a managerial assistant to come on to the promoter to secure his services.

"You have so much to learn, Miss Stewart. So much to learn."

The painful way he gripped my arm above my elbow left me no choice, short of making a scene, but to accompany him into the restaurant. He marched me to the back room where Diane had laid an elegant table for nine. Garrett deposited me rather than seated me in the seat to the right of the head of the table. "Stay right there," he ordered then he turned and left the room.

As I sat by myself, my back to the door, I pondered my choices. Why did I feel almost like I had to goad Garrett? As he'd made so clear in our meeting this afternoon, I owed my future to his good opinion of my work. Doing as he asked seemed prudent. Yet the way he looked at me sometimes, like he wanted to strip me bare and run his greasy hands all over me, invade me, made my skin crawl. Insinuating that I needed to prostitute myself to the promoter for the good of the band went way beyond the pale, even for him. No business school would find that action an attractive line item on my résumé.

A few minutes later, he returned, his hearty fake laugh preceding him into the room. I turned to see him escort a tall, lanky man whose designer suit hung on him like a scarecrow, his receding hairline lending prominence to his sharp cheekbones and lack of chin. The guy reminded me of the creepy butler on some old sixties sitcom that used to play on cable when I was a kid.

Still, he was the promoter, so I needed to be professional. Standing, I extended my hand to him when Garrett said, "This is Annabelle, the intern I told you about. Annabelle, this is Barton Barton, the promoter for Balefire's West Coast tour."

"A pleasure, Annabelle. You may call me Barton—or Bart," he said as he took my hand in a limp-wristed handshake. The gesture gave me an idea of what it would be like to hold a dead fish. The high pitch of his voice, so at odds with his height, jarred me. He stood considerably taller even than Tron, who at somewhere around six three was the tallest member of the band.

As though my thoughts materialized him, Tron strolled through the door. "Garrett. Annabelle."

Barton had been using his impressive height advantage to try to steal a peek down my blouse, which thankfully I'd had the good sense to button up one extra than usual. I'd added a delicate gold chain as further incentive to draw attention to my neck rather than to my rack, but apparently, I overestimated the man's manners. It took Tron's entrance to draw Barton's attention away from my chest.

"This is Barton Barton, the promoter for this tour," Garrett said, introducing the two men.

With a smirk, Tron extended a hand. "Bart."

In the short time I'd known him, I'd noticed that while Tron could be open and animated and funny when he was with the band, with outsiders, including me, he hoarded his words like he thought he should save them in case of emergency. Either the promoter didn't notice Tron's reticence or didn't care because he launched into rapturous gushing about Tron's virtuoso bass playing that left me grinning at Tron from behind the man's back. Tron listened stoically though his eyes danced with mischief while I tried to hold it together.

Interrupting my mirth, Blu and Ashleigh and Jack and Clio showed up simultaneously, and Garrett made introductions. I thought Barton might sprain his brain as he tried to give effusive praise to each of the band members all at once. Garrett slowed down Barton's obviously rehearsed litany of Balefire compliments to seat us. Before I realized what he'd planned, I found myself sitting to the right of Garrett at the head of the table with Barton beside me, Tron, Blu, and Ashleigh across from me, and Jack and Clio to the right of Barton. That left one seat for Dakota at the far end of the table. The man himself walked into the room right as we all sat down and a waiter appeared behind him to take our drink order.

Dakota scowled at his seat and a sound from Garrett drew my attention to the smug look on his face a second before he literally wiped it off with his hand. When Dakota looked up the table at Garrett, Garrett stared neutrally back at him. Glancing back at Dakota, I saw his narrow-eyed glare at Garrett, and my stomach flipped as I braced for the coming explosion. Instead, Dakota sat in his designated chair and ordered a beer from the hovering waiter.

Barton spent dinner describing—or maybe bragging—about all the work he and his company had done to promote Balefire's upcoming tour. When he wasn't ramming my arm with his elbow as he sawed up the succulent steak Diane had cooked for him, he was sliding his hand under the table to cop a feel. I managed to choke down a small amount of Diane's delicious shrimp creole using my left-hand while I used my right to block Bart's advances.

During the meal, Dakota remained unusually silent, but I noticed he put away at least five beers before dessert. Since Barton kept me busy trying to block his advances without being rude, I didn't have many opportunities to gauge Dakota's expressions. Though whenever I glanced at him, I caught him staring down Barton, or more specifically Barton's left hand, with something lethal in his eyes.

Oblivious to the drama going on between Dakota, Garrett, and me, Barton turned to me. "So, Annabelle, will you be touring with the band?"

"Uh, I'm not sure at this point," I said.

Garrett inserted himself into our conversation. "Annabelle is learning the marketing and management aspects of a successful band. She'll be working from the studio during the tour."

"Seems a waste of good talent," Barton commented to Garrett over the top of my head. He returned his attention to me. "You could work on promotions from my office in LA. We're always on the lookout for talented interns."

Beneath the table, he went for my thigh again, but I preempted him with an emphatic push of his hand into his own lap. A snort coming from across the table snapped my eyes to Tron who looked at the ceiling in an effort not to burst out laughing. Blu wasn't as circumspect, turning to laugh into Ashleigh's neck. The expression on Ashleigh's face told me she didn't share the guys' entertainment at my expense.

Whatever Garrett's game was, I'd had enough. "Thank you for your offer, Barton, but I'll have to pass." I gritted my teeth behind my smile. Turning to Garrett, I said, "I'll have to pass on dessert too. I just remembered I need to finish some mock-ups of an ad I promised to have on Caroline's desk first thing in the morning."

Abruptly, I slid my chair away from the table and stood, leaving Barton's hand in midair as he reached for me for at least the twentieth time. Reversing course, he grabbed my hand. "Don't go yet, Annabelle. We were just getting to know each other. Garrett suggested you'd be up for a drink with me after dinner."

If anything, the man's high-pitched voice climbed even higher as he squeezed my hand with much more strength than his earlier handshake indicated he possessed. Glaring at Garrett, I said, "Garrett doesn't speak for my downtime." When tugging my hand steadily didn't work, I jerked back and ground out through my teeth, "Let go of me."

Suddenly, I came free as Dakota growled from beside me, "Take your hands off Annabelle."

Apparently, Barton was a little slow. "But Garrett said his intern was my date tonight," he whined.

At Barton's words, Jack and Blu stood too. "Thought we went over this, Garrett," Blu began.

"It's not the same. We're talking about Annabelle here. She's an intern, not a girlfriend—or a wife," Garrett replied, the last two words sounding like they stuck in his throat.

"She's with me, Garrett. You knew that," Dakota said through clenched teeth.

The atmosphere in the room crackled with unspoken history and too much testosterone. Fearing for Diane's beautiful private dining room, I put my hand on Dakota's arm. "I'm going to go, okay? No harm done."

Dakota continued to stare down Garrett like he hadn't heard me, hadn't felt my touch. Beneath my fingertips, the muscles in his arm tensed to strike. Before I could say another word, Diane breezed into the room. "I have a special dessert specifically for you. We'll clear and—" She froze as she took in the tableau in front of her.

Everything happened at once. Jack grabbed Dakota while Tron stood between Blu and Garrett. Ashleigh grabbed Blu to prevent him from taking on Tron, and Clio cried out Jack's name. I pushed against Dakota, trying to move him away from both Barton and Garrett, but it was like trying to move a solid brick wall. In the middle of it all, I heard Diane cry out, "LeShaun!"

Almost instantaneously, the former pro football player appeared in the doorway. In a booming voice I had no idea he possessed, he called, "Not in Diane's place. Not even if you are her boys. Especially since you're her boys. Sit your asses *down*." He stared down the room. "Now."

As quickly as the testosterone in the room intensified, it dissipated in the face of LeShaun's command. Within a couple of seconds, I was the only member of the dinner party still standing. Clearing my throat with as much dignity as I could muster, I said, "Excuse me. I was leaving."

I slung my purse over my shoulder, pushed my chair under the table, and walked toward the door.

"But you haven't had dessert," Diane lamented and looked at my plate. "You haven't even had dinner. Was there something wrong with your meal?"

"No, it was fabulous as always, Diane. I wasn't all that hungry."

"You wait right here while I have it boxed up. You can reheat it and enjoy it when you are hungry."

I kept moving toward the door. When I reached her, I whispered, "Could you bring it to the maître 'd's stand, please? I'd rather not wait here."

Diane slanted me a look and nodded. Keeping my eyes trained forward, I walked out the door. I understood that I probably lost any opportunity I might have had to go out on tour with the band, which looked like it might be for the best. But all I could think about was escaping two smarmy men who could only see me with their eyes and one beautiful man who had no business even considering risking his million-dollar hands on either of them days before his tour.

CHAPTER SEVENTEEN

Dakota

AS FLASHY AS I enjoy being, I've learned over the years that sometimes it's good to be somewhat discreet. Like when you visit the girl you can't get out of your head, and she lives above her parents' garage. I left my beautiful neon green brute of a truck parked in my driveway and drove the Lexus over to Annabelle's in the wee hours of the morning of the day we were headed out on tour.

Waiting on the landing for her to open the door, I surprised myself by experiencing a weak sauce version of stage fright. Rolling my head and shoulders, I literally shrugged it off and rested my hand on the doorjamb. Which is how Annabelle found me when she opened her door.

"Dakota! What are you doing here?"

"I think the polite greeting is 'Hi Dakota. Would you like to come in?'"

In the glow of the lamplight, I noticed a faint pink stain her cheeks. I grinned.

"Please, come in."

She stepped back, pulling the door with her, and silently invited me into her place.

Though I was on a mission, I took the time to give her a once-over, noting the sexy robe that barely covered her. Cotton-candy pink, and she looked delicious in it. My mouth watered, and I nearly forgot my mission.

Annabelle reminded me.

"Dakota, why are you here?"

"I heard you're not coming with us on tour. I want to know why."

Those gorgeous green eyes I saw even in my dreams widened before she closed herself off from me. Literally. Crossing her arms over her gorgeous rack, she replied, "I'm not needed on tour. My tagging along is an extraneous expense, and since I'm trying to learn how to streamline your operation, it's counterproductive to add to the tour's price tag."

"Isn't one of the perks of working for the band getting to watch us play?" I tempted her.

"Well, sure. And I love your shows. The one you played in town two years ago was over the top, and I've seen your specials on Netflix too," she gushed then caught herself. "But I'm only interning with you guys, well, with Garrett. So, like I said, I'd be an extra expense."

What a load of bullshit. Arching a skeptical brow, I stared her down. "I want you to come out on tour with us, Annabelle."

"Dakota. I'd only be in the way."

I raised both brows, and she rushed on. "You guys are all about the music and the party. I know I've probably given you a different impression, but the truth is, I'm not that wild."

"Really," I said dryly.

She puffed out a nervous little laugh. "I mean it. In college, I played a part, which girls like Clio believed. Even that first night with you, I was playing a part. Never before or since have I initiated sex like I did with you. The whole strip show and climbing all over you was a first for me."

"I know."

She blinked. "You do?"

If the situation weren't so serious, I would have burst out laughing at the incredulous look on her face and the rose blush that lit up her cheeks. But the situation *was* serious. I hadn't engineered her entire internship only for her to bail on me when I had the chance to have her with me for a couple of uninterrupted months.

"I gotta tell ya, babe, that show you put on for me after Red Rocks was so fucking hot. I think about it all the time. That night in the studio and that incredible afternoon in the front seat of my truck play regularly through my head too."

She opened her mouth to say something, probably something contradictory, so I cut her off. With the pad of my finger, I traced the petal-soft contours of her cheek, cupped her face in my hand, and smoothed my thumb over the plump softness of her lips. Whatever she wanted to say disappeared in the tiny gasp that escaped her at my touch.

"Matter of fact, I think about you all the time," I continued. My voice sounded rough to my own ears as my concentration centered on the way her breath hitched at my touch. "I want you to finish your internship with all the perks. I want you on tour with me." I leaned in, brushing my mouth against hers and whispered, "I want you."

Then I smashed my mouth down on hers, nothing subtle in my technique at all. Annabelle stiffened against me for a second, but I didn't stop. It had been almost two weeks since I'd last been with her, and the sensual line of her lips beneath mine sent a lightning bolt through me straight to my dick. I pulled her into me, let her know what she did to me. With relief, I sensed her relax. A second later when she joined me in the kiss, she drove me absolutely wild with the quiet hum of excitement she couldn't contain in the back of her throat, her hands sliding up my arms until she wrapped her arms around my neck. Her braless breasts felt like heaven pillowing the hard wall of my chest as I slid my hand from her face to her back to pull her even closer.

All the reasons for why I was there with her came down to my mouth on hers, my body flush with hers, her whimpered responses to my touch. I backed her up to the edge of her couch, breaking the kiss only enough to spin her around and pull her with me as I sat, Annabelle straddling my lap. Giving her a stern look, I demanded, "What are you hiding beneath this sexy little robe, my pretend party girl?"

I anchored her to me with one hand on her hip while I explored the deep vee of her robe with the index finger on my free hand. She sucked in a breath, and I watched in fascination as her nipples pebbled beneath the satiny fabric. "S' matter? Cat got your tongue?"

"A rather naughty rock star had it a minute ago, but I've got it back," she sassed.

"So—my question?"

"Guess you're going to have to find out for yourself."

Oh yeah, I absolutely would take that dare. I slid my finger down to the knot at her waist and gave the sash a tug. It came apart with little persuasion, revealing an even sexier hot pink lace nightie, and—oh, hell yes!—no panties. My lady apparently slept nearly naked. Good to know. I looked into the endless green of her eyes and said, "Very good, Miss Stewart. You're appropriately dressed for the occasion."

"What occasion is that, Mr. Perri?" she mimicked.

"The occasion of me giving you another reason to go out on the road with us."

I emphasized my point with a fingertip tour of her pussy and tried not to surge up into her through my jeans when I discovered exactly how slick and ready she was for me. Revving both of us up even more, I put my fingers to my nose and inhaled her sweet scent then slid my tongue along my fingertips to taste her. Annabelle's eyes darkened as she watched me, and a tiny moan escaped her as she rocked her hips into me.

Her sounds drove me crazy. It took me about two seconds to lift us both up so I could retrieve a condom from my wallet. She was about as quick as she slipped her hands between us to open my fly and free my cock. A wicked grin stole over her beautiful face as first she palmed then stroked my length, driving me right out of my head with her perfect touch. I'd been stroked many times in the past. But damn, what was it about this particular woman's touch that took me places I'd never been before?

Annabelle left me little coherent thought when she touched herself and then spread her sweet slickness over my naked cock.

"Annababy," I groaned. "Hold on a sec. I gotta protect us first."

I tore open the condom with my teeth, but Annabelle snatched it from me and did the honors herself. Her eagerness matched my own. I sucked in air and fought for control as I grew harder beneath her busy hands. She gave my shaft a squeeze and feathered her fingertips over my balls, and I thought I might lose it before I had the chance to be inside her.

Grabbing her wrists, I put a stop to her games and pulled her hands up to my shoulders, "You're gonna wanna hang on for this, Annababy."

Gripping my shoulders, she lifted up, and I centered myself at her entrance. But even previous experience couldn't prepare me for the aggressively hot way she sheathed me fully inside her on one beautiful down stroke.

"Fuck, Annabelle!" I shouted as I clamped my hands on her hips.

With a naughty grin, she wiggled her body, seating me even deeper inside her as she tightened her inner muscles around me.

"Yes, Dakota. Fuck Annabelle," she commanded in a sugar-sweet voice that had me grinding my hips against her as I tried to push even deeper inside her.

I'd come to her place to convince her to go out on tour with me, and yes, I'd come prepared to use sex to get my way. Yet somehow, Annabelle had flipped the game on me. And she felt so good I didn't give a rat's ass.

Lifting her nearly off me only to slam her back down, I took over the show again, setting a rhythm that left both of us panting. Beneath my calloused fingers, the satin smoothness of her bathrobe contrasted with the patterned texture of her lacy nightie, giving me ideas. While I continued to guide her hips with one hand, I slid the other up to cup her breast, holding her to my mouth where I tongued a hard nipple through the layers of her pajamas. She cried out and arched into me, silently begging for more of this particular attention. Being in no position to deny her anything she asked in any way she asked for it, I sucked her nipple into my mouth, reveling in her response as I pistoned my hips and drove into her over and over and over.

"Dakota!" she moaned and clamped her legs to mine, her pussy pulsing wildly around my cock as she came.

Her response made me feel like Superman—again. My own release gathered at the base of my spine, and I pumped into her hard once, twice, and I was flying with her.

Afterward, it took a few minutes for our breathing to even out, time spent with Annabelle collapsed against my chest as I smoothed my hands over the lovely curves of her spine and ass.

"Are you convinced?"

"About what?"

"About touring with me?"

She tensed, and I could feel her closing herself off from me again even though my cock was still enjoying aftershocks inside her body.

"Annabelle, we're loaded. We can easily afford your expenses. We won't even notice them, probably. Not with the whole tour sold out already."

"I don't know, Dakota. Will the other guys look at it that way?"

"They better since Blu is bringing Ashleigh and Jack is bringing Clio and Angel along with us."

"What about Garrett?" she asked, and I swear her voice shrank as she said his name.

"What about him?"

"Well, he's my direct boss," she began, "and-he-thinks-I-should-stay-in-the-front-office-and-work-on-marketing-with-Caroline," she finished in a rush.

What the fuck is the deal with Garrett?

My thoughts must have projected across my face because she hurried on. "I do work well with Caroline, and we have some kick-ass ideas for marketing the tour," she trailed off. Her arguments probably sounded as lame in her ears as they did in mine.

"What about sold out did you not hear, Annie-girl? Between Balefire's awesome sound and the excellent marketing work you two have already done, we don't have any open seats left at the venues we're scheduled to play. Tell me again why you think you're not going with us?"

Blinking at me, she bit her kiss-swollen lip. "I'm not sure about the whole rock 'n' roll party that's part of going on tour. Contrary to what happened here a few minutes ago, I'm not a huge party girl. Somehow, you bring out the naughty in me."

"Exactly. Now get your pretty ass off my lap and go pack, woman. Our plane leaves in a little less than two hours, which means we need to be at the airport in less than an hour."

"Why are you leaving so early? Don't you fly your own plane?"

I rolled my eyes. "We do fly our own plane, but since Jack is now a dad whose kid gets him up the butt crack of dawn most days, he thinks the rest of us need to see the sunrise too. He only gets his way when we fly though, 'cause none of us wants Angel to be cranky on the plane. You need to move it, babe."

Annabelle slid off my lap. Before I could dispose of the condom, my phone chimed an incoming text. I put myself together and checked my message as I followed her down the short hallway to her bedroom.

Get your sorry ass up, Perri. It's time to go wow the fans.

I smiled at Jack's text. Guess he thought turnabout was fair play, but his candy-ass version of a wake-up call couldn't compare to the fun I'd had with him before he hooked back up with Clio.

I laughed as I texted him back: *I got up. Then I got it up. Race you to the airport.*

Jack responded right as I entered Annabelle's bedroom: *Unless you were getting it up in your car, you're in second place, Diva-boy.*

Shit!

Since I'd had to stop teasing him with wake-up calls, I'd resorted to competitions with the winner exacting some sort of amusing—read that embarrassing—shit for the loser to do. Fuck all if I was going to arrive at the airport after Jack and Clio, 'cause no doubt he'd have me doing something I'd rather not do in front of Annabelle.

"We're on a schedule, woman. Let's go," I demanded.

"But I need to shower and pack. When do we have to be there?"

"You have ten minutes. Twelve tops."

"You're out of your mind, Dakota Perri. I can't pack for two months and shower in ten minutes."

I gave her a look. "*Ten* minutes, Annabelle."

She squeaked and raced into her bathroom. Five minutes later—yes, I timed her—she emerged looking damn fine with her hair up in a messy bun, her face made up enough to play up her eyes and those lips I loved so much. She smelled amazing, something musky and spicy and citrusy. Hustling over to her closet, she pulled out a monster suitcase and tossed it on her unmade bed. I leaned against the door to her bedroom and watched in fascination as she threw in the toiletries bag she'd brought with her from the bathroom followed by several pairs of jeans she grabbed from a drawer in her dresser. Racing back to the closet, she didn't bother to pull clothes off their hangers. She tossed a haphazardly folded armload of what looked like T-shirts, blouses, skirts, and dresses into the case.

Her packing speed stunned me as she grabbed a duffel bag she filled with shoes and boots and tossed it on the bed beside her suitcase. Only then did she acknowledge me. "Do you mind? I need to get dressed."

I cocked a brow. "It's not like I haven't seen you naked."

Planting her hands on her hips, she huffed, "It's not the same."

"Uh-huh." I smirked, but I turned around so the woman could dress. After all, we were on the clock. "Don't forget to pack the outfit you're changing out of."

She squeaked out an "Oh!" which had me chuckling, but I heard the sound of soft fabric landing on the pile of clothes in the suitcase, so I'm pretty sure she gave me what I wanted—again.

A minute or two later, I turned around. Yeah, yeah, I wasn't playing by the rules. Like I ever did anyway. But she surprised me by being dressed in a sweet little blue minidress and some damn sexy high-heeled sandals that made her legs go on for days. My dick perked right up when she bent over her suitcase to try to force the lid down enough to zip it closed.

"Need some help?" I drawled, because I definitely was enjoying the view.

She blew a stray strand of hair from her face. "That would be good since you're the one who said I needed to be ready in ten minutes."

"Twelve tops," I reminded her with a grin as I pushed the top of the case down and slid the zipper closed around it.

"How did I do?"

"Twelve minutes on the dot. Nice work, Annababy."

Because I couldn't resist, I gave her a quick, hard kiss and grabbed her beast of a suitcase off the bed. "I've got this. That all you need?" I asked.

She nodded, and I headed out of her room and down the hall carrying her suitcase and her duffel.

Annabelle was right behind me until I reached the door. When I looked back, I found her stuffing her laptop into a messenger bag. She gifted me an apologetic smile, slung the strap of her bag over her shoulder and snagged her purse from a side table as she caught up to me.

"You ready now?" I asked more to tease her than because I was annoyed. Honestly, I didn't think there was a woman alive who could pack as fast as she had.

"I'll need to let my parents know I'll be gone for a while. It'll take me only a minute," she said as she preceded me out the door of her apartment.

"One minute, Annabelle," I called as she hustled down the stairs. For a woman in heels, she moved with a lightness that left me half hard again. I grinned at her back as I lugged her massive suitcase over to the trunk of my car and hefted it in.

She disappeared through a side door into her parents' house that even at this early hour was lit up like Christmas. By the time I stowed her things in my trunk and shut the lid, she reappeared with her whole family in tow.

"Mrs. Stewart. Mr. Stewart," I greeted them and turned to her sister. "Hey, Pita."

"Emma," she corrected me.

Grinning, I said, "Sorry. Last time I saw you, you were kind of a pain in the—"

As my meaning dawned on her, she gave me a solid punch to the biceps that smarted. With a laugh, I rubbed my arm. "You've proven my point."

"Emma! Jesus." Annabelle sighed.

Alan interrupted his daughters by extending his hand. His grip left me no doubt what he meant when he said, "Take care of my daughter, Dakota."

"Absolutely, sir," I replied, but I don't think his idea of what that meant exactly meshed with mine. In fact, it was a little awkward shaking hands with Annabelle's dad after what I'd done with her in her living room less than half an hour earlier.

"Stay in touch, please, Annabelle," Ellie added as she pulled Annabelle into a hug.

"Bring me home something cool," Emma said. "That means my idea of cool, Annabrat." She smirked.

"There's a reason Dakota calls you Pita, Pita," Annabelle said with a smile then she hugged her sister. "Apparently, we're on some kind of schedule." She gifted me with a side-eye. "I'll keep you posted on our travels. Love you guys."

CHAPTER EIGHTEEN

Annabelle

TOURING WITH BALEFIRE blew my mind.

I tried to follow Clio's lead and act like I'd been there before. But since I'd never even flown first class, the private jet overwhelmed me with its plush captain's chairs, comfy couches, the full bar tucked into a back corner, and a full bathroom with a shower. The king-size bed in the bedroom at the back of the plane tempted me. I couldn't help but think about what it would be like to join the mile-high club with Dakota.

With the standard excuse, "It's five o'clock somewhere," the man in question retrieved a beer from the bar, cracked it open, and took a long pull. "Here's to Annabelle for not making me come in second to Jack."

Jack rolled his eyes at Dakota and directed his attention to his daughter who studied him with great intensity from her perch on his lap. "Timing, Angel. Timing," he said to her in a solemn tone. "As a drummer's daughter, you need to get your timing down."

Angel babbled a response to him and Clio laughed delightedly. "Oh, Jack. You tied this time. That's not so bad, is it?"

"It's not as good as after the show watching Dakota serve all of us beers while wearing nothing but an apron," Jack grumbled.

At Jack's description, Dakota nearly spit out the swig of beer he'd taken. I had to hide a grin both at his response and at the image Jack had put in my mind. If I'd known Jack's penalty for Dakota being late to the plane, I might not have packed so fast.

"You thought you'd have me walking around bare-assed at the first after-party? Jesus! Well, that ups the ante for you next time," Dakota replied as he threw himself into the captain's chair beside mine.

Right as Jack asked what Dakota had in mind, Garrett entered the cabin. He took one look at me, and the smile on his face pinched into a grimace. "Aren't you supposed to be at the office, Annabelle?" The frost in his tone sent shivers over my skin.

"What the hell, Garrett?" Dakota said.

Ignoring him, Garrett narrowed his eyes at me. "I gave Caroline and you a specific marketing plan yesterday. How are you going to work with her from the tour?"

"Garrett, I, um—"

"Annabelle should have the whole experience, don't you think, Garrett? How else is she going to learn how to manage a band?" The patience in Dakota's tone in no way matched the thunder in his eyes.

Something happened between them, judging from the looks they exchanged. I watched in terrified fascination and knew I'd made a mistake in letting Dakota talk me into doing exactly what I wanted to do—go out on tour with the band.

With everyone's eyes on the drama playing out between Dakota, Garrett, and me, I knew what I had to do. "If you could have someone send back my luggage, that would be great since unloading it now will put your flight behind schedule," I said with as much dignity as possible as I stood to exit the plane. If I could hold it together until I stepped back onto the tarmac at least, then maybe I could manage the way things were going at the moment with my internship.

A hand clamped down on my wrist, halting my progress. When I looked at my arm, I found Dakota holding me, but he stared at Garrett. "I don't know what your problem is, Garrett, but Annabelle is going out on tour with us."

"Really?" Garrett drawled, his hands on his hips, challenging Dakota.

"In case you forgot, Blu oversees our books, and I oversee the business. You book us, but you don't boss us." Dakota spoke low and deadly, his grip on my wrist tightening a fraction. "Sit down and strap yourself in, Annabelle. Enjoy the ride."

In the short time I'd known him, Dakota's playful demeanor held center stage. This intensity was something new, something unexpected. As was my reaction to it. Dakota standing up to Garrett for me warmed me to my toes. That is until I caught the anger flashing across Garrett's face. I'd made an enemy, one who could make my life hard, possibly ruin my career before it even started.

Tron, blessedly, drew Garrett's attention away from Dakota and me. "Garrett, my man, join me for a beer, wouldja? With the rest of these suckers all mothered up, I need someone normal to drink with. We're starting a sold-out tour. Let the party begin."

Garrett shot daggers at me then with a shrug, he walked over to join Tron at the bar.

Dakota leaned back in his seat. "Relax, Annababy. Everything's cool." He closed his eyes and held out his hand. After a second's hesitation, I took it. Garrett's reaction and Tron's suggestion about Dakota and me somehow being the same as Blu and Ashleigh, snuggled together on one of the couches, and Jack and Clio, entertaining their daughter on another couch, tumbled around in my head. Other thoughts joined the mix, mainly thoughts about what I was doing with Dakota and how I was going to handle Garrett. Luckily, the flight itself was smooth, but then again, I doubt anything Mother Nature could have thrown at the plane could compete with the turbulence in my head. Two and a half hours later when

I stepped off the jet in LA, a headache that dwarfed Jack's massive drum kit pounded behind my eyes, and a snaky sense of foreboding constricted my chest.

♪

Clio told me once that when Balefire traveled, they booked an entire floor of the hotel for the band and the floor below for the road crew, creating a buffer of sorts between the fans and the band. With Balefire taking up the whole floor, I assumed I'd have my own room. Yet when we checked in, Dakota took a key card from the sleeve the hotel clerk gave him and handed the other card to me.

"What's the room number, Annie?" he asked as we boarded the elevator with the rest of the band for our ride to the top floor.

"Um, thirty-two ten." I lowered my voice for his ears only. "Are we sharing a room?"

Dakota didn't do discreet. "Of course we are. What did you think this morning was all about, Annababy? I wanted you to go out on tour. With me."

I stared up at the mirrored ceiling of the elevator car and willed my face not to burst into flames. Throughout college, I'd actively cultivated a reputation as a wild child. However, it wasn't something I wanted to follow me into my professional career. Luckily for me, only the band shared the elevator with us.

"Don't worry about it, Annabelle. That's the reason Clio and I are traveling with the guys too," Ashleigh said, laughing.

"See what you started, Jack?" Tron said. "Before you insisted on reconnecting with your girl, we were all about sex, booze, and rock 'n' roll. Now even Dakota's mothered up."

The twinkle in Tron's eyes alerted me that he didn't feel the least bit upset about being the only band member flying solo at the moment. His words implied a relationship between Dakota and me, something I wasn't sure was on the radar—for either of us.

"What are you on about, Tron? Nothing's changed about sex,

booze, and rock 'n' roll other than I prefer one lady rather than a crowd," Blu said with a special smile for Ashleigh as he pulled her closer to his side.

"You know, now that I think about it, you kept the panties Annabelle threw onstage for you after Red Rocks, didn't you Dakota?" Tron teased.

"We need to write more complicated rhythms for you, Tron. Keep you occupied so your mind doesn't wander so much when we play," Dakota said.

Before I could decide what Dakota keeping my panties after that show meant, and that Tron noticed, the elevator stopped. When we exited the car, Tron's chuckles echoed behind us as Dakota hustled me down the hallway.

He keyed us into our room—check that—our suite. I tried to process by what magic our luggage awaited us along the wall to the right of the door. Then my attention wandered to the minibar, the soft leather couches in the middle of the room, the muted lighting of the wall sconces, everything done in a tasteful shade of deep burgundy accented by taupe and cream paint on the walls and the plush cream area rug on which the furniture rested. Rich, yet understated, the room exuded class.

An open doorway across from the entrance to the suite revealed a king-size bed covered in a burgundy duvet and piled with burgundy, cream, and taupe throw pillows. As though pulled by some unseen force, I walked over to inspect the bedroom further, discovering a massive closet that took up half of one wall and gave way to floor-to-ceiling windows with a view of the city stretching out to the ocean. With the day being unusually clear, the view stole my breath.

After staring out the windows for several minutes, I turned toward the room and spied another door opening into the bathroom. As incredible as I found the rest of the suite, the bathroom rocked my world. It was easily as big as the bedroom in my apartment—maybe even bigger. A full Jacuzzi tub beside a walk-in shower took up one wall while across from them stretched a long vanity with two sinks. Everything was done in dark gray marble. Brass fittings gleamed in the lights and reflected in the mirrors covering the wall above the sinks all the way to the ceiling.

Standing in the middle of the bathroom and admiring the space reminded me that I hadn't showered yet today. As I walked back through the suite, I noticed Dakota casually leaning against the bar, a bottled water in his hand. He looked scrumptious and tempting standing there, but more than anything, I wanted to test out that incredible shower. Grabbing the handle on my suitcase, I'd barely taken a step toward the bedroom when Dakota materialized beside me and relieved me of my burden.

"You're good with this?" he asked as he carried my bag into the bedroom.

"Do I have a choice?" I teased.

He stopped midway through the room and faced me. "You always have a choice, Annabelle." His tone turned deadly serious, a side of him that was new to me.

"Including going with you on tour?"

"Don't even pretend you didn't want to come with us." He cleared his throat. "I don't know what Garrett's problem is, but you going out on tour with us was always the plan. If you wanted to, that is." A grin played over his lips.

He strode the rest of the way into the bedroom and set my case on the stand waiting inside the closet. "We're playing three nights here, so you might as well move in."

"Actually, I was hoping to take a shower. You should see the shower. It's amazing," I gushed then caught myself. The shower would only be amazing to me, not to Dakota who had probably seen hundreds of suites exactly like this one, probably some that were even more opulent.

"Amazing is it? Let me see."

He sauntered over to the bathroom and poked his head inside

the door. A second later I heard him give a low whistle. "Fancy. Mind if I try out that shower with you?"

Like I could say no to that.

After rummaging around in my disaster of a suitcase, I retrieved my toiletries bag and left my sandals on the floor in front of the closet. When I stepped inside the bathroom, a naked Dakota adjusting the water temperature in the shower stopped me in my tracks. I'd noticed the broken heart tattooed on his left pelvic bone and the series of notes inked over his heart. Though I'd tried on several occasions to map the images making up the sleeves tattooed over both of his arms, I'd only managed his stable of guitars, the one of his truck, and the massive wall of flames inked up his right bicep and over his shoulder with the faces of his bandmates staring out from inside the flames. Judging from his placement near the bottom, Jack had been a late addition to the image.

Yet somehow, I'd missed the tat on his lower back. Tentatively, I reached out to trace a teardrop about the size of my hand resting above his ass on the right side of his back. The Aegean blue of the ink exactly matched Dakota's eyes. The intricate Celtic knotwork making up the perimeter of the image was hauntingly arresting. For some reason, the tat tugged at my heart.

Dakota sucked in a breath and stiffened at my touch.

"I've never noticed this one," I whispered. "What does it mean?"

He hung his head, looked up at the ceiling, then blew out a breath. "That story is too long for today. At least if you want a shower." He faced me, and his somber tone did a one-eighty. "What the hell, Annabelle? What are you still doing in your clothes? I thought you wanted a shower." The playfulness in his voice sounded a little forced.

"I do, but…"

He spun me around and lowered the zipper on my dress, pushing the fabric off my shoulders. It puddled at my feet as he rained kisses from the base of my skull down my spine, flicking my bra open on his way to the small of my back. His mouth felt so good on my skin, and I bowed my back to push myself into his caress, my bra dropping to the floor in front of me, all questions about his tattoo and the story behind it lost in the sensations of his lips on my body.

He knelt behind me, his hand skimming my panties down my legs as he applied his tantalizing lips to my ass. With his hands caressing my outer thighs, he lulled me into a lust-filled lethargy with his kisses, a lethargy he brought me out of abruptly when he bit down on one plump cheek.

"Dakota!" I shrieked as I tried to step out of his grasp.

Laughing darkly, he said, "Jesus, I do love your ass."

His hands on my hips held me in place as he laved the tiny hurt with his tongue. When he bit down a second time, he practiced some restraint, the result driving me a little wild and making me push myself back into him. Again, he laughed and slid his hands up to squeeze my ass as he stood behind me.

"So, Annabelle. Shower?"

Still with a hand on my ass, he guided me into the space, the spray feeling heavenly after my whirlwind of a morning. Like he understood somehow without me having to say it, he didn't push for another round of sex, not that I would have been averse to the suggestion in my half-aroused state. But I did need to wash and unwind and try to find my bearings after the way the day had begun.

As though he knew exactly what I needed, he stood behind me, gently pulled the clip from my hair, and nudged my head beneath the falling water. His fingertips on my scalp as he massaged shampoo into my hair relaxed me, and I dropped my head back for more. I could have dozed off standing up, which he must have figured out. He pushed my head back under the water then turned me to face him so I could reach up and sluice out the rest of the shampoo myself.

When my hair was squeaky clean, I opened my eyes to find him staring at my breasts with a hungry look, but he didn't touch.

Smiling, I ran my hands over my body, touching myself for both of our pleasure. When he said, "Jesus, Annabelle," and took over touching me, he delighted me. It seemed only a second passed before he slid his hands from shaping my breasts and plucking my nipples to cupping and squeezing my ass again as he pulled me tight against him.

"I was going to wash you first, but then you had to go and touch yourself, so now washing will have to wait," he growled and crushed his mouth down on mine.

Good thing the bathrooms in the suites on the top floor came equipped with industrial-sized hot water heaters. It took Dakota a long, pleasurable time before he finally made good on his promise to bathe me.

CHAPTER NINETEEN

Annabelle

"GREAT! FREAKIN' PEACHY!" I grumped as I rummaged through the epic mess of clothes filling my suitcase.

From somewhere behind me, I heard Dakota drawl, "What's the problem, babe?"

I blew out a breath and faced him. "Apparently, when *someone* insisted that I pack in under ten minutes for a two-month trip, after he'd woken me up at the butt crack of dawn—"

"And sexed you up rather nicely," he added with a smirk. "Don't forget that part."

Ignoring him, I continued, "I managed to leave home with only the underwear I had on. I don't have one single other pair of panties or another bra. Fan-freakin'-tastic."

"That's the problem? From the way you were acting, I thought it was something serious."

"Being without underwear *is* serious, superstar."

I shoved my way past him and marched bare-assed back into the bathroom to retrieve my one set of underwear, only to discover that both my bra and panties were soaked from the two of us spilling out of the shower, kissing and hugging in the afterglow of some wow-worthy sex. Even in my moment of distress, I had to admit Dakota was the best lover I'd ever had. One touch from him could make me forget my own name—let alone that I needed lingerie for two months.

He leaned against the doorframe of the bathroom and watched me as I processed my current predicament. Pushing away from the door, he relieved me of my wet panties and pulled me into his arms. "I don't see what you're getting so worked up about, Annie-girl. Put on some clothes, and we'll go shopping. We need to find a black lace thong to replace the one you tossed at me the night we first met," he said with an exaggerated leer that had me laughing in a second.

My eyes widened. "You really do remember what I tossed at you onstage that night?"

"Why do you suppose I sought you out at the after-party? Hot panties like that warrant an investigation into their owner."

He held me close, his hands, as usual, on my ass. Somewhere in the back of my mind, I thought I should probably be uncomfortable with the imbalance of power between us. After all, he was fully dressed while I remained naked. But his words empowered me. I'd intrigued him from the night we met. At least I wasn't alone in this, not that I had any illusions that my current fairy tale would last. I might not be a total wild child, but Dakota and I were both too free-spirited for the whole white picket fence thing.

An image of a Celtic design teardrop intruded into those thoughts. For a fleeting second, I wondered if there were invisible tethers on Dakota, tethers that maybe gave him quite a bit of latitude but not complete freedom.

Something of my thoughts must have flashed across my face because he pulled back to look closely at me. "Hey, babe. You're with me on tour. We're going to have a blast. Beginning with lingerie shopping."

I blinked at him.

"Since women are so generous with their pretty things when we play, I've never had to shop for panties before. Buying them for you is going to be fun." With an eyebrow waggle, he turned me to the door and gave me a stinging slap on the ass.

"Dakota! What is it with you and ouching my ass today?" I demanded as I hustled over to my suitcase.

"You have such a pretty ass. Now it's a pretty pink ass that's moving so we can go have some different kind of fun together."

With an unladylike snort, I turned back to my suitcase, pulled out a halter dress with a built-in bra, and slipped it over my head. The flared skirt skimmed the tops of my knees, so I had to hope we didn't experience any breezes before I had my privates decently covered.

A town car awaited us when we stepped outside the hotel. I raised a brow in question. Dakota shrugged and said, "What? You thought I'd call an Uber? Come on. Get in."

I stepped past him and lowered myself onto the seat, sliding my legs around and into the car, acutely conscious of my nakedness beneath my dress. I knew a girl in college who never wore panties, saying the sensation of going without made her feel free. My current experience did not mirror hers. Even though I knew better, it still felt like everyone I passed knew I had absolutely nothing on beneath my dress.

It didn't help that the second Dakota joined me in the back seat, he slid his hand beneath the hem and up my thigh. I crossed my legs, pinning his hand in place before he reached his destination, and he chuckled low in his throat. "Don't worry, Annababy. That partition is made of one-way glass, and I've turned off the intercom. Our driver can speculate all day, but he has no idea what we're doing back here."

"Oh, I bet he has an idea. Especially if he chauffeurs rock stars often," I replied wryly.

He grinned but pulled his hand out from beneath my dress and slid it along the seat behind me.

"Since it's my fault you came out on tour with us so woefully underdressed," he began with an exaggerated sigh, "it seems only right that I take care of rectifying the situation. That also means I get a say in what you pick out."

"Department store selections aren't all that impressive, but they do the job," I said with a smirk.

"Who said anything about a department store?"

"Where else would we go to buy underwear?" I asked, genuinely confused.

"I said I don't go out and buy lingerie, but I do appreciate it. And I pay attention to it. We will not be shopping at a department store today."

The car came to a halt outside a boutique. Leaning forward, he pushed a button and lowered the dividing glass. "Wait here, please," he instructed the driver. "We have some shopping to do." He grinned in my direction.

After glancing at the discreet sign on the door, I sat back in the seat and crossed my arms. "Agent Provocateur? I can't afford this."

"Like I said. It's my fault you need some lingerie, so I'm taking care of it." Taking my hand, he gave me no choice but to accompany him inside the store. "Come on. We need to shop now 'cause I have a rehearsal this afternoon."

"Yeah, and Garrett said something about needing me to work this afternoon too," I said, remembering his parting shot to me in the lobby before we went up to the suite.

When we stepped inside, I forgot all about Garrett and my worries concerning him. The boutique exuded sex and class with tasteful displays of hot lace, sheer silk, rich colors, and every design and style of bra, panties, slips, bustiers, garters, nighties—I couldn't believe the selection of beautiful underthings. For a second, I forgot Dakota was with me as I fingered the barely-there silk on a table of boy shorts panties while I stared at a row of lace push-up bras that looked like they could fly my girls almost to the moon.

Dakota brought me back to myself with a familiar squeeze of his big hand around mine. "See anything you like?"

"I like everything," I whispered.

At that moment, a saleswoman greeted us. "Were you interested in something special today?"

"We're always interested in something special," Dakota said, his smooth voice matching the playful look on his face. His words, his tone, his expression put butterflies to flight in my belly. I had to stand with my legs squeezed together as I teetered on the precipice of creaming myself from his look, his voice, his hand in mine as we stood in the middle of sex central.

Though I worked to control my response to him, I had no choice but to look around the store. The displays of hot lingerie did nothing to cool me down as pictures flashed across my brain. Pictures of me wearing sheer white boy shorts panties with a matching bra as I strutted through our suite in front of Dakota. Pictures of me strolling out of the bedroom in a lacy black thong and matching black push-up bra as he watched from his casual stance near the minibar. Pictures of me standing in front of the closet trying to determine what to cover the sexy red-and-white-polka-dot bikini set with as he watched me from the bed.

I blinked away the pictures as the man himself purred softly into my ear, "Pick out whatever you like."

His hand on the small of my back felt both proprietary and hot through the thin cotton of my summer dress. His touch alone sent my thoughts skittering.

I sucked in a deep breath and pasted on a smile for the saleswoman, who apparently either didn't recognize Dakota or was so jaded by celebrities frequenting her store she didn't react to him. "I need panties and bras. Your selection is beautiful. I'm sure I'll have no trouble finding something I like."

However, when I picked up a pair of the sheer boy shorts I'd first admired and saw the price tag, I put them back down like they'd scalded me.

"Annabelle." There was a warning note in Dakota's voice.

"That one pair of panties is a quarter of a week's pay for me," I hissed back at him.

He leaned in close, setting his luscious lips on the shell of my ear. "For the last time. I'm buying." Before pulling away from me, he gave me a little kiss that sent shivers sliding all over my body.

As he stared at me, he came to a decision. "Go to the changing room, and I'll bring you some stuff to try on." He winked at the saleswoman who smiled back at him.

When I opened my mouth to protest, he said, "Don't argue, Annababy. I told you on the drive over here that this little shopping trip was going to be fun."

Dakota took me by the shoulders and turned me toward the dressing room. Knowing what to expect next based on his antics at our suite earlier, I arched my back and scooted off in the direction of the changing rooms. He laughed, his hand in midair after I deprived him of the swat he so clearly intended to hustle me along. A secret smile ghosted over my lips as I anticipated what he would bring me to try on.

While he chose my lingerie, I checked out the stunning dressing room in the boutique. Floor-to-ceiling mirrors covered every wall. The plush champagne-colored carpet underfoot begged me to bare my feet. The velvety pink Chablis-colored benches seemed more suited to a boudoir than to a dressing room, but that was probably the point.

A cream silk wrapper lay tastefully across one of the benches, so I slipped off my dress and slipped on the wrapper then sat to await Dakota and his selections. A couple of minutes later, he entered the room with lingerie draped over his arms, a huge grin splitting his face.

"This place is fuckin' awesome," he exclaimed as he dropped his choices onto the bench beside the one on which I sat. Easing himself into an antique-looking mahogany chair with velvet cushions, which had been strategically placed in a corner of the room, he sat back and grinned.

The mirrors revealed my bemused expression as first I stared at Dakota then at the pile of underwear then back at him again.

"All right Annababy. Time for you to give me a private fashion show." Clasping his hands behind his head, he leaned back in the chair and waited expectantly.

Ooookay, so that was the game. After a beat, I took his dare. I untied the sash at my waist, letting the wrapper whisper to the floor as I stepped over to the mound of lingerie awaiting my inspection. I started with a leopard-print bustier and matching thong. Pretending to ignore my audience, I turned this way and that, examining the fit in the mirror. A smile bloomed inside me at the sight of Dakota's eyes deepening to midnight blue as he watched me model the underwear.

"This works, I think." I gazed at myself in the mirror. "What do you think?" I turned to face him.

"I think"—he cleared his throat—"I think I like that one very much. Buy it."

"Great."

I changed out of the leopard print into a sheer champagne colored bra and bikini panty set. Little bows held the front of the panties together, leaving inviting openings from the waistband to my clit. Though the cups of the bra were sheer, the construction with the underwire and the tapes up the centers of the cups and across the top of the bra lifted my girls quite nicely while revealing my now erect nipples. After only two sets, I found myself sizzlingly turned on as I modeled them for Dakota.

He'd remained in his laid-back power pose for the first set, but the champagne set had him sitting forward, his hands clasped between his knees. He didn't say anything, but his nostrils flared as he nodded toward the set we'd already chosen, silently telling me to add this one to it.

Next up was a black lace thong and matching black lace push-up bra. After I put them on, I faced him but turned my head to look over my shoulder and check the fit in the mirror. I already knew it was perfect from the feel of the lace on my body, but his increasing arousal in the darkening of his eyes and the flexing of his hands made me want to show off.

"I like this one. What about you?" I asked with a smile.

"Definitely. We'll get two of those." His voice dropped an octave.

My next choice was a sheer pink teddy with magenta lace trim along the boy shorts-style legs and over my breasts. By now, his breathing was audible, and I couldn't help but want to tease him even more. I ran my hands over the silky material, watching myself in the mirror then turning to skim my palms over the globes of my ass. When I walked past him to remove the teddy and add it to the growing pile of keepers, he reached out and pulled me to him.

"You're doing this deliberately, aren't you?" he growled.

"Doing what?" A grin threatened, but I schooled my features into something resembling innocence.

"Driving me crazy."

"Hey, superstar. This whole shopping spree was your big idea, remember?" I straddled his lap and ran my hands over his deliciously broad shoulders made more interesting by his tight white T-shirt.

"Tell me something, Annabelle. Have you ever had sex in a dressing room before?"

I blinked. "Um, no. But I don't think—"

Loud laughter burst through the shop, and both of us stopped for a second to listen. After several raucous comments about the racier the better and some vulgar responses to some of the toys on display—handcuffs seemed to be the object of most interest— Dakota and I smiled at each other.

"Bachelorette party," I whispered.

"Perfect cover," he replied.

Reaching between us with one hand, he petted my pussy and unsnapped the teddy. As he freed his cock from his jeans, he said, "Stand up and turn around."

Given I'd been turned on from the moment my borrowed wrapper hit the floor, he didn't have to tell me twice. I waited breathlessly while he removed a condom from his wallet and sheathed himself. He grasped my hips and guided me back to him, urging me back down to his lap. As he filled me with one long beautiful thrust, I smacked my hand over my mouth to keep from crying out in surprise and pleasure.

"Don't worry about them. They won't hear us, Annababy. Put your hands on the arms of the chair and ride me," he demanded, his sexy voice sliding up my spine and stealing any reserve I might have had at the prospect of getting caught.

He slightly lifted his hips, seating himself even deeper inside me. Involuntarily, I clamped my inner muscles around him because he felt so damn good.

"Come on, Annie-girl. Take a ride," he said. "And enjoy the view."

The fiery desire in his eyes reflected in every mirror in the room, ratcheting up my own need. I couldn't help it. Stunned at my own wantonness, I gladly gave him everything he wanted, becoming more and more turned on as I watched us move together. I was wetter than I could ever remember being, and I wondered vaguely if I'd leave a telltale spot on the front of his jeans.

He gripped my hips and urged me to move faster before he took over thrusting into me. Never in my life had I seen anything as erotic as Dakota's mask of ecstasy reflected all around us as he ramped up our rhythm. After one final hard thrust, I closed my eyes and clamped my mouth shut against my orgasmic screams when I flew with him through outer space.

Coming down at last, I opened my eyes and stared in wonder at the infinity of reflections of the two of us. Dakota was still inside me as I lay back against his chest, one hand resting on top of the one he'd splayed over my belly to hold me to him. His other hand cupped my breast, his thumb lazily rubbing my erect nipple as he nuzzled the side of my neck. "Lingerie shopping was a good idea. Glad you suggested it," he said in a low tone. The mirrors revealed the twinkle in his eyes that hadn't quite returned to their normal sea blue color after their trip into the deeps.

"And I'm only halfway through modeling what you picked out."

The saleswoman must have remembered we were in the dressing room as she chose that moment to call through the door, "Everything going okay in there? Do you need anything?"

In a surprisingly normal voice considering our current state, Dakota answered, "We're fine in here, thanks."

I stifled a giggle at his double entendre, which caused me to clamp my inner muscles tight around his still partially erect cock. He shifted in the chair and gave me a look in the mirrors, one that made me want to laugh out loud.

"I think we've finished shopping today," he said as he lifted me off his lap.

He tied off the condom we'd used and dropped it in the wastebasket in the room. When I shot him a side-eye, he shrugged. "You want me to take it with us?"

I rolled my eyes and stretched, returning to the lingerie I had yet to try on. "Are we really finished? I haven't tried this lavender and black lace bustier, thong, and garter set yet," I said, sighing dramatically.

Loud giggles from the dressing room across the hall interrupted the pretend tantrum I'd considered throwing to mess with Dakota. I stared at the door and turned back to him. "Fine. I have enough for a few days. I can always wash them out in the sink at night."

"Annabelle, we both know I got your size right for all of it, so we'll take it all. I want you to leave that one on under your dress." He nodded at the teddy I still wore. "That way, whenever I look at you today, I can imagine it on you and remember what we were doing the first time you wore it."

For a long minute, we grinned at each other. Someone jiggled the handle on the door. "Is there someone in here?" a high-pitched feminine voice called out.

"Yes," Dakota and I said simultaneously.

"Oh!" the anonymous woman squeaked.

He chuckled. "Get dressed, Annababy, while I take care of this stuff." He scooped up the piles of lingerie and headed toward the door.

He should have looked ridiculous with his arms full of silk and lace underthings. Instead, he looked mouthwateringly hot, no doubt because of the relaxed just-fucked way he moved. When he reached the door, he winked at me in the mirrors and disappeared into the store.

I slipped my dress over my head, adjusted my new teddy beneath the halter top bodice, and followed him out of the dressing room a couple of seconds later. He stood in front of the counter in a relaxed stance with his impressive arms crossed over his broad chest as he casually chatted with the saleswoman who rang up our selections.

As we waited, the bachelorette party spilled out of the dressing rooms, and chaos broke out as one of the women recognized Dakota. The saleswoman did her best to ring up our items quickly, but in the end, he was late for rehearsal after he signed eight bra and panty sets for the wild women who surrounded him and wouldn't let him move until he gave them at least that much. From the way a couple of them tried to cop a feel of his crotch, he was lucky all we were was late to the concert venue.

CHAPTER TWENTY

Annabelle

"I'D LIKE TO say that little scene in the lingerie store surprises me, but I've seen some version of it every time I've gone out on tour with Jack," Clio said as we sat together in the hotel bistro enjoying a late lunch.

"The surprise is that Dakota didn't bring back one or two of those women," Ashleigh said with a smirk. "Which begs the question, Annabelle. What's going on with you two?"

A long swallow of my iced tea only allowed me to stall for a few seconds. "Nothing."

Two sets of eyebrows lifted simultaneously, but Clio spoke first. "I call bullshit. Emory said Dakota didn't take his usual vacation when the band broke for Jack's and my honeymoon. In fact, she said Dakota spent the entire month hanging around the studio, especially in your office."

"What's the deal, Annabelle?" Ashleigh prodded with a grin.

"We're having some fun together. It's nothing special—for either of us. I mean, we *are* talking Dakota Perri here, guitar virtuoso and rock god." Turning to Clio, I added, "You forget. I've seen the man in action already. I know what the score is."

Clio gazed fondly at her daughter who, from her perch in her mom's lap, played happily with the french fries on her mom's plate. "You made no secret of wanting to hook up with Dakota before we went to the show that night." Her expression turned speculative.

"Which proves my point," I said, heading her off.

"Today's little excursion to Agent Provocateur was only to replace the pair of panties you threw at Dakota *two years ago*?"

Angel gave a tiny squawk at her mother's tone, and I laughed. "My thoughts exactly, Angel-baby."

"It means something that Dakota bought you underwear," Ashleigh forked a bit of salad. "After all, it's not like he needed to do that."

"Well, he kind of owed me."

Ashleigh leaned back and sipped her Coke, shooting me a look over the rim of the glass.

"I guess Dakota has some kind of bet with Jack?" I glanced at Clio who grinned. "So he insisted I pack in under ten minutes. I forgot to grab undies, and Dakota helped me out. That's it."

"'Course it is," Ashleigh drawled.

Trying to direct the conversation to something else, I asked, "What does the band do with all the underwear that ends up onstage after one of their concerts?"

"The roadies gather it up, send it to a cleaners, and the band donates it to a local women's shelter in whatever city they're playing," Ashleigh said.

"Seriously? In every place they go? Even overseas?"

"Everywhere," Clio added. "Which is another reason to love the guys in Balefire so much."

"Or one of them in your case," I teased. After taking a sip of my tea, I asked, "Why didn't I know this before?"

Ashleigh raised her brows. "You didn't ask?"

"It didn't matter when Dakota obviously kept the pair Annabelle threw at him," Clio said, laughing.

Angel interrupted by executing a perfect toss of a french fry into Clio's lemonade. "No, no baby. We don't throw our food at the table," she patiently admonished her daughter as she fished the food from her drink.

"Sharing that info would probably tarnish the bad-boy rock 'n' roll image of the band, but I'm filing it away in case we ever need some good PR," I said as I finished the last of my seafood salad. "Speaking of PR, I need to check in with Caroline to see what she needs me to do for tonight's show."

"Actually, I think you're going to be checking in with Garrett. He's standing at the door scanning the room," Ashleigh warned. "He's coming our way."

I wondered at the acid I thought I heard in her tone, but I didn't have long to contemplate it.

"There you are, Annabelle. Is your phone out of juice?" Nodding at my friends, he added, "Ashleigh, Clio. Have a nice lunch?"

I pulled my phone from my purse where I discovered I had six waiting texts: two from Dakota and four from Garrett. I pulled some bills from my wallet and placed them in the middle of the table. "I'm off to work, ladies. Thanks for sharing lunch with me. Enjoy your afternoon." I slid out of the booth and stood beside Garrett.

"See you at the show tonight," Garrett said to Ashleigh and Clio. Taking my arm, he led me from the restaurant, starting his lecture within earshot of my friends. "I realize you're doing an internship, Annabelle. But it is paid, and you are on the clock, so I expect you to be available and to pay attention to your phone while on this tour."

For a guy who had to be in his midthirties tops, he sure had officious down. Gritting my teeth to hold back what I wanted to say, I hustled along beside him out of the bistro. Knowing that for some reason he didn't want me on this tour in the first place kept me in check, but I wondered how long I'd last if he continued treating as he had so far.

We arrived in front of the hotel to my second town car of the day. If this was the way Balefire usually traveled, I could get used to it—the one bright spot in what looked to be an otherwise trying afternoon. The driver held the door, and Garrett slid in ahead of me. I gave the driver an apologetic smile then chastised myself for trying to make up for Garrett's rude behavior, which, after all, he'd directed at me.

"Garrett, I get it. You don't want me on this tour," I began before he cut me off.

"Actually, Annabelle, you *don't* get it. You don't get it at all. What Dakota sees in you is beyond me. You're not any different from any other groupie who throws her panties at the band during a show," he snarled.

The venom in his voice, in the way he stared determinedly out the opposite window, the way he'd treated me from the moment he entered the bistro converged on me and almost smothered me. It was obvious he had no intention of telling me what I'd done so wrong as to warrant his vitriol, but I couldn't sit there and take it. Some instinct told me in this moment of moments, I needed to do something proactive.

While I tried to decide what to do, LA sped past us in a blur of Spanish broom bushes and mall sprawl as we navigated the freeway out to the Coliseum where the band would play the first three shows of the West Coast tour. Garrett extracted a beer from the minibar and popped off the top, which he tossed carelessly to the floor before taking a long pull. The fact that he didn't offer me a drink served as an additional reminder that he didn't want me along.

A visual of a rejection letter from grad school briefly clouded my mind. I pulled in a deep breath, let it out slowly, and retrieved my laptop from my bag. *Good thing I grabbed this at the last minute*, I thought as I booted up my email with the latest spreadsheets from Caroline. Somehow, I had to execute an end around on Garrett's attitude toward me if I wanted to complete my internship successfully.

Dakota had made it clear he had no intention of treating me as just another professional on this tour. That meant I had to make my business skills stand out even more. For a second, I resented him for that. Then I shifted in my seat and felt the silky teddy slide over my skin beneath my dress, and memories of our shopping trip crowded my thoughts. Smiling to myself, I scanned the information for something I could use to get back on Garrett's good side.

His growl startled me out of my thoughts. "What's making you so happy?"

Mentally chastising myself for jumping at his tone, I wiped the smile off my face and turned my laptop toward him. "The numbers for the advanced sales of tour shirts for the show. Looks like our social media challenge is a success."

He softened his tone a fraction. "Impressive. Guess we'll see for sure at the show tonight. Do you have the photographers lined up?"

"They're supposed to meet us at the Coliseum at four today to go over optimum locations for the best shots."

"Good thing I managed to find you when I did, then, isn't it?"

Aaand we were back to square one.

I busied myself on the rest of the drive emailing Caroline and texting the photographers. Back at the office, Garrett had loved our idea of showcasing the crowd in concert T-shirts for the album cover for Balefire's latest release. The T-shirt sales demonstrated the idea's merit. I needed to concentrate on that initial success and on my job until showtime and do my best to ignore my surly boss.

Dakota

The guys and I were on break from sound checks when Annabelle and Garrett walked up to the stage. She still wore the electric pink sundress from our morning shopping spree. The front of my jeans grew tight at the thought of what she had on underneath it and how hot she looked in the dressing room in nothing but that sheer teddy. She and I would be going underwear shopping again on this tour for damn sure.

Jumping down from the stage, I stood in front of her and gave her a private smile, one she could interpret only one way. Her eyes widened as she took in my meaning, but to be sure, I leaned in and whispered in her ear, "I know what you have on under that dress. Makes me hard thinking about it." I kissed her jaw below her ear, and the tiny shiver that stole over her at my touch made me feel like Superman like always with Annabelle.

"Excuse me, Annabelle," Garrett interrupted, "but last I checked, you're on tour to work, and I don't mean the band."

She flinched like Garrett had slapped her, and I saw red. "What the *fuck* is your problem, Garrett?"

"The album cover shoot is Annabelle's idea. I thought she might want to meet with Bailey and the photographers to go over locations and protocol for that part of the show," he replied without an ounce of apology in his tone.

He stared me down and turned to our road engineer who had materialized out of nowhere. "Annabelle will explain what she has in mind for the shoot, and you can tell her what's going to work and what won't, Bailey. By the way, how'd the sound check go?"

Bailey looked from Garrett to Annabelle to me, his eyes tracking my hands, which still rested on Annabelle, one on her hip, the other caressing the back of her neck where I could feel all kinds of tension.

At last Bailey returned his attention to Garrett. "No problems. Everything sounds great, the pyrotechnics are all set, the hydraulics work exactly the way they're supposed to. We're all ready to go for the next three nights."

"The photo shoot is only for tonight. We'll need all hands on deck to sell T-shirts in the merch tent. You won't mind helping out there will you, Annabelle?" Garrett asked.

I didn't like the way he was looking at her, like she'd fucked up somehow. He knew damn well I wanted her on tour. When he'd seen her college transcript and her portfolio, he'd been all over having her be our first intern. Whatever his problem was now was his problem—not hers.

"Annabelle will watch the show from the VIP section with Clio and Ashleigh, Garrett. She will *not* be working merch. Understood?"

Annabelle, who'd been uncharacteristically silent throughout this little pissing match, finally spoke up. "I should probably take a look at locations for the photo shoot."

When she tried to step away from me, I gave her hip a little squeeze. "The whole band loves your cover idea, babe. Go on and direct those photographers, but I'd better see you in the area during the show." Facing Garrett, I said, "Right, Garrett?"

He shot me a look, shrugged a shoulder, and walked over to the rest of the band who'd been watching this whole exchange with smirks on their faces. *Screw 'em.* Pulling her close, I whispered against her mouth, "You're doing great, Annababy. You keep doing your job, and I'll take care of Garrett."

Of course, I had to kiss her then. Those plump rosy lips of hers so close to mine begged for my touch. Which might have been a mistake given where we were and what still needed doing if we wanted the show to go on in about four hours. Didn't matter. Kissing her lit me on fire like always, her soft lips molding perfectly to mine, her desire for me mirroring mine. As I gathered her flush against me, I could still sense tension along her spine and the long muscles of her back. I traced the outline of her mouth with my tongue, and she opened for me so sweetly I dove right in to taste all her hot sugar. Nothing else could compete with the taste of Annabelle Stewart on my tongue.

My Annie-girl responded completely to me, fisting her hands in my T-shirt over my pecs and pushing her hips into my pelvis. The way she danced her tongue over mine left me nearly incoherent with want, and I held her hard against me. That kiss made the earth move, and I never wanted it to end. After all the girls I'd known, I couldn't remember a single one who could rev me up as hot and fast as she could with a single kiss. My blood pounded through me, concentrating in my dick, which pushed hard into the front of my jeans.

Having lost myself in that kiss, the throat-clearing sound I heard seemed to come from a long way off. The tension I'd noticed in Annabelle when I first started kissing her thrummed back through her, making her body stiff instead of pliable beneath my hands, and she pulled away from my mouth.

When I registered the location of the noise, it sounded like Bailey stood close enough to be taking notes on my technique. He cleared his throat again. "Sorry to interrupt, but the photographers showed up around half an hour ago. They're waiting in the backstage area."

Annabelle pushed at me, and I slanted her a look before I reluctantly let her go. A light pink stain covered her cheeks, which surprised the hell out of me. What did my girl have to be embarrassed about?

As she walked away with Bailey, I called out, "Don't be too long, Annababe. We need to go back to the hotel to shower and eat before the show."

Though she nodded to let me know she'd heard me, she didn't look back. Damn. What had Garrett said to make her act so uncomfortable with me? When I looked around for the asshole to set him straight, I discovered he was MIA. But the rest of the band remained standing right where they'd been when Annabelle and Garrett showed up.

Blu started in first. "You've really got a thing for Annabelle, don'tcha, buddy?"

"Don't get your shorts in a knot, Blu. Annie and I are having some fun right now is all. Nothing like you putting a giant rock on Ashleigh's finger or Jackie-boy tying the knot with Clio."

I shuddered, but the guys laughed.

"Tell yourself whatever you need to so you can sleep at night,

Dakota," Jack said with a smirk. "Or keep sleeping with Annabelle. Whatever works for you."

"You really should refrain from sleeping with the help, Dakota. It's bad for business," Garrett said as he appeared out of nowhere to join us.

His snide tone pissed me off, but I held it in. "What the fuck do you mean, Garrett? I've never even made a pass at you," I corrected him. "No offense, but you're not my type."

The guys busted out laughing. Anger clouded Garrett's face for a second before he gave in and joined them. I grinned at the rest of the band. "Later, dudes."

With a wave over my head, I headed in the direction of backstage, intending to catch up with Annabelle. We'd started the day with too much fun to end up with her walking away from me with a blush on her face that I didn't put there.

CHAPTER TWENTY-ONE

Annabelle

CLIO GRINNED AS we made our way to the VIP area before the show. "This is totally different from the last time we attended a Balefire concert together, isn't it, Annabelle?"

"I don't know. We're still pregaming with caramel vodka," I replied with a wink as I downed a healthy swig of my drink. While we waited backstage with the band, Bailey Saunders had given each of us girls a flask with Balefire's signature flames etched over it and filled with yummy vodka. After the day I'd had, I needed it. Especially after Dakota insisted on using our downtime before the show for activities other than resting—or talking about how I needed to keep my job separate from playtime with him. Judging from how awake the rest of the band and my friends were, *they'd* spent at least some of their downtime napping.

"What's the story there?" Ashleigh asked.

"Not something that should be included in the annals of the band," Clio said with a pointed look in my direction.

Sometimes I forgot that not only was Ashleigh Blu's gorgeous and sweet fiancée, but also, she was a freelance writer and music reviewer for *Rolling Stone* among other prestigious music mags and blogs.

She pulled a face. "I'm not working on anything about the band, Clio. Now spill."

Clio sighed and rolled her eyes.

"I'll tell you," I drawled. When Clio didn't offer to stop me, I kept going. "While we were still in college, Jack arranged for me to have tickets and backstage passes to the after-party for the band's show at Red Rocks provided I bring Clio along. I didn't know why until after Angel was born. Seems Jack and Clio were high school sweethearts before Jack signed with his first band. He wanted to reconnect with her, and because I'd met Bailey at a party once, Jack used the whole weird six-degrees-of-separation situation to see Clio again."

Ashleigh gave me the universal gesture for *Go on*.

"I brought along a bottle of caramel vodka for the preshow, even sneaking a flask of it into Clio's purse. She downed all of her share and half of mine after Jack acknowledged her in the front row of the concert. I guess someone remembered those details and set us up for this tour." I lifted my flask for a toast. With a big grin, Ashleigh joined me. After a beat, Clio clinked her flask to ours as well.

"To caramel vodka, hot rock stars, and us," I said.

"Oh yeah," Ashleigh seconded.

"And baby girls," Clio added with a soft smile.

Tipping back our flasks, we finished our toast.

"That's a great story, Clio. Don't know why you wouldn't want it included in the story of the band if someone ever wrote it someday," Ashleigh said as we clicked along down the hallway toward the area designated for the band's special guests.

"Some things in Jack's life can remain private. Undoubtedly, you feel the same about some of Blu's secrets too." Clio gifted her a knowing look.

Ashleigh smiled. Having my own secrets with Dakota, I kept moving. Even though Ashleigh and Clio were my friends, I didn't want either of them to ask me about private times between Dakota and me.

As we neared the stage, we could hear the loud excitement of the stadium filled with fans. Hopefully, the vast majority of them were dressed like us—in the latest iteration of a Balefire T-shirt. I wore mine over a pair of skinny jeans and sky-high stiletto ankle boots. Ashleigh said she put Blu in a state when she paired her T-shirt with white crop jeans and the high wedge sandals I noticed she preferred. Clio wore hers over a black miniskirt that, paired with the four-inch heels of her Louboutin crocodile pumps, accentuated her long legs. Everyone noticed how Jack couldn't take his eyes off his wife backstage before we had to leave the guys for their last-minute show prep. I loved how Clio had revived her shopping mojo following some dark times in college after she became pregnant with Angel.

I'd positioned one of the photographers on a scaffold behind the band, diametrically opposite the VIP section. The three of us, along with the other guests in the section, were bound to end up in several of the photos, which meant we all had to wear the band shirts. The way the guys responded to us in those shirts gave me a few ideas for some shots of Ashleigh, Clio, and Angel with the band. Or maybe some shots of only the girls. A nebulous marketing idea started forming in my mind, interrupted by the raucous noise of ninety thousand screaming fans as we entered the stadium behind a small army of security personnel.

Over the years, Balefire had grown in stature and popularity to rival acts like Springsteen and Beyoncé, so they no longer traveled with an opening band. Instead, their live shows sold out because the fans knew they'd be treated to two or three hours of nonstop Balefire hits with a sound and light show so big it needed a stadium-sized venue in which to perform it.

Once we found our places, we pulled out our flasks and saluted each other, downing another swallow of lovely vodka. As we returned our flasks to our purses, the lights dimmed and a roar went up in the stadium. The crowd quieted as the distant sound of drums emanated from beneath the stage, the audience holding their breaths for Balefire's signature concert opening. As the drum solo grew louder, lights flashed across the stage. Jack Whitehorse rose from the floor at the back of the stage like a sorcerer behind his massive drum kit, his platform soaring a full story above the stage floor. Gold and silver lights ricocheted off the polished chrome stanchions of the lift and the chrome on his drums. The crowd exploded in a frenzy of screams, and I sensed Clio beside me vibrating with excitement at the reception her husband received from the band's adoring fans.

Blue lights pulsing in rhythm with the deep sounds of Tron's bass guitar announced his entrance onto the stage. He stood near the base of Jack's platform and grinned up at Jack before turning his attention to the crowd. The women in the front row screamed at ear-piercing decibels, and panties and bras rained down on the stage, landing at Tron's feet.

A rainbow of laser lights bounced off every surface in the stadium. An intricate guitar solo accompanied the lasers and a spotlight illuminated Dakota at the edge of the stage opposite where we stood in the VIP section. I couldn't take my eyes off him, his fingers a blur over the fretboard as he whipped the crowd into hysteria with his virtuoso skills. Watching the ripple of muscles over his arms and chest as he ripped scores of notes from his axe left me wet. The sound of his music reverberated through me, fizzing my blood and stealing my thoughts. Then he looked straight at me, his sea blue eyes so intense they were almost black, and his mouth broke into a huge grin, a grin I was powerless not to return.

An explosion of fireworks behind the stage broke my connection with Dakota. A primal scream tore from the speakers, and like an apparition or something, Blu landed in the middle of the stage. The band dropped into its rock anthem "Feed the Fire," and the crowd lost its mind. Clio, Ashleigh, and I stood together, our arms around each other as we joined in the screaming of the stadium full of fans.

We sang along to the lyrics, each of us smiling broadly at each other as we enjoyed the show from our premium vantage point.

Later in the concert when the band slowed things down and Jack joined Blu to sing "Missing You," I noticed tears shimmering in Clio's eyes. Ashleigh tugged me back when I tried to lean in to ask Clio what was wrong. "She does this every time they sing this song. She's even more emotional when they sing 'Far Away.'"

Overhearing our conversation, Clio turned to Ashleigh. "You're a fine one to talk." Addressing me, she added, "Wait till Blu sings 'My Beauty.' Ash blubbers through the whole song."

Ashleigh shrugged, offering a sheepish little smile.

Nodding, I turned away from the conversation. I didn't want either of my friends to see my own longing for Dakota to write something for me. My heart tripped, and I hauled myself up short. Dakota and I were fooling around. Nothing more. I certainly didn't expect a rock on my finger at the end of the tour. Heck, I wasn't entirely sure I'd still be sharing a suite with him by the end of the tour, no matter how regularly my stupid heart had started dreaming of exactly that.

The man himself interrupted my morose thoughts. The band barely finished performing "Missing You" before Dakota launched into a sexy, bluesy guitar solo. As my ears tuned in to the sound, I recognized the solo as the one he'd been working on in the studio during the band's hiatus for Jack and Clio's honeymoon. While he played, he started rising above the stage on a hydraulic platform. From where I stood, it looked like he could plummet two stories from the platform to the stage, and my heart jumped into my throat.

Unconcerned with my fear, he played for several minutes, the crowd cheering its approval for the solo and its death-defying delivery. When he finished, he called out, "Did you like that one?"

The crowd roared its appreciation.

"Yeah? It's a little something I've been working on. Now Blu needs to get his ass in gear and write me some lyrics. What do ya think?"

Again, the crowd screamed its agreement.

Blu strolled back out onstage. Looking up at Dakota, he taunted, "How 'bout you do your own work, Dakota? Write your own lyrics?"

He slanted Blu a look from his high-flying vantage point before flipping him the bird, and the crowd broke into laughter at their antics. Launching into the opening riffs of "Helluva Ride," Dakota egged on the audience's reaction that no doubt contributed to the fault lines running the length of California. His platform visibly swayed beneath his feet, and I worked to swallow my nausea at the sight.

With the last notes of the song echoing around the stadium, Dakota's platform slowly returned to rest flush with the stage. Only then did I notice Bailey Saunders discreetly unhooking him from a harness and unlocking a back stand set into the platform that Dakota had stood against as he played so high above the crowd. Seeing that he didn't fly utterly without a net made me feel marginally less ill.

During the next song, he strutted his way across the stage to the VIP side and leaned down toward us. Catching my eye, he waggled his eyebrows and grinned wickedly. Guess I should have expected his antics. Dakota was nothing if not a show-off in everything I'd ever known him to do except for maybe that night he jammed with my dad at my parents' house. Still, I couldn't help but smile back at him. The fun he had entertaining the fans was infectious, and I wanted to share in it, especially now that he was safely back on solid ground.

By the time the band played their third and final encore, I couldn't coax even a drop of vodka from my flask. But the show itself left me higher, more excited and energized than I could ever remember being. Ashleigh, Clio, and I laughed and danced the whole way to the backstage area where we'd meet the guys. My friends said the guys liked to grab a quick shower immediately following the show, but they were always out by the time everyone made their way backstage to see them. I could hardly wait to see Dakota and tell him how much I enjoyed the concert.

Chapter Twenty-Two

Dakota

POURING SWEAT AND testosterone, the boys and I jogged off the stage after the last encore, the sounds of ninety thousand screaming fans ringing in our ears.

"That was fuckin' epic!" Blu shouted as we rocked our way to the locker room behind the stage.

"Best damn show we've ever done," Tron echoed.

I think he fist-bumped everyone from the roadies to the security team, the band, and anyone else he saw as we ran off the stage and down the corridor to the showers. I couldn't blame him. Playing in front of a sold-out show—in a stadium no less—made me feel like a fucking rock god.

Letting out a primal yell, I jumped on Blu's back and rode him halfway to the locker room, the two of us laughing our asses off. We were so fucking jacked that I don't think we could have flown any higher. Jack slapped Tron on the ass as he ran by us, laughing and yelling as he led us the rest of the way to the locker room.

My clothes were soaked right down to my socks as I tore them off to jump into the shower. As excited and high as I was from playing the show, more than anything, I wanted to see Annabelle. Throughout the concert, I kept stealing glances at her, and every time I looked, her eyes remained locked onto me. As much as I wanted to believe the success of our first show on this tour was about that stadium full of fans, a part of me knew I played to impress one particular girl. I had no doubt Jack and Blu played their hearts out for their women too. Tron's steadiness on the bass never wavered, as usual, but I couldn't help but think even he played a little better tonight to match the rest of us. Or maybe he played for all the ladies who literally carpeted the stage for us in sexy underwear.

Thinking about underwear reminded me of the late-afternoon impromptu runway show Annabelle gave me with some of the rest of the stuff I'd bought for her. With a grin, I remembered how that little modeling exhibition eventually ended up. Playing the show left me semihard already—it always did. But thinking about Annabelle's sexy little body and what she was wearing under her band T-shirt left me showing off in the showers.

Even though I wasn't the only one in that state, it didn't stop the catcalls from my friends. "Looks like your new toy inspires you, Dakota," Tron commented with a laugh.

"Which one?"

"It doesn't take hydraulics to give me a lift," Blu said over Tron as he toweled himself off in front of a bench where one of the roadies had stacked fresh clothes.

"Fuck you, Blu. You're just jealous. Maybe if you're a good boy, you can talk Bailey into lifting you up for the next show," I teased as I stepped over to my own clothes and pulled on boxers and jeans.

"Don't be ashamed, Dakota. Those hydraulics get me off every time," Jack said, and I gaped at him. Jack backing me? Did hell freeze over? *Damn.*

"Better not let your wife hear you say that," Tron joked from where he sat on the bench pulling on his boots.

"Oh, she knows," Jack said. "One of these days Clio's going to take a ride with me on that drum kit. See why it's such a rush."

"I bet you'll give her a rush, Jackie-boy," I said with a smirk, tugging my T-shirt over my head. Tonight my shirt was a tribute to "Spaceship" by Puddle of Mudd. Yes, I definitely had plans for taking Annabelle on a little ride later.

As usual, every one of us zipped the flies of our jeans last. Playing a big show was such a fucking turn-on. It just was.

When we joined the after-party backstage, the first thing I did was seek out Annabelle. I didn't analyze why I bypassed several fawning fans who reached for me as I walked through the room. I'm not sure I even saw them. What I needed was a sizzling-hot brunette in a pair of jeans that fit her like a second skin and heels that made her legs look endless. Having experienced them several incredible times already, I knew how long those legs were. They led all the way up to heaven.

At last I spotted her near the bar chatting with Bailey Saunders. Since we were doing two more shows in the LA Coliseum, he didn't have to oversee the teardown of the sound system. Which meant he could attend the after-party. Not something I usually thought about until I saw him chatting up my Annie-girl. Something Garrett said once scratched at the back of my mind, but like she sensed me, Annabelle turned in my direction and smiled. The whole world fell away in that smile.

Before she had a chance to say anything, I pulled her flush to me and set my lips on hers. There was nothing subtle in my technique as I claimed her, plunging my tongue inside her mouth and tasting caramel and sugar, alcohol and Annabelle, an intoxicating combination. The hard-on I'd barely controlled after the show roared back to life as I molded her soft body to mine. For good measure, I ground my hips into hers, making sure she understood exactly what state I was in.

She pulled back, panting. "I may be a bit of a show-off too, but there's no way I'm giving you that in a room full of people."

"Awww, come on, Annababy. Where's your sense of adventure?" I pretended to whine.

"I left it in a dressing room on Rodeo Drive this morning," she sassed.

I couldn't control the smirk on my face. Good to know that underwear excursion played in her head too.

With her safe in my arms, I'd completely forgotten about Bailey until he spoke up from somewhere beside me. "Nice talking to you, Annabelle. Great show, Dakota. Best one I've seen you boys play." Grinning, he gave me a slap on the back and slid off the barstool. He grabbed his beer and ambled off into the room.

Judging from Annabelle's tiny gasp when he interrupted us, she'd forgotten Bailey for a minute too. I had to admit that made me happy. Over the last month, I'd discovered that unlike other women I'd met, Annabelle was too special to share with anyone.

"Thanks, man," I said over my shoulder and returned my attention to the hot woman in my arms. "I'm always horny after a show, but tonight was epic, and I can't jack down." Moving slowly and deliberately, I dry-humped her right there in front of the bar, leaving her no doubt what I wanted—what I needed right then.

"Dakota!" she hissed. "This place is full of fans with backstage passes and cell phone cameras. I don't want to end up on *TMZ*."

"All right then, come with me."

With my arm wrapped tight around her waist, I kept her tucked up close and guided her toward the hallway back to the locker room. When people called out for my attention, I gave them a wave over my head and kept moving. If I didn't get inside Annabelle in the next few minutes, no doubt I'd explode.

One second after the locker room door closed behind us, I pinned her to the wall and devoured her mouth with mine. I filled my right hand with her full breast while I held her steady with my left hand at her hip. Kneading and squeezing her through her clothes only marginally satisfied me, so I slipped my hand up her shirt, pushing it and her bra up to expose the naked weight of her breast to my needy palm. Her nipple pebbled at my touch, and I didn't even try to stifle the groan that escaped my throat as I pulled away from her mouth.

For a second, I stared at her luscious body in the harsh glare of the overhead lights. If anything, she puckered even tighter, her nipple hardening under my gaze as I swooped down to take her into my mouth. As I sucked her hard, a scream tore from her throat, and I hummed against her, her response turning me inside out. While I continued pleasuring her nipple, I feathered my fingers over her taut belly until I reached the waistband of her jeans. After making quick work of the fly, I slipped my hand inside to discover that she was 100 percent in this with me. Her sexy lace panties were soaked. Making this discovery, I smiled wickedly against her skin and sucked her hard one more time, pulling off her with an audible pop.

"Dakota!" she shrieked.

"Oh yeah, Annababy. I do love the sound of my name on your lips, especially when I'm sexing you up."

As I knelt in front of her, I tugged her jeans and panties down to her ankles. Leaning forward, I gave her clit a long slow delicious lick. She rewarded me with another shriek. Standing, I said, "Turn around, Annie and widen your stance. Put your hands on the wall and push your ass back to me."

She slanted me a saucy look and did what I demanded. After she situated herself, she looked over her shoulder and taunted me with a quirk of her brow. My eyes never left hers as I freed my cock from my jeans, rolled on a condom, and grabbed her hips to hold her steady as I thrust into her hard and deep. Jesus. Her heavenly body contracted around me, and I had to reach down and take hold of myself to keep from turning back into a sixteen-year-old and coming right then.

She dropped her head between her outstretched arms, her fingernails scratching against the wall as she pushed herself harder against me, silently begging me to keep going. How the fuck could

I say no to that pretty plea? As keyed up and turned on as both of us were, once I started thrusting into her, it didn't take long for both of us to take that ride into outer space.

Always horny after every show, I never had any trouble finding a woman willing to take care of me. But I'd never been this turned on before. Though I'd just climaxed like it was my job, pulled out of her, and sandwiched her between the wall and me to keep us both upright, I wanted her again. Now. I tried to attribute my hyper-horny state to the kick-ass show we'd performed, and certainly that was part of it. Still, I knew in some dark corner of my mind where I deliberately never shined a light that the intensity of my physical response to her came from something growing between us. And it wasn't only my Energizer Bunny dick.

So I tried distracting myself. "You enjoy the show, Annababy?"

"Which one?" she asked with a twinkle in her eye.

"The one on the stage, wicked girl." I couldn't help grinning. She elevated surprising me into a science. "What did you think of the hydraulics?"

"I think they're not quite finished doing their job."

My cock twitched against the cleft of her ass as she pushed back into me.

"The ones on the stage?" I asked, deliberately obtuse.

"The ones in this locker room."

She rubbed herself against me, and that was it. I pulled another condom from my wallet, and we blasted each other into space again.

By the time we returned to the backstage area, the after-party had started its migration back to the hotel.

"Hey Dakota, there you two are. We thought we"—Blu coughed into his hand—"lost you. We're continuing this little partay back at the hotel."

"We're coming," I said.

From somewhere in the background, Tron chimed in. "Thought you already did that."

Flipping him the bird, I said, "Fuck you, Tron." But I was laughing.

"Isn't that what I said?" he shot back with a smirk.

I aimed a half-assed punch at his shoulder that missed as he snickered and danced away from me. The other two with their arms around their ladies smiled knowingly at me. I exaggerated an eye roll and tightened my hand on Annabelle's shoulder, hugging her even closer to my side. We followed Tron out the back of the stadium to the line of town cars waiting for the band and the VIPs who were invited to the after-party.

"This looks familiar, Clio," Annabelle said over her shoulder as we neared the car in the front.

"Sure does," Clio replied with a grin.

A stab of jealousy pierced my chest as I thought about how many other rock band after-parties Annabelle had attended. Then she made it all better when she looked up at me and whispered, "But this time I've already had the hot lead guitar player—twice—with a promise for a third time. After the Red Rocks show, I only had hope as I climbed into a VIP car."

She gifted me with a wink and a wicked grin. Her expression shot directly to my groin, leaving me to adjust myself behind the fly of my jeans before I could slide into the back of the car after her.

Apparently, banging random rock stars hadn't been her MO when we met. The thought spread a warm glow through my chest, something maybe I should have worried about. In the moment, though, I could only care about celebrating the monster opening of our West Coast tour with its promise of being one of our best tours ever—in every possible way.

CHAPTER TWENTY-THREE

Annabelle

THE AFTER-PARTY DIDN'T wind down until nearly four in the morning. Somewhere around two as I exited a hallway bathroom outside the party suite, I spotted Garrett walking out with two groupies tucked beneath his arms. So engrossed with impressing his conquests, he didn't notice me.

Or so I thought.

When my phone chimed a text at the ungodly hour of 10:00 a.m., I couldn't believe he expected me back on the clock. Since Dakota—okay, yes, and I—wanted another round of hot sex after the party, sex which lasted a little longer than the exciting moments in the locker room right after the show, I'd only been asleep for about four hours.

With a groan, I covered my head with my pillow while beside me, Dakota snored softly, completely oblivious to his manager's demands on me. When another insistent text interrupted the quiet of our suite, I knew I couldn't risk ignoring Garrett or waking Dakota for the chance of a little more sleep.

Though I tried to stifle it, a deep sigh escaped me as I rolled out of bed and stumbled to the bathroom for a quick shower. Not wanting to wake Dakota, I skipped blow-drying my hair, opting instead for a French twist I thought would carry me through the day. Considering Garrett's current mood, I needed to be prepared for anything, so I slipped a neon green and turquoise knee-length sheath dress over my head and stepped into a pair of low heeled sandals I could wear all day. After applying a light touch of makeup—mascara, a flick of blush, and a lick of pink lip gloss—I slid my makeup bag into my oversized purse along with my laptop and tiptoed to the door of the bedroom.

All the while I readied myself for the day, Dakota slept like a stone. His cheek rested on one forearm while he'd flung his other arm across the mattress where I'd been sleeping twenty minutes earlier. The covers had slid down his beautiful broad back to rest over his perfect ass. I gave myself thirty seconds to take in every aspect of his sexy bed hair, the dark beard stubble shadowing his jaw, the gorgeous lines of his muscular arms and back, defined even in sleep. Damn. Dakota Perri could induce *People* magazine to release a "Sexiest Man Alive" edition every single month of the year with him gracing the cover. With any luck, however, no one else would ever see him like this.

I jerked my wayward thoughts to an abrupt halt. I had no claim on him. No matter how hot—and frequent—the sex, that's all it would ever be with him. This whatever-it-was between us would only last the duration of the tour—if even that long. With a shake of my head, I chastised myself for my silly thoughts and shrugged on another layer of armor to shield my emotions. Hopefully, it didn't have any chinks in it. My phone signaling another insistent growl from Garrett mercifully pulled me out of my head and back into the moment.

With a soft snick of the door locking behind me, I exited the suite, careful to make sure the Do Not Disturb sign remained attached to the door handle. As I hurried to the elevators, passing the suites belonging to the other members of the band, each with a Do Not Disturb sign, I couldn't help the uncharitable thoughts invading my mind. Though I knew I was the only woman with the band who had an official job to do, I couldn't help resenting my friends a touch for not being at Garrett's rather capricious beck and call. Apparently, I'd need to adjust my party attendance if I planned on catching even a little sleep during this tour.

Quick on the heels of that thought ran another. If I didn't attend the parties, wasn't I inviting Dakota to find other women to enjoy? If he did, where did that leave me—literally? Sharing a bed with Dakota and some stranger? The thought left me cold, something that must have shown on my face when I stepped off the elevator and nearly walked straight into Garrett Phillips who seemed to be timing my arrival in the lobby.

"About time. As I recall, you're being paid to do a job here."

The snide tone set my teeth on edge. Forcing myself to pull in a discreet breath, I said, "No one told me there were specific hours while we're on tour. Since the band is playing three shows at the Coliseum before moving on to San Francisco, I thought—"

"It's not your job to think, Annabelle. The band goes out and plays tourist when we're not en route to another venue. The help has work to do."

He turned on his heel and walked away, clearly expecting me to follow him like some lackey. Glaring daggers at his back left me feeling childish and powerless, something his condescension had reduced me to. However, I had no choice but to follow him as he led the way through the lobby and outside to a waiting town car.

When I climbed into the car behind Garrett, I looked up to find Bailey Saunders seated across from me. The questions in my mind reflected in the dark chocolate of his warm eyes.

Slanting me a look, Garrett explained, "We're meeting the promoter for breakfast to do some advance planning for the shows in San Francisco. He's been making some noise about the band's requirements concerning the hydraulics on the stage and the fireworks. I need you to explain the safety basics to him, Bailey." Turning to me, he added, "I need you to smooth over any rough spots in his attitude, Annabelle."

My blood first ran cold then flashed fire. "Exactly what are you asking, Garrett?"

"You know. Be nice to him. Maybe linger after breakfast and show him the photos from last night's show, explain the T-shirt challenge."

Behind the oiliness of his tone, I could hear steel, but before I could challenge him, Bailey stepped in to defend me. "You wouldn't be suggesting Annabelle prostitute herself for the band, would you Garrett? Because I don't think any of the guys would appreciate that, least of all Dakota."

Garrett waved him off. "Of course not. She can lead him on a little, make him think he has a chance as long as he plays ball with us."

Garrett held my future in the palm of his hand, and he knew I knew it. Yet, no matter what I did here, I couldn't win. If I gave in to his demand, he could come back at any time and out me for using my body to promote a business goal. If I didn't do what he wanted, he could end my internship in a second and send me home.

There was no choice.

"No."

"What do you mean, 'No'?" he demanded.

"No," I repeated. "No. I will not throw myself at that scarecrow with the pretentious name so you can use me to get more out of him. The shows are sold out for the entire tour. Beyond making sure the venues are ready for when the band arrives, he doesn't have much to say about it."

"Exactly. Weren't you listening?" Garrett rolled his eyes at me like he was talking to a toddler. "Barton is making noise about not preparing the venues for the style of show Balefire plays. We need you to convince him to play along with us. It's not asking much for you to flirt with the man, Annabelle. It's not like you haven't already used your considerable talents to flirt your way onto this tour."

Involuntarily, my head snapped back as if he'd physically slapped me across the face.

Before I could respond, Bailey rescued me—again. "That was low, Garrett. It's also kinda surprising after what happened with Ashleigh Baker on the band's last tour."

"Not the same thing at all."

There was something petulant in the way Garrett replied, but I was too preoccupied with his implication that I'd slept my way onto this tour to give it much attention.

Bailey interrupted my thoughts. "Annabelle won't need to flirt with anyone she doesn't want to. By the time I finish explaining to the promoter how we roll, he won't have any concerns. We have a spotless safety record for a reason, Garrett. Something you should have already convinced the man of."

Bailey stared him down until he finally looked away through the tinted glass at the passing scenery. Then Bailey turned those dark brown eyes on me, the concern in them clear as he mouthed, *You okay?*

I nodded and turned unseeing eyes to the other window. The ride to breakfast lapsed into tense silence. I didn't know who was vibrating the most—Garrett, Bailey, or me. It felt like the men teetered on the edge of something explosive while all I wanted to do was return to the safety of the suite I shared with Dakota. And what did that make me?

♪

"There you are, Annabelle! Where the fuck have you been all morning?" Dakota demanded when I keyed into our suite.

Bailey stood behind me in the hall. After escorting me away from Garrett, he'd spent the elevator ride up to my floor reassuring me that the band would see to Garrett and his shenanigans. Which

Dakota made hard to believe when he spotted Bailey standing there. "What the fuck were you doing with him?"

Before I could answer, Bailey said, "Chill, Dakota. Garrett demanded that Annabelle and I have breakfast with him and the promoter. Since that creeper decided to ride back to the hotel with us, I thought I'd make sure he didn't try to bother her when she returned to her room." He pointed a look at Dakota. "You're welcome."

Dakota's eyes never left mine as he said, "Thanks."

"Thanks, Bailey. For everything this morning. I truly appreciate it."

"Anytime." He nodded. "You don't ever need to ask."

With a tiny salute, he turned on his heel and walked back to the bank of elevators.

I closed the door to the suite and sagged against it.

"You wanna tell me about it?"

"I don't think it was such a good idea for me to come out on tour with you guys. Maybe I should pack my stuff and fly back to Denver, help run the tour from the studio."

Feeling defeated had never been in my repertoire before now. Then again, I'd never had to deal with someone as hostile to me as Garrett Phillips. When I'd started my internship, he'd made a run at me, but I thought I'd deflected him rather deftly without any hurt feelings. Guess I was wrong.

Yet I had the weird sensation that this morning had been more about throwing Bailey and me together than about smoothing things over with the promoter who seemed fine with all the arrangements Bailey explained to him. Not that Barton Barton didn't make a clumsy pass—or six—at me during the ordeal otherwise known as breakfast. Still, he hadn't been the big problem. The big problem sat across the table from me watching me with the soulless eyes of a shark circling blood in the water. Whatever drove Garrett Phillips meant nothing good for me, I had no doubt. Better to walk away before everything I'd worked so hard for disappeared from my résumé with one keystroke.

Dakota smoothed his fingertips along my hairline and rubbed away the crease between my brows with his thumb then cupped the side of my face with his big hand. Staring intently into my eyes, he said, "*I* want you on this tour, Annabelle."

The deep timbre of his voice echoed through me, and I closed my eyes to hide my response. The power he held over me scared the hell out of me. I didn't need to add to my predicament by letting him see.

"Look at me, Annabelle."

It was no use. I couldn't deny his whispered command. Blinking my eyes open, I stared into the endless sea of his eyes and tried not to drown.

"I'll take care of Garrett. Stay with me. Please."

He set his mouth on mine, and the gentleness of his kiss nearly undid me. This was a side of Dakota Perri I'd never experienced as he held me quietly and explored my lips as much with his breath as with his touch. Without any conscious decision, I fisted my hands in the waistband of his board shorts as I held his body to mine and tried to capture his lips with my own. Framing my face with his calloused hands, he thwarted my efforts at deeper contact. Instead, he held me where he wanted me and continued his sensually delicate exploration of my mouth.

Every other time, Dakota dove right in, disarming me, claiming me, demanding I give him everything he wanted. This time, he butterflied his lips over mine, sipped me, teased my senses with his breath that tasted and smelled like mint toothpaste and Dakota. Vaguely, I thought his kisses might melt me into a mound of soft putty he could mold into anything he wanted.

Time disappeared as we stood in the middle of the suite quietly, easily, gently holding and kissing each other. When at last he pulled away, I swayed a little as I tried to right the world he'd tipped on its axis. Blinking several times, I focused on his beautiful eyes, which had darkened to midnight depths. I thought I saw desire there; then his nostrils flared as he sucked in a long breath and let it out slowly, his eyes returning to their normal sea blue.

"Hello Annabelle. You're back right in time to join me for a trip to the beach. Close the bedroom door when you put on your suit so you don't distract me, woman. I need some beach time."

With his hands on my hips, he turned me toward the bedroom and gave me a not-so-subtle push with his hands on my ass to make sure I'd follow his command. Gracelessly, I stumbled two steps then righted myself and hustled into the bedroom. Despite how aroused Dakota made me with his drugging kisses, the beach sounded like the perfect antidote to the morning I'd had.

♪

The water of the Pacific Ocean off the coast of Southern California in late summer definitely grabbed my attention when I raced head-long into it. I could hear Dakota laughing at me as I stood up in the frosty surf sputtering my surprise. "It's September, Annabelle. What did you expect?"

"It's Southern California. It's eighty degrees outside," I huffed.

He smiled and ran into the water. As he surfaced beside me, he shook freezing water all over my torso.

"Hey!" I shrieked as he picked me up high in his arms, turned, and launched me into the in-coming waves. When I came back up for air, I sputtered. "You are unbelievable!"

"In that perfectly tiny bikini, you're beautiful, all slick and wet," he said as he swam out to me. Catching me up in his arms, he planted a hard kiss on my mouth, pulled back, and licked his lips. "Saucy and salty too. Mmm, I think I could eat you up right here."

"Oh," I breathed as he slid his hands up my waist to cup my breasts through the thin fabric of my leopard-print bikini bra. My already hard nipples stiffened into needy little points beneath his clever thumbs, and I leaned in to his touch. A big wave lifted us high enough for my chest to clear the water, the sensation reminding me where we were.

"Dakota, you have a rather scary penchant for public sex. And I don't want to be part of the latest story on *TMZ*."

"Annabelle, look around. We're all alone out here. Relax."

Being a big-time rock star came with the perk of meeting and making celebrity friends. In Dakota's case, he counted Parker Malone, the popular bad boy of action movies, as one of his buddies. Parker owned a gorgeous bungalow with a strip of private beach in a quiet gated community populated with several millionaire businessmen and a few other celebrities. An outfit like *TMZ* would be hard-pressed to breach this exclusive little slice of Los Angeles. Which, of course, would make it even more enticing to them.

"Dakota," I warned.

He laughed and slicked his hands down my body to cup and squeeze my ass. "Their cameras can't penetrate the surf." He kissed me again, making me forget everything but his hard wet body pressed to mine, his hands stroking and kneading the globes of my ass, his tongue dancing erotically with mine.

A wave crashed into us, breaking the kiss and the spell he'd woven over me. Like he could read my mind, he smiled wickedly. "Play with me, Annabelle." He splashed water at me and swam away. The afternoon quickly devolved into a water fight that I lost rather badly.

At last, I dragged myself from the surf and made my way back up the beach to Parker's house. After rinsing off in the outdoor shower on the edge of his flagstone patio, I walked a few steps back out onto the sand and stretched out on the towel I'd left there before my initial foray into the ocean. Closing my eyes, I savored the heat of the sun drying the droplets of water on my skin and warming my body. I might have drifted off if not for the naughty man responsible for bringing me to the beach.

Freezing cold water splashed over my chest, rolling in rivulets down my belly to pool in my navel. Screaming my indignation at Dakota's games, I surged up only to be met by his big hands on my shoulders urging me back down on the towel as he proceeded to cover me with his hard wet body.

"Dakota Perri, you're an asshat."

"Worth it to watch your nipples pucker up." He grinned without a shred of apology.

Before he could finish what he clearly had intended to start, Parker's housekeeper called to us from the patio. "Mr. Perri, Miss Stewart I've set out some refreshments for you. Please help yourselves whenever you wish." Carissa, Parker's pretty housekeeper, smiled at us and disappeared back into the house.

"Whenever we wish, Annabelle," Dakota rumbled from deep in his throat.

My reaction to the plans he'd been developing for us behind his board shorts—where I currently cradled him at the apex of my thighs—was pretty obvious. With the first words out of the housekeeper's mouth, my entire body stiffened. At the mention of food, my stomach gave a gauchely loud grumble, ending the discussion about beach sex before it began.

While we enjoyed the ocean and private beach, Carissa worked on showing her appreciation for Dakota's generosity with the concert tickets he'd given her when we arrived. A feast of seafood cocktail and exotic fruits like mango, papaya, pineapple, guava, kiwi, and some I didn't recognize awaited us on the patio. Alongside the food, a pitcher of sangria sweated in the afternoon heat.

Dakota poured a tall glass and handed it to me then poured one for himself, downing half of it in one long swallow. "That's Carissa's specialty. The best sangria you will ever drink. Try it," he said, finishing off his glass and pouring himself another.

Watching his throat work as he downed the cool drink mesmerized me. When he pulled the glass away from his mouth and winked, I grabbed my own glass and gulped half of it down without tasting it at all. As hard as I tried to maintain some self-control, the man was sex on a stick, and he knew it. And exploited it.

"Like what you see, Annababy? You can have it anytime—any-where—you want. Just say the word."

Pretending to maintain my equilibrium, I lifted my chin. "I'll keep that in mind."

A laugh burst out of him, and I knew my little show of bravado hadn't fooled him a bit. It didn't matter that I was serious about not wanting to end up in the tabloids in some compromising situation that would derail my chance for acceptance into a top graduate business program. Dakota didn't want me resisting him—for any reason—and went out of his way to make sure I understood that. If not for the timely interruptions of big waves and a tiny housekeeper, he would have enjoyed public sex with me at least twice already on this trip to the beach. We'd already gone there in a dressing room in a boutique and in a locker room after last night's show, and today was only the second day of the tour.

Oh, boy, was I ever in trouble.

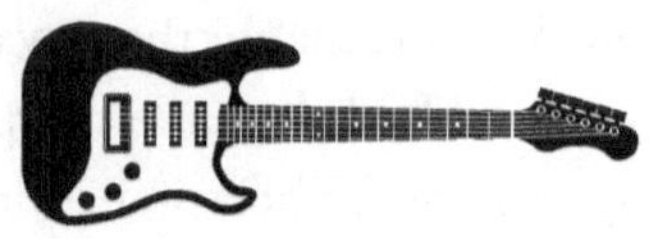

CHAPTER TWENTY-FOUR

Dakota

THAT WOMAN. SHE slays me. A leopard-print bikini. Hottest damn thing I've ever seen. But she wouldn't let me take it off her until we were in the shower back at the hotel. She let me have her in a public dressing room with a crew of giggling bridesmaids in the rooms beside us but wouldn't give in on a private beach. Annabelle was an enigma. And she was going to need more animal-print underwear in the near future. The champagne lace thong and bra I'd watched her put on beneath her leather miniskirt and tight red T-shirt would be on my mind all through tonight's show, though, no matter what the fans threw on stage.

A smile stretched my lips as I recreated the picture of her in nothing but her underwear while she stood before the closet deciding what to wear. All that dark hair cascading down over her shoulders in waves. The light-colored lace of her thong framing the perfect globes of her ass and showing off the way the sun had painted her skin golden over the course of our afternoon. Thoughts of my day with Annabelle left me half hard.

"What the fuck, Dakota? Where'd you go?"

I shook my head as Blu waved a hand in front of my face close enough to bump my nose. Batting his hand away, I growled, "Whoa! Are you trying to mess up my face before the show?"

"Wouldn't be hard to do with you being so far into your head that you're MIA to the rest of us," he said laughing. "You have a good afternoon, buddy? Heard you took your girl to the beach."

Ignoring his reference to Annie being my girl, I replied, "The beach was awesome. Parker's got a sweet place."

"I notice he didn't contradict you when you mentioned 'his girl.'" Tron used air quotes from his seat across from me in the town car. "'Another one bites the dust,'" he sang, his hands banging out the rhythm of the old Queen song on his thighs.

"Fuck you, Tron. Annabelle and I are just having some fun on this tour."

"It's your story, Dakota. Tell it any way you want," he said, a grin spreading wide across his face.

"Heard you took her underwear shopping yesterday," Jack chimed in with a smirk. "What's up with that?"

"Since *someone*"—I stared pointedly at Garrett—"implied to Annabelle that she wasn't going out on tour with us, she wasn't packed when I arrived to pick her up. Since *someone* else"—I shot a glare at Jack—"thinks he can one-up me all the time, she forgot to pack underwear before I hustled her out of her place and out to the airport. So she needed some. But if you haven't done it already, you two should take your ladies underwear shopping. I highly recommend it," I finished with a grin none of my friends could misinterpret.

"Aren't the groupies supposed to throw the panties at you rather than you buying panties for them?" Garrett groused from the corner of the limo where we always made him sit.

"For the last time, Garrett, Annabelle isn't a groupie, and you damn well know it."

For a fleeting second, even I wondered at the intensity of my immediate response to his bullshit. Instead of the guys flipping me shit over it, they jumped to Annabelle's defense.

"Watch it, Garrett. She's one of Clio's best friends."

"Like Ashleigh, Annabelle has worked her ass off for us. And I don't mean between the sheets."

"Pokin' the bear is never a good idea, man. You should have learned that already, Garrett. What the fuck is wrong with you?"

"Fine. Whatever," Garrett replied, but he didn't sound in the least apologetic.

Honestly, I couldn't figure out the man's problem. Neither could the rest of the guys, judging from the rolled eyes and arms crossed over chests as everyone sort of relaxed back into their seats. Yet Garrett's comment hung in the air like he'd fouled it.

"I was thinking, after my solo, maybe I could play two songs from my hydraulic stage. Good idea, huh?" I asked to detonate the silence Garrett's remarks dropped inside the car.

"Compensating for something?" Tron drawled.

"Not from the reactions of the ladies," I reminded him. But the only lady I could see in my mind's eye was driving me crazy with her combination of wicked-awesome bedroom skills and general gorgeousness and willingness to have fun with me.

"They're jealous, Dakota. Don't mind them," Jack said with a smirk.

"If all of you are using hydraulics, the crowd on the floor won't be able to see you, much less be able to throw their pretty underthings at you. You ever think of that?" Garrett grumbled from his corner.

"Awww, someone in the cheap seats made a point, and it's not even on top of his head," I teased.

The guys cracked up. Tron reached into the minibar, grabbed some beers, and passed them around, mellowing out the mood. The hydraulics jokes devolved into something raunchy, relaxing us by reminding us how much we enjoyed being together and playing music and leaving Garrett's bad mood in the dust. By the time we reached the Coliseum, we were psyched for the show.

♪

Like the night before, the girls were waiting in the VIP section when we stepped out onstage. Once again, my focus zeroed in on Annabelle, whose megawatt smile shined hotter than the spotlights illuminating my entrance. We were halfway through the first song before I could jerk my eyes from hers. Somewhere during the second song, I noticed Parker Malone standing next to her when he leaned down to say something into her ear. She nodded, looked straight at me, and winked. I didn't even realize I'd tensed up at seeing Parker speaking to her so intimately until my fingers relaxed against my fretboard.

Parker waved and gave me a thumbs-up. His action drew my attention to the blond bombshell standing on his other side, and I recognized his costar from the movie he was currently filming. I winked back at Annabelle and turned my attention to the crowd on my side of the stage, opposite the VIP section. Annie's focus remained on me. I could sense it almost like a caress over the skin on my back, an encouragement that left me feeling ten feet tall and bulletproof. And I played like I was both of those things. In response, the crowd lost its shit in a screaming and cheering frenzy with bras and panties raining down on us like a monsoon. When I looked back at Blu and Tron, they were grinning and nodding, our sound even tighter, more focused than usual. The opening night of our tour had been over the top, but this show was shaping up to be epic.

By the time Bailey came out to rig me to my hydraulics, I was sweating a river. "When you come out to unclip me, could you bring me a fresh T-shirt, buddy?" I asked as he made quick work of prepping me for liftoff.

"Sure thing," he said and melted back into the shadows.

Earlier in the day when I'd awakened alone in the suite, I'd been pissed until I saw the note Annabelle had taped to the bathroom mirror. While waiting for her, I worked on adding more bars to the song I'd been writing most of the summer. As the hydraulics raised me up into the air, I turned loose with those new notes, and the crowd rewarded me with a roar of approval.

"Yeah, that's right. Being out here in LA sharing all your sunshine and energy inspires me," I said into my head mic as I finished playing the solo. The crowd gave me what I wanted, and I grinned. "Wonder if it will inspire Blu to add some lyrics." From my perch two stories above them, I couldn't see the rest of the guys when they returned to the stage, relying instead on the change in lights to alert me that they'd finished their midconcert break.

"We're back to that, are we, Dakota? Lazy bastard just writes notes and leaves the hard work to me," Blu informed the crowd, much to their amusement. "Fortunately for him, I know exactly what words to add to his notes."

Blu let out a primal scream, my cue to play the opening bars of "High On You," and to my surprise, I remained high in the air for the entire song. Huh. Someone took me seriously when I said I should fly for more than my solo. Of course, I hammed it up on my axe, giving the crowd even more of a show. When at last Bailey lowered me and unclipped me from my personal stage, my legs were wobbly from holding my balance up there for so long. For a second, *be careful what you wish for* flashed through my brain. Bailey handed me a fresh shirt along with a different guitar tuned down for playing "Missing You," and I had to switch gears in a flash for Jack's mellow poem for Clio.

I couldn't be sure, but I think Annabelle looked relieved when Bailey lowered me back down to earth. Jack had already started into his opening drum solo for "Missing You," giving me no time to think about what her expression meant. When we segued into "Something's Gotta Give," I made my way across the stage to play for her, and she rewarded me with a smile and a salute from her flask, tipping it back for a swallow. The little worry I thought I'd seen in her eyes earlier vanished in her mischievous wink as she licked what was probably caramel vodka from her lips, leaving me half hard right there in front of God and everybody.

Later. I mouthed to her and turned my attention to the rowdy throng at the front of the stage.

After the show, she greeted me with a cold beer in the green room backstage. What I really wanted was a repeat of last night in the locker room, but the presence of my buddy Parker Malone and his date standing with Annabelle tossed cold water all over that plan.

"Damn, Dakota. That was a helluva show you boys put on out there tonight," Parker said. "Thanks for the tickets."

"It was the least I could do after you let us use your place today."

Parker Malone and his date Jennifer Hartwell weren't the only Hollywood types in attendance at the show and the after-party. Which meant I wouldn't be enjoying any alone time with Annabelle anytime soon. Because I couldn't help it and because I knew it was all I was going to get for a while, I dragged her into my embrace and kissed the shit out of her. Or lost myself in her soft, pliant body and the delicious taste of caramel vodka and pure Annabelle. Whichever. When she whimpered in the back of her throat and tightened her arms around my neck, I deepened the kiss and forgot all about where we were and who we were with.

An insistent, irritating poking against my bicep brought me out of my Annabelle-induced trance. "Save that for the hotel, huh?" Parker said, laughing as he gave me one last hard jab with his index finger.

Desire dilated Annabelle's gorgeous green eyes almost to black, and her plump full lips remained slightly parted in invitation. Somewhere in the haze of lust clouding my brain, I thought my expression probably mirrored hers. Never looking away from the pure hotness that was Annabelle, I replied, "Easy for you to say. You probably already got yours after work." I knew I sounded pouty, but I didn't care. I wanted—no I needed—twenty minutes of alone time with my girl, and it pissed me off that I had to wait for it.

Not caring one bit about my current state, Parker burst out laughing and nudged my hand where I still held the beer Annie had handed me earlier. "Drink up, Dakota, old man. Take the edge off. I liked the hydraulics in the show. Da-amn, they lift you right up into the sky. How cool is it to fly like that?"

At Parker's question, Annabelle tensed in my arms. *She* does *worry for me*, I thought. The idea heated the center of my chest.

"It's fuckin' awesome, man. We only practiced it with the solo. I'm going to have to do more squats in the weight room if I'm going to fly for several songs in a row," I said with a chuckle. I downed a long swallow from my beer and squeezed Annabelle tighter to my side when I sensed her go board stiff.

"I'm perfectly safe up there, Annabelle. I've got a back brace clipped into a belt under my T-shirt. You know that." I brushed a reassuring kiss over her temple, but she only marginally relaxed against me. Guess we were going to talk about my hydraulics later. The thought brought a smile to my face.

"What's that look for?" Parker asked.

"Nothing much." For Annabelle's ear only, I added, "Thinking about how I'm going to convince you later about the safety of my hydraulic lift."

As I hoped, she softened as she used her whole body to exaggerate an eye roll at my double entendre.

"Is the rumor true?" Jennifer asked. "Is Cristy Valor joining Balefire for tomorrow night's show?"

"Yeah. But don't be releasing that on Twitter. We want it to be a surprise."

"That's going to be quite a show with two stadium-filling acts on the same stage together," Jennifer said with a coy grin.

"Fine, Jennifer. You can have tickets for tomorrow night's show."

I sighed melodramatically. "I s'pose you'll want to bring him along too." I gestured toward Parker with my beer.

"How nice of you, Dakota," she said as she gifted Parker with a self-satisfied smirk.

"Did I miss something here?"

"Only Jennifer assuring me that no man can deny her when she truly wants something," Parker growled.

"Huh. Walked right into that one, didn't I?"

"Lucky me," Jennifer said.

Her hungry expression made me glad I had Annabelle beside me, and I squeezed her hip to let her know I had absolutely zero interest in the barracuda Parker brought along as his date.

"Whose idea was it to bring Cristy Valor onto the tour?" Jennifer asked.

I couldn't figure out why she was fishing, but it didn't matter. "It was Annabelle's suggestion. She's our marketing ace," I said not bothering to keep the pride out of my voice.

Inviting the hottest female act on the planet to guest on a couple of stops on our West Coast tour had been a stroke of genius, one that probably would mean more shows added to the tour before we finished it in time for Christmas. When Annabelle had suggested it at a marketing meeting with us early on in her internship, we'd all jumped on the idea. In fact, I was more excited than usual for rehearsals tomorrow afternoon.

Jennifer stared at Annabelle with renewed interest. "Your idea? Wonder what you could do if we turned you loose on our movie. What do you think, Parker?"

"Something to consider," he drawled against the lip of the bottle before he downed a long swallow of beer.

I didn't have to look at Annabelle to gauge her reaction to Jennifer's suggestion. Touching me from my chest to my hip, her body vibrated with the energy of her smile.

"That would be epic," she gushed. "I'd love the opportunity."

"Well, then. We'll have to run it by the producers," Jennifer said in a way that made me think she wasn't kidding when she said she always got what she wanted.

"Enough shoptalk. This is a party. Let's party," Parker said.

"I'm with you, man," I added as I finished off my beer. "I need another one of these." Holding Annabelle tight to my side, I headed to the bar.

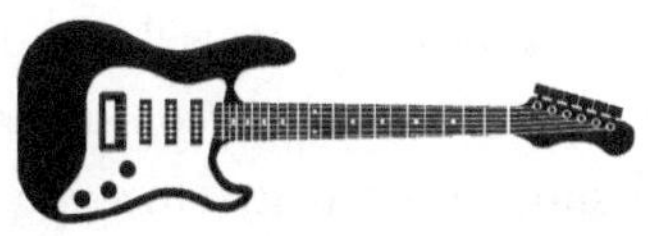

Chapter Twenty-Five

Annabelle

EXPECTING GARRETT TO ruin my day with another early morning wake-up text didn't stop me from staying out into the wee hours of the morning with Dakota and his friends. The band rocked the second show on the tour even harder than the first, so they were in a euphoric mood. Add to that all the celebrities in attendance—yeah, turns out Parker Malone and Jennifer Hartwell were the tip of the proverbial iceberg—and the after-party morphed into something nearly as epic as the show itself.

Tron started it by demanding everyone do Twangers. Then Blu lined up Scooby snacks, daring the rest of us to keep up. Somewhere along the way, Dakota decided to sip tequila—from my navel. After that, things became hazy.

By some miracle, I woke up in the correct suite, in the correct bed, with the correct roommate, and with no additional party people joining us. It took me several minutes to realize the reason I woke up emanated from the insistent chiming of my phone. When at last I located it in the pocket of my skirt lying on the floor half under the bed, the chiming had stopped, replaced by an angry red light indicating a waiting message. I didn't need supernatural skills to divine exactly who would be leaving me a message at the ungodly hour of—noon?

Shit.

I scrambled out of bed and raced into the bathroom with my phone stuck to my ear. Coming fully awake to the sarcastic tones of Garrett's voice did nothing for my burgeoning hangover, so I clicked off the message and shot him a text. Hopping into a mostly cold shower, I hoped it would stave off the nastier effects of too much alcohol and too little sleep.

For the second day in a row, I twirled my wet hair into a French twist and applied the most basic makeup. I prayed my outfit for the day—a pair of white Capri pants, a floral scoop-neck T-shirt in shades of peach, and a pair of medium-heeled Roman-style sandals—would be appropriate for whatever was on the agenda. After retrieving a bottle of water from the minibar, I let myself out of the suite.

Throughout all my preparations for the day, Dakota slept like a rock.

Lucky him.

As I exited the elevator into the lobby, I nearly smacked right into Bailey Saunders.

"Whoa, Tiger! Slow down! Nothing's on fire—yet." He laughed as he held me by the shoulders. His warm brown eyes danced as he grinned down at me.

"I overslept, and I have a meeting with Garrett and some of Cristy Valor's people in"—I checked my phone—"fifteen minutes. At the Coliseum. Obviously, I'm going to be late."

"No worries. I had some of the guys stay after last night's show to do some prep, so we're ahead for rehearsals today. Garrett sent me to pick you up for the meeting that's been moved back half an hour. You have time to eat something if you want."

At his suggestion, I must have turned a little green because he chuckled and said, "That bad, huh?"

Taking me by the elbow, he steered me into the bar off the lobby. When I gave him the stink eye, he laughed again and said, "Trust me."

A few minutes later, we walked out of the bar with two huge go-cups filled with some smoothie concoction both Bailey and the bartender guaranteed would make me feel better than normal before we arrived at the Coliseum for the meeting. In my current predicament, however, I would have tried anything. I needed to make a good impression on these people since their presence on tour had mostly been my idea. Not only that, but I didn't want to let Dakota—and the band—down.

Clearly, my most pressing problem was to figure out what to do about the after-party aspect of touring.

"What was that?" Bailey asked.

"Nothing. I need to rethink letting Dakota do shots from my navel is all." I sighed.

Bailey grinned and shook his head. "Don't worry. You'll have a rest day when we head north to San Francisco."

"That would be nice." I sipped at the fruity concoction with hints of coconut and something green—green tea and kale maybe?—and noticed a marked improvement in my headache and upset tummy. Maybe Bailey was right and things weren't as bad as I thought.

Dakota

We arrived for rehearsals with Cristy Valor at two in the afternoon, each of us in various states of hungover—even Jack, formerly known as the monk. Probably not the best way to meet her, but then again, we had a reputation as the bad boys of rock 'n' roll for a reason.

We earned it.

With pleasure.

Mostly.

When I stumbled into the green room, the first sight to greet my eyes was an intimate tête-à-tête between Bailey and Annabelle in a quiet corner of the room. For the second day in a row, I'd awakened to an empty suite, and I had to admit, the situation pissed me off. I wanted her along on tour for me. And I didn't feel like sharing.

Before I could walk over to interrupt that cozy little scene, Garrett sidled up to me. "Yeah, they've been like that since they arrived for meetings an hour ago."

"What time were your meetings?" I asked, though I never took my eyes off Annabelle.

"Noon. I sent Bailey to pick her up, and they got here around one I think. The rest of us were out onstage working on logistics, so I can't be sure if they showed up then or later." Garrett shrugged in a what-can-I-say sort of gesture. "Anyway, you need to meet Cristy."

He literally tugged me away from the scene I couldn't ignore in the corner of the room and walked me over to where the rest of the guys were making the acquaintance of our new partner on the tour.

"I caught last night's show from one of the VIP boxes. I love the hydraulics, but Jack only rises up once at the beginning of the show and stays there. With his huge drum kit, rising up once and staying there makes sense. The smaller hydraulic stage you use, Dakota, has lots more potential. I was thinking we could black out the lights, lift me up on that stage, and put a spot on me for my first song. What do you think?" Cristy was saying when Garrett and I joined her and my bandmates.

"I don't know, Cristy. Dakota won't share it with any of the rest of us, and we've even asked him nicely," Blu said with a smirk.

I flipped him the bird, which earned a laugh from all the guys. Addressing Cristy, I asked, "You come on after both Jack's and my solos, right?"

"Yes, in the last third of the show."

"Well, then. Make an entrance, girl." I grinned. "Light the place up."

"What the fuck, Perri?" Blu crossed his arms over his chest and stared me down.

I shrugged. "She's gorgeous, talented, and willing to let me have my stage first. She's our guest. What the hell? Sharing is caring," I singsonged at him, which had Jack and Tron cracking up.

"He's got you there, buddy," Jack added.

"Like we keep saying, Jack, it's easy for you to back Dakota because we lift you up on hydraulics every damn night," Blu grumbled.

"Clio hasn't mentioned one thing about Ashleigh complaining about your hydraulics, Blu. What's the problem?" Jack asked, his expression all innocence until you caught the gleam in his eye.

"Fuck you, Jack."

"Now, boys. I didn't ask about the hydraulics to start a fight. In fact, I didn't suggest it at all. It was Annabelle who thought it might be cool if I stayed true to form and made an unusual entrance," Cristy said.

"It was Annabelle's suggestion, huh?" I looked over to the corner where I'd seen her with Bailey. But she wasn't there.

"What was my suggestion?"

That voice I'd needed to hear since waking up alone in the suite came from almost directly behind me.

When I turned to acknowledge her, she peeked up at me and gave me a flirty half grin. All I wanted was to haul her into my arms and kiss the shit out of her, but we were in the middle of talking business.

"Hello Annababy. Missed you when I woke up."

She blinked at me.

"I think maybe we need to discuss your hours."

"Now is not the time for that, Dakota," Garrett butted in. "Shall we start the rehearsal?"

Never taking my eyes from Annabelle's beautiful green ones, I addressed Garrett. "Do something about Annabelle's hours, Garrett. While you're at it, remember who she's with."

Her eyes rounded at my words or maybe my tone. Didn't matter. She was mine, and I wanted people to remember that.

"Does that mean you like Annabelle's suggestion, Dakota?" Cristy asked, a speculative expression crossing her face.

Annabelle slanted me a look, and I blinked away the spell her presence alone seemed to cast over me. "Yeah. If it's not using the hydraulic lift too much. Right, Garrett?"

"No one's likely to want to throw panties at Cristy, so it'll probably work."

Cristy planted her hands on her hips. "Hey. I appeal to the ladies too, Mister."

Her comment broke the tension. We grinned at each other, and everyone headed out to the stage for rehearsals. I slid my arm across Annabelle's shoulders and held her back, letting the others move several steps ahead of us.

"I missed you when I woke up, Annie-girl. Why didn't you wake me before you left?" I whispered against her temple as I inhaled the sunshine and coconut smell of her hair.

"You were sleeping so soundly, and I knew you didn't need to be here as early as I did, so I let you be."

I liked the way she stilled and then melted against my side—even though her words didn't make me happy. "What time was that?"

"Garrett called and left a message at noon. I was supposed to be here at twelve thirty, but I desperately needed a shower, so I took a cold one, which is why I didn't look all that professional for my first meeting with Cristy Valor. They moved the meeting back, so when Bailey came to pick me up, I made the meeting on time, miraculously."

"Maybe you don't need to spend so much time with Bailey, hmm?"

"But—"

I cut off her protest with a kiss. I meant it to be a little reminder that on this tour, I was her man. As usual when it came to Annabelle,

I couldn't stop there. Hauling her body flush to mine, I deepened the kiss, and she came along for the ride, pressing her luscious breasts into the hard planes of my chest and wrapping one hand around the back of my neck while she anchored herself to me with her other arm around my shoulders. The round globes of her ass filled my hands perfectly as I held her to my groin and let her feel exactly the effect she had on me.

Our lips fit together like they were made for each other. Our tongues playing together lit my whole body on fire. I felt as much as heard her whimper as I kissed her exactly the way I'd wanted to since I first saw her when I walked into the green room.

A rather loud throat-clearing penetrated the lust-induced fog in my brain, and still, I had to take a couple of additional sips of sweetness from Annabelle's lips before I could clear my head enough to pay attention to anything else.

"Yeah?" I growled, my eyes never leaving the gorgeous green of Annabelle's eyes softened by the same lust overwhelming me.

"You're needed onstage, Dakota." Bailey turned and slapped his hand against the frame of the door.

"Duty calls, Annababy," I said with a grin. "From now on, I want you to wake me up exactly like this before you hare off to some meeting or whatever shit Garrett dreams up. Got it, babe?"

"But Dakota—"

I stilled her argument with a finger to her lips. "No buts. I used to be a big fan of sharing, but I'm finding I like it less and less these days. Promise me."

"Dakota, I have an internship with the band. That means I'm working on tour too."

"Not instilling a lot of confidence there, Annababy."

She huffed out a breath. "You ask a lot, Dakota. I don't want to blow this opportunity."

"Better. Now we gotta go see about making something epic, what with bringing Cristy in with us being your big idea and all."

I grinned and grabbed her hand, pulling her along behind me to the stage.

♪

"That was fuckin' awesome!"

"Best show we've ever done!"

"I'm going to kiss Annabelle all night for coming up with that idea!"

"Damn, that was fun. I want to kiss her for that idea too."

"Not sharing, Blu. Besides, you've got your own lady."

We were in the passageway between the stage and the green room after coming off probably the best show of our career. The energy and the crazy Cristy Valor brought with her considerable talent complemented our set like we'd been playing together for years rather than for the first time.

The woman in question strolled down the hallway behind us. "Boys, I absolutely loved working that show with you. That was almost better than sex."

"Someone needs to help you with sex, Cristy." I laughed. Turning to Tron, I added, "You hear that, buddy? As fucking outrageous as that show was, it's not as good as sex. Maybe you need to change that for Miss Valor."

"Or you could, Dakota," Cristy purred in her sultry voice that sounded like whiskey and sin when she wasn't using it to sing.

"Sorry, gorgeous, but my bed's taken. As are Blu's and Jack's. But Tron's is available. Ain't that right, Tron old man?"

"Gotta hit the showers. Wouldn't want to miss our own party," Tron said as he pushed his way past the rest of us.

Blu and I exchanged a look. *What the hell?* I mouthed.

Blu shrugged and followed Tron to the locker room.

Jack, as ever, stepped in to keep the peace. "See you at the party, Cristy. Fuckin' fantastic work you did out there tonight."

She didn't seem fazed by the lot of us at all. "Thanks, boys. That was definitely a good time."

Her entourage hovered behind her as she took another hallway to her private dressing room. Even for the short set she did with us, the woman changed four times, so she'd required her own space near the stage.

Jack and I hustled to catch up with Blu and Tron. Wanting private time with Annabelle vied with my euphoria over the outcome of the show. I'd barely seen her all day, and even as epic as our show had been, it absolutely didn't compare to sex with my hot lady.

Which I wouldn't be getting anytime soon. When we finished showering off the sweat and smoke from the show, we returned to the green room to find it swarming with VIP fans and several members of the press who wanted interviews. Garrett being Garrett and a pretty damn good manager when he wasn't being a douche to my girl, had arranged for extra publicity for the tour by setting up an impromptu press conference.

I didn't need to ask if my mates in Balefire were still buzzing with adrenaline and pent-up testosterone. My own body told me all about it, and I knew, like always after a big show, the other guys were in the same shape. No matter how wild Cristy acted, it was anyone's guess what she felt. We gave the press exactly ten minutes before Jack, Blu, and I sought out our women.

I'd be lying if I didn't admit to feeling relief at finding Annabelle chatting with Clio and Ashleigh rather than sitting at the bar having a drink with Bailey. 'Course tonight Bailey would be busy overseeing the teardown of the sound boards and amps to prepare for transport to our next show in San Francisco. It might make me an asshole, but the thought made me smile. No matter what, I'd be waking up with Annabelle in my bed in the morning.

CHAPTER TWENTY-SIX

Annabelle

IT HAD BEEN easy to keep my promise to Dakota the day after the band's first collaboration with Cristy Valor. In fact, waking up with him had meant the most incredible sex I'd ever had without the risk of having an audience. When he'd whisked me off to the end of a dark hallway behind the green room after the show, I couldn't resist him—like always. But I knew it was only a matter of time before his penchant for public sex would land me in an embarrassing situation. Yes, I was daring. Yes, I wanted to play with Dakota. Yes, locker room and dressing room sex were fun, in part because of the risk of being caught. The hallway last night? Not so much. Even though I think I was every bit as pumped after the show as he was, I'd taken it easy on the yummy vodka. Which meant my sense of reputation preservation made an appearance. Though I enjoyed myself because, well, it was Dakota, and I couldn't help it, I also couldn't get into it as much as usual.

He tried to mollify me by pointing out how Blu and Ashleigh walked ahead of us back to the green room, holding hands and looking at each other with blissful smiles. Clearly, they'd been the ones taking advantage of the locker room and the reason why the door had been locked when Dakota tried it. Pointing out that fact hadn't helped since it only served to highlight how close we'd come to someone catching us.

The morning after in our hotel room though was magical. If I wasn't careful, I knew I'd lose myself in the golden net of desire and fun he wove over me without even trying. He could be such a clown and a diva in public, but when it was only the two of us, he turned on the sweet. He didn't do charming with me, only sweet, and the more time I spent with him, the more I craved that sugar.

We ate a leisurely breakfast of bacon and eggs, croissants, fruit, and a pitcher of the mystical green smoothie hangover cure. By the time we'd showered—another experience in out-of-this-world sex— dressed, and packed, it was time to catch the tour bus. He grabbed my suitcase as well as his duffel bag, and we joined Blu and Ashleigh in the hallway outside our suite. Blu handled all of their luggage as well, and for a second, I felt like I belonged with Dakota and his friends. The overhead lights in the hallway flashed off the giant rock on Ashleigh's left hand, and I remembered myself.

"You look pretty good for as hard as you partied last night, my man."

"It's the smoothie. Looks like green slime, and I kinda have to hold my nose when I drink it, but it kills a hangover like a champ," Dakota said, setting down my case to fist-bump Blu.

"Prolly a good thing we didn't discover that cure sooner in our career, or Dave might not have been the only one to have to leave the Balefire party before it's over."

"You being all mothered up slowed you way down, Blu," Tron said as he closed the door to his suite. "I bet you didn't even need a smoothie this morning." He fell into step with the rest of us making our way to the elevator.

Blu shared a grin with Ashleigh. "Nah," he said. "That show last night was too epic not to celebrate properly. Ash and I both needed a smoothie this morning. It's all good now, right babe?"

She winked.

"The monk still sleeping?" Dakota asked as we awaited the elevator.

"I heard a bunch of noise about fifteen minutes ago. I don't think a smoothie takes care of a toddler who wants to see her daddy first thing in the morning," Tron said with a chuckle.

"Good thing we aren't racing to the plane today, then," Dakota said, visibly shuddering at the memory of what Jack planned for him if Jack beat him to the airport.

The doors to the elevator opened, and we crowded in together.

As though the conversation hadn't been interrupted, Blu said, "Actually, I'd like to see that."

"Fuck you, Blu."

"Yeah, me too," Tron added as though Dakota hadn't said anything. "'Course, we'd have a groupie riot on our hands that would likely put us all over social media for all the wrong reasons."

"Or maybe the right ones. We are the bad boys of rock 'n' roll, after all."

Dakota sighed and rolled his eyes. "Of *course* there would be a riot. Don't know if I can say the same if either of you paraded around an after-party in nothing but an apron though."

The guys and Ashleigh laughed at the image of Dakota serving drinks in nothing but a scrap of cloth, but the idea left me awkwardly uncomfortable. The history the band and Ashleigh and Clio shared didn't include me, and from the way I became invisible during the conversation, likely wouldn't include me much past the end of the tour—if even that long. I needed to remember that and keep my focus on the right prize. A positive review from my internship would open all sorts of doors for me. Fantasies of a future with a certain wild-ass lead guitar player needed to hit the exit sign in my head pronto.

♪

While the band partied, the roadies had spent the night tearing down the stage and the light and fireworks show and headed up to San Francisco ahead of us. The band had a day off for travel, which meant I could work at my computer from the luxury of a captain's chair on their gorgeously appointed tour bus. That was if Garrett—or Dakota would let me work.

As the bus pulled into traffic, it was Clio who interrupted me. "Annabelle, what did you think of the opening of the tour? Was it everything you hoped it would be?" She made herself at home in the seat beside mine.

"Where's Angel?" I asked when I noticed the toddler wasn't with her mom.

"She and her daddy were both cranky this morning," she said with a wink. "They're trying to catch a nap." She nodded in the direction of the master suite at the back of the bus.

"Too much fun last night, I take it?"

"That and Angel is teething again, so we didn't sleep much."

"Don't you have a nanny for that?"

"Yeah, but when you're hurting, nothing beats your parent. Last night, Angel insisted on that parent being Jack, even in his rather wasted state. Not even the magic hangover smoothie can make up for no sleep though," she added, a gleam in her eye.

"You seem rather gleeful at your husband's distress," I said with a chuckle.

"Do I?" She waved her hand. "Huh. After all those nights when Angel needed feeding, and she didn't care a bit that I had a test the next morning, maybe it's Jack's turn." The grin on her face was positively wicked.

"Sometimes, Clio, you can be pure evil."

"Me?" She widened her eyes. "There's not an evil bone in my

body. Naughty, maybe. Never evil." Turning sideways in her chair, she returned to the subject. "What do you think of the tour so far?"

The conspiratorial way in which she leaned over to ask left me no doubt what she wanted to know.

"There is so much more to touring than I thought. I had no idea how much behind-the-scenes work went into making a successful show," I deflected. "The opportunity to have VIP seats at the shows is epic. I love that part."

"I know what you mean. This is my second tour with Balefire, and every night is a new adventure." An impish expression flitted over her face. "But what about the best part of the tour?" she whispered. "What about you and Dakota?"

I stole a glance over my shoulder. The man in question kicked back in a captain's chair toward the rear of the cabin, a baseball cap pulled low over his gorgeous face, sculpted arms crossed over his impressive chest, long legs stuck out in front of him and crossed at the ankles. As I looked at him, I wondered when he'd had time to work out to look like he did. Of course, the tour had just begun, so maybe he gave himself a few days off at the start before he went back into a gym. I didn't know. I didn't know a lot about Dakota Perri, least of all how to answer Clio's questions.

"We've had fun, Clio. That's all it is. We're nothing like you and Jack or Ashleigh and Blu. We're both too wild for that."

"It's your fantasy, Annabelle. You can spin it any way you want. But I've noticed the way he looks at you when he thinks no one else is paying attention."

I slanted her a dubious stare from beneath my brows.

Carrying on like I hadn't responded, she said, "I've seen the way you look at him too."

My brows shot up.

"Like he's the sunshine lighting up your world. Honestly, Annabelle, I don't think I've ever seen the kind of wattage you flash when you smile at him."

I rolled my eyes and shook my head. "Whatever, Clio."

Her self-satisfied smile made me nervous.

"You being married and all, living your dream, has you building castles in the air for everyone else. Dakota and I aren't like Jack and you. In any way."

"You forget that I've seen Dakota in action. On the last tour, he was the definition of manwhore. The fact that he didn't have to share groupies with Jack and Blu absolutely delighted him. This time he hasn't even noticed when the groupies fall all over him. After the shows, he single-mindedly seeks you out and disappears with you for a while. When you two reappear, he never lets you out of his sight." Her eyes danced as she shared her observations. "He rarely lets you out of his arms."

Crap.

If Clio noticed that Dakota had spirited me off for a few minutes at each of the after-parties so far, who else saw us? Guiltily, my eyes drifted to Garrett who chose that moment to look up from his laptop. He raised one eyebrow and stared pointedly at the closed machine in my lap then back up at me, leaving me no doubt what he thought I should be doing.

"You're having such a good time in your happily-ever-after you think that's the destination for all of us. Some of us are pretty happily-in-the-moment, Clio." I leaned toward her conspiratorially. "And some of us become grumpy when interns don't work." Subtly, I nodded in Garrett's direction.

She wrinkled her nose and whispered back, "He's a good manager, but not such a great human being. I'll let you work."

She stood and made her way back to the master suite, presumably to check on her family, and I opened my laptop to check in with Caroline, Trevor, and Dan.

♪

One Dakota mystery solved. When we arrived at the hotel in San Francisco, Tron suggested the band hit the weight room, a suggestion the guys jumped right on. That explained how Dakota built and maintained that sculpted rock-hard body. I heard Jack invite Garrett to join the band, but apparently, the guy had a workout aversion or put his reps in by harassing me. At any rate, he declined the invitation in favor of dragging me out to the Fillmore where the band would play an intimate show the first night in San Fran before their stadium-filler at Levi's Stadium the second night.

"Do you have photographers lined up for this show, Annabelle?" Garrett demanded once we arrived at the venue.

"Our idea was to have the massive stadium crowds dressed in the T-shirts. Caroline and I didn't market the idea in the smaller venues."

"Rather shortsighted of you, hmmm? Perhaps you should make sure to have photographers on-site tomorrow night since it's an historic occasion."

"It is?"

"It's the fifth time the band has played the Fillmore, only the most storied concert hall on the West Coast, Annabelle."

The man was trying—and spectacularly succeeding—at making me feel imbecilic. Bobbing my head, I pulled out my laptop to research photographers who wouldn't mind dropping everything to take pictures of the fans at tomorrow night's show. I had the good sense to alert Caroline to the change in plans so she could put out a Facebook alert to the fans for the Fillmore event and every other show on the tour, including the smaller ones. It was going to take us years to go through all the photos to find exactly the right ones for the album cover, but I don't think Garrett cared about that—or about the marketing concept he'd signed off on in the first place.

After we finished inspecting the set-up at the Fillmore, we rode in silence all the way out to Levi's Stadium to see how the pyrotechnics and staging progressed there. By the time we finished inspecting the venues, Garrett dictating tweaks and changes to me the entire time like I was his secretary or something, we were long past dinner. My whole body sagged with exhaustion as I dragged myself into the lobby of the hotel. Only then did I realize I had no idea about my room.

He strolled purposefully to the elevator bank while I stood in the middle of the lobby trying to figure out what to do next.

As though he'd been waiting for me, Dakota materialized in the lobby and called out to Garrett, "Hey, asshole. Where the fuck have you had my girl all the damn day?"

Garrett turned around right as the bell above the elevator chimed a car's arrival. "She's along on this tour to work. Remember? We were working. At least when Annabelle could pay attention long enough to do that."

The triumphant gleam in his eye scared the shit out of me since I couldn't understand it or his words. I'd worked my ass off for him the whole day, so what did he even mean? But I was too tired to stand up for myself.

Turns out, Dakota had me covered. "Garrett, for the last time. Annabelle has done a kick-ass job on everything she's been asked to do for this tour. From now on, she gets off the bus, settles into our room, maybe grabs a meal." He stopped as if a thought occurred to him. "You did feed her today, didn't you?"

"We were busy. We had two venues to oversee you know."

"Seriously? You didn't eat?" Dakota asked me.

I shook my head.

"Dammit, Garrett. Didn't you learn fucking *anything* on the last tour? Come on, babe. Let's put some food in you."

Dakota draped an arm over my shoulders and led me away to the hotel restaurant, a five-star affair for a five-star hotel. Dinner was basically lost on me though. It was all I could do to keep my head off my plate during the appetizer. Dakota had the rest of the meal boxed and sent to our room. For the first time since I met him, our night didn't end with sex. Instead, he carefully undressed me and tucked me into bed. I don't remember him joining me there.

CHAPTER TWENTY-SEVEN

Dakota

"WHERE THE FUCK is Tron? For once, you guys aren't waiting on Annie and me," I said with a grin.

Annabelle stiffened at my side, but before I could process what that meant, Blu chimed in. "Cristy's missing too. Wonder that means." He waggled his eyebrows and grinned.

At that moment, Tron, looking pretty damn satisfied, strolled back into the green room behind the stage at Lumen Field, and two groupies slid beneath his arms like they belonged there.

"Huh." Blu shrugged. "Thought something might be happening between Tron and Cristy."

"Someone from Cristy's entourage said she'd meet us back at the hotel," Ashleigh said.

With her being a reporter and all, guess I shouldn't have been surprised she knew about Cristy's plans somehow. Too bad. I was kinda of Blu's opinion about Tron hooking up with that outrageous woman.

"Well then, let's get this party on the road!" I pulled Annabelle along with me as we headed out of the stadium to our waiting limos.

We'd rocked San Francisco *hard*. Even the intimate little party we threw for the fans at the Fillmore. I don't know how they managed it, but Garrett, Annabelle, and Bailey had everything in place for a live recording session at that show, and we brought the house. Cristy Valor's cameo teaser for the stadium show for the next night nearly fractured the fault lines beneath the city with her style and sass in that tiny concert space. When she joined in on "Outta This World," I thought the fans' thunderous response might bust that old place at the seams.

After a little foray inland to blow out Boise, we overpowered Portland. Tonight we took Seattle by storm. Every damn show on this tour so far topped the last one.

Cristy seemed to be baiting Tron at our shows now, sashaying up to him, running her hands across his shoulders, leaning in close as she sang her part. Watching her, you would have thought she sang duets with Tron rather than with Blu. Tron even missed a beat once, something I don't think he's done even in practice in five years. Yet tonight, when he joined the rest of us headed for the party at the hotel, he had a groupie under each arm and was giving each girl equal attention. From the way he and those girls were kissing, I wondered if they'd make it back to the hotel before they shared with him exactly how much they appreciated his musicianship at the show.

"Hello Dakota. Where'd you go?" Annabelle asked from my side. The look on her face told me I needed to set her straight about my thoughts real fast.

"I was thinking the way Tron and Cristy have carried on with each other onstage lately, maybe they were collaborating in other ways too." I smirked.

"Dakota Perri, I would have never taken you for a gossip," she teased as she relaxed against me.

"I'm not about spreading rumors." I grinned. "But I do like to razz the shit out of my friends whenever they present the opportunity. Thought Tron might give me that, but I guess not, dammit. Now, what did you think of the show?"

"I loved every second of it."

"Even when I lifted off into the skyline?"

"I might always be a little nervous when you do that, but I admit it's a cool effect."

I brushed a kiss over her temple and whispered, "I kinda like it that you worry about me, Annie-babe."

She rolled those gorgeous green eyes of hers, making me want to drag her off for another round of hot sex right there, but there wasn't enough privacy in the town car with the whole band piled in it together. I'd thought about indulging in two rounds when I sneaked her off to a private and conveniently unlocked office beside the locker room back at the stadium. Shoulda followed my instincts. Now I had to wait until at least a while into the party before I could steal her away for another round of epic sex.

When we arrived back at the hotel, I had to admit to feeling relieved at not seeing Bailey there for once. Made me wonder how much time the two of them spent together when Garrett dragged her off to "work."

Like he read my thoughts, Garrett materialized beside me as I watched Annabelle dancing with Clio and Ashleigh to some Cristy Valor number the after-party band covered.

"Annabelle is hot. I can see why guys gravitate to her."

"What do you mean, Garrett?" I growled.

"Oh, you know. It seems whenever we're working, she has two or three roadies—and Bailey Saunders—hovering around her, vying for her attention."

"Prolly 'cause you've given her some task that's not necessary for her to market the band."

"Everything I ask her to do is for the benefit of the band, Dakota. There's no question where my loyalties are."

The song ended, and Garrett melted away as Annabelle returned to me.

"Whew! Those girls wear me out. Honestly, I don't know how

Clio has so much energy after she's chased Angel around all day before a show," she said, panting.

The shine in her eyes, the gorgeous way her rack heaved as she caught her breath, the smile on her face at a wattage to blind a spotlight made me forget all about how much Garrett pissed me off.

"You girls know how to tear up a dance floor. I hope you've saved some moves for a private dance later," I said, smiling back at her.

Because I couldn't help it, I wrapped my arm around her and slid my hand down to palm her ass. The woman had one very fine ass, and the way she'd been shakin' it on the dance floor made my fingers itch to touch. Her hot pink minidress drove me crazy, hugging all her luscious curves perfectly. That and the fact I knew all about the sheer lacy teddy underneath it. Thinking about our last lingerie shopping trip yesterday in the Bellefleur boutique left me half hard, especially with Annabelle snuggled up tight to my side.

"Dakota, we're in public," she hissed in my ear, dragging my hand up to her hip.

"All the more reason to make sure all the assholes in the room know you belong to me."

She narrowed her eyes at me. "Marking territory is for some other species—I hope."

But she didn't move away from me. Instead, she reached for my beer and snagged a long swallow then ran the back of her hand across her luscious lips.

She baited me with that move, marking me as her man as surely as I'd laid claim to her. I threw my head back and laughed. "You're a piece of work, Annabelle Stewart."

I'd leaned in to nuzzle a kiss along the beautiful column of her neck when two fans chose to interrupt our moment.

"Dakota, you're the best lead guitar player in the world," the one in the barely there strapless minidress gushed.

"Yeah," her overly made-up friend chimed in. "Watching your hands move over your guitar mesmerized me." Her breathy delivery accompanied with the batted eyelash cliché would have cracked me up if I didn't feel Annabelle stiffen against me.

"Thank you, ladies. Glad you enjoyed the show."

"We loved it," the two said in unison.

"We'd love to show you how much we loved it," minidress purred as she boldly ran a neon green fingernail down my bicep.

"Have you met Annabelle?" I asked, nodding in her direction. "I'm with her tonight—and every night on this tour. But thanks for the offer."

They were fans after all, so I couldn't be rude and tell them to shove off. Didn't change Annabelle's attitude. If anything, her body hardened to stone beside me. Makeup looked like she wanted to say something, but I stared at her in a way she couldn't miss the message.

Minidress pressed on. "If you change your mind or you get tired of her, we'll be around." She flashed me what she must have thought was a winning smile, but all I could see was teeth.

"Ladies." I nodded in the direction of the dance floor, a clear signal for them to move on.

Minidress gave me a finger wave, and the two wandered over in the direction of Blu and Ashleigh. I might have warned my buddy, but one look at Annabelle, and I knew I had bigger problems to deal with.

"Dakota."

I cut her off. "Don't even go there, Annababy. I have zero interest in girls who dress like escorts and hide their other assets under six inches of makeup. I like my girl in a sexy dress, her hair in a ponytail, and a touch of color on her face." Emphasizing my words, I eyed her up and down, lingering on her breasts, her legs, leaning back for a view of her ass, and finishing up with a long gaze into her eyes. Because I couldn't help myself, I stared at her full mouth and gave in. I meant to reassure her with a little taste, but as usual with Annabelle, the kiss turned hot and dangerous within a nanosecond of our lips touching.

Without any conscious thought at all, I tucked her between my legs and filled my hands with her sweet ass while our tongues danced together the way I wished our bodies were dancing at that moment. Holding her, I kissed the world away from us. A loud throat-clearing from somewhere nearby penetrated the fog of lust kissing her always created in me. Slowly, I pulled away, leaving her with light pecks on those full lips before I acknowledged the person interrupting us.

"You two might want to take that somewhere more private if you don't want to end up in all the tabloids," Blu said, a smile playing over his mouth.

He nodded at something behind him, so I leaned back to see what he meant. Sure enough, some photographer had a zoom lens trained on us. At the short distance he stood from us, he could have practically taken a shot of my hard-on where it stood at attention against Annabelle's beautiful body.

"Shit. Who let them in here?"

"Hard to say, but short of making a scene, we're not going to avoid showing up in some rags. Just a heads-up."

"Thanks, man."

Annabelle kept her face turned away from the photographer, which probably was good since her cheeks were a delightful shade of pink. For someone who could make as much noise as she could in the sack, dance like a maniac with her girls, and indulge me with hot sex in some rather public places, she definitely had a shy side.

I willed her to look at me, but she kept her eyes averted. Blu's warning blew over us like a blast of Arctic air, and this time, I knew I wouldn't be able to kiss and cajole her back into playing along with me.

"It's too early to leave the party, Annie. We need to spend time with the folks who sprang for backstage passes. But we can put distance between us and *TMZ* over there. Come on."

I slipped off the barstool and with my hand at the small of her back, guided her into the crowd, surreptitiously moving us as far away from the photographer as I could. When we were on the side of the dance floor opposite the bar, I stopped. Annie still refused to look at me, directing a stony stare at the crowd in the middle of the room.

"Annabelle."

She wouldn't look at me.

"Come on, Annie-girl. Tell me what scary thoughts are sneaking around inside that gorgeous brain of yours."

With the pad of my index finger beneath her chin, I gently turned her face to me.

"I don't know, Dakota. Between the groupies who never stop coming on to you and the paparazzi who never stop invading your privacy, it's hard to be with you sometimes."

"They're part of the rock 'n' roll road show known as Balefire, babe. Nothing for you to worry about."

She raised a skeptical brow.

"I mean it. As weird as it is for me to admit, with you on this tour, I have zero interest in the groupie scene. I'm with a classy babe who makes me laugh and gives me regular and fucking outrageous sex. Why would I give that up for underdressed and overly made-up girls who have no interest in me as a person?"

"I can't imagine." The dryness of her tone alerted me to my error.

"Shit, Annabelle. I've never seen you underdressed or wearing too much makeup. Based on the way we reconnected, I'd say you thought about me as a person once or twice after that night too."

I grinned and sensed her relax.

"Dakota, you've seen me naked," she clarified.

"Which was the perfect outfit for the occasion. In fact, I'm looking forward to when you're wearing that outfit again after we jet from this party."

That pulled a smile out of her right as a camera flash lit up her face.

Dammit.

She turned her face into my chest, hiding from the photographer who kept snapping pics.

Honestly, her attitude didn't make a damn bit of sense to me. "Annie, what's the deal? You line up photographers for every show, and I know you've even aimed a few at the VIP section when you and your girls were sporting band tees. What's wrong with the guy taking a few shots of us at a party?"

"It's one thing to be one fan in a crowd and something else completely to be speculated about as Dakota Perri's latest conquest," she mumbled into my shirt.

"People knowing you're with me is a bad thing? What the hell?" I pulled back for a look into those eyes that haunted my dreams even when I lay in bed dreaming beside her.

"No, nonono, it's not that." She spread her hands over my chest. "It's just...I want to earn my MBA. You know that. But if admissions officers at business schools read the tabloids, they might have the wrong idea about me."

She started to piss me off. "What idea would that be, Annabelle?"

"That I'm a groupie for the biggest band on the planet rather than a marketing intern."

"Or maybe, you're my girl, huh? Ever think of that as a possibility?"

"Maybe we should discuss this some other time—in some other place," she said with a pointed look over my shoulder.

I turned slightly to find the paparazzi had stopped taking photos in favor of trying to move in close enough to eavesdrop on us. A picture of another woman who rejected me long ago flashed in through my thoughts. Ruthlessly, I shoved it out of my head.

"You're right. We'll finish this later. I see some people I want to talk to."

I walked away, letting Annabelle make up her own mind if she wanted to be seen with me anymore tonight or not.

CHAPTER TWENTY-EIGHT

Annabelle

THE BAND PLAYED two shows in Seattle then crossed the border to perform in Vancouver, Canada. After the concert, we spent a little downtime in Vancouver where Ashleigh led us on garden tours. The way she obsessed over flowers and the way Blu played right along with her gave everyone the warm fuzzies. I had no doubt the two of them would marry in late spring or early summer in some enormous flower bed somewhere.

What surprised me was how much Dakota played along with Ashleigh's love of flowers. The morning after the Vancouver show, he hustled me out of the room so fast I forgot to swipe on some makeup, and I think he zipped up my dress in the elevator because he didn't want to miss some botanical wonder Ashleigh gushed over at dinner.

Though he remained playful and never passed up a chance to sex me up, shadows rolled across his face sometimes when he looked at me. More than once, I also caught him glaring at Bailey Saunders for no apparent reason. Especially the day Garrett invited Bailey along on the garden tour. I don't think Dakota stopped touching me in some way—holding my hand, resting his fingers in the small of my back, draping an arm over my shoulders—that entire morning. Not that I was complaining, but I sensed something was off.

Obviously, Ashleigh had spent time researching Dr. Sun Yat-Sen Classical Chinese Garden since she chattered on like a tour guide as we wandered through it. We learned all about the garden serving as a symbol of peace between China and Canada and being the first "scholars" garden outside China. All the while she gushed over the balance of rocks and water, flowers and shrubs, Dakota kept shooting daggers at Bailey to the point of being embarrassing. Bailey mainly hung with Garrett or Jack and Clio who were taking their time letting Angel smell and touch the flowering plums and miniature rhododendrons.

Bailey must have picked up on Dakota's mood because as we left the private park and wandered into the adjacent public park, he stepped over to us. "I'm going for a soda. You guys want anything? Annabelle, would you like me to grab something for you?"

"A water would be good. Thanks," I said with a smile.

Dakota scowled. "I'll come with you, Bailey."

I shot a perplexed look at Bailey who shrugged and said, "Sure," before the two walked over to a refreshment stand set up on the edge where the public park segued into Chinatown.

What was that all about?

I barely finished the thought when Garrett materialized beside me. "Playing one off against the other, Annabelle? Are you trying to cause friction in the band?" he sneered.

"I have no idea what you're talking about, Garrett. There's absolutely nothing going on between Bailey and me, and you of all people know it."

A few minutes later, Dakota and Bailey returned. Bailey carried several cans of soda and a bottle of water, which he distributed to Jack and Clio, Ashleigh and Blu, and Garrett. Dakota tossed a can of soda at Tron and handed me a bottle of flavored water.

"Thanks, Dakota."

He nodded, so I cracked open the top, took a sip, and tried to figure out what I'd done to make him think he had a rival for my affections.

After the tour of the Chinese gardens, Ashleigh decided we should see another garden out on Victoria Island. But Angel needed a nap, so Jack and Clio called a cab to head back to the hotel. Before I realized what he had in mind, Dakota hustled me into the car with the Whitehorses, and the five of us returned to the hotel together. I had the good sense to wait until we were in our room to ask him why he cut our outing short.

"In case you didn't notice," he said, "I was having a lot of trouble keeping my hands off you this morning. Though I kept an eye out, I never could find a place secluded enough for a quickie. If you didn't look so hot in this sweet little sundress, maybe I could have restrained myself."

He trailed his index finger from the hollow of my throat down the middle of my chest, brushing the sides of my breasts with his fingertip. With his eyes following his finger, he couldn't miss the goose bumps his touch elicited, and he chuckled.

"Guess we're on the same page, huh Annie-babe?"

He leaned down and placed a hot kiss on my chest, tingling my skin and puckering my nipples into hard peaks. With a grin, he rubbed his thumbs over the front of my dress, and I couldn't stop the moan that escaped my lips.

Still, his playfulness in the moment made me wonder exactly what the deal was. Ever since Bailey offered to buy me a drink at the gardens, Dakota had been in a mood. Then his hand found its way under my dress to caress the top of my thigh, and I forgot all about gardens and drinks and weird vibes.

Every time he touched me like this, he made me forget every-thing but him. His calloused fingers and his breath on my skin always turned me on. The groans rumbling in his throat as he touched me left me no doubt I turned him on too, ratcheting up my desire. I buried my hands in the soft blond-brown waves of his hair and tried to push my body into his.

"Slow down, Annababy. We're gonna get there." He chuckled against my skin, yet his actions opposed his words when he grabbed the hem and whipped my dress up and over my head, dropping it on the floor beside us.

"Mmmm, delicious." His voice rumbled as he stared at the cerulean blue lace bra and panty set I wore. "Have I ever told you how much I love blue curaçao? Holy water is one of my favorite shots."

The question was rhetorical as he hauled me into him and kissed me senseless. His firm lips, his demanding tongue, his even teeth taking tiny nibbles of my full lower lip before he plunged his tongue back in for another drugging taste drove me to the edge of wild. An undercurrent of urgency vibrated below the surface of our lovemaking. In hindsight, I should have paid more attention. But Dakota demanded my body's complete attention, and I willingly gave it to him. Along with another piece of my heart.

♪

When we arrived in Las Vegas for three nights of concerts, the whole team—band, roadies, staff—came alive. Everyone enjoyed Sin City, which came as no surprise. After all, the band had a reputation as hard partiers always up for a good time.

The day we arrived, everyone headed for the blackjack tables. Apparently in the early days when the guys took turns driving their old bus, they passed the time playing poker. The roadies still spent much of their downtime playing cards, but somewhere along the way, monetary wagers went out of favor. Once when Garrett gave me two minutes to breathe and I asked Bailey about it, he said something about having to fire a good roadie over a bad wager on a previous tour.

But in Vegas, everyone could do whatever they wanted with

their money. Obviously, they wanted to risk some of it. Though Balefire paid me well, especially for an intern, I decided to follow Clio and Ashleigh's leads and be arm candy for Dakota while he challenged the house at the card table.

He played well enough to go up five grand before he decided to switch games. We strolled over to the craps table where people recognized him, and a crowd surged around us.

With a wink, he leaned in and whispered in my ear, "Hold on tight, Annababy. We're about to take a ride."

He placed some chips on the table, grabbed the dice, and rolled them around between his hands. Offering them to me, he said, "Give 'em some luck, Annababy."

I blew on the dice, and he tossed them across the table with a wild flick of his wrist. Rather than rolling, the dice bounced drunkenly, but he still managed a natural seven. The fans surrounding the table cheered, and he executed an exaggerated bow then grabbed his dice from the stickman. We repeated the ritual with me blowing on his dice and him tossing them wildly, and he won again. The shouting and applause at our table attracted more and more people until it looked like the audience stood at least five deep around us.

Dakota signaled for another beer and, laughing, turned to me. "Having fun?"

His hair had flopped down over his brow the way it usually did by the middle of a concert, the boyish grin on his face reflected on the faces of the fans closest to the table.

Smiling back at him, I nodded.

He glanced past my shoulder, and his grin disappeared. I shivered at the coldness in his expression and hazarded a peek over my shoulder. There were so many people there, I couldn't be sure who Dakota saw who upset him.

The stickman cleared his throat, and after a beat, Dakota turned back to the table and grabbed the dice. Instead of the ritual this time, though, he handed them to me.

"Your turn, Annabelle."

Slipping behind me, he wrapped his arms around me and took my hands in his to rub the dice together.

I glanced back at him for a second to see the grin back on his face, but his eyes looked like a storm at sea. I couldn't figure out what his problem was.

"Annie, you're too stiff. Relax, or we'll lose this bet. Come on, seven!" he called as he continued moving my hands over the dice. "Now, blow."

He lifted our hands to my mouth, and I dutifully puffed some air between them.

"On you now, Annabelle. Go for it."

Having never played craps before, I tossed the dice a little too hard, sending one over the edge of the table.

"Hey there, Ace. Jack it down, would ya? We're throwing dice not fastballs here."

I heard the playfulness slip back into his voice, and I relaxed into him. After losing the next five throws, though, I faced him. "I don't think dice is my game."

"Oh, I don't know, babe. I like the way you're throwing yourself into it."

"But I'm losing all your money."

"Are you having fun? 'Cause I definitely am."

It took me a second to register his pelvis pushing hard into my backside, with hard being the operative word. "Dakota! We're very much in public here," I hissed.

"A certain part of me doesn't pay much attention to that when your sweet ass is rubbing against it."

I could feel his smile against my ear, and I closed my eyes to control the way my body reacted to his words and to his body. Pulling in a deep breath, I willed myself to stay under control. When I opened my eyes and tipped my head back to look at him, I caught the flaring of his nostrils and the dilation of his pupils as he looked into my face. I guess he came to some kind of decision as he nodded once and turned his attention to the stickman.

"Apparently, the dice have turned against my lady. Time to call it a night."

Dakota smiled at the groans of protest from the gathered crowd and added, "Besides, someone else needs a turn. How 'bout you, Bailey?"

He looked over his shoulder, and I noticed Bailey Saunders standing near us. Somehow, I'd missed him earlier. Before I could acknowledge Bailey, Dakota collected the remainder of his chips, tossing several large denominations in the middle of the table for the stickman, and threw an arm over my shoulder to lead me away from the table.

"Thanks for the fun, party people. But we need our beauty sleep if we're going to entertain you tomorrow night."

Several people in the crowd snapped photos as we walked away, and I fought the urge to cover my face. I had to hope none of them were Facebook or Instagram friends with college admissions directors. Then the way Dakota revved me up in the elevator, I forgot all about camera phones and college admissions directors and crowds—in short, I forgot about everything but him. I barely kept my clothes on until we reached our suite.

Dakota

Annabelle lay quietly beside me, one arm flung across my belly, her legs tangled with mine, her soft breaths gusting over my chest as she slept. With my head propped on my hand, my other arm wrapped tightly around her waist, I lay awake, unwanted thoughts swirling in my brain. I knew the story of how Jack used Bailey's acquaintance with Annabelle to reconnect with Clio, but exactly how tight had Annabelle been with Bailey in the past? Judging from the way he looked at her his first day back to work, he'd had a thing for her at some point. Judging from the way he always showed up wherever Annabelle happened to be, he still had a thing for her.

Trouble was, I *really* had a thing for her, and for once in my rock 'n' roll-rodeo life, I did *not* want to share. All I could think whenever I looked at her, listened to her laugh, held her in my arms and made love to her was—*this girl is mine.*

Damn.

Bailey Saunders needed to realize that, believe that. Which is why I pulled her out of the casino when I saw him move in close. Unless he had the sensitivity of a brick wall, he couldn't have misunderstood the look I gave him when I saw him eyeing my girl. I didn't give a shit about their history. The only thing I cared about was my relationship with Annabelle, something important that was happening in the present.

Relationship? Where the fuck did that come from?

Yet as the word bounced around with the other thoughts keeping me awake, I couldn't help but smile. Dakota Perri in a relationship. Who'd a thought?

The idea of settling down with one girl should have terrified me, but somehow it didn't. Annabelle sighed in her sleep and tightened her arm across my waist. Maybe she was on the same page? Her unconscious move reassured me, relaxed me. I inhaled her spicy, citrusy scent and the smell of sex in our room. The woman tied me in knots, but I didn't want to be untangled. The last thing I remember before drifting off was thinking how happy my girl made me.

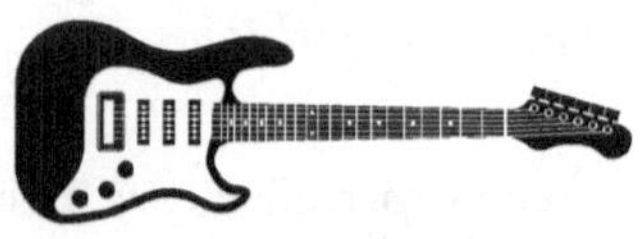

CHAPTER TWENTY-NINE

Dakota

"ANNABELLE, I'M NOT sure you know this, but it's hard to keep secrets from Dakota."

"He does have a way of looking at a person that makes you want to give it up, doesn't he? His eyes focus in on you like lasers and turn almost cobalt blue. Sometimes, though, his smirk lets you off the hook." She giggled. "Still, we only have to keep this secret for another day. Then he'll know all about it."

"Everyone will know all about it." The male voice paused then added, "You sure we shouldn't tell a few more people? It might make things a little easier."

"Like you said, Bailey, it's hard to keep secrets from Dakota. The fewer people who know on the front end, the better it will be."

I heard a shuffling noise then Annabelle said, "I gotta go. No doubt Garrett's on a rampage somewhere because I didn't do ten minutes ago whatever he only now decided needed to be done. I'll catch you after the show."

"See you then, Annabelle."

I stepped farther back into the shadows behind the massive

crates for our gear the roadies stored behind the stage. Annabelle hurried past where I stood, her gaze on her tablet as she seemed to unconsciously avoid cables on the floor like she'd been touring with us for a decade rather than a couple of months. Bailey whistled softly as he headed in the opposite direction behind the stage, and my hands fisted until they shook.

What the fuck? She's been playing me? For how long? She thinks I can tell when someone is lying to me? Really? 'Cause she sure as hell fooled me all night long. And this morning. And every damn day of this entire tour.

Vibrating with anger—and yes, hurt—I stood there and tried to process what I'd heard, fire flaring across my chest. I clawed at my throat as I struggled to breathe until I doubled over to steady myself with my hands on my knees as the worst pain I'd ever experienced threatened to suffocate me. My eyes swam as images of my eight-year-old self watching my mom drive away rose up in my vision while Annabelle's words echoed in my brain. *Still, we only have to keep this secret for another day. Then he'll know all about it.*

News flash, Annabelle. I knew the secret already. Only I wasn't a helpless eight-year-old anymore. I wouldn't be standing around tearfully watching as she walked out of my life. Dad was right. A man could never trust a beautiful woman. Good thing I figured her out before I did something really fucking stupid—like tell her I loved her.

Gritting my teeth, I held in my breath until I thought I could suck in air without risking vomiting my breakfast. At last I straightened, shook out my hands and feet, rolled my neck—a prizefighter prepping for the next round. Yeah, Annabelle might have knocked me on my ass, but I wasn't down for the count.

As I stalked out from behind the stage, Garrett materialized by my side. Not in the mood to talk to anyone, I ignored him, but as usual, he didn't catch on.

"Have you seen Annabelle, Dakota? I need her to check on the merch, and then she needs to catch up with Bailey—"

"I have no idea where Annabelle went, Garrett. She's your intern," I growled and kept walking.

"Trouble in paradise?"

"Fuck off, Garrett. You need to find Annabelle? Go find Annabelle. I've got a sound check to do."

I shouldered past him and leaped onto the stage, the only place where I ever felt truly safe, truly in control. The roadies had already lined up my guitars in their designated slots in the rack, so I grabbed my favorite metallic blue Fender Stratocaster, flipped on the amp, and started playing. Distant shouts tried to penetrate my mind, but I couldn't focus on them. Instead, I let my fingers dance over the strings, channeling my emotions into the riff that played on a loop in my head. It wasn't until Blu put his hand on my wrist that I finally came to.

"Damn, son. That was some intense shit you were playing there. Like you put that solo you've been working on into over-drive. You okay?"

Shit. I didn't even realize I played the song I'd come to think of as Annabelle's until Blu pointed it out. What the *fuck* was my problem?

"Too much for the sound guys?" I deflected.

"Only if they didn't record that. Da-amn. I don't know what got into you, but that was fucking amazing. Like you gathered all the energy in the universe and channeled it into your guitar. You better check it, though. I think it might be on fire," he said, laughing.

"Just like you better be if you're keeping up with me tonight."

As I slipped the strap over my head and racked the guitar, Blu said, "I was born on fire, Dakota. Ask Ashleigh."

Pasting a grin on my face, I flipped him the bird and hopped off the stage.

Ripping out that solo hadn't done one damn thing to ease the ache in my chest, the ache I promised myself at eight years old I'd never feel again. So I headed out of the concert space in the hotel and somehow managed to end up in the gym. I grabbed a set of dumbbells and started lifting. After a couple of reps, I discovered Tron nearby pushing iron like a freight train. The look on his face mirrored my emotions, so I walked over and spotted for him. I didn't ask him, and he didn't ask me. After about an hour, we were both dripping sweat, but at least our expressions had returned to something resembling human again.

♪

"I don't understand why Garrett works Annabelle so hard. He's not even letting her take a break to have dinner with us tonight," Clio said as she sat next to Jack who held their daughter Angel in his lap.

I couldn't seem to stop myself. "Sure she's with Garrett?"

Confusion flashed across Clio's face. "What does that even mean?"

Shrugging, I took a big gulp of the double Jack and Coke I'd ordered before dinner. "You tell me."

"I have no idea what you're talking about, Dakota. Do you know what he's talking about, Jack?"

Jack shook his head and shot me a look.

Before Clio could pursue the conversation further, Blu and Ashleigh and Tron joined us.

"Ah, Vegas. I fucking love playing this town," Blu said. "Everyone is here to have a good time."

"Except for Dakota," Jack said, directing a dark look my way.

Blu laughed. "Especially Dakota. Did you see the crowd gathered around the craps table he was playing last night? They love us here. Tonight's show is going to be epic—again." He saluted the table with his beer and downed a swig.

At Blu's pronouncement, Angel started patty-caking her tiny hands and squealing in apparent agreement with him. Between the two of them, they defused the tension at the table, and by the time we finished dinner, we were primed to give our fans exactly what they came for.

Annabelle

Half an hour before the show started, I finally sneaked a few minutes away from Garrett. I don't know what crawled up his butt for this series of Vegas shows, but he'd been on a tear all day. My stomach growled loud enough to echo through the green room, and I realized I hadn't eaten anything since breakfast. The covered platters the caterers had left for the band called to me, and I snitched a couple of chicken wings and mini quesadillas. I doubted the guys would miss them when they came off the stage after the show.

Thinking of the band naturally led to thoughts of Dakota and the incredibly intense way he'd made love to me last night after we left the casino. It seemed like he used his body to try to tell me something, but I feared losing myself to my own fantasies to read anything more into it than that gambling and winning made him almost as horny as playing a show did. Aside from witnessing the incredible solo he unleashed during sound checks, thanks to Garrett, I hadn't seen him all day. In fact, I hadn't even been able to return to our suite to change into my concert clothes. I checked the time on my phone and sighed. The guys would be here any minute with showtime in less than thirty. My copper-colored, flared, silk pants and rainbow floral-design halter top would have to do. "Garrett didn't need to keep me so busy I didn't have time to go back to the suite and change into the cute lime green sequined minidress I splurged on in the hotel shop," I muttered to myself.

Sighing, I glanced at my tablet one more time, making sure I'd completed all the tasks Garrett had listed for me to do. Right after I sank down on one of the plush couches and slipped off my heels, the door to the green room swung open. "Hey, Annabelle, what are you doing here?" Bailey asked, a worried frown creasing his brow. "Everyone else is backstage and wondering where you are."

I stared at him for several beats and hurriedly slid my feet back into my platform sandals. "Garrett told me to wait here, so I did," I gritted out. "That man has gotten on my last nerve. For once I wish he'd remember what he tells people."

"He's not usually like this. I don't know what his problem is, but we need to be backstage five minutes ago."

Bailey ushered me through the door and all but pushed me down the hall to meet the rest of the band and crew.

Garrett's smooth snarl greeted us when we arrived backstage. "There you two are. Where the hell have you been?"

I opened my mouth to remind him I'd waited exactly where he told me to wait, but he cut me off. "Never mind. You need to join the other women in the VIP area now. They waited, but you didn't show, so they went out there without you."

How long has everyone been here? Why didn't they come to the green room first like usual?

I caught Dakota glaring at me, so I hustled over to him.

"Where have you been all day, Annabelle?" he asked, frowning.

"I'm sorry, Dakota. Garrett's had me working all day," I began.

"Really?" The sarcasm dripping from that one word froze my blood to the marrow. "'Cause Garrett spent the last half of the afternoon at the hotel bar, and he didn't seem to have any idea where you were."

Closing my eyes against the implications of Dakota's words, I opened them again to see him walking away from me. Across the room, a look of triumph crossed Garrett's features before he literally wiped it off with his hand, returning his face to a neutral expression.

What the hell?

As he passed me to join the rest of the band, Jack leaned in to whisper, "Whatever is going on between you two, you need to take care of it, Annabelle. Dakota can be a diva, but we need him to be on top of his game."

I might have remained gaping after him like a fish on the pier if Clio hadn't shown up at that minute.

"There you are, finally. Come *on*, Annabelle. The opening is the best part of the show."

She linked her arm through mine and hustled me down the opposite hallway from the band, chattering on about how Jack's entrance to start a concert always stole her breath. Before I could even begin to process what had happened backstage, I found myself standing between Clio and Ashleigh in the front row of the VIP section and taking hold of the flask Clio pressed into my hand. The distant thunder of Jack's drums alerted the crowd to the start of the show, the screaming throng rivaling the band in decibels.

I might have lost myself in everything Balefire—the lasers beaming throughout the concert space, the flash pots tearing open the dark, the wild energy of the band's music, the excitement of hearing them playing live in front of a hyper enthusiastic crowd—except that not once during the show did Dakota seek me out. He played for the crowd and made a bigger than usual show of accepting the lingerie the eager women in the front rows sacrificed to him. When he lifted off on his hydraulic stage, he didn't spare even a glance at the VIP area. I drank down a sense of dread with the suddenly sour vodka Clio so thoughtfully provided me.

By the time the guys took their final bow after their third encore, I knew something terrible had happened between Dakota and me. I couldn't figure out what and how it happened. I hadn't been anywhere near him since I'd left his bed before ten on Garrett's summons. Maybe that was it? Dakota was in a snit because I hadn't seen him all day? Yet somehow, it felt so much bigger than that.

♪

When I caught up with Dakota after the show, something was terribly wrong. Gone was the playfulness, the insistent horniness he always showed me in the adrenaline rush that followed a concert. Instead, he stared at me with a look of detachment, like I'd become a stranger to him. The coldness of his voice couldn't compete with the deep freeze of his eyes on mine. My bones turned to ice in the chill of his gaze, and I feared if I moved, I'd shatter into a thousand frozen shards.

"You know, Annabelle," he began conversationally, "when Dave was with the band, we all shared everything. Especially the groupies. The things we did. Damn, it was fun."

If he intended for his words to hurt, he'd succeeded, like daggers piercing my chest. I'd known it was only a matter of time before he decided I wasn't enough for him. Obviously, I'd fooled myself into believing I'd been keeping up with him, exciting him, making him happy—like he'd been doing for me.

"Then Jack joined the band, and he didn't want to share, didn't want to do the groupie thing at all. Which was cool. Just meant that many more girls for the rest of us." He grinned, seeming to enjoy the memory.

"Blu threw me a curve when he took up with Ashleigh and definitely didn't want to share, didn't want to play at all except with her. I couldn't understand it. Then I spent a night with you and found myself thinking about you every now and then until we reconnected."

He narrowed his eyes. "These last couple of months with you showed me why Jack never wanted to play, why Blu stopped wanting to share. Too bad for me I picked a girl who likes to be shared."

I nearly landed on my ass as I staggered back under the blow he dealt with his words, his accusation robbing me of air.

"Wh-what did you say?" I croaked out.

"You heard me, Annabelle. I was never interested in sharing you. Thought I made that clear, but I guess you and Bailey never got the message. Or you chose to ignore it. Either way, we're done."

"*Bailey?*" Dakota's words rendered me stupid. "Bailey?" I asked his retreating back.

He stopped walking. "Don't play innocent, Annabelle. It doesn't suit you," he tossed over his shoulder. Then he was moving again while I stayed rooted to the spot, unable to move, unable to think past—*Dakota thinks I'm sleeping with Bailey?* How could Dakota think I'd sleep with anyone but him?

Dakota

When I'd walked into the green room following the show, my atten-tion zeroed right in on Annabelle standing with Clio, Ashleigh—and Bailey Saunders. Bailey said something, and Annabelle's pretty laugh carried across the room to tease and torture me. Bile caught in my throat, forcing me to swallow a couple of times to keep it down. From out of nowhere, Garrett appeared at my side, his raspy voice slithering into my ear. "She sure spends a lot of time with our head road engineer, doesn't she? Of course, they knew each other a long time ago."

I'd walked over to her, demanded her attention, and tore out my heart. Afterward, I stalked to the bar and ordered two beers, downing the first in a single long pull. I slammed the empty down, grabbed the full one, and told the bartender to keep 'em coming.

As I tried to drink Annabelle out of my head, a blonde in a barely-there white dress joined me. "That was some show you put on out there, Dakota. Makes a girl wonder what else you can do with your talented hands."

Nothing about this one was subtle. Which made her exactly what I needed.

"Come on over here, darlin', and I'll give you a preview," I invited, opening a space between my legs as I finished off the second beer.

"My friends call me Sylvie."

She stepped right into me and wrapped her arms around my neck.

"Oh, I definitely want to be your friend."

I pulled her in for a kiss and felt—nothing. Pure, empty nothing.

So I deepened the kiss, Miss Subtle enthusiastically coming along for the ride. This woman was so my type. With her skimpy outfit and the way she kissed me, she was ready and willing to give me as much sex as I wanted, all of her attention squarely on me.

Yet my dick stayed quiet behind my fly, didn't even twitch, which left me highly pissed off. What had that traitorous witch Annabelle done to me?

"Dakota?"

As though I'd conjured her with my thoughts, Annabelle stood in front of us, the look of hurt and confusion on her face almost convincing—until that conversation I'd overheard before sound checks invaded my mind.

I looked at blondie and said, "Present, meet the Past. Past, as you can see, I'm a little busy here."

As Annabelle continued to stare, tears gathered in those gorgeous green eyes of hers, but I was in no mood to believe her lies. "Feel free to read that as get lost, Annabelle."

I turned back to blondie, grabbed two handfuls of her ass, and locked my lips with hers. Obligingly, she ground her pelvis against the front of my jeans. When I let her up for air, I noticed two things: Annabelle was gone, and she'd taken my libido with her. *Dammit.* "Hey barkeep. I need a bottle of Jack and two more beers."

Gently disengaging myself from blondie, I said, "You know what, doll? It appears I left everything out on the stage. We're in town for another night. You take a rain check?" I gave her the boyish grin that worked on all the ladies, and the tantrum I felt stiffening her body melted away.

"I'll hold you to that, Dakota," she said with a smile. "In case you change your mind before tomorrow's show." She wrote her name and number on a napkin, tucked it into the front pocket of my jeans, and brushed her hand lingeringly across the fly. My dick paid no attention whatsoever to her caress. *What the fuck?*

I stood and grabbed my drinks, retreating to a couch across the room where I found Tron nursing a cocktail in one hand and chasing it with a beer in the other.

"Looks like tonight's a drinkin' night," I said as I invited myself to join him.

"Looks like," he grunted.

That's the beauty of lifelong friendships. You don't need to spend all your time talking to make a point. I sat on that couch with my drinks, and the next thing I remembered was waking up alone on the couch in my suite.

CHAPTER THIRTY

Dakota

"OPEN UP YOUR fucking door, Bailey!" I shouted as I pounded my fist against it. "I know she's in there. I can hear her. Open the fuck up!"

Bailey's roommate Todd opened the door bare-ass naked. "What the hell is your problem, Dakota?"

Pushing past him, I didn't even bother to answer. Nearly tripping over the clothes strewn across the floor, I rounded the bed nearest the door and descended like a bomb on it. Bailey scrambled up out of the sheets, a T-shirt and boxers covering his body as he tore earplugs out of his ears. "What the fuck is your problem, Dakota?" he snarled.

"You're my fucking problem, Bailey. Where is Annabelle?"

"How the hell should I know? She's your girlfriend."

A sexy purr coming from Todd's bed interrupted us. "Dakota, are you here for your rain check?"

Glancing briefly at the girl who lay barely covered in Todd's sheets, I saw blondie from the after-party had found a partner for the night. Good, 'cause I didn't have time for that anymore. "I changed my mind."

"But you said she was in the past," the girl insisted. The sheet slipped as she knelt on the bed, but she made no attempt to cover herself.

Bailey coughed. "Is she talking about Annabelle?"

"Don't play dumb, Saunders. I heard you two talking yesterday. You said today everyone would know about you two. Where is she?"

Bailey started laughing, and I lost it. Walked right over to him and would have landed the punch if Todd hadn't grabbed me.

"What the hell, Dakota? You lost Annabelle?"

"You seriously don't know where she is?" I demanded.

"Not a clue. But if she were my girl, I'd damn sure never have lost her."

"Watch yourself, Saunders. You're not irreplaceable you know."

"What the hell does that mean?"

Narrowing my eyes, I said, "I heard the two of you planning to tell everyone about your surprise today. Guess you can start with me."

Bailey shook his head, the look on his face souring my stomach. "*Annabelle's* surprise." He lifted a brow. "For you."

I shrugged out of Todd's hold and strode from the room. *Annabelle's surprise for me?* A cloak of dread settled over my shoulders the minute I found Bailey alone in his bed looking like he'd spent the whole night that way. His words only added to its weight.

When I stepped off the elevator onto my floor, I ran into Jack and Clio pushing Angel in her stroller.

"You look like hell, Dakota. What were you and Tron doing last night anyway? Trying to see who could be the most drunk and stupid? How would you know who won?" Jack asked, laughing.

I shook my head. "You're a funny guy, Jack." Turning to Clio, I sucked in a breath and tried to be casual. "Have you seen Annabelle?"

Clio stared at me. "She's not in your suite?"

"No."

"Did you try to call her?"

"I can't find my phone," I grudgingly admitted.

"After all the stupid wake-up calls you jerked me around with—and cost me my girl for nearly a year—you can't find your phone?" Jack smirked. "That's rich. I hope you have it locked, or someone's going to have a lot of fun with you." He sounded way too pleased about the situation.

"Maybe Annabelle's with Garrett?" Clio asked.

"It's eight o'clock in the fucking morning."

Jack growled a reminder. "Language, Dakota. There are children present."

Running my hands through my hair, I sighed. "Sorry, Angel."

The baby looked up at me and grinned. Probably the only bright spot in my otherwise totally fucked-up morning.

"Dakota, what happened?" Clio asked, concern written across her face.

I didn't answer. Instead, I walked back down the hall to the suite I shared with Annabelle, hoping somehow the scene I'd awakened to had changed. Swiping my key card over the lock, I pasted a smile on my face, turned the handle, and walked in. Silence echoed around me while I smiled stupidly at an empty suite. Instead of catching the soft scent of Annabelle's spicy perfume, the odor of sweat and stale alcohol assaulted my nose. The door to her closet in the bedroom stood wide open, mocking me with the lack of clothes hanging there. Nothing had changed. Annabelle was gone.

What the fuck have I done?

CHAPTER THIRTY-ONE

Annabelle

EMMA MIGHT BE a pain sometimes, but she's my sister. Today of all days, she came through big-time when she picked me up at the airport and waited to ask the questions burning in her eyes until we were in the car and pulling away from the curb.

"Annabelle, what the hell happened? You look like somebody died."

"I can't talk about it right now, okay, Emma?"

"Is it Dakota? Did you two break up?"

Closing my eyes against the tears I couldn't seem to control, I whispered, "You can't break up with someone you were never really dating."

"Geez. This is bad. This is really bad."

"Can you just drive? Please?"

I'd walked through Denver International Airport in a daze. I'd probably still be wandering around there if Emma hadn't literally stuck her nose in my face in the baggage claim area. As it was, of all the passengers on my flight, I retrieved my suitcase last.

For once, she didn't argue with me. Which left me to replay the scene with Dakota at the bar on a loop in my head. Like I'd been doing ever since the moment I walked up to see him locked in with a blonde in a nearly transparent white minidress.

After I left the party, I somehow arrived at Dakota's suite and managed to gather up all my things. By some happy accident, no one else rode the elevator as I headed down to the lobby. When I dropped my key card at the front desk, I must have looked terrible because the concierge tsked and asked me where I was headed and what airline I needed. When the man asked for my credit card, I realized he'd made my flight reservation for me, putting me on the first plane back to Denver. He told me I could stay in the office until the time came to head to the airport since I couldn't fly out before six in the morning, but I couldn't stay one more minute in the same place where I knew Dakota entertained my replacement.

So I spent the night in the airport checking my phone every five seconds in the silly hope the whole scene had been a mistake. When my phone mercifully ran low on battery, I put it in my bag and willed myself to keep it together long enough to board my flight. Bailey Saunders? Dakota thought I had something going on with Bailey? How could he ever think that? It made no sense, but that didn't change the fact he'd jettisoned me like space waste on the shuttle.

Somehow, I'd convinced myself that I'd meant something to him. The way he'd treated me on tour, as though I was his girl, made me feel like I was a star. After our first night in Vegas, the way he'd so attentively made love to me, I'd even gone so far as to believe we had started something special. I should have known better. Dakota earned his reputation as a bad boy rock star. It was the core of his appeal. Who the hell was I to think I'd be the one to make him want to settle down, share himself only with me? He'd never once implied that sort of relationship was even on the table. Sure, he'd acted possessive of me sometimes, but he never said anything I could even deliberately misinterpret as commitment. I'd based all my dreams on his actions. Then his actions suffocated those dreams.

When we arrived home, I barely thanked Emma for the ride before I trudged up the stairs to my apartment. I don't know how long I sat on the couch staring into space. I still wore the outfit I'd had on all of yesterday. My unpacked suitcase stood against the wall inside the door to my apartment when my mom knocked and let herself into my place.

"Annabelle? May I come in?"

"Listen, I'm not very good company right now, Mom. Could you come back later?" I said as I slowly came to my feet on legs that didn't want to support me.

Ignoring me, she asked, "Have you been sitting on your couch since Emma brought you home?"

"I guess?"

"Oh, Annabelle," she said, folding me in her arms.

I silently inhaled Chanel, my mom's one nonnegotiable indulgence, all my tears spent.

"Where is your phone, Annabelle?"

"In my purse I think. Why?"

"Your office manager, Emory she said her name was, left a message with me. She needs you to call her. When I tried calling, your phone rang in to a full inbox."

"Oh," I said numbly. "My battery died at the airport, and my charger was in my checked luggage."

"Annabelle—"

"Don't start with me Mom. Please."

Disengaging from her embrace, I wandered over to where I'd left my things and pulled my phone from the bottom of my purse. After a few minutes, I finally located my charger in the middle of the mess of my packing. Plugging in my phone, I saw it had blown up with voice and text messages. As I scrolled through them, I saw about a hundred from Clio, a couple from Ashleigh, far too many from Garrett to bode well for a recommendation from my intern-ship, a couple from Bailey, and at least three from Emory. None of the messages, however, came from Dakota.

Skipping the others, I went straight to Emory's. "I'm not sure what all has gone down there in Vegas, but Dakota's dad made it in for Dakota's birthday as you requested. Also, everything's a go for Cristy Valor's performance with the band tonight. Nice job on that, by the way. Give me a call when you get this message."

I'd totally forgotten that I'd asked Bailey to keep Dakota's dad company until the show, my little birthday surprise for Dakota. Now I had to wonder if I'd screwed up there too.

On the next one, Emory said, "Garrett's in a snit. No one seems to know where you are. Could you give me a call, please?"

The third one sounded a bit frantic. "Annabelle, you're scar-ing me. You never let a message linger without a prompt response. Where are you? Are you all right? Call me."

As I saved the message, I looked up at my mom who stood near enough to overhear my messages. "Mom, thanks for stopping by. I have some work stuff to do. Maybe we can talk later?"

"Annabelle, whatever happened, you know you can talk to me."

"I know, Mom. But not right now. Please?"

She stared at me for several long seconds then nodded and walked toward the door. Before turning the doorknob, she qui-etly said, "We thought he was something special too, sweetheart. Guess he fooled us all." With that, she let herself out into the cool fall night.

Though I knew she meant to comfort me, Mom's parting words punched me in the chest. It took several long minutes for me to catch my breath after she left. When I thought I had myself under some control, I called Emory's personal number.

"Hey, Em. Sorry I didn't return your message. I was en route to Denver and my phone died. What's up?"

The cheerfulness I tried to inject into my voice didn't fool her.

"What's wrong, Annabelle? What happened? Garrett's been on the phone with me all day demanding to know if I've heard from you."

"Garrett didn't want me on the tour from the start. Probably he forgot he changed his mind on some minor detail for the hundredth time and needed someone to blame." A terrible thought intruded. "Did he fire me?" I asked, and grabbed the edge of my island for support.

"He didn't fire you. That's not in his wheelhouse. Apparently, Cristy Valor would rather work with you than with him. Why are you in Denver?"

The abrupt change of subject threw me. Before I could stop myself, I answered honestly. "Dakota was the one who wanted me on tour with the band. Now he doesn't want me around. So I came home." I could hear Emory draw a breath to question me, so I plunged on. "I have several voice mails from Garrett. I'll get off the phone with you and give them a listen. Whatever it is, I'm sure it can be worked out before the show."

"Um, Annabelle, it's eight o'clock. The show's been going for an hour already."

"Damn. Sorry, Emory. But surely Garrett could fix whatever the problem was, right? I mean it's not like he hasn't been managing the band by himself for ten years."

"No doubt. Listen, Annabelle. Come in to the office tomorrow morning. Let's make sure everything is in place for the rest of the concerts on the tour, yeah?"

"I'll be there at nine."

"Ten is fine. Take some time and get yourself unpacked."

Guiltily, I glanced at my suitcase and nodded. Involuntarily, I giggled at my silly response to a phone conversation.

"You sure you're all right?"

"No, but I'll be good to go in the morning. No worries. See you tomorrow, Emory."

I rang off and stared stupidly at my phone. Did I even want to keep working for the band? What choice did I have? I needed an internship on my résumé if I wanted to apply to a prestigious MBA program. Why did Clio have to be so generous in securing this opportunity for me? I shook myself. Clio's generosity most definitely wasn't my problem. My problem stood six feet tall, pierced me with his beautiful sea blue eyes, and stole my heart with his charm and intelligence and music. It went without saying that he owned my body. Only he didn't want me anymore. Right when I figured out I'd fallen wildly in love with him.

♪

The jangling sound of my phone ringing shot me like a Roman candle straight off my couch. Sometime after my conversation with Emory, exhaustion claimed me, and I'd fallen asleep. Disoriented, I tripped over my coffee table and sprawled on the floor in front of it. Scrambling on my hands and knees, I made it to my kitchen and dragged myself to standing so I could snag my phone before it went to voice mail.

"Finally! Where are you, Annabelle?" Clio demanded.

I could hear the sounds of a party in full swing in the background and checked the clock on my microwave. One in the morning. The show with Cristy Valor no doubt warranted a kick-ass after-party. Pain shot through my chest as I wondered about Dakota's choice for the night, his birthday no less. I'd had such fun planned for us. I choked down a sob as Clio interrupted my wretched thoughts.

"Annabelle?"

Clearing my throat, I replied, "I'm at home. In Denver."

"Why? Why would you leave Dakota on his birthday?"

"Because he asked me to."

"That can't be true. Are you sure he wanted you to go home?"

I doubled over as the pain of my last conversation with him rolled through me—again. "Clio," I said at last, "whatever Dakota and I were doing is over. Trust me."

"I'm talking to Jack about this. If you saw Dakota right now…"

"I knew from the start there was an expiration date on my time with him. Please, Clio. Let it go, okay?"

"We're staying an extra day in Vegas while the roadies pack up the show and head down to Phoenix. I'll call you back tomorrow. Don't let my call go to voicemail, Annabelle. You scared the heck out of me when I couldn't reach you all day."

"Sorry."

"I'll talk to you tomorrow."

She clicked off, leaving me standing alone in my kitchen in the dark hours of the night. Her words echoed in my head. *If you saw Dakota…* Visions of Dakota's hands all over a petite blonde in a barely-there dress swirled through my brain, leaving me nauseous. Wrapping my arms around myself, I remembered I still wore the same outfit from nearly two days ago.

Wearily, I dragged myself down the hall to my bedroom, stripped out of my clothes, and discovered I still wore the pretty Mimi Holiday baby blue lace bra and panty set Dakota bought for me at Bellefleur in Seattle. Memories of that afternoon flooded my mind. Dakota's eyes darkening nearly to cobalt as he watched me try on bras and panties. Dakota stalking me in the confined space of the dressing room as I teased him by covering my breasts or my pussy or my ass with my hands depending on where he wanted to look. Dakota pulling me down to straddle his lap as he licked and kissed my nipples through the lace of a bra he had yet to purchase. The feel of his hard thighs supporting my ass, his calloused hands tickling the skin over my rib cage, his practiced tongue coaxing my nipples into hard peaks as I covered my mouth with both hands to contain my moans of pleasure.

As I squirmed in his lap, to escape or move closer I didn't exactly know, he kept shushing me, reminding me where we were and that we didn't want to be caught. Then he let me go long enough to free himself from his jeans, sheath himself with a condom he seemed to produce from thin air, and push aside the delicate lace of the panties so he could enter me with one slow, delicious thrust.

Dammit, Dakota. Do you even know how you changed me?

I tore off my bra and panties and kicked them under my bed. After pulling on an oversized T-shirt, I padded to the bathroom, brushed my teeth, and headed back to my bed. When I pulled back the covers, I remembered how Dakota "talked" me into joining him on tour. Before more memories could assault my mind, I grabbed the blanket from the bed and returned to the couch where I spent the night willing myself back to sleep.

Somewhere around dawn, exhaustion reclaimed me. The next time my phone rang, sunlight painted my living room in late-morning light.

Time to face reality.

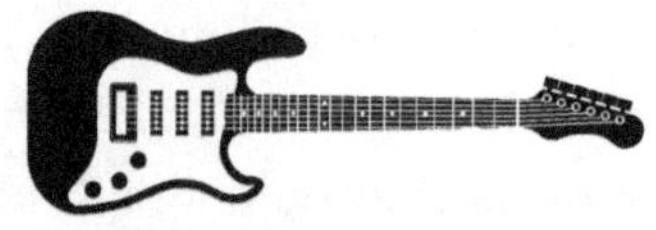

CHAPTER THIRTY-TWO

Dakota

ANNABELLE'S SURPRISE FOR me was inviting my dad to see our show in Vegas. When he showed up backstage, he told me a woman with a happy voice had arranged everything. A happy voice could only mean Annabelle. Guilt joined pain to party in my head, and I'd spent another night trying to numb myself with alcohol. Not a great plan considering how my dad wanted to spend our down day together.

"Seriously, Dad? Golf? When did you start playing such a sissy-ass game?" I asked as our driver shuttled us to the golf club on the Strip.

"It's good for stress," my dad replied, a sly grin stretching his features.

"Throwing and bending clubs and such? Yeah, I can see how that could lower your blood pressure."

"We're going to the driving range, knock some balls into the stratosphere."

"I'd rather tear up the track racing exotic cars."

"Those boys at the track would catch a whiff of your hangover and nix that idea pronto," Dad said, laughing.

"Jerk," I said under my breath.

"Dumbass."

We grinned at each other and kicked back in the plush leather seats of the limo.

When we arrived at the club, Dad asked for two drivers and a bucket of balls while I smirked at the caddy behind the counter who obviously had no idea who I was. All he could see was my Jimmy Page T-shirt, tats, ripped jeans, and biker boots. The way he'd stare first at one thing and then the next, I knew he could only see low-life, so I stretched and belched for effect. Dad rolled his eyes as he walked past me, but I caught the smirk that flitted briefly across his lips as he strolled out the door in front of me, looking oddly respectable in khakis and a polo shirt he'd actually tucked into his pants.

After he teed up some balls and gave me a quick lesson on hitting them, we started swinging. I was finding a rhythm and thinking this golf thing might not be so ridiculous when he blindsided me.

"You gonna talk about it?"

"What?" I asked, checking my swing.

"What happened between you and the girl who arranged for me to see you guys last night—on your birthday. The girl who wasn't there."

Closing my eyes against the vision of Annabelle's tears that plagued me even after I'd drunk enough booze to drown a bus, I hung my head and tried to figure out where to start.

"I fucked up, Dad."

"She catch you cheating on her?"

"Worse. I thought she was cheating on me, so I kicked her to the curb—hard. Only afterward, I discovered I'd misinterpreted everything I thought was going on. 'Course, I had some help from Garrett who kept whispering in my ear, but in the end, that's no excuse for me not giving her a chance to explain herself at least."

"Well, son. You're a better man than your old man."

"How do you mean?"

"At least you recognize you need to give her a chance to explain. Which you need to do sooner rather than later. Wish I'd done that with your mom."

"She walked out on us and never looked back. Nothing to explain there."

"That's where you're wrong, Dakota." He sucked in a breath, blew it out, and stared at me hard. "There's something I should have told you years ago. By the time you graduated high school, you were on your way with the band, so it seemed easier to let it go."

"Let what go?"

"Your mom walked away because I gave her no other choice. I could never believe a woman as beautiful and perfect as your mother could ever truly love me. So I made myself unlovable. I accused her of cheating and wouldn't believe her when she swore she would never cheat on me." He puffed a sigh up at the heavens.

"Eventually, she tired of trying to defend herself against a man who couldn't get over himself enough to believe her. She tried to take you with her when she left, but I made sure she couldn't have you."

I didn't think I could experience worse pain than going to bed and waking up without Annabelle next to me. Turns out I was wrong. The driver hit the turf as I flexed my hands into fists and gritted my teeth against taking a swing at this stranger masquerading as my dad.

"What the fuck, Dad?"

Jesus, I needed to hit something.

"You can take your swing, and I'd deserve it, but remember what you do for a living and how many other people depend on you," he warned.

I paced away, turned back, paced away again. "What are you saying?"

"I'm saying that before I arrived in Vegas, I talked to your girl.

She wanted to surprise you, make you happy. I know what a woman in love sounds like, and that girl loves you."

I gaped at him.

"Maybe you should be a smarter man than your old dad and make it right with her." He sucked in a breath. Let it out slow. "Judging from the way you ignored every woman who came your way after the show last night and the way you drank yourself into a stupor, you've moved on from the groupie sideshow."

While I stood there silent and staring, he proceeded to tee up several balls and systematically sent each of them down the range.

"Come on, son. Tee 'em up. Put my face on every ball if it helps."

I watched him hit a few more balls before I picked up my club again. By the time we finished the bucket of balls he'd bought, my shoulders, back, arms, and hands ached. Yet my body couldn't match my heart. At least I'd calmed down enough to be able to think somewhat rationally again. What I thought was how I'd been played. Dad and I had a lot more to talk about, but first I needed to call a Balefire meeting.

CHAPTER THIRTY-THREE

Annabelle

CLIO HAD BEEN calling or texting me every day for a couple of weeks, trying to coax me into taking Dakota's calls. That meant hearing his voice. It meant being reminded that he thought of me like any other groupie eager to get it on with anyone connected to the band. I still couldn't believe he thought I'd been sleeping with Bailey Saunders on the side.

"Annabelle, you need to talk to him. For yourself at least."

"Clio, there's nothing to say. When he tired of me, he moved on. It shouldn't be a shock to you. After all, you've known him better and longer than I have." I sighed.

Sure, Bailey was hot with his buff body built by moving heavy equipment for the band. His light brown skin and velvety dark brown eyes definitely drew the attention of more than one groupie. His mile-wide smile always made me feel better whenever Garrett came down on me extra viciously. But Bailey had only ever been my friend. How could Dakota not see that?

In the end, I couldn't do it. I couldn't listen to Dakota accuse me again of cheating on him, but for the sake of the band, he would "forgive" me.

"Annabelle, where'd you go?"

"What? I'm sorry Clio. I've been putting in some long days finishing up the details for the end of the tour and putting the final touches on the new album cover Carolyn and I designed. Guess I was distracted."

"Annabelle, I'm worried about you. You sound like someone else, not the bouncy Tigger who's been one of my best friends since we met on the first day of sorority rush."

"I love you for your concern, Clio, but let it go. Besides, you know I always bounce back."

"Annie, there's something I have to tell you. Jack keeps telling me to stay out of it, let you two work it out, but since you're not talking to Dakota, you don't know what happened after you left Vegas. It's good Ashleigh is a journalist who knows how to pry information out of people, or I might not have known this either." I gripped my phone tight and waited. "Jack's been tight-lipped about what's happening with the band."

"What do you mean? They aren't breaking up, are they?" I cried in alarm.

"Nothing like that. Jack, Tron, Dakota, and Blu are as tight as ever. Maybe tighter than ever after Dakota tried to fire Bailey."

"Dakota tried to fire Bailey? Why?"

"Because of you."

My voice squeaked up an octave. "That's all wrong. Bailey is only a friend. It's because of him that you and Jack were able to reconnect."

"Fortunately, Bailey's roommate Todd had his back. Which was when the truth came out."

"The truth?"

"It's kind of like that Shakespeare play my teacher made me read sophomore year of high school. *Othello*."

"Huh?"

"You know, *Othello*. The story where the villain makes it look like the hero's wife has a thing on the side with the captain of the hero's army?"

"Come again?"

"The hero sends the captain on a suicide mission and smothers his wife with a pillow—that story."

"Clio, it's obvious you read too many books. That story has nothing to do with me."

"It's *exactly* like you."

"What do you mean? I'm still here. No one's smothered me."

"Not literally—" her voice gentled—"but emotionally for sure."

I sighed, and Clio could probably hear my eyes roll through the phone.

"Hear me out. When Dakota called a band meeting, they brought Garrett in because Dakota wanted to fire Bailey for being with you. Ashleigh told me some things didn't add up with Garrett's version of events. The more the guys questioned him, the more his story changed."

"Clio, what are you saying?"

"Apparently, Bailey came in and told his side. Turns out, like in Shakespeare's play, Garrett set up Bailey—who's kind of Dakota's captain with how he sets up Dakota's guitars and flies him on his hydraulics." Clio took a breath. "Garrett threw Bailey at you and worked on Dakota to make him think you were cheating with Bailey."

I sat down hard on my kitchen chair. "Why would he do that? I know he didn't want me on the tour, but why try to hurt Bailey too?"

"Bailey was convenient since you two knew each other from before. Turns out, Garrett was afraid Dakota was falling for you."

My breath caught. "What would that have to do with Garrett?" I whispered.

"Groupies, Annabelle."

"What?"

"Think about it. With Jack married and Blu engaged, the boys weren't partying as much, which meant fewer opportunities to hook up with groupies."

"So?"

"Garrett's pushing forty. The only women he meets are through the band. He thought if another member of the band settled down, he'd stop getting some action."

"Wow. That explains a lot." I stood and walked over to my fridge. As I cracked open a Coke, Clio circled back to her theme.

"Exactly. You need to talk to Dakota."

Sitting at my dinette, I traced my fingers over the lettering on the can. "No, Clio. You weren't there. You didn't hear what Dakota said to me. And he was so into the groupie he replaced me with." I choked back a sob. "Every time I close my eyes, I can see his hands all over her, hear him telling me I was in his past."

"Are you sure he meant that?"

Wrapping my free hand around my waist, I held onto myself and whispered, "I know he did."

Living alone had its advantages since no one could see the silent tears slipping down my face as I listened to my friend's hope, knowing I couldn't share it.

She continued on like she hadn't heard me. "This is the second stunt Garrett's pulled with one of the guys. When the tour finishes up, Jack said he thinks there could be a shake-up in management. Will you talk to Dakota?"

"Clio, it won't change anything." I stood and walked over to the window overlooking my parents' backyard. "Listen, if you guys are worried I'll be a problem when you all come home, stop. The only member of the band I ever hung out with before my internship was Jack. Which was because of you. When you come home, we'll go back to the way things were."

I stopped talking to trap the sobs threatening to escape my throat. Clio waited quietly on the other end of the line while I gulped down several breaths.

Hoping to sound cheerful, I pasted a smile on my face as salty tears filled my mouth. "I'll be finished up with my internship by then anyway, so I won't have any reason to run into Dakota."

"Oh, Annabelle."

The sound of her compassion undid me, and I couldn't hold back my emotions anymore. Being my best friend, she hung in there until I hiccupped my way back to something resembling coherent.

"When the tour ends, we'll go out for a girls' night. We'll call Stacy and MandMs. It'll be like in college. We'll dress up and drink and dance and be fabulous. Okay?"

I gave my phone a wobbly smile. "Sure, Clio. Sounds fun."

CHAPTER THIRTY-FOUR

Dakota

I BANGED ON ANNABELLE'S door until she had no choice but to come to it. But she didn't open it.

"Dakota. It's the middle of the night. What are you doing here?" she asked from the other side of the oak barrier separating us.

"It's freezing out here. Can I come in?"

"No."

"Please?"

"Go away, Dakota."

She was hurting. I could hear it in the catch in her voice. "If you hit the bars now, no doubt you can have a new girl in your bed every hour for the rest of the night."

The old me deserved that. The old me who hurt her at a party definitely deserved that. But I wasn't that man anymore.

"This isn't a booty call, Annabelle. I need to talk to you. You wouldn't take my calls or return my messages or texts. Please, Annabelle. I know I royally fucked up, but if you'll just talk to me. Please."

The soft thump against the door was probably her forehead hitting it as she fought with herself. Then I heard the snick of the dead bolt sliding back, and I grinned in triumph for a second before I wiped it off my face in time for her to open the door a crack.

"We have nothing to talk about, Dakota. You made yourself clear in Vegas."

I put my hand on the door and pushed it steadily back until she huffed with indignation but stepped aside enough for me to enter her place. When she closed the door, I reached around her and shot the dead bolt home. She crossed her arms over herself, a question in her eyes.

For several seconds neither of us spoke before she found her voice. "Just because you're a big-time rock star doesn't mean you can toss me aside like yesterday's trend and then walk back into my life like nothing happened. Go away, Dakota."

"No."

I took a step toward her, but she held her ground, lifting her chin defiantly at me.

"I'm spending the night here. With you. In your bed."

Her mouth formed a perfect 'O' then she opened and closed it several times like a fish out of water. It would have been comical except for the stakes.

I took another step, and she found her voice.

"Like hell you are." She tightened her arms around herself. "You don't believe in me. You think I cheated on you."

That last part came out in a whisper, and I saw her eyes were glassy with unshed tears. *Shit.*

I took another step.

"You left some of your clothes behind. Don't worry. I packed them up and brought them home. They're in your closet in our bedroom back at my place. I want to see you in the skirt again. You know the one."

"Dakota, I don't know what game you're playing, but you have to stop. Please. Can't you see you're killing me here?"

When the tears spilled down her cheeks, *she* killed *me*.

"Annababy, please don't cry. Jesus, I can't take the tears."

If anything, her arms tightened around herself even more as I reached for her. Didn't matter. At last I had her back in my arms. Her tears soaking through the front of my T-shirt sobered me up though.

"I fucked up, Annabelle. I was wrong. So wrong. And I hurt you, the one person in the world I should never, ever hurt. I'm sorry, baby. So sorry."

I ducked my head to see her face, but she pulled away from me, putting her little island between us.

"Annabelle, let me in. Let me prove to you how much I believe in you, how much I trust you."

With the back of her hand, she swiped at the tears falling down her cheeks. "Why? What changed? Your groupie didn't work out?"

The sarcasm landed like a blow, one I deserved.

Closing my eyes, I sucked in air. Opening them, I stared directly into the green depths of the eyes that haunted me every night. "You asked me once about the tattoo on my hip. The teardrop."

She tilted her head and waited.

"It's for my mom. When she walked out, she left a big hole in my heart. Since I was eight, I've been trying to fill that hole with music, alcohol, women, traveling, whatever. Then you came along and filled it up to the brim with your sass and your playfulness and your understanding."

She looked away from me.

Flattening my hands on her counter, I leaned toward her. "All my life, I've been trying to be whole, and with you, I finally was. I was just too scared to believe you could be real. That made it easy for Garrett to work me over, convince me to believe something far different from the truth."

At last she blinked up at me through the tears staining her beautiful face.

"Why didn't you fight? Why didn't you fight for us?" She had to hear the rough emotion in my voice, and I didn't care. As far as

I was concerned, there would be no more hiding from ourselves or from each other.

"I thought you wanted to be free. So I gave you what you wanted. I always give you what you want," she finished on a whisper.

Rounding the island, I cupped her face in my hands and thumbed at her tears. "We set each other free, yet neither of us is free unless we're together," I said.

"But?"

For a second, I thought I heard hope in her voice, but she kept her eyes on my chin and wouldn't look at me. Time to lay it all on the table. "That surprise you gave me for my birthday? The one with my dad?"

She nodded, her brow furrowed.

"He took me out to a driving range, and we had a heart-to-heart." I rested my hands on her shoulders, and miracles, she let me. "Turns out, so much of what I believed about my mom was never true. Especially the part about her walking away from me. After you left, after the tour broke for Christmas, I spent some time with her."

Annabelle puffed out a breath. "That's great, Dakota. I'm glad for you."

There was still so much hurt swirling in those eyes I loved so much. And she still shielded herself with her arms over her chest.

"After you left, the tour stopped being fun."

Her brow shot up.

"Forget sex. I couldn't deal with sex unless it was with you. That's when I realized how much you'd changed me, made me better in every way. It's why I sucked it up and gave my mom a chance."

I ducked down a touch to look her in the eyes. "What I want, what I need is you, Annabelle. I need you to take up all the room in my heart where the hole was until you slipped inside me. You made me see how good it is to put someone else ahead of myself. You make me better." I stroked her jaw with my thumb. "You make me whole. I need to be whole again, baby. Please."

She choked out a sob.

"Please, Annababy. Take me back. Let me prove I'm a better man."

"Dakota, what are you—"

Framing her face, I stared at her oh-so-beautiful mouth and cut her off with a kiss, our tongues tangling together like the long-lost lovers they were. As I kissed us both breathless, I felt her hands on mine before she gently pulled herself away from me.

Fuck, I wanted her, needed her so much, and it had been so long. I leaned into her and sensed her softening.

Taking her hand, I led her to the love seat where I pulled her down onto my lap.

"Thank you for inviting my dad on tour for my birthday."

She blinked at the change in subject. "You're welcome."

"It gave him the opportunity to set me straight on how I fucked up with you and how I needed to let go of the resentments I'd harbored against my mom for most of my life."

Annabelle tilted her head but didn't interrupt.

"Turns out, my mom left my dad because he drove her away. He punished her for his irrational jealousy of her by keeping me from her. All these years I thought she didn't want anything to do with me."

Alarm flashed in the depths of Annabelle's deep green eyes. "You're not estranged from your dad now? Please tell me I didn't do that to you."

I watched my fingers as I tangled them in the silky strands of her hair. "We're good. Rich and I are good. So is my mom."

"Dakota, that's great. I'm happy for you."

She sucked in a breath. "I never thought I'd be exclusive with you. After all, I was one of those fans who set out to sleep with you when I had the chance after that concert at Red Rocks."

Clearly, we'd both never forget that night.

"Watching you on tour, seeing how much you love to flirt, seeing you walk into an after-party with a dozen groupies trailing you, I realized I'd fantasized my way into something more substantial with you, something that didn't exist," she trailed off, her tone so sad she broke my heart as she simultaneously sent it flying.

"You're crazy about me," I said with a smile.

She blinked and rallied. "Don't put words in my mouth Dakota."

"But I want to put words, my tongue—my dick—in your mouth Annabelle," I said with a wink.

I couldn't help but laugh at the look on her face. "We'll save my dick for later, then."

Her eyes flashed fire, and all I wanted to do was start later right now, but we weren't done talking.

Sobering, I said, "Annabelle, you're right. I do like to flirt with the ladies. My *job* is to flirt with the ladies. It keeps 'em coming to the concerts and buying our music. Plus, it's fun." Her eyes narrowed, but I talked over them. "The biggest reason I pursued a career in music is the fun factor, and nearly every aspect of playing music for a living is fun."

She tried to slide off my lap, so I wrapped my arms around her.

"But the best part of being a rock star came along when a certain gorgeous brunette put on a private strip show for me in my hotel room after a concert one night. Baby, I couldn't stop thinking about you after that. When it turned out you were best friends with Jack's new wife, all I could think about was how I could score a repeat performance."

She pursed her lips, and I fought to maintain my focus.

"At the risk of making you mad, Garrett offered you the tour internship because I asked him to."

"*What?*"

She'd been softening all the while I talked, but at that little revelation, she stiffened tight enough to strike.

"I pulled some strings, did some sweet-talking, and discovered you had a rockin' GPA, graduated top of your class." I smiled my pride in her. "Garrett wouldn't have taken you on without your considerable credentials."

She relaxed slightly, but her arms crossed over her luscious chest told me I still had to work at it. Smoothing one hand up and down her back and gently squeezing her thigh with the other, I continued. "I wanted you on tour, but I knew you wouldn't tag along like a groupie."

Her arched brow confirmed it.

"Shit, I didn't want to you to be a groupie. I had other interests in you, interests that didn't make sense to me at first, but I couldn't walk away from you."

I traced the contours of her face with the pads of my fingers.

"Annabelle, I haven't had sex, haven't even wanted to have sex with anyone but you since I walked into Jack's parents' place the night of the wedding rehearsal and saw you sitting there with Clio."

"Not even with that groupie in Vegas?"

She couldn't let go of that—my fault after how I acted. "My dick didn't even twitch with her. When you left, I suggested she find another party for the night. Tron and I competed for who could do blinding drunk best." Pulling a face, I said, "I think it ended in a tie."

She sucked in a breath. "You hadn't had any other stripteases even on all your exotic tours around the world?" she asked, a twinkle in her eye.

I relaxed. She was coming with me. She might make me beg a little—hell, I hoped she did—but she was still coming with me.

"Annabelle, when you started your private show for me in my suite that night, a look of worry flashed for a second in your pretty eyes. Then it was gone, replaced with a sassy determination that told me you hadn't ever done what you were about to do, but that wasn't stopping you. It was sexy as hell to watch."

I grinned.

"You started slipping buttons down the front of your dress while you rolled your hips from side to side, rocking on those stiletto boots you wore. I kicked back on the bed to enjoy the show. The way you moved made my cock rock hard, and you were barely undressed."

For a second, I closed my eyes as the memory flowed through my head. "You slipped the top of your dress off your shoulders and raised your arms above your head, dancing to a tune only you could hear, but you never took your eyes off me."

Remembering our first night put my cock on alert, and I had to reposition Annabelle on my lap.

"That turned me on more than anything else because you performed only for me. You turned around, winked at me over your shoulder, and kept dancing as you lowered the zipper on your tight leather skirt. When you shimmied it over your ass, revealing your pretty thong and a garter belt holding up your stockings, I nearly came right in my jeans."

A tiny smile ghosted her lips like I was telling her something she already knew.

"You turned and smiled at me as you stepped out of the circle of your dress, smoothed your hands up your sides, and pushed your strapless bra up off your beautiful tits before you let it drop casually from one finger onto your clothes on the floor."

Tipping my head back on the couch cushions, I took a minute to keep myself from pushing before she was ready.

"You topped anything I'd ever seen. Watching you was the biggest turn-on of my life."

"I would have never guessed by the cool way you lay there watching me with your hands behind your head, your feet crossed casually at the ankles. Except maybe I heard you groan when I dropped my skirt." A tiny grin tugged at her lips.

She'd relaxed enough to drape an arm over my shoulders and to rest her hand on my forearm.

Progress.

"I almost drew blood, I was grinding down so hard on my jaw. You left your panties, stockings, and boots on as you crawled up the bed to straddle me, unbutton my jeans, and pull my T-shirt off me. You leaned down, brushing your pretty nipples across my chest and whispered in my ear, 'Do you want to do this with my stockings and boots on or off?' It took all my control not to explode right there." The memory still made me smile. "Jesus, Annabelle, I'd never met anyone as fucking hot as you were that night. You should have come with a warning label—dangerous when wet."

"On, as I recall," she said with an impish grin.

"Oh yeah, definitely on. You proceeded to ride me into the wildest orgasm I'd ever had. I couldn't let you go when you offered to leave after one round. And that was hot too, like you had no intention of making a claim on me." I smoothed my hand over hers where it rested on my arm. "Baby, after that night, I compared every woman to you, no matter if I bedded them or not. None of them could ever come close to you. You ruined me for anyone else, but I didn't know how to find you again. Then I walked into that wedding rehearsal, and that was it."

She remained quiet.

My girl insisted on making me beg.

"I was an asshole in Vegas. From the bullshit accusation to using the groupie to make you hurt as much as I hurt. The problem with that thinking was if you were involved with Bailey, you wouldn't have felt a thing. The look on your face when I sent you away—" I dragged in a ragged breath. "Your expression has haunted me ever since that night."

With the backs of my fingers, I caressed her petal-soft cheek. Staring into her eyes, I laid everything out there. "You're the most important person in the world to me, Annabelle, and I need you in my life. Whatever I need to do to convince you that I've changed, that I've learned I need to talk to you first, listen to you first, believe you every single time—tell me what that is and I'll do it. Please, Annababy, give me another chance."

For the next eternity, she stared back into my eyes, and I held nothing back. At last she blinked twice, long and slow, and snuggled into me.

"It's late Dakota, and I haven't slept in weeks. Let's go to sleep."

I set her on the couch, stood, and took her hand to help her stand. In one smooth movement, I lifted her high into my arms and carried her to her bed. She didn't remove her robe before she slid between the covers, and I took the hint. Stripping down to my boxers, I joined her, wrapping my body around hers. It seemed like only a few seconds later, light sneaked beneath the curtains, and someone was pounding on Annabelle's front door demanding she wake up for breakfast.

Chapter Thirty-Five

Dakota

WHEN SHE SAW me standing behind Annabelle at the door, Emma, AKA Pita, dropped her jaw to the deck.

"Why are you banging on my door at this hour, Emma?" Annabelle demanded.

"This hour," Emma parroted, "is after eight. The pancakes are getting cold." She slanted me a look. "But maybe you don't care about that."

"Ask Mom to set another place at the table, would you please?"

"Um, Annabelle, is Dakota *naked* behind you?"

"Go away, Emma. Tell Mom and Dad we'll be down in a few minutes."

I didn't need to see Annabelle's eye roll. I could sense it in the tension in her shoulders beneath my palms.

"Some things are better left to the imagination, Pita." I couldn't help teasing both of them. "Don't worry, Emma. I'll wear all my clothes when I come down to breakfast."

Annabelle rewarded me with a huff as she turned in to me.

Emma's eyes grew three sizes until she realized I stood at the door in my boxers.

"Bye, Emma," Annabelle said, catching the back of the door with her heel and pushing it closed.

♪

Though Annabelle assured me her mom's pancakes were gourmet fare, I couldn't taste the stack I devoured past the hostility in the room. When the ordeal of awkward attempts at conversation followed by even more awkward silence ended, at long last, I knew the only way back into the Stewarts' good graces would be through music. So I asked Allen if he wanted to jam.

Up in his office as we tuned his axes, he said, "You hurt my daughter. Took all the fire right out of her. Are you doing something about that?"

"I know I screwed up, sir. But I think I know how to get it right this time—and keep it right."

Annie's dad stared me down for a long minute then nodded. "Hope you can convince her mother of that."

We started playing, and before long, all the ladies joined us in Allen's office. As usual, I took advantage of the situation.

"Remember that song I was working on last summer and during the tour, Annabelle?"

"The solo you wowed the audiences with when Bailey lifted you two stories into the air?" she asked with a shudder.

"I need to lift you up on that platform sometime, Annababe. Let you see how freakin' awesome it is." I grinned at her. "Anyway, yeah, that solo is in a whole song I wrote, a song I've never played in front of anyone before."

"Do we get to be the first people to hear an original Balefire song?" Emma gushed in a way that made me think she might wet herself.

"If you want," I replied nonchalantly. "Annabelle?" I asked while I worried almost to the point of wetting *myself.*

Gifting me with a small smile, she nodded.

Overdoing the drama of flexing my fingers and clearing my throat, as much to calm myself as to entertain Annabelle's family, I prepared to bare my heart. Closing my eyes, I strummed the opening chords then launched into the words.

Your eyes flash
A warning, an invitation
I took you for a rocket ride
Cuz I know, oh yeah, I know

You want to be sexy and hot and wild for me.

Pretty girl
Come a little closer
Come on be a little bolder
I wanna ride this roller coaster
Cuz I know, oh yeah, I know

You want to be sexy and hot and wild for me.

Please, sugar
Don't walk away
I need you more and more
Every day
I miss you more and more
In every way
You're my everything and
I gotta say

Pretty girl

Come a little closer
Come on be a little bolder
I wanna be your only lover
Cuz you know, oh yeah, you gotta know

You want to be sexy and hot and wild for me
Sexy and hot and wild for me
Sexy and hot and wild for me
Cuz I'm wild for you, so wild for you,
I'll always be wild for you
Wild for you
Wild for you.

As I let the final chords reverberate, I didn't take my eyes off Annabelle. Silence echoed the last chord and still she didn't say anything. Ducking my head, I raised my eyebrows at her. At last she spoke.

"You finally convinced Blu to write some lyrics, huh?" she whispered.

"Nope. He flat-out wouldn't work with me on this one. Said he knew the melody held a special meaning, so I'd better make it clear with my own lyrics."

"What do you call the song, Dakota?" Allen asked.

Never taking my eyes from Annabelle's, I said, "'Wild For Me.' I wrote it for you, Annabelle. It's been all about you since we reconnected last summer." I paused. "I love you."

She burst into tears, and I barely had time to set the guitar aside before she leaped into my arms. "I love you too, Dakota. So much."

"I kinda figured that, but it damn sure took you long enough to say the words. Say it again, Annabelle."

"I love you, Dakota Perri. So very much."

She made me feel ten feet tall and bulletproof. Damn, my Annie was *something*. I smiled at her with my whole body, and she started sobbing all over again.

As she soaked the front of my T-shirt with her tears, I looked helplessly to Allen who shrugged as he wrapped the other two Stewart women in his arms. The two of them soaked his shirt in stereo.

Even Allen seemed a little misty-eyed as he said, "You know, Dakota, I think every dad hopes to see his daughter's choice of a man look at her the way you look at Annabelle." He smiled. "You better get used to this, son. Stewart women cry when they're sad *and* when they're happy."

Annabelle laughed a little into my chest. Her smile broke through her tears like a rainbow, stopping my breath in my throat. "Can we go back to my place to talk about this? Somewhere without an audience?" she said for my ears only.

I nodded. "Guess it's time for us to go. Thanks for breakfast, Ellie."

Wrapping my arm around her, I guided Annabelle from the room. As we walked past the rest of the family, Allen pointed at his wife's back and gave me a thumbs-up. I grinned and kept walking. Yeah, I wanted to be back in Ellie's good graces, but I needed to be alone with my Annie.

♪

Annabelle bowed her beautiful body, her inner muscles pulsing in rhythm with my favorite song: Annabelle chanting, "Dakota! Dakota! Dakota!"

A beat followed her refrain as the entire universe held its breath.

Then she clamped her pussy down on me and screamed, "I love you, Dakota Perri!"

An electrical storm gathered in my muscles, and I pumped into her once more—hard. That's when lightning struck, crackling down my spine. I started pumping again because I couldn't stop coming.

She tightened even more around me, her body plastered against my chest and abs, her heels digging into my ass as we rode out the storm together.

When at last the explosions of our lovemaking subsided into seismic aftershocks, I stared in love-drunk wonder at her. "Every time we're together, you rock my world. But this time you tipped it right on its head."

She tightened her arms around me and stared into my eyes like she was trying to see all the way to my soul. "Ever since the first time after Red Rocks, it's only been you Dakota. Even though I believed that night was a one-night stand. I tried to convince myself you were a fantasy, that that night was a dream so I could live like a normal person in the real world. But it was no use. You changed me."

She stopped, sucked in a breath, her green eyes clouding with an uncertainty I damn sure didn't want to see. "And now—"

"Now?" I prompted.

"Now, after the tour, after being without you, after what we just did, I've passed the point of no return. There can never be anyone for me but you."

I didn't even know I'd tensed up until her words let me relax.

"Because you love me."

"Because I love you so much, Dakota."

"Sometimes, Annabelle, when you'd sneak into my head after Red Rocks, I pushed you out—hard."

She stiffened, a frown creasing her forehead.

"Because I thought I'd never see you again. Sometimes when I was feeling alone, I'd invite you in on purpose. I must have relived that night a thousand times before I saw you at Jack and Clio's wedding."

Her body softened, molded to mine, and I smiled. "Watching Jack with Clio, watching Blu with Ashleigh, I could see how one woman was enough—more than enough for them. I couldn't under-stand that—until I saw you again." I ran the tip of my nose down the length of hers and gave her a gentle kiss on the mouth. "It will always only be you, Annabelle. I love you."

Because I couldn't help it, I kissed her again.

"By the way—" I smiled against her lips, "all that pretty lingerie we bought for you, the stuff you left in a pile on the bed when you left Vegas? It's waiting for you in your closet back at my place," I said and held my breath for the fallout.

She reached up and took my face in the palms of her hands, mischief dancing in her eyes as she looked into mine. Holding me where she wanted me, in typical Annabelle fashion she turned the tables on me. Ravaging my mouth, she kissed me with her lips, tongue, and teeth, tugging and nipping at my lips, plunging her tongue inside my mouth to demand my response, moving my head up enough to leave space for her to kiss and nibble at my lower lip.

The woman drove me wild.

After the first round, I should have been exhausted. So should have Annabelle, for that matter. But it seemed our honest confessions reenergized us, and my cock, still half hard from before and still inside her, roared back to full strength.

A long time later when we lay quietly in each other's arms, a conversation I'd had a lifetime ago with Jack and Blu slipped into my thoughts. Finally, I understood what it meant to make love naked, to trust someone enough to believe she'll keep your heart safe when you give it to her. Annabelle owned me—heart, body, and soul. I was safe with her—at last.

Wild For Me Playlist:

"Dancing on Nails"—We Are Harlot

"Spaceship"—Puddle of Mudd

"Control"—Puddle of Mudd

"Paralyzed"—Failure Anthem

"Addicted"—Saving Abel

"How Did You Love"—Shinedown

"Better Than Me"—Hinder

"Not Strong Enough"—Apocalyptica (featuring Brent Smith)

"Rolling 7s"—Dirty Honey

"Here Until Forever"—In Flames

"Rest in Pieces"—Saliva

"Save Me"—Burn Halo

"Life After You"—Daughtry

"Reckless"—Papa Roach

Thank you so much for reading *Wild For Me*.

Turn the page for an excerpt from *Hot For Me*, Book Four in the
Balefire Series coming in January 2022.

CHAPTER ONE

Adam

MY BLOOD SIZZLED at the thought of all the glitz and glamour waiting for the boys and me to dirty it up with our kick-ass show. Our music absolutely begged the ladies to lose their minds—and their lacy panties and pretty bras, which they were only too happy to toss at us when we played. Every. Single. Show. Damn, the fans' response to us never got old. Kicking off our West Coast tour in L.A. only pumped me up more as I looked around the interior of our jet at my band mates—my brothers.

After ten years on the road, I still anticipated a tour like other people looked forward to vacations. That additional variable popped into my head—*Cristy Valor.*

This tour promised to be epic.

"What put that smirk on your face, Tron?" Blu asked from his comfy seat on one of our jet's three couches.

"Just thinking about the tour. Damn, I do love playing to a sold-out Coliseum. Makes this rock 'n' roll circus of ours too fucking fun."

Blu grinned. "I know what you mean, brother. Next to being

with my girl here," he gave his fiancée Ashleigh's thigh an affectionate squeeze, "playing the big venues is the greatest rush in the world."

"Adding in that wild thing named Cristy Valor is definitely going to make this tour a circus," Garrett groused from his captain's chair beside me.

"Are you pissy because it wasn't your idea or because we all agreed to the experiment?" Dakota asked.

Huh. I thought Dakota was sleeping off his early morning after squeaking out a tie in his newest race-to-the-airport competition with Jack.

Then I noticed instead of answering, Garrett tried to use his eyes to burn a hole through Annabelle Stewart's sleeping head resting on Dakota's shoulder. Without another word, he turned away with a look of disgust.

I'd joined him in a little day drinking during the flight, but apparently my brand of beer had a more mellowing effect than his. Either that or he thought he'd been shown up by the band's intern. Whatever his problem, he needed to get over it.

"Lighten up, Garrett. The whole point of this gig is the fun factor. Have another beer," I said as I popped the top off a bottle of Fort Collins' finest microbrew, the good stuff we always kept stocked on the jet, and handed it to him. I didn't know who or what put a bee up his ass, but our manager had radiated attitude almost since he boarded the plane.

"I'll have one of those too, since you're buying," Dakota said.

"Count me in," Blu added.

"Jack? Ladies?" I asked Ashleigh and Jack's wife Clio as I uncapped beers for my friends.

"I'm good." Jack's response surprised no one as he played with his daughter on his lap.

"Really, Jack? Are you still pissy 'cause Annie and I almost beat you and Clio to the airport this morning?" Dakota taunted.

"Think you guys already established the consequence when

either of you loses your game, Dakota. Drink a beer and give it a rest," I said as I handed him an opened bottle.

Jack made a face, but he aimed it at Angel. "It's your mom's turn for this one, little girl."

"How is it you always get the easy ones?" Clio demanded.

"Timing, Clio." Jack grinned. "Remember what I do for a living? Drummers are not only good with rhythm," he waggled his eyebrows at her, "but we have excellent timing."

Clio rolled her eyes, but she smiled as she took their daughter from Jack.

"I'll help you," Ashleigh volunteered.

"Guess that means you ladies don't need a brew right now." I stated the obvious just to be a pain.

"Not unless you'd like to take over?" Clio pretended to hand Angel to me.

Waving a hand in front of my nose, I said, "I'll pass. Angel's adorable, my all-time favorite kid, but diapers give me hives."

"One day some woman is going to call you out on that, Tron," Blu said with a smirk as I handed him his beer.

"Fat chance of that. As part of the last half of the band still standing," I saluted Dakota with my beer, "I think it's incumbent upon me to uphold the reputation of Balefire. Music, girls, and booze." I grinned and downed half my beer to punctuate the point.

"Incumbent? Are you for fucking real?" Blu asked, laughing.

"Hey, if that online college you got your degree from didn't teach you any vocabulary, you should probably demand your money back," I shot back.

"Jack, I think we need to give this guy more to do when we write in his parts. Obviously, he has way too much time to think."

Jack smiled at Blu. "Or he can write more songs himself. Slacker." The last part Jack directed at me.

I flipped him the bird and looked over at Dakota who hadn't chimed in with his usual off-the-wall shit. He'd pulled down the bill of his hat to pretend sleep, but he brought his beer to his mouth and took a pull. Which of itself didn't mean much. His other hand, however, tracing patterns on Annabelle's knee where she sat beside him on the couch definitely warranted my attention.

Raising my eyebrows at Jack and Blu, I drew their attention to the tableaux on the third couch, and both raised their brows in question. I couldn't help but notice Dakota's interest in our new intern at Jack and Clio's wedding during our summer hiatus. The developments on the couch warranted further investigation—or torture. Whatever.

"It's not enough at least two of you are whipped," Garrett shot a venomous glance in Annabelle's direction, "but we have to bring a kid along on tour these days too. Are we a rock 'n' roll show or the goddamn Brady Bunch?"

"Jesus, man. Relax. Have another beer," I said, uncapping a bottle and handing it to him.

"Don't know what's up your ass, Garrett, but get over it. You booked us on a sold-out tour. We're going to blow the minds of every fan in attendance at our shows, the press is going to love us, and the party starting in L.A. isn't stopping until we hit Houston after Thanksgiving." Blu downed the rest of his beer for emphasis, I think. "Hit me with another, Tron. Since you're up."

"Since when did I become the freakin' bartender on this ride?"

"Since you're the only band member not shackin' up with some woman," Garrett mumbled, turning his back on the rest of the cabin.

As I pulled another beer from the fridge, I shot Blu a look and caught him glaring at Garrett's back. Right when I thought I might be stepping in to clean up the mess before he made it, Blu stuck out his tongue and blew a raspberry at Garrett. One second it felt like the cabin pressure might blow out our eardrums, the next, the whole place filled with air and morphed into peals of laughter.

Cristy

"Balefire wants you to tour with them."

When Gretchen Hoff, my manager and oldest friend, first approached me with a request from someone associated with Balefire, I thought she was joking.

"You know, Gretch, the hottest band in the universe doesn't need anyone to help amp up their popularity—or their sound. Neither do I. I've played sold-out shows in major stadiums all over the world." I raised a brow. "Shows you've booked and organized."

"You've made a name for yourself, especially these last four years, Cristy-girl. For sure." Gretchen kicked back in a lounge chair and slugged back some of her favorite vodka cocktail. "But this is a hell of an opportunity to showcase your range, launch you beyond pop diva and into the realm of mega-star."

Lying now on the massage table in my hotel suite, I remembered our conversation from a couple months back. The idea of being a mega-star, whatever that was, wasn't one of my biggest goals. Yet, the more I'd thought about it, the more the idea of playing some shows with the Balefire boys intrigued me. The bad boys of rock 'n' roll teaming up with the naughty girl of pop presented all sorts of possibilities for fun.

The kind of fun that would mortify my parents. Geez, I hated it when they invaded my head whenever I thought about cutting loose. Though I'd traded my long brunette locks for a bottle-blonde pixie cut, sometimes I could still feel the tightness of the severe bun my mother insisted on. These days I wore tops with plunging neck-lines and tight mini-skirts. But every now and then, I could still feel the collar and top button of my thick, formless shirt chafing my neck, the constriction of maxi skirts falling to my ankles. The censure in their voices as they bombarded me with cherry-picked Bible verses chastising me on my behavior, my dress, my songs echoing in the corners of my mind. Because of course, everything about me had always been wrong. My growl of frustration at myself resulted in the extra pressure the masseur exerted on my shoulders.

Sighing, I turned my thoughts to the other consideration involved in going on this tour—one-upping my former BFF. Picturing Mali Tatum's claws scratching ineffectually at the news of me touring with Balefire, I purred with self-satisfaction. She'd been doing a number on me in the tabloids for weeks. Rumor had it, she'd also started working on a song—or maybe an entire album—documenting all the ways I've "wronged" her. Except for the real reason—the part where I have more number one songs than she has on every outlet from Spotify to iTunes to the good old *Billboard* Hot One Hundred. A no-holds-barred war in the tabs loomed when she found out about me joining Balefire's most recent tour. If *she* weren't such a diva, the two of us could have rivaled Balefire with a tour of our own. Now she could sit her jealous tush on the sidelines and try to disguise her whining in her pathetic little songs.

No doubt the grin spreading over my features looked feline as I stretched lazily and rolled over onto my back. Not that I cared. The masseur repositioned the drape, and went to work on my legs, his strong warm hands relaxing and energizing me at the same time. Obviously, he'd taken Gretchen's instructions well since he hadn't said one word to me. Exactly the way I liked it—a man keeping his mouth shut while he took care of me.

"Sorry to interrupt," Gretchen said, not sounding the least bit sorry as she breezed into the outer suite of my hotel room. "The team wants to know if you're planning to glam it up tonight to watch the show or if you'd rather stay on the down-low."

My entourage had taken up residence with me in the hotel the night before my debut concert with Balefire. Even though we all lived in L.A., I wanted us together for my shows. Gretchen and my make-up, hair, and costume team took up most of a floor in the Hotel Bel Air near the Coliseum.

"Tell them to dress me like a casual fan. Oh, and I'll need a wig. Something long and dark."

Gretchen ticked off something on her iPad. "Annabelle Stewart, the intern I've been working with, said everyone at last night's and tonight's shows are wearing Balefire T-shirts. Something about photos for the cover of their new album." She glanced up from her tablet. "Shall I get one for you?"

"Yes, absolutely. And I want to be in some of those pics."

Her eyebrow arched. "Hard to do from a private V.I.P. box."

"I'm sure you'll figure out something, Gretch. You always do." Resettling on the table, I focused on the masseur's talented hands working over my legs.

I hadn't mentioned to anyone in Balefire I'd be attending their second L.A. concert. I wanted the pure experience of seeing one of their shows live before I performed with them. As part of the contract for joining their tour, I'd asked the guys to record instrumental versions of my songs that I planned to sing with them so I could practice in my studio. Balefire's versions of my pop music gave it a rock edge, which I liked. It remained to be seen how our little experiment would play with the fans. Thinking about the band backing up my songs put a genuine smile on my face. My masseur lifted a brow when he caught me smiling, so I closed my eyes.

♪

Gretchen and I arrived at the Coliseum incognito. One of the roadies for Balefire met us at the V.I.P. gate and led us to an unused locker room backstage. Garrett Phillips, Balefire's manager, awaited us there.

"Miss Valor. A pleasure," he said, gripping my hand about ten long seconds too long.

"Mr. Phillips. I believe you already know my assistant, Gretchen Hoff."

He inclined his head at Gretchen, but I noticed he looked her over from her five-inch Jimmy Choos, up her net stocking-clad calf, and all along her tight black pencil skirt. He lingered on her hips before continuing his perusal of her Balefire T-shirt straining to cover her girls before giving her face a cursory glance.

I growled my impatience with the man. "Don't get your hopes up, Mr. Phillips. Gretchen already has a girlfriend."

To her credit, Gretchen tortured the man, resting one blood-red manicured hand on her cocked hip and subtly lifting her chest while she pulled out and played with the emerald pendant nestled in her cleavage. "You were able to meet Cristy's request to be pho-tographed with the other fans during the show." The command in her voice required only one response.

Apparently, Garrett wanted to send his own message.

Jerking his attention to me, he replied, "It's going to be tricky, but I think we have a way of including you in the photos for the album cover. That wig is going to waste the effort though."

"Not if you alert the photographer to who's under this wig." Licking my lips, I twirled a lock of long chocolate-colored hair around my finger and rocked on my six-inch boots. Flirting like a sixteen-year-old seemed to work with this guy. How again was he the management genius behind the biggest act playing in the world?

"At my direction, my intern stationed a photographer at the top of the stairs leading to the V.I.P. boxes. I'll see to it he knows to look for your wig. Are you sure you don't want to join us at the party after the show? We could solidify your plans for tomorrow night."

He took a step toward me, a smarmy smirk on his lips. No doubt he thought he looked and sounded sexy, but the man made my skin crawl.

"I think that's what tomorrow afternoon's rehearsal is for."

Softening the rejection with a sexy wink, I turned and headed out of the locker room, giving my tight fuchsia mini skirt a little extra sashay. Knowing she always had my back, I didn't wait for

Gretchen to catch up as I strided down the hall to meet the roadie guiding us to my box.

"Is that guy for real?" she hissed as she caught up with me. "I know he manages a monster rock band, but you aren't just any woman. Certainly not a groupie he can impress into a hook-up." Attitude rolled off her in waves. "And what the *fuck* is up with his outfit? A leather vest over a cut-off band T-shirt paired with five-hundred-dollar dress pants and Italian leather shoes? Does he even know what effect he's going for?"

I grinned at Gretchen's indignation at Garrett's not-so-subtle come-on. Her description of his terrible fashion sense made me giggle, which of course infected her.

"What a self-important asshat. 'At my direction, my intern,'" she mimicked him perfectly. "Could he sound any more pretentious?"

When we reached the stairs leading to our box, we were nearly in hysterics. That's when the flash lit up our faces.

"Wow! It really is you," the photographer gushed as he continued snapping photos.

I struck a pose, tossing my flowing locks over one shoulder before I pulled my oldest and most loyal friend into the frame with me.

"On three," I whispered. "One, two, three."

Together, we crossed our eyes and stuck out our tongues, just touching the tips to each other while making sure our chests with the Balefire logo faced forward. The photographer nearly lost his balance on the step as he leaned down for a closer angle.

"Have a nice night," I said as I stepped past him, Gretchen in tow.

"You know that shot's going to be all over the tabloids in the morning," Gretchen said as we found our way to the mini-bar in our box. "People are going to speculate like crazy. Again."

"Let 'em speculate. At least this way I get to set the narrative."

She slanted me a look.

"Gretch," I began, "Kelsey knows the truth."

"I'm not worried about Kelsey. She and I are solid." Gretchen fingered the monster emerald dangling from her neck. "You, however, need to look around for someone who's going to snag the fans' attention, someone they think they know. That's the only way to solve your little problem."

Blowing out a breath, I stared at my best friend. "You're right. As always. Have a drink." I handed her a glass of champagne. "The tour dates with Balefire offer all kinds of opportunities for solving that, beginning tomorrow night." I flipped back a long curl on my wig. "So how 'bout we let our hair down and have some fun tonight?"

We mingled our way to the front of the box where we found to my delight most of the members of Metallica in attendance along with Gwen Stefani and Rhianna. Since I'd opened for Gwen early in my career, she held a sacred place in my heart. As for Metallica and Rhianna, I was just another big fan. However, everyone in the VIP box buzzed about Balefire. Gretchen and I exchanged a secret smile at how people were going to react to my part at their next show.

The lights dropped down in every part of the stadium. Somewhere beyond the roar of ninety thousand frenzied fans, the unmistakable rhythms of Jack Whitehorse's drums rumbled to life. Gold and silver lights sprayed across the stage as he rose up from beneath it, a wizard commanding the heartbeat of the crowd. His drums crescendoed, his hands and sticks a blur as he tom-tomed in the flashing red lights signaling the arrival of Dakota Perri. The wail of Dakota's electric guitar intensified as he made his deliberate way into the light from stage right.

The tension in the Coliseum ratcheted up like a too-tightly wound guitar string when the lights turned green and a throbbing bass rhythm signaled the arrival of Adam Tron. As if by magic, he appeared at the base of Jack's platform. When the lights changed to electric blue, the crowd went bananas. Lingerie of every style, color, and fabric rained down on the stage as Blu Connelly belted out the opening verse to "Helluva Ride" from his place at stage left.

Flash pots burst flames from the sides and back of the stage. A massive shower of fireworks lit up the night sky above the crowd. The gravitational pull of Balefire's sound coupled with their crazy-good pyrotechnics and mesmerizing light show sucked me right into their rock 'n' roll universe. When they finished playing their opening song, I was both elated and wrung out. And they'd only started the show.

Judging from the shouts, high-fives, wide open grins, and the general need to fill our lungs with air, everyone else in the box experienced the same thing I did.

Holy buckets! These boys came to *play*.

"That was some opening," Gretchen shouted in my ear.

"They definitely blew the doors off this place." No doubt everyone in the box could hear the awe in my voice.

That was all the time Balefire gave us before they launched into their next song. For a solid hour, the band didn't give the crowd a rest. Sweat poured down my back from beneath the heavy hair of my wig because I couldn't stay still. It wouldn't have surprised me if we cracked the cement floor of our V.I.P. box with the way we all danced together to Balefire's kick-butt music.

Then the band took it up a notch. All the lights dimmed except for one spot on Dakota Perri. His guitar solo wowed the whole house—before he started slowly rising into the air. When he stopped about fifteen feet above the stage, someone sling-shotted a lacy red thong, landing it perfectly to dangle from the neck of his guitar.

Dakota burst out laughing. "Fucking beautiful shot, babe. Makes a guy wonder what else you do well," he said into his head mic.

The screams from the adoring female fans in the audience drowned out whatever else he said. The rest of the band showed back up on stage to play a new song off the album they were touring. Watching Dakota play from his perch high above the stage,

I knew exactly how I wanted to make my entrance at tomorrow night's concert.

Throughout the show, though, I kept homing in on Adam Tron. Like the rest of Balefire, he had his fans, and he wandered out to the edge of the stage often to give them a show. But there was something steady about him, something not so rock-star show-off that drew me to him. Even when he melted back to stand near Jack's platform, I couldn't help but watch him. He was easily the tallest man on the stage, but it wasn't his size, his black hair and dark brown eyes, the muscles rippling down his arms exposed by the tank top he wore to show off his ink that drew me. No, there was something in his expression that reached inside me and told me to relax. Everything was under control. Everything was fine.

By this point in the show, Blu, Dakota, and Jack had soloed already, which was regular for a rock band. Usually, the bassist stood back and drove the beat—except, apparently, for Adam Tron. He stepped to center stage and launched into a solo with his four-string bass, rivaling Dakota's prowess with his six-string lead guitar. Adam mesmerized me as he pulsed, throbbed, and thumped his way into my blood. It took me nearly to the end of the song after the other guys rejoined him to discover I'd locked my legs together as an orgasm rolled through me.

I sucked in air. He did that with his bass? Adam Tron had never met me in his life, and he gave me an orgasm that left me reeling.

"Hey, you okay?" Gretchen asked. She waved her hands in front of my face. "You look a little flushed."

"It's the wig. There's a reason I wear my hair so short."

"Uh-huh. Wouldn't have anything at all to do with tall, dark, and steady out there, would it?"

Her left eyebrow arched in a look that said she knew everything. Good thing for me, Adam Tron didn't have a clue.

ACKNOWLEDGEMENTS

Dakota drew me in from the minute he showed up in *Play For Me*, Book One in this series. His playfulness and devil-may-care attitude hid a deep wound, and I desperately wanted to discover it. But Blu Connolly stepped in front of him, making me wait to tell his story. Likewise, Annabelle was a ball of fun in *Play For Me*. She was the perfect person to fill the hole inside of Dakota—and learn some things about herself along the way. I truly loved writing this book, and I hope you enjoyed reading it too.

I owe a ton of thanks to my critique group: LindaRae Sande, KJ Gillenwater, Sara Vinduska, and Jacque Coburn. Your catches, comments, and encouragement for these characters and this story have helped me give readers the best experience I can. I appreciate our bi-monthly dinners more than you know. Your expertise and your friendship make this writing journey even more fun.

As always, I can count on you, Bri Weigel, when I need a last minute opinion on any aspect of my books. Your enthusiasm for the cover and your ideas for the blurb truly helped me through some anxiety about those all-important aspects of this book. Thank you.

Nikki Busch, you are a rock star editor. Knowing that you once sang in a rock band and wrote music reviews gives me even more confidence that I'm getting the details for this series right based on your edits and suggestions. These books truly wouldn't exist without you. Thank you.

Most of all, thank YOU for reading *Wild For Me*. Readers are the reason for authors to write books, and I appreciate every one of you who spends some of your time with my characters. If you enjoyed this story, perhaps you would leave a review on your favorite review sites? Indie authors need reviews to connect with new readers, and your review would go a long way toward helping me reach a bigger audience. If you'd like to hang out with me, check me out on Instagram @tamstales32, on Facebook at Tam DeRudder Jackson Reader Group, and on BookBub at Tam DeRudder Jackson. You can also get in on sneak peeks, what's new, and giveaways by subscribing to my newsletter. You can find the link at my website: *https://www. tamderudderjackson.com.* Let's connect!

About the Author

Tam DeRudder Jackson is the author of the paranormal romance Talisman Series and the contemporary romance Balefire Series. Her favorite "room" in her house is her patio where she dreams up stories of romance and risk. When she's not writing her latest paranormal or contemporary romance, you can find her driving around in her convertible or carving turns on the slopes of the local ski hill. The mom of two grown sons, Tam likes to travel, attend rock concerts, watch football and soccer, and visit old car shows with her husband. She lives in the mountains of northwest Wyoming where she spends most of her free time trying to read all the books. Her TBR piles are threatening to take over her office, and she's fine with that.

www.ingramcontent.com/pod-product-compliance
Lightning Source LLC
Chambersburg PA
CBHW061557190726
48288CB00007B/2063